# THE
# DRYAD'S
# CROWN

# THE DRYAD'S CROWN

## DAVID HOPKINS

SEVEN COINS MEDIA

"Aubec Skarsol" created by Michael Brown. "Estrid the Armorer" created by Ashley Georgakopoulos. Used with permission.

**Developmental Editors:** Betsy Mitchell (book one) and Holly Lyn Walrath

**Copy Editors:** Kara Robinson and Tricia Klapprodt

**Cover Design:** Rena Violet | coversbyviolet.com

**Cover Art:** Calvin Nicholls | calvinnicholls.com

**Illustrations:** Daniel Irving Decena | penslingerart.com

**Cartography:** Francesca Baerald | francescabaerald.com

**Audiobook Narrator:** Lindsey Dorcus | lindseydorcus.com

**Audiobook Music:** Ensom Lokk by Sissel Morken Gullord | gullord.no

All artwork commissioned by the author and used with permission.

ISBNs: 9798218186432 (paperback), 9798988140191 (ebook), 9798988140108 (audiobook)

*To my daughters, Greta and Kennedy*

# AMON
## Northeast Region

*Ringaré Sea*

Mahynfleth
Llambe Oromór
Winterhaven
Drymill

Fel Harbor

Silva

Brayford
Guldur

Ebernok

Eloe Vale

Hollywell

Toelan

Barcombe

House Varyn

Asher

Whitewood

Star's Path
Laew

Mountain Keep

Taruithorn

Yére

Il Strig

Il Strie Deep

Ferndale

Elm

Overlook
Aulebridge

Maynor
Settlement

Klein

Mountain Palace
of Lord Vauoner

The Boundless
Ruins

Welton

Dzayn

Coventant

Ryvenmoor

Senach

Qualheim
Elind

The Kat'tari
Tower

Qual's WayStation

Kengwé

Atwen

# A STEADY JOURNEY AND A CLEAR PATH

If you enjoy this novel, tell others. Leave a review. Post and share. To keep this airship flying, Seven Coins Media depends on the enthusiasm of people who love fantasy literature.

And honestly? We wouldn't have it any other way.

Join our Discord community to talk about this book: discord.gg/uney7VT

Note: This book contains monsters. Scan the QR code if you'd like a detailed list of content warnings (possible spoilers).

*"Whether she ran a long way or a short way,*
*and whether the road was smooth or rough,*
*towards evening of the next day,*
*she came out of the dark, wild forest*
*to her stepmother's house."*

*— from Vasilisa the Beautiful and Baba Yaga,*
*a Russian fairy tale*

# I

A MOTHER WOKE up in the middle of the night.

Jori thought she heard her son crying. But when she checked on him, he was fast asleep. Then she heard it again, so unimaginably faint: a baby crying out in the forest.

She grabbed the hand axe and a blanket. Jori ventured from the cottage and farther into the forest, hearing the baby's cry more clearly. Did a caravan get lost in the woods? Refugees from a sacked city? The cool air chilled her breath. The child must be freezing.

Then, she came to an oak tree in a clearing illuminated by moonlight. Dust twinkled, suspended in the air. The crying came from within the tree! Jori walked forward, too bewildered to consider the impossibility of it all. She placed her hand against the tree. It hummed with life. She chopped at the tree with her axe until warm, pungent water poured out, and she saw a newborn baby inside. Jori cut a larger hole and pulled the baby out, a human girl with her umbilical cord attached. Jori cut the cord and wrapped the baby in the blanket. The baby was perfect and beautiful in every way, as are all fragile things that require care and protection.

Jori cared for the baby. Jori's breasts still gave milk, as she had not weaned her son. She nursed the infant. She called her "Ald'yovlet," a Volir phrase meaning "tree born."

With the first rains of spring, four druids arrived at the cottage. Jori welcomed these visitors with the usual customs of hospitality. The druids spoke with a Raustfweg accent. They festooned acorns into their long, braided hair, and tattooed their faces with runic patterns, including a tattoo of a seven-point star. Jori could tell these four were gifted with power. It was undeniable. The druids had traveled for months, directed by a vision proclaiming the nativity of a true fey, a child born from a tree. Jori ached to keep the infant, but the child did not belong to her. A child of the forest should be with the people of the forest.

With the child in their possession, the druids camped near a river. The four, each in their own way, could sense something was wrong. The wind wavered. The campfire burned too hot. The earth trembled gently. The forest animals were eerily quiet. None of these portents would have been noticeable, except to their kind, who spent a lifetime listening to nature. The druids traded fearful looks. And before any of them could put words to this concern, a pack of gnolls burst from the thicket and charged. They wielded jagged, battle-worn pikes. They bared their teeth. When the War of the Hounds raged across Amon, these filthy dog-like creatures were the eponymous hounds. They often fought at the front lines, but raiding parties would break from the larger army to torment farming villages. No place was safe during this cruel season.

The gnolls slaughtered every druid except one.

Ausdre, holding the baby, was able to flee. She threw pomegranate seeds at the ground and whispered an incantation. The wind picked up, and Ausdre strode upon the air—over the gnolls—carrying her to the far end of the camp. She touched lightly on the ground again and ran. The gnolls pursued. Ausdre could hear the yips and snarls not far behind. She called upon a swarm of bees to hinder the gnolls, and then she turned toward the river. She waded into the cold, rushing waters.

Ausdre cast no spell, but the gods must have shown some divine sympathy, because the baby transformed into a fish. The fish slipped out of the surprised druid's hands and into the river. Ausdre swam to the other side. She had survived the gnolls, but what did it matter? She could not find the fish. Ausdre clawed at the wet ground and screamed. She screamed until her voice gave out. The fey child was gone.

That is the way of the gods. When they intervene, everyone loses something.

* * *

PIPER WAS UP LATER than usual. She refused to go to bed until Timon told her a story. Her favorite story. The priest sat on a cushion next to the girl's cot and took a deep breath, which was his way of saying, "You win."

"Afterward, you'll go to bed. No complaining?"

"No complaining. I promise."

"Here's the story as it was told me and as I remember it. An old Penderyn farmer fished along the coast. Every morning, before the sun rose, he would walk from his shack to the beach and cast his line. He enjoyed the noise of the waves. He enjoyed his routine. The farmer had lived alone for some time. His husband died during the plague, before the War of the Hounds. During those lonely years that followed, the farmer discovered a secret. He could work half as hard and still manage the livestock just fine. There was time to fish, time to reflect. If he could have done anything differently in his younger years, he would have slowed down sooner. He and his husband should have had more time for fishing and walks."

Timon began this story the same way every time. He loved to talk about the farmer and his routine. Timon thought of himself as being like this farmer—called to a boring and methodical life.

"One day unlike any other, the farmer felt a pull at his line. A fish! He held onto the pole, tucking the end under his arm. With his other hand, he pulled at the cord and looped the cord under his elbow. He did this again and again until the hooked fish was on the shore. The fish flopped about, mouth opening and closing. It was a large river fish. They sometimes found their way along the coast in the brackish water near the estuary. The farmer transferred the fish to his net, which he left in the water until he was ready to leave."

Timon lifted Piper out of her cot. Pretending to be the farmer, he carried her around the room as if she were the fish. He swung her around as she giggled.

"Once home, after fanning the room, he placed the fish upon the kitchen table and grabbed for his knife. He chopped at the fish's head to prepare it for breakfast. As soon as the knife struck, the fish began to expand, twist, stretch, and convulse until it transformed into a little girl! The girl sat up. She took deep gulps of air. She looked around, wide-eyed. Blood trickled from the side of her neck."

"And I'm that girl? The fish girl?" Piper interrupted, even though she knew the answer.

Timon smiled. "That's what I was told."

"That's silly." She held out her hands to indicate her utter lack of fishiness.

Timon raised his finger. He had expertise to share. "What about the named goddess of the wilderness? She can turn into any animal she wants—some fey can as well."

"Fey aren't real."

"So, the farmer," Timon continued the story undeterred, "dropped his knife and stumbled backward. The girl—that's you—fell off the table and scrambled to the other side of the room. You hid behind a chair. The farmer could hear you struggling to breathe, pulling in the air with great effort, learning something that should come naturally. Soon, your breathing settled, and the farmer approached you. He reached out his hand. You flailed about in a panic. He stepped back. Your head moved about as you looked at everything. You focused on a mobile, which the farmer's husband had made. It hung in the open window with chunks of blue glass, suspended by twisted wires. Sunlight hit the mobile. Rays of shimmering blue danced and swayed around the room. You smiled. The farmer inched forward, not wanting to disturb you, and then sat next to you. The cut on your neck was minor and no longer bleeding. You and the farmer sat there as you took in the surroundings, wiggled your toes, and sniffed at the air. Then you fell asleep on the floor."

Piper took over the telling of the story. "And the farmer knew I was a gift from the gods, a gift he had no interest in. He wrapped me in a blanket and carried me to you, a Taraki priest. The farmer shared his fish story. And you were dumb enough to believe it."

"I make space for a few miracles, and maybe you're one of them." Timon tucked Piper into bed as he finished the story. "Yes, I took you from the farmer, and I said I would raise you in the temple as an act of devotion to the benevolent Taraki. That first night, I had a dream where a beautiful queen said I should name you 'Piper' after the fish that are plentiful along the coast. That's you. My fishy foundling. My child."

For a while, Timon was successful in caring for the girl. He taught her what he could. But sadly, he had no real interest in being a parent, even if it would honor Taraki. Like the farmer, Timon had his routine, which he preferred to any higher calling that broke from his regimen. The girl had a feral impulse that was difficult for a priest who enjoyed cleaning the temple more than disciplining a child.

As the girl grew older, she kept running away, choosing to

live on the streets of Penderyn—where merchants sold their goods, sailors shared stories of distant lands, and children played games of their own invention. She could not endure the rigidity and boredom of temple life. She preferred to wander free.

Eventually, the priest stopped searching for her, knowing she would come back when it suited her. She would be gone for a day or two, and then return like a stray cat. Which she did until one day when she did not.

\* \* \*

Piper prowled the wealthier north end of the city. She was tired of begging for alms or being offered small jobs around the docks and the east gate. However, this patrician district was not as generous as one might hope. As she worked her way along the street, she became aware of the judgmental glares, the upturned noses. Her ambitions dimmed, and she shifted her agenda to sightseeing. She wanted to explore their domain. The main thoroughfare of the city ended at the north gated section. Here was where the elite lived—an entire neighborhood of large homes with personal guards patrolling each property.

Piper peered through the wrought iron gate to this dazzling world beyond. One house caught her eye at the far end. The two-story manor had stone pillars all along its exterior. Polished stones accented the trim at the first and second levels, and gilded owls roosted at each corner. Windows were small, but plentiful—not to let light in, but to give the occupant several eyes on the city.

Piper noticed the lush garden outside this house. Penderyn was a city of trade and commerce. It wasn't known for its beauty or public gardens. This garden was a verdurous paradise. The ivy twisted along the pergola. The untamed shrubs stretched into awkward poses. The white flowers, luminous and alluring, did not even seem possible in Piper's cobblestone world. She had to pick one flower, just one, and keep it for herself.

A light breeze carried the fragrance of the plants to her. Piper gasped in recognition. It all felt familiar. Her eyes watered, and a lump formed in her throat. She wiped her tears, not sure why she was reacting this way. The pain was so primal, a longing for home.

Piper climbed the gate and landed on the other side. She might have reconsidered had she known the estate belonged to Dahlia Tulan.

In the garden, Piper touched everything. She pressed her flat palms against the broad ivy leaves. She ran her fingers along the flower petals. She inhaled the floral redolence. She closed her eyes. A shiver shot across her arms, up her neck, and along her scalp. Then she heard the crunch of boots upon gravel. She turned to see a woman.

The woman had a stern face punctuated with dark, sharply angled eyebrows. Her black hair was cut short, shaved on the sides. Piper noticed her ears, which had several small hoops along the pierced ridges. The woman dressed like the mercenaries at the taverns—with intricately patterned leather straps and armbands, all fashioned to accentuate her muscular arms. She held a rapier. The sword was the only thing about her without a trace of ostentation. The sword was not ceremonial. Unambiguous in its purpose, used and used often.

Dahlia Tulan raised her sword, pointing it at Piper.

"If I let you live, every urchin in the city will scale that gate to visit my garden. Let me know if you have parents. I will toss your body at their doorstep so they don't think you've gone missing."

Piper ran. She fled with the panicked realization that her life was at stake. Piper rounded a corner in the garden. Her foot slipped as she turned. She reached out for something to keep her from falling. Her hand landed upon a gnarled staff, lodged in the grip of a horned fey statue. She pulled the staff free and tumbled onto the ground.

Piper looked up to see Dahlia approaching.

"Did you honestly think you—"

Piper did not wait for the woman to finish. She swung the staff around. Dahlia did not expect the girl to fight back. The swing caught her unaware. It struck Dahlia across the face. She wobbled, reeling from the hit. Dahlia took a step back, and then another to get out of range. She rubbed the side of her face and looked at the girl with new eyes.

"What is your name?"

"People call me 'Piper.'"

"That's not a name. That's a fish."

"Timon, the Taraki priest, says I spent my first years as a fish."

Piper's response was so genuine and spontaneous. It caught the guildmaster off guard. Dahlia laughed.

"Do you have parents?"

"No."

Dahlia's eyebrows arched higher, incredulous.

"I'm going to ask you again. Do you have parents?"

"No. The priest takes care of me sometimes. But for the most part, I'm on my own."

Piper could not tell if this was the right answer, but she was too afraid to lie. She wouldn't get far if she ran again. Dahlia's sword was aimed at Piper's chest. Piper knew her life hung by a spider's web. The wrong movement, the wrong word, and she was dead.

"You like those flowers?" Dahlia gestured to the white flowers.

"Yes."

Piper wanted to cry, but she would not cry, not in front of this monster. She trembled. That was involuntary, but she could hold back her tears. That she could do. The corner of Dahlia's mouth twitched. Whatever thoughts were crawling through the twisted maze of Dahlia's mind, Piper could not tell.

This preternatural attention to facial details: this is how it is for the child of an abusive parent. Piper would soon become an expert at reading every twitch of Dahlia's face. Every movement, no matter how slight, might signal the warning of violence.

"I'm going to name you 'Silbrey.' It's Volir." Dahlia's tone was even as she declared her claim upon the frightened girl. "Means 'beautiful flower.' *Sil* is flower, and *brey* for beautiful. The object and the descriptor are reversed. Do you know Volir? It's the language of the elite and the educated. I can teach you the language."

"Why do I need new words?"

"With the right words, you won't need to climb the gate. The gate will be opened for you."

"Are you going to kill me?"

"You're going to stay with me. I have an empty room with a view of your garden."

The girl, who was now Silbrey, noticed Dahlia did not answer her question.

Dahlia had a question of her own. "Where did you get that staff?"

"In your garden. The fey statue held it."

"Don't lie to me."

"I'm not lying. I pulled it from the statue."

The girl looked over to where the statue was, the place where she had fallen. No statue existed. No horned fey. She had tripped over overgrown brambles that extended across the path. Whatever she saw had been a deception of her peripheral vision, the phantasm of a distressed mind.

Yet there it was. A gift. Her staff.

The next morning, Silbrey woke up in her new bed in her new room that overlooked the garden. The bed was wooden with tall posts at the corners that held up drapes. The drapes had a beautiful pattern, Karkasse design, embroidered in green thread. The mattress was stuffed with down.

She had slept with the staff under the quilted blanket. Every time she stirred during that first night of fitful sleep, she would grab for it. As the sun broke over Penderyn and the city roused with the sounds of a new morning, Silbrey rolled over to look out the window. She saw a crown wreath of the white flowers laying on her bedside table, a gift that signified adoption.

\* \* \*

Dahlia Tulan was both feared and loved in Penderyn. She had made her fortune as a guildmaster over several industries in the city. She controlled the docks, the taverns, and any artisan with a storefront—almost everything except the open market in the center of the city. She took payment from each in exchange for arbitrating disputes, setting fair prices, controlling outside competition, and providing protection against accidents. She was generous in her own way. If a merchant fell upon hard times, they could go to Dahlia, and she would help them. Repayment might come later in the form of a favor: smuggling stolen goods, sowing a dangerous rumor, or even spying on a person of interest. Dahlia had purchased something worth all the gold in her vault—the loyalty of an entire city. No one defied her. No one would dare.

Dahlia Tulan leveraged two skills.

First, Dahlia had an ability to sense when someone was lying. Dahlia understood that there was no consistent pattern of behavior for a liar. Some liars would talk too much, some too little. Some would not look straight at her, and others lingered too long with their eye contact. Deception came in many varieties. Dahlia observed people as if it were an art. She knew when someone was being untrue. On the day she met Silbrey, Dahlia knew the child was being honest about not having parents. Dahlia would need to keep an eye on the priest Timon, that he wouldn't stake a claim on the girl.

Second, Dahlia could identify gifts in people. She would meet a boy at the docks rolling barrels upon the quay, and know he'd be an ideal apprentice to the bookkeeper on the south end of town. She would find a destitute man, starving outside the city gates, and appoint him to the city guard. He would thrive in his new role with only Dahlia to thank for his good fortune. Such stories were common in Penderyn. If anyone needed a job, Dahlia would find them a suitable occupation or apprentice them to a master if they required training.

In Silbrey, Dahlia saw a warrior and a killer. This assessment was not a moral one. Dahlia never thought of killing in terms of right and wrong, but in terms of what was beneficial and expedient.

The common street urchins played at being dangerous, but they were filled with unease and insecurity, longing for a home and a loving parent to care for them. Silbrey didn't carry herself like most children on the streets—that anxious desperation. She didn't play at being tough. No posturing. No threatening body language to read. That was why, Dahlia told herself, when Silbrey struck her across the face, she was taken by surprise. And Dahlia's ability to spot a lie meant she knew Silbrey sincerely believed she found that staff from a statue that does not exist. Curious, but not surprising. Scared children see ghouls in every shadow, goblins in every cave. Silbrey only saw Dahlia. She would follow instructions with an uncomplicated desire to stay in the good grace of her guardian.

Dahlia taught Silbrey to speak Volir and to fight. The fighting took priority. It started with the basic concepts of stance, grip, and balance, then to the importance of speed, strength, and focus. Every time Silbrey held the staff, she felt power, a connectedness, that was hers alone. She did not tell anyone else about it.

Silbrey knew the weight and balance of her staff with such familiarity that she could, with eyes closed, pick it up and identify it from a thousand imitations. Like a mother who recognizes her baby's cry in a crowded nursery or a wolf that rejoins its pack after long estrangement, some things are innately felt. Silbrey knew her weapon by its heft alone.

The staff was not cut properly, shorter than a standard quarterstaff. The wood was gnarled with the slightest curve on one end, and heavier on the other end, where the wood twisted around like a blunted screw. A trained soldier would not handle it comfortably. But to Silbrey, everything was as it should be. The staff felt soft to the touch, worn smooth from countless hours of being held and manipulated—smooth as only cherished items can be, from a lifetime of use.

Woodworkers of Penderyn could never identify the wood's origin. Most presumed an exotic hickory, sturdy with the slightest give. After years of striking, blocking, parrying, tripping, dislodging, and outright walloping anyone who opposed Silbrey, the staff gave no indication it would crack.

Silbrey spent hours each day—even on the fifth day of rest —fighting against wrapped hay, which served as a dummy. Once Silbrey beat the effigy to a pulp, it would be replaced with another. Silbrey's hands blistered. Muscles ached. During those early months, Silbrey was always exhausted, always hungry, and always sore. Every time she closed her eyes, she saw the hay dummy. Then Silbrey graduated. Dahlia took the dummy's place, and the girl wished for those easier days. The dummy did not move. It did not mock her. It did not hit back.

Silbrey's adeptness with the staff pleased Dahlia. Just as a prodigy might have a talent for poetic verse or song, Silbrey was masterful in her movements. One afternoon, Silbrey landed a series of painful strikes. Dahlia lost her temper and broke Silbrey's arm. This forced Silbrey to wield her staff one-handed with a shield strapped to her upper arm to protect the injury as it healed. Much to Dahlia's delight, Silbrey was even better one-handed.

Dahlia stepped down as teacher, replaced by her second-in-command, Keote. At first, Keote terrified Silbrey. Here was a goliath, a true goliath with the giant ancestry that he could name back several generations. The most terrifying man one could ever face in battle.

Silbrey cried in her room, begging Dahlia not to let the goliath kill her. The girl had reached a breaking point. The physical and mental fatigue had taken its toll, and she believed Dahlia had some sadistic intent behind pairing Silbrey with this staggering brute.

Keote was formidable, a more skilled fighter than Dahlia and twice as tall. But Silbrey was relieved to discover that Keote had a mild disposition. While sparring, he didn't hit with any force. He gave a slight tap to say, "I got you. Let's try this again."

Whereas Dahlia taunted and degraded, Keote was encouraging and insightful. He respected Silbrey as an equal, a fellow student of combat. Dahlia might say, "You stupid cow, you're going to get yourself killed." But Keote would say, "Your swing is a little wide. You're giving your opponent too much time to react." Dahlia might say, "You're wasting my time." Keote would say, "Let's try that again. I think you're catching on." Dahlia might say, "I will beat you until you learn how to not get hit." Keote would say, "Keep your shield up. Much higher. It may feel odd at first, but it's the right thing to do."

Silbrey did not have a brother. But if she'd had a sibling, she couldn't imagine one better than Keote.

Even after her arm mended, Silbrey held the staff in her dominant right hand. In the other hand, she carried a tattered shield. This unique approach had its advantages. She often braced the staff against her inner forearm. She could jab with either end or twirl it around, back and forth. The rhythm of her melee was uncommon, syncopated. And yet, she fought with an airy confidence. In Silbrey's hands, the interplay of shield and staff was ideal, no matter how peculiar.

The secret to her skill went much deeper than any training. Silbrey did not just feel the wood in her palm. She held the whole tree. The whole tree held her. She sensed the deep roots digging into the rich soil, the soil that contained moisture from the sky and the lakes and the rivers, which all fed into the ocean. The soil contained the diverse decay of life. So multitudinous, it became all one: several generations of animals and plants, worms and insects, bacteria and magic. All within her grasp.

The tree inhaled the air around it, tasting and consuming the smallest particles carried thousands of miles on the breeze. Over its lifetime, the tree sampled the whole world. When holding her staff, Silbrey breathed in. The forest breathed with her.

Silbrey felt the sunlight upon the leaves of the branches, the branches of the tree, the tree of the forest that was her staff. And that light was an extension of the sun, a celestial giant circumnavigating Efre Ousel. The sun spoke to Silbrey through her staff, reminding her that on the most crucial level, everything was radiant energy.

She did not strike with a staff. She struck with the force of creation, the force of the primordials Ignasi, Aylo, Cael, and Terron, as well as Al'taru, which wove them together. Silbrey did not rely on her strength in a fight. She was not that strong. She relied on the fullness of what she held, greater wisdom guiding every move.

No one taught her about the interconnection of nature. The wisdom she possessed was true as love was true, like rocking a sleeping child in the night, intimate and essential.

Something to treasure, knowing that a moment could be held forever. True, as fear was true. Terrible creatures lurked in the dark. Anything and everything could be taken away at any moment. True, as a flower petal placed in her hand. Light enough to be nothing, yet there it was.

That was her power.

Silbrey lived on Dahlia's estate, but not as a prisoner. She freely roamed the city after her training. She was the ward of Dahlia Tulan. Piper-now-Silbrey wore a crown wreath of adoption, and Penderyn opened to her. Every meal was on the house. Every store welcomed her.

A clothier decided Silbrey should have a wardrobe worthy of her station. A jeweler insisted Silbrey come to her if she needed anything, anything at all. A maid from a respectable household washed, combed, and braided Silbrey's hair whenever she was in the neighborhood. These kindnesses accompanied another truth. The tavern cook's hand twitched when he placed a meal before her. The clothier appeared distracted, as if he was being watched. The jeweler once jumped at a loud noise outside her shop. The maid apologized profusely when the comb pulled too hard. And the children of the city no longer played with Silbrey. They were all too afraid.

* * *

One evening, Dahlia Tulan asked Keote to slaughter a goat for dinner, but he would not do it. The duty fell to him because the butcher and the cook were preoccupied—or was this always intended to be a test of loyalty? The goat was innocent, Keote said. The goat could not offend. Keote reminded Dahlia of their covenant. Keote's violence would not extend to any animals.

Keote's goliath clan did not eat meat or anything that came from an animal. Keote had forfeited his former life when he chose service to Dahlia, but he continued with the traditions of his people. Dahlia dressed him as a noble in an ill-fitted doublet and a floppy hat with exotic plumage. But underneath it, he was still a proud goliath who did not belong to Penderyn or its ways.

Dahlia was livid. She left the room. A minute later, she returned with the goat. She dragged the panicked creature into the parlor. Then she bludgeoned that goat with anything and everything she could wrap her hands around. The animal cowered and bleated, writhing in pain. It kicked at the air in spasmodic, involuntary movements, but it did not die.

"Keote, my friend," a breathless Dahlia gestured to the goat with her bloody hand. "Would you please put the damn beast out of its misery? For me? This once?"

After Keote left, Dahlia turned to Silbrey. "When I ask you to kill something, it is a mercy. It is a kindness that you do it, rather than me." Dahlia rubbed her cheek, smearing blood on her face. "Because I take too much pleasure in the suffering of others. Do you understand, my sweet flower?"

"Yes, Dahlia."

"Mother," Dahlia corrected her.

"Yes, Mother."

Afterward, Dahlia referred to Keote as "Keote the Goat-slayer." She required Silbrey to call him that as well.

* * *

Silbrey was impressionable and expendable. Under Dahlia, her training had been a series of lessons grounded in blind devotion. Do whatever she was told to do. Believe whatever she was told to believe. Go wherever she was sent. And if Silbrey ever failed to return, she would be replaced.

Silbrey delivered messages and picked up payments. She reveled in the authority she had over people. She strolled through Penderyn, and shop owners would wonder if it was their turn to settle an old account with the guildmaster. Silbrey could feel what it was like to be Dahlia. It felt good. But she also knew she could not fail Dahlia. If she had to retrieve silver coins from the dockmaster and she returned empty-handed, she would be the one to get a severe beating. Silbrey saw her work as a strange kindness. It was better for the dockmaster to receive his beating from a young girl with a wooden staff than for Guildmaster Tulan and her rapier to pay a visit. If someone was too proud to do business with a child, Silbrey would correct them on that matter as well.

Every day, Silbrey walked into dangerous situations, reveling in her power. Every night, Silbrey went to bed fearful, hiding under the covers. All her power was gone. She thought about the beautiful queen who came to Timon in a dream and gave her the name "Piper." She wished that queen would come save her and give her a new life in a faraway land. But no one came. Day or night, Silbrey was always on alert. Being in that heightened state does something to a person over time. They are broken down and rebuilt into something monstrous.

Her first kill was the bookkeeper's apprentice. The apprentice was secretly working a second job and was often late to his post. One morning, he didn't show up to either. His body was found in an alley. He was holding a dagger, but that wasn't the detail people remembered. His head was caved in. The body twitched for several hours after his death.

After that was the immigrant family. Dahlia had been charitable. They came from Raustfweg, and Dahlia found work for them at the Welton estate. They worked hard and saved their coin. Word spread they were leaving to start a farm near Illuin Faire. Many warnings had been given: Do not take Dahlia's gift for granted. But they intended to leave, anyway. The entire family was found dead in the fields they worked. Maybe the children should have been spared, but orphans might end up in the care of her employer. Silbrey saw it as mercy.

* * *

Silbrey was a young adult when she met Callis. The girl who had taken such joy in exploring the garden had matured into a woman with an icy indifference to everything around her. Silbrey's severe expression mirrored the person who raised her.

On a misty, moody day in spring, Silbrey walked through the open market. Normally, she avoided this area. It was the only section of Penderyn outside of Dahlia's control. Not that Dahlia hadn't tried, but the people who sold their goods were visitors to the city. They could travel elsewhere, and their contributions to the local economy were worth more than any coppers Dahlia could shake from them.

Silbrey had received a black eye from Dahlia earlier, and Silbrey needed to walk around to collect her thoughts. The scattered showers kept many of the market regulars away.

One young man was drenched while he kept a flock of sheep dry underneath a makeshift tent. The man's long, dark hair framed his clean-shaven face. The wet tunic clung to the muscular form of his body. Silbrey's gaze lingered too long, and she tripped over the person walking in front of her. That person turned around, annoyed, until they saw who it was and scurried away.

The beautiful man laughed. No one had laughed at her in a long time. He moved his hair back, tying it in a bun. With his arms up, she noticed his biceps.

"Damn," Silbrey whispered, not realizing she said this invocation aloud. She had never seen anyone so striking.

"A steady journey!" He gave the standard Amon greeting in a cheerful tone. It didn't occur to Silbrey until much later that his salutation might have also been a teasing reminder to watch where she was walking.

"And a clear path," Silbrey responded.

"It's not a great day to sell sheep, but I have the tent at least. No one wants to buy a lamb if it looks like it's been hauled through the mud."

"Uh huh." Silbrey didn't hear a word he said.

"Fortunately," the beautiful, muscular man gestured to his soaked appearance, "I'm not for sale."

"That's a shame."

"Excuse me?"

Silbrey shook out of her stupor. "Nothing. I said nothing."

"Why are you walking about in this weather?"

It was a reasonable question. Silbrey had no response, just a pathetic shrug.

He smiled again. Silbrey realized she too was smiling and tried to stop.

"Do you live in the city?" the man asked.

"I do. I—live at the temple near the east gate. I serve as a scullery maid."

The man nodded. He was impressed by her fabricated, pious upbringing. Silbrey wasn't sure why she needed to lie, except to mention Dahlia might scare him away.

"Is it a rough life washing dishes for priests?" He tapped below his eye, referencing her black eye. He was observing her closely as she was observing him.

"Oh, this," Silbrey tried to play it as a joke. "Most of the gods are fine. You need to watch out for Aegir and Tian, though. They don't mess around."

"I'll keep my distance from sailors and gamblers. Good advice."

"You can't reduce those gods to sailing and gambling." Silbrey was leaning into her alter ego as a theological expert. "They represent randomness and chance. Sailors and gamblers know better than most that your life can fall apart in an instant."

The man pointed to the floral crown. Silbrey always wore one, ever since she started living with the most feared person in all of Penderyn.

"And the flowers?"

To the people in Penderyn, that crown was a cold-blooded reminder of her position. But to an outsider, it must appear childish. She reached up to remove the crown, but he took her hand, and every hair follicle on her body awoke.

"The flowers look nice."

"You're not from around here," Silbrey observed.

"I've only been to Penderyn a few times. My parents and I raise our livestock a couple of days southeast of here. I have more sheep outside the city walls." He waved to his flock. "My father has them penned where we set our tents. These are the prize specimens."

"You're going to be here a few more days."

"All week unless we sell our sheep sooner." He stuck out his hand. "My name's Callis."

She took his hand. "I'm Piper. I mean—Silbrey."

"Are you sure? I've never heard either name before."

"No." Silbrey couldn't stop smiling like a buffoon.

For the size of this port city, Penderyn's temple was modest. The exterior walls of the cylindrical tower were white limestone. The wooden dome roof had twelve square windows cut into it, so that the sunlight would hit particular stations inside, depending on the time of day and the season. The inside walls were paneled with wooden boards, and the flooring was also wood, in the style common for most temples. The altars to each god were arranged around the perimeter—three gods of life, three gods of death, three gods of society, and three gods of the self. The altars were adorned in a fashion suitable to the tastes of each god.

Taraki, the most beloved of the named gods, received the most attention. Gifts and tokens of devotion were piled before the statue of the two-headed, four-armed god, both male and female. Taraki was the great savior. According to legend, after the firestorm, Taraki walked among those who survived. Taraki took the form of forty-seven avatars across Efre Ousel, planting seeds and healing the earth, which began *Cora Aspru'eir*, the Age of Many Kingdoms. It was a lovely story, unless one paused to question why Taraki hadn't prevented the firestorm in the first place.

Silbrey entered the temple and saw Timon sweeping the floor with a broom. Timon smiled. He had changed some. He had lost the hair on his head and grown a peppered beard. His round belly expanded further—a sign of Taraki's blessing, he would often joke before patting his stomach.

"*Yakost!* Piper, it's been too long. How have you been?"

Silbrey ignored the pleasantries. She pointed at him with her staff.

"*Ya.* I need a favor."

"Name it."

"If anyone asks, you tell them I've been a temple servant since the day I first came to Penderyn."

"Is this a favor or a threat?" Timon raised his broom to meet her staff.

Silbrey parried the broom. "You know who I work for."

"So, both favor and threat." Timon returned to sweeping.

"Always both."

"If you need anything, I'm here," Timon's tone changed to one of priestly sympathy. "I can help you escape."

"I already told you what I need."

"You're asking me to tell the truth. You've always served the gods. Maybe you're the one who needs reminding?"

"You know who I work for," she repeated.

"Do *you*?" Timon said these words, but Silbrey had already left.

That week, Callis was not able to sell a single sheep. The people of the market avoided him. Silbrey visited as he closed every night. Then, on the final day, inexplicably, he was able to sell the entire flock to the Weltons.

A month later, Callis returned as promised. He visited the temple, looking for Silbrey. Timon sent a message to Silbrey at

Dahlia's estate, saying she was "forsaking her duties." Silbrey took the hint and rushed there.

Callis sold the sheep much sooner than expected. No sense in turning back around. He stayed the week.

Silbrey got him a room at the Bronze Spoon—a favor from the owner to the so-called temple servant. The lodging was near the docks, but small, quiet, and clean. Pricier than most, it catered to ship captains more than a ship's crew. Callis wouldn't need to sleep in a tent outside the city. As it turned out, neither Callis nor Silbrey left the room much that week.

And so it went. Callis would visit Penderyn under the pretense of important sheep business, and Silbrey would disappear from Dahlia for a time.

Silbrey would wait at the east gate, watching for him to arrive with his mare pulling the green cart. She would then run down the road toward him. He would dismount. They would kiss, deeply and desperately. Then they would pull back and look at each other, amazed at what they saw.

Silbrey discovered something tender and unguarded in herself. The knots of fear and anger loosened. Life was more than the brutal world she had been raised in—a world where people either served the interests of the guildmaster, or they were a threat to eliminate. Joy was possible in this world with Callis. There was love, compassion, kindness, pleasure, and faith. She could possibly have a family, raise children, and build a legacy that would outlive her. That could be a good life.

She had to push the dark thoughts down. It was hard to not think about the people she killed. People who fought back, people who ran away, people who never saw it coming: she killed them. She was young and manipulated, trained and conditioned—impressionable and expendable—but she was the one holding the weapon, not Dahlia.

When these thoughts surfaced, Silbrey would become melancholy. She would lie to Callis and say it was because she didn't want him to go. She could never tell him the truth because who could forgive such a person?

\* \* \*

"Thank you, Silbrey, for coming to see me."

Silbrey was the only person, other than Dahlia herself, allowed in the vault. A trap door underneath the rug in Dahlia's private quarters revealed a staircase that spiraled down to this stone block dungeon where she stored the overflow of her wealth. The guildmaster of Penderyn always kept a bag of gold and silver coins on hand, but down here was a hidden treasure, more than anyone could hope to spend in several lifetimes.

Large trunks crowded the vault. Each trunk overflowed with coin. The trunks fanned out from the center of the room like a web. In the middle of the web was a round table where Dahlia often sat to write letters.

Maybe it was by design, but there was no easy way to approach the center table. Silbrey had to weave around the trunks and step over a few of them. But she found her way and sat at the table.

There was another locked door behind them. Silbrey had never been through that door, but she knew it was a tunnel that went under the walls of the estate and connected to a tower in the heart of the city. Dahlia had guards posted at this tower day and night. The citizens wondered what was inside—

but the theories were boring and unimaginative. Most assumed it was a prison for those who wronged the fearsome Dahlia Tulan. In truth, the tower contained enough weaponry to equip an army. Much like the gold in her vault, it was more than Dahlia would ever need.

Dahlia leaned forward to feign interest in her surrogate daughter. The gesture said, *I know what you've been doing. I know about the shepherd.*

Silbrey nodded to acknowledge this truth.

Dahlia leaned back again. She surveyed the room. *If you stay here with me, all of this will be yours someday.*

Silbrey gave a shrug. *I don't want your gold.*

Dahlia smirked. *A fool would turn her back to this.*

Silbrey smiled. *I found love. I have all that I need.*

Dahlia rolled her eyes.

Silbrey reached over and placed her hand on Dahlia's. *I want to be with him. I want to start a new life.*

Dahlia pulled her hand away as if she had been stung. Dahlia had offered Silbrey the world, but Silbrey said no. Rejection was not something the guildmaster could accept.

"If you leave, you can never return to this city. Not you or your shepherd. Not ever again." Her words were low and spaced.

Silbrey looked at Dahlia, a woman who tried to be a teacher, who tried to be a mother. All she was ever capable of was cruelty. It was her nature. Her kindest act was giving Silbrey a head start on the escape. Without a word, Silbrey placed her floral crown upon the table and left the vault.

\* \* \*

Silbrey knew about menhirs, the standing stones, but she had never seen one, real or fake. A hundred imitations existed throughout Amon. Only a few were genuine, dating back to the age of giants and dragons—before the firestorm. On the day she and Callis traveled to the family farm, her new home with her new husband, she saw a menhir on the side of the road. She recognized it as ancient and authentic. She knew by sight alone.

The menhir was smooth from centuries of wind and rain. It was taller than a standard imitation. Not even a goliath could touch the top of it. The menhir was broader at the base to keep it stable in the ground. When Silbrey saw the standing stone, she felt focused. A power pulsed through her.

The newly wedded couple stopped to pay tribute to the menhir, older than any temple, placed in honor of unnamed gods preceding the named ones. Silbrey placed a hand on the stone. It was unyielding, hard and smooth. Small trinkets, coins, and items only valuable to the original owner littered the ground. Raccoons and ravens, and other clever creatures, would steal the shiniest offerings, relocating them to a burrow or nest. For this reason, people joke that the forest contained more gold in hollowed trees than the wealthiest guildmaster.

Masons could never identify the menhir's origin. It did not come from Amon. No one knew why these massive rocks had been dragged from parts unknown to be placed here. The rock was unbelievably durable. Give it a good wallop with a hammer, but the menhir would never crack.

Silbrey placed two hands on the stone. She rested her forehead against it. In her old room, whenever she was stressed, she would brace her forehead on a firm surface, sometimes rolling back and forth. This ritual relaxed her. But right now, she was already at peace. She exhaled deeply, an airy invocation to the quieter gods: *Please let me have this life with him. Don't take it away from me. I will tear down this entire world to keep us safe.* The stone vibrated a response, almost indiscernible, but Silbrey felt it. *Life can fall apart in an instant.*

The twelve named gods—Olar, Cyruth, Golwin, Taraki, Fen, Aegir, Hebren, Wedril, Sarna'vot, Yoon, Verin, and Tian—were more popular than the unnamed gods, but this appeal may have been the result of charismatic priests who enchanted their followers with the promises of benevolent, intervening forces. But first came the endless speculation of religion: Taraki would never do that; Sarnva'vot was at work here; or Yoon likes flowers, so we must gather the flowers before giving birth. Why should Silbrey or anyone have an opinion about Tian? She had never met this god. She knew of her reputation for being loud and crass, deceptive and reckless. A strange, unfortunate god. Silbrey did not want to deal with her. The twelve named gods were needy, wanting devotion or a portion of the harvest.

The unnamed gods could be seen as an anonymous alternative. Silbrey always felt closer to them.

The unnamed gods brought order to primordial elements. Their divine spirits imbued everything with a sense of harmony and balance. No one knew how many unnamed gods there were, but some sages have suggested "one less than infinity." To worship them was, in a sense, to worship nature itself.

The unnamed gods were indifferent to the kings in their castles and the farmers in their fields. They were gods who wanted nothing, gods who couldn't be bribed with devotion. So why place tokens before the menhir? Silbrey saw the tokens as a friendly nod to the transcendent. Nothing more. With the unnamed gods, no one left behind a gold coin expecting five gold coins waiting for them at home. Silbrey preferred this. She was wary of prosperous masters and their favors.


The silent, secret vibration that Silbrey felt at the menhir went much deeper than any actual words—difficult to explain. But the message was clear: *you do not need to tear down this entire world; only Dahlia must fall.* Silbrey, with her forehead against the standing stone, pressed harder against the whole edifice. Dahlia's control over Silbrey dug deep like roots. The tree could grow upward to the sky, but it could not sever its connection to the earth. Likewise, Silbrey was allowed to extend toward the clouds and feel something akin to freedom—a new life, a new identity, a new family—but she was forever entangled with the guildmaster of Penderyn. She could not set upon her adoptive mother. Matricide was the worst of crimes.

The air around the menhir was still. An entire lifetime passed in those moments as Silbrey reflected on her former world and what the future may hold. Then she felt Callis's hands on her waist. A gentle touch that asked, *Are you well?* She breathed in, and her husband breathed with her.

Silbrey turned around to look at him. She smiled and then closed her eyes. She felt his hand caress her cheek and her neck, her collarbone. They kissed, and Callis was an extension of her —and she of him. They laid upon the ground. He navigated her body with his touch and his mouth. On an intimate, crucial level, they became an offering at the base of the menhir, as their passion rose into a mounting, rushing energy.

She did not want this moment to end. After all those

months behind closed doors and in hiding, now Silbrey and Callis were part of creation, part of Al'taru, free and open. Their bodies were woven together. Her legs and arms wrapped around him, until his strength and hers gave out in that final fullness, which guided every move.

No words broke the quiet that followed. They both looked up at the sky with the standing stone obscuring it. In a few hours, they would arrive at the farm, later than intended. She would meet his parents. She would see her new home, smaller than the Tulan estate, but hers. No hidden vaults or secret tunnels. No gates, locks, or walls. The clouds reminded her of the white flowers in the garden, plucked and drifting on the wind. Silbrey closed her eyes and dreamt of a long life.

The man she loved was true and constant. He was her menhir, unchanged and essential. She would place all the treasure of her heart before him, to be held forever. But in that love, there was a fearful realization. Anything and everything could be taken away at any moment. The entire world was nothing in the hands of the gods, yet there it was.

\* \* \*

Silbrey never shared with Callis much about her life as Piper. He knew she had been abandoned as an infant and delivered to the temple in Penderyn, and that she had grown up as an orphan, living at the temple under the care of Timon, a priest of Taraki. He knew that, as Silbrey, she met Callis, and she left the temple to marry him. Then, she had moved to his parents' farmhouse with the intention to raise a family.

That was the story Callis knew.

At the farm, Silbrey had her first stillbirth and then her

second. Callis's father, Wardi, a well-meaning but meddlesome man, believed Yoon the Great Midwife, one of the twelve named gods, demanded garlands and bouquets throughout the birth room. During Silbrey's third pregnancy, she conceded to Yoon and her father-in-law. She felt foolish—naked, sweaty, and covered in blue powder—in a room filled with flowers. No one could walk through the room without knocking over a floral arrangement. Birth, such a natural process, was rearranged and distorted by a ceremony.

However, this Yoon must have some value because Silbrey gave birth to her daughter, Gydan. Later, following the same stupid ritual, she gave birth to her son, Yurig.

In keeping with custom, she gave each of her children a never-to-be-spoken name—so that Golwin, one of the three gods of death, could never speak it. Even if Golwin could not claim them, that still left two other gods up to the task, Olar the Warrior and Cyruth the Hunter. Silbrey wasn't sure what this meant for her children or for herself. She didn't give much credence to the superstitions surrounding names, but she also decided there wasn't much harm to naming a child twice.

Silbrey had neither a true name nor a true parent to provide it. "Piper," an orphan nickname. And "Silbrey," what was Silbrey? Did it count as a true name? Silbrey wondered what name would be spoken when Golwin came for her in that final moment. What made a name true?

The unknown gods served no one, but Silbrey remained faithful. Thank Yoon for her two children, and curse Yoon for her two stillbirths. The named gods got credit where credit was due. But whenever Silbrey felt lost, she stood before the menhir and left her tokens among the grass, the gravel, and the sticks.

* * *

"One day, unlike any other, a raven, as he was flying, saw a great darkness—"

"Is this the only story you know?"

Gydan glared at her mother, Silbrey, who never understood why children did not want to hear bedtime stories about the world ending, all because of a lazy raven. Her mother was not one to nurture or comfort. That role fell to her father. With Mom, Gydan had to be direct about everything.

"I don't like that story."

"Who does?"

"Why do you tell me stories that give me nightmares?"

Gydan was missing two front teeth, which gave her a lisp on the words "stories" and "nightmares." These teeth had been stubborn about coming out. Until a few days ago, when Silbrey pinned her daughter down and pulled them out by hand. Gydan was still upset.

"It's a fable," Silbrey explained. "A child's story. These stories aren't meant to be safe or happy or make you feel good. They are meant to prepare you for a world that is monstrous and unfair. And when you're an adult, and you've worked the fields and tended your flock, all for a few silver coins in the market, you will say to yourself, 'At least I'm not lazy like that raven.' That's why those stories exist."

"But is it real?"

"I don't know. A lot of things are possible in this world."

Gydan gave a tiny grunt. It was a sound of diminutive resignation—to understand and still be displeased with the answer.

After the story, Silbrey patted Gydan's shoulder and left the children's room. Yurig had been asleep for an hour and was already twisted around in his blanket. He could fall asleep anywhere, but Gydan required more attention.

Silbrey's lantern guided her through the dark house. She walked past the guest room, which had once belonged to Callis's parents. Wardi and Igvan had stayed to care for the children while they were still infants, but then they moved to a small cabin on the other end of the farm. The new place suited them. Igvan still cooked all the meals, which suited Silbrey. She helped where she could, often relegated to the task of fanning the kitchen beforehand, but she had neither the interest nor the patience for cooking.

Silbrey found Callis in their bedroom, in their bed, waiting for her.

"You told Gydan the bird story again, didn't you?"

"How did you know?"

"It takes too long. Children prefer shorter stories. The grandmother witch turned the princess into a pig and ate her. The end."

"That's not how the story goes," Silbrey corrected him. "The clever princess tricks the grandmother witch into turning herself into a pig. The princess eats her."

"That's terrible. Children will go around thinking they can outsmart their elders."

"Grandmother witch did eat the princess's friends and family first."

"That's better." Callis smiled as Silbrey joined him in bed.

Their bed at the farmhouse was not as nice as Silbrey's bed in Penderyn. The bed had no wooden frame or embroidered drapes. It was simply a mattress, stuffed with straw, on the floor. Callis assured her that this mattress was much nicer than what he had slept on as a child. Silbrey loved their bed. Callis and Silbrey could not have done what they just did in her Penderyn bed without rattling the frame and waking up everyone in the house. The mattress on the floor was sensible and soundless.

Sweating and recovering their breath, they lay on the bed. The quilt was on the floor. Callis had an innocent smile on his face as he ran his fingers along Silbrey's belly.

Callis said, "I love you." He always broke these quiet moments.

"Shh."

"Have you thought about talking with our neighbor?" Callis ventured.

"Maricel? You want me to get her?" Silbrey teased, feigning to get out of bed.

"Not now," Callis reached for Silbrey. "But you wanted to see if she's interested in coming over for dinner, perhaps for some evening company."

"Evening company?" Silbrey laughed. "You idiot. Is that what you call it? You're bold enough to proposition her, but not bold enough to say we want to ravish her senseless in our marriage bed?"

"'Ravish' is crass. It's violent."

"The word can also mean to take delight or pleasure. We *are* hoping she enjoys our company?"

"I mean, yes, I hope she does."

Silbrey liked how Callis would respond to every teasing comment with an honest answer. His sincerity could not be deterred.

And yes, Silbrey was also interested in Maricel.

Maricel had purchased a few acres from their farm. She built a small cabin with help from her neighbors. Within a month, she was planting a variety of herbs, which she dried and sold at the markets along Tu'enya Bay. Maricel's stock was easy to transport, and she had a strong horse. While Maricel traveled among the coastal cities, Penderyn included, Silbrey and Callis kept an eye on the property and maintained her garden.

Callis and Silbrey didn't know much about Maricel's life before she arrived—nor did they inquire. Silbrey, in particular, believed that digging into one's past was an unkind trespass. They knew Maricel had been married to a woman from Aberton at one point. They knew Maricel had a clever, dry humor that could sneak up on a person. Her beauty was much the same. She had long blonde hair, which she did not braid. She had soft green eyes and a prominent hook nose. Her neck was long and exposed. Individually, these features were notable. Collectively, it was hard to keep one's eyes off her.

Silbrey did not want to presume at Maricel's preferences, but she sensed the woman might only want another woman's company. Silbrey saw how Maricel looked at her during their chance encounters. This was fine with Silbrey, but she didn't want Callis to be a spectator to anyone new in their bedroom.

When Silbrey was young, she had watched other people her age sneak off to the wilderness beyond the city walls for their assignations. They would disperse into the secluded woods, chasing each other like squirrels at play, not to be seen until the next morning. Many loves were made, many hearts were broken as they groped their way into adulthood.

But Silbrey did not have this experience. While others were rolling around in the undergrowth, she was the right hand of Dahlia Tulan, striking out against any merchant who didn't pay for the guildmaster's protection. Silbrey was not desired. No one broke her heart. No one wrote poetry about her. No one said to her they wished the night would never end. That wasn't until she met Callis. And Callis was wise enough to know Silbrey was still trying to understand her heart, to learn how to be vulnerable.

Silbrey found she was attracted to men, to women, and to people who didn't fit into these crude categories. Male, female: this language, like water, fills the container, but not the entirety of one's experience. It was expedient, but sometimes words fall short. She was attracted to people—some, not all—like everyone else. Her heart belonged to Callis, but her heart was large enough to include others. She could love more than one child, more than one friend. She could love more than one lover. Her heart was open. Callis and Silbrey saw the openness as the mark of a loving marriage that allowed them to grow and adapt.

Silbrey planned to talk with Maricel the next day.

After a long silence, Callis spoke again. "You're not going to like this, but I need to take our flock to the Penderyn market. Sales have been low. We have an excess of sheep, too many wethers. A butcher in Penderyn could use them for mutton, especially before the winter feasts."

"We're not going back to Penderyn."

"How did I know you would say this?" His tone was more hurt than angry. "What is it this time?"

Originally, Silbrey lied to Callis and said she didn't want him to return to Penderyn because she heard rumors of a pestilence in the city. But over the years that lie wore thin, and she replaced it with new lies. The city was becoming more violent, or the city's market was now closed to outsiders. She always pushed for rural markets closer to home or other cities farther away. He knew there was something Silbrey wasn't sharing. Silbrey had been anticipating this argument, one where Callis would insist on the truth. She would often play it out in her head, conjuring every possible rebuttal to whatever Callis might say. She had all the points she wanted to make, all the clever insights. This was the one fight she couldn't lose. For all their openness and honesty, she had been neither open nor honest about her past. He knew who Dahlia Tulan was, because her reputation loomed throughout the region, but he did not know about his wife's connection to the infamous guildmaster. He did not know how fortunate and precarious his time with Silbrey was.

"Gydan and I can go. She's old enough, and she's better at numbers than I am. It's time she learned how to offload the cart and keep the ledger." Callis pulled his long hair back and tied it into a bun. Somehow this act always made Silbrey weak. He was such a beautiful man. "I don't know why you won't return to Penderyn. The story keeps changing. But you don't need to set foot in the city if you don't want to."

In the moment, Silbrey's carefully planned counterattack faltered. She didn't know what to say. Their daughter had been asking when she could travel with her father to market. Gydan was tired of staying behind with her grandparents and looking after Yurig while they were away.

Dahlia would notice if Silbrey returned. But would she even bat an eye at a shepherd and his daughter in the market? Would Dahlia recognize Callis if she saw him? It had been so long ago. Silbrey relented. She knew she shouldn't, but she did.

"Gydan may go with you. Stick to the market. Do not venture anywhere else in the city. Not the docks and not the

north end. There and back. I want you home as soon as the last
sheep is sold."

Callis gave Silbrey a kiss. He was happy for a resolution. He
wanted the truth, but it could wait for another day. "There and
back."

* * *

Callis and Gydan walked alongside the green cart, packed with
a dozen wethers. The mare dutifully pulled the cart. They
stopped throughout the day to allow the sheep to graze, so the
flock would appear healthy and energetic in the market.

Gydan was elated to see Penderyn for the first time. An idea
formed in the child's head that High General Bren Caius and
her troops could be in Penderyn.

There was no reason for the high general to be there. Bren
Caius lived on the bay island of Rhyll. She was born in the
town of Eloe Vale, much farther west. But the notion of Bren
Caius in Penderyn stuck in Gydan's head, and she clung to it—
and that merited a marathon retelling of the Northern Light's
many adventures.

Did you know Bren Caius, as a child, fended off a pack of
wolves using a sling and a few rocks? Did you know Bren Caius
won a bet where she wrestled a stag to the ground? She knew
she couldn't overpower the beast. So, she spent weeks
befriending it with treats, and Bren trained the creature to lie
down. She used the coin from that bet to buy her first sword.
Did you know, without formal training, Bren learned to use a
sword by picking fights with mercenaries at local taverns? She
wielded a wooden sword out of mercy to her unwitting tutors.
Did you know Bren Caius gained the service of her faithful

companion, Oren of Angnavir, by defeating him in combat while she was blindfolded? Did you know Bren Caius received her pet owl, Ruth, by climbing a mountain to rescue the owlet from a goblin witch? And did you know, during the War of the Hounds, Bren Caius and her soldiers would often use Kret Bonebreaker's own tactics against him? As the gnolls would raid villages—never staying anywhere for long—so would Bren scout and track smaller units of the army to attack before retreating again. Did you know Bren Caius did not kill Kret at Pynne's Field, despite every eyewitness account to the contrary? Instead, Bren spared his life. And to this day, she keeps the gnoll warlord as her prisoner *and advisor* in a jail cell beneath her estate. Did you know—

"Gydan! Who told you that?"

Callis had been half listening, but this one caught his attention. Gydan looked at her father, confused that he had interrupted her narration.

"When that theatre company traveled through and stayed near our house. They were telling stories around the fire."

"You were supposed to be in bed."

Gydan was unconvinced by her father's attempt at authority.

"You can't believe everything those actors say." Callis fumbled through his explanation. "They will say anything to entertain their audience. Anything. We all know Kret Bonebreaker died at Pynne's Field. Everyone saw Bren slay him. There would be no reason to keep him as a prisoner."

"Bren had her reasons."

Gydan was ever confident about the folklore regarding Bren Caius. She resumed her stories, which continued without a break until they reached the east gate.

· · ·

The open market was busier than Callis remembered. Everyone pressed against each other in the crowded aisles, a disturbed anthill of activity.

Wending through the masses, Callis saw Penderyn as a giant wheel, a hub for all other bay towns. The entire world, it seemed, revolved around Penderyn. He spent an hour searching for an open space. Meanwhile, Gydan kept watch over the family's mare, the green cart, and the remaining sheep.

Gydan surveyed the crowd, hoping to see some indication of High General Bren Caius's presence in Penderyn—a standard-bearer with Bren's red sun sigil, an elite guard patrolling the streets, horns and drums to declare her arrival, but there was nothing. Gydan frowned. If the high general were coming to Penderyn, she wouldn't visit the market.

Gydan took a chance on asking a merchant, carrying a basket of dyed cloth. "*Yakost!* Have you heard any word about the Northern Light coming to Penderyn?"

This question caught his attention. He stopped and put his basket down. "The high general is coming to Penderyn?"

With this, a few more people stopped what they were doing and looked at Gydan.

"I heard—" Gydan couldn't remember who she heard it from, or if this were a farmer's fabrication, her own wish to see Bren Caius. Either way, she couldn't stop now. "I heard the high general and her troops were stationed nearby. If they plan to return to Rhyll, wouldn't they set sail from the ports of Penderyn?"

Another merchant spoke up. "I saw some new and

unmarked ships in the harbor this morning. Maybe they belong to Bren?"

"I saw a white barn owl as I readied my table for market," said another.

And with that, rumor spread throughout the city that the Northern Light, the woman who single-handedly defeated Kret Bonebreaker and won the War of the Hounds, the great high general, the legendary Bren the Beloved, was on her way to Penderyn. Gydan, the innocent instigator of this rumor, was even more convinced of its truth.

Once Callis and Gydan claimed a spot in the market, most of the sheep sold without much effort. A boy, about Gydan's age, stood near a stack of crates farther down their aisle. He looked feral—in need of a bath and new clothes. Half of his left ear was missing. This boy held an apple, which he shined on his pant leg every so often, but he did not take a bite. The boy made Gydan nervous.

Gydan pointed out the boy to her father. As soon as Callis noticed him, the boy raced toward their cart. He tossed the apple to Callis. Then the boy grabbed the coin purse—which hung loose off the side of the cart—and ran. Callis took off after the boy as he weaved in between the people in the market. Callis called back to Gydan, "Mind the flock!" Callis yelled for people to move out of the way. Then Callis disappeared from Gydan's view as he ran after the thief.

Gydan obediently waited with the remaining sheep. She thought about the feral boy with half an ear. He had wanted to be seen. He could have taken the purse while customers distracted them. The boy did not act until her father noticed him. He did not want to be caught. He wanted to be chased.

Her father never returned.

The sun was low, and the sky was now purple and orange. As other merchants packed for the day, Gydan left the mare tethered to a post and the flock in its cart. She walked to the other side of the market and onto the cobbled streets past the market. She looked down every alley and around every corner. She looked into every tavern and storefront window. She called out, "Dad! Dad!" Each time, her voice was a bit more panicked, a bit more broken. She was alone, and she wanted to go home.

Gydan turned down a narrow alley. A cloud of dust filled the empty space. Light glinted off the suspended particles. She saw an unblemished apple on the ground. Next to it was her father's body. Three arrows stuck out of his chest. His dagger was still in its sheath. Whatever happened, he had not had a chance to fight back. The coin purse was also there. The boy had not kept what he had stolen.

Gydan was stunned. All responses failed her. Her father, who had been alive earlier, was dead. He was dead. She couldn't make sense of it. She did not know what to do. Gydan wanted to leave him there and walk away. Later, she would hate herself for having such thoughts.

She forced herself to walk deeper into the alley. She knelt before her dad. His eyes were half closed. The iris was not visible. This image of her father would stay with her until her last day. She hated that, too.

"Dad? We have to go."

She touched his chest. It was not warm; it was not cold. Touching his dead body felt like nothing at all—and that unsettled her.

"Dad? We have to go. It's not safe here." Her lisp on "it's" and "safe" was more pronounced than usual. Everything was quiet.

Gydan unsheathed her father's dagger. She grabbed the apple. She cut the apple in two, revealing the seeds at the core. With her fingers, she dug out the seeds. There were five seeds. She put them in her belt pouch. Her mother and father often saved the seeds and kept them in folded wax paper in a box at their house. She needed to get home.

Gydan walked out of the alley and saw a pull wagon in front of a shop. The wagon looked like it was used to haul trade goods from the docks. She had seen these wagons in the market. She took the wagon and rolled it into the alley. She pulled her father onto the wagon. He was a large man, but Gydan had spent much of her life wrangling sheep. With a bit of effort, she was able to get his body into the wagon. She bent his knees so he would fit on his side. She took a cloth tarp from behind a tavern and draped it over his body. Then, she pulled at the wagon, and she made her way with her father's body out of Penderyn. She did not want to go back to the market for the mare or the green cart or the few sheep they weren't able to sell.

* * *

Gydan pulled the wagon down the road leading home. The road was empty at night, so she kept going, fighting the desire to rest her heavy eyes. The cool autumn air helped. Her muscles ached from pulling the wagon, but she reminded herself that Bren Caius had once climbed a mountain to save a baby owl. The woods on either side of the road were dark with unfamiliar predatory animal noises. Fallen leaves crunched under unseen, padded feet. But she remembered that Bren Caius had fought a pack of wolves to save her family.

If Bren Caius was coming to Penderyn, Gydan would not see her. Gydan was taking her father home.

Gydan sang a song to stay awake and keep focused.

> *Il cunet akel tunorofel.*

> *My friend, dear moon, lend me your light.*
> *I cannot see in the dark to write.*
> *My love must know I will soon return.*
> *The candle is spent. No fire will burn.*

> *Il cunet akel tunorofel.*

> *My friend, dear moon, please shine bright.*
> *I cannot see in the dark to write.*
> *My love will leave if I do not reply.*
> *My heart will break, and I will die.*

> *Il cunet akel tunorofel.*

> *My friend, dear moon, why tonight?*
> *I cannot see in the dark to write.*
> *My love will wonder if I'm still true.*
> *Alone with my pen that I use to woo.*

> *Il cunet akel tunorofel.*

> *My friend, dear moon, heed my plight.*
> *I cannot see in the dark to write.*
> *My love will wander alone on the street,*
> *Without hopeful words to guide her feet.*

*Il cunet akel tunorofel.*

The song had nearly a hundred verses. Gydan had heard many of them, but not all. Bards would add their own verses or switch the order around, changing a word or two. It was a bawdy tavern song intended to go on forever. With each verse, the foolish lover begs the moon to shine brightly, so he can see what he's writing—and in each verse, he's more desperate. The foolish lover rationalizes that Efre Ousel will cease to exist if the moon won't shine. The "moon shining" had a double meaning. Every adult knew the song was about convincing a lover to consent to sex. The pen, the candle, and so on, all phallic. To Gydan, it was just a silly song. The song always ended the same way. The foolish lover sings all night long. He finally sees the sun rising and tells the moon he doesn't need her anymore. He has found a greater light by which to write.

Gydan walked all night long, singing *Il cunet akel tunorofel* to distract her from every horrible thought that might prevent her from taking another step. By morning, she pulled the wagon off the road and into the woods. When she was sure they would not be spotted from the road, she made a bed upon the soft earth and dead leaves next to the wagon and slept.

Around nightfall, she pulled the wagon back onto the road and continued.

For two nights, she journeyed this way until she was close enough to the farm—with the surroundings more familiar— that she made the rest of the trip by day. She passed the menhir, which felt like the true signpost for her home. While she was still a long way off, her mother ran to her. Gydan had no words, and none were needed.

Heroes like Bren Caius always came of age through some

marvelous, gut-wrenching tragedy—orphaned as a child or losing a lover (or several in Bren's case). The epics are obsessed with orphans and dead lovers. Gydan knew if she were going to be like Bren someday, the story of how she walked home from Penderyn pulling a wagon with her dead father in it would be part of the tale. She felt stupid and childish and would trade it all to keep her dad from chasing after the boy who wanted to be chased.

\* \* \*

Wardi laid his son upon the wooden pyre. He had spent the day building the pyre in the field behind the farmhouse. Silbrey, Gydan, and Yurig were silent as they watched the ritual. Wardi and Igvan both sobbed. Maricel stood at a distance to show her support for the family, observing but not interfering. Igvan lit the torch and offered it to Silbrey. The gesture confused Silbrey. She wasn't expecting to be involved. She shook her head. Igvan frowned and handed the torch to Gydan, who obediently walked around the base of the pyre, lighting all sides.

Wardi began the invocation.

"Our son," he paused to collect himself. "Our son, we return you to the elements, Ignasi, Aylo, Cael, and Terron, as well as Al'taru, which weaves them together. You have been claimed by the named god Golwin—"

"Cyruth," Silbrey interrupted. "Callis was hunted. Someone shot him with arrows. Cyruth claims him."

Wardi, who prided himself on how much he knew about the twelve named gods, stood corrected.

Golwin claimed a variety of deaths—sickness, old age,

dumb luck. However, the hunted belonged to Cyruth. And Callis's dagger was still in its sheath when he was found. If it had been drawn, Olar the Warrior would have claimed the death. Such a small, sad detail for the gods to be concerned over. Why did it matter? Wardi removed the folded cloth over Callis's eyes, traditionally placed in honor of Golwin, and continued.

"You have been claimed by the named god Cyruth, and we release you to her care."

Wardi struggled to get the words out. For Callis to be claimed by Cyruth, like some animal pursued for sport, felt shameful. Silbrey understood. She had sent many to Cyruth. She struck most people down before they ever had a chance to draw a weapon in defense.

Silbrey watched as the flames grew, fed by the wind and the dry wood. Wardi sprinkled water onto the body. All the elements would be represented. Silbrey looked at her husband upon this final bed, one that did not include her. She wanted to be with him. She could be his air and earth.

The people of Raustfweg, the eastern continent across the sea, believed that warriors did not return to the elements. They instead went to some other world filled with eternal warfare. The fallen soldiers would reform daily to continue the fight. The only pause was to gather at the dining hall to drink and eat. Once they sobered, the fighting would resume. This other world sounded boorish and fabricated, a story invented by commanders who had to send vanguard soldiers to their deaths. But if this was true, Silbrey would probably die a warrior's death—and she would never reunite with Callis. If Silbrey had a choice, she would like her body to be buried, placed in the earth to decompose, to nourish the trees that would grow through her. That sounded peaceful and pure.

The family watched the flames consume Callis. The smoke filled the sky. As Silbrey watched the flames, she thought of war and of that strange Raustfweg afterlife, which she hoped did not exist.

That night, Silbrey sat at the edge of the bed. The one with no wooden frame or embroidered drapes, merely a mattress, stuffed with straw, upon the floor. It had been perfect with Callis. She could not think, and she would not sleep tonight. She held her hands out in front of her. They shook. She focused on her hands until they were still. She clenched them into fists and released, once and then twice.

Silbrey walked over to the trunk where she kept a change of clothes and another quilt for the cooler months. Underneath was a small notch. With her finger, she lifted the wood panel, which revealed a second compartment where she kept her staff, her tattered shield, and a breastplate, crafted to fit her slight frame, embossed with leaf flourishes. The breastplate had been a gift from Dahlia.

In the bedroom, Silbrey stood with staff in one hand and shield in the other. Silbrey swung her staff to one side and then the other. She brought it around in a sweeping arc. She spun the staff around and then steadied it across her shield, a jab against her imaginary foe. A quick breath, and then she swung the staff back and forth, back and forth, until it popped like a whip.

. . .

In the middle of the night, Gydan woke up to a lantern's light to see her mother looking down at her.

"Where's the flock?" she asked, disoriented at this uncustomary hour. She had been dreaming about the sheep and her father.

"We have fifty head in the pen. It's not morning yet."

Gydan drifted back to sleep, but Silbrey nudged her awake again.

"What?"

"Gydan, I'm going to Penderyn tonight. In the morning, tell your grandparents they need to look after you and your brother for a few days."

"Are you going to get the sheep we left in the market?"

Her mom was wearing a breastplate. In Gydan's tired state, it made sense. If her father had been wearing armor in Penderyn, he might still be alive. Only when morning came did Gydan wonder why her mom was dressed as she was. She looked like a knight about to charge into battle. She looked like Bren Caius, except Bren carried a sword. Her mom walked out of the room carrying a broomstick—or perhaps it was a crook for the sheep.

Silbrey saddled their last remaining horse, Feste. The colt had not been ridden in some time and was enthusiastic to leave the stable. He was a fast horse with a beautiful, speckled chestnut coat. Callis had purchased him from a breeder in Oulent. Silbrey was furious when Callis came home with the foal. The family had little use for such a horse, but Callis had a broad smile and a handful of excuses on why this horse was an investment, suggesting they could put him to stud for extra coin.

Silbrey saw all the things they could've purchased, evaporating in the presence of this magnificent, overpriced horse. She supposed every spouse had dealt with an impulsive, extravagant purchase from their partner. Better to forgive these weak moments since they went both ways. But as Silbrey rode Feste through the night, she marveled at the speed of this horse—and gave thanks to her husband for such a gift. No, Feste was not a farm horse. He galloped with a sense of purpose that reminded Silbrey of a cavalry steed.

* * *

Silbrey and Feste arrived at the east gate by daybreak, an amazing feat even without a cart to pull. They did not go through the gate. Dahlia Tulan had spies everywhere. One was invariably at the gate, keeping an eye on who entered the city. Instead Silbrey dismounted Feste and led him on foot along the wall, heading north, past the large oak where the roots stretched along the ground and disrupted a portion of the faded roseate stonewall.

The back entrance to the temple was an arched alcove in the wall leading to a wooden door. The door was bolted shut. Silbrey placed the end of her staff against the door. She closed her eyes. Maybe it was the death of her husband, shaking something loose inside of her, but she sensed a power—long ignored —returning. The heft of the wooden staff, the wood that was part of a tree, the tree with roots digging into the soil, the soil with the decay of life and the moisture from the sky and the lakes and the rivers, the tree that inhaled the air around it, the sunlight upon the leaves. Silbrey breathed in. The whole forest breathed with her. A simple thrust and the staff knocked the door to the ground with a dull crash.

On the other side, two priests sat at a table enjoying tea and a hearty morning meal. They looked at the fallen door, not sure what to make of it. They looked at Silbrey with her staff, her shield, and her horse, standing where the door at been.

"Good morning," she said. "I'm here to see Timon."

Timon walked with Silbrey. He hadn't seen her in years. He didn't need a cane back then, but his knees were not built to hold the weight of a lifetime at the temple. The main tower was quiet, except for Timon's cane tapping on the wooden floor as Silbrey and Timon strolled the perimeter. The light from the windows shone at the base of Aegir's altar.

"Piper, most people come through the front entryway. They don't knock down the back door. And it's not customary to stable a horse in the priests' living quarters. For future reference."

"I would've gone through the east gate, but I'd like Dahlia to not know about my return."

"Crashing through the back door was another favor, I take it?"

"Always."

"Last time I saw you was at your wedding. A rushed and private ceremony, if I remember correctly—"

"Callis is dead," Silbrey said the words, but they felt strange. "He was murdered outside the market. Do you know anything about it?"

"Oh, Piper. *Il mot golé laith.* That is terrible news. I knew someone was killed, shot by an archer. I didn't know it was your husband."

Silbrey ignored Timon's pithy Volir condolence. "One of Dahlia's soldiers?"

"Most likely a child recruit from the docks."

"My daughter told me a boy stole some coin from them. He did it to lure Callis into a chase, which led to an ambush."

Timon remained focused on the dead. "I will offer grain to Yoon in honor of your husband and your family."

Silbrey bristled at his kindness. "I don't need whatever it is you do here all day."

"The gods are good, Piper. Always good. But they are too big to be of any use to us. My job is to make the gods a little smaller, for our sake. It's a profane act to be an intermediary for the divine, but I do it for the people I love."

"What would a small god say to me in my circumstance?"

"Something along the lines of, 'Think of your children. Be strong for them. Everything happens in its season.'"

Silbrey thought of Taraki, a god who could plant seeds and anoint monarchs but wasn't strong enough to prevent the firestorm from consuming Efre Ousel.

"I do not like these small gods."

"No one does, but I cannot bring myself to tell people that big gods are indifferent while the world is in pain."

"Is that the truth?"

"My trade is not one of truth."

On this, Silbrey could agree. She had been waiting her whole life for someone else to acknowledge how absurd it all was. What had Timon's faith given him? A fat belly, while others starved. A walking cane to accessorize his long life, while others died young. Timon would be remembered long after his death for his devotion to these twelve altars, while Callis died like a hunted animal.

Timon broke the tapping silence. "Don't blame yourself, Piper."

Silbrey's cheeks flushed with anger. She wanted to hurl so many hateful words at the priest, but they came out at a steady, controlled pace. She sounded like Dahlia.

"I don't. I blame you. The old farmer found me. He handed me to you, believing I was a gift worthy of a priest's care. What did you do with that gift? You let me—as a child— roam the streets. You treated me like a stray. You left the scraps of your meals at the door so I would come back now and then. But when I wandered off and found a better meal, a better master, you were happy to be rid of me. You gave me over to a monster who abused me and made me into a soldier. When I was younger, I thought it was a cruel twist of fate. But now that I am a mother, I realize you are the monster. You aban- doned a child in your care."

Timon stopped walking. His cane shook.

Silbrey's words had injured him, so she continued.

"There was a time when I would've killed anyone without hesitation. No remorse. Dahlia pointed me in a direction, and I did what I thought she wanted. But my husband taught me compassion, and my children taught me how precious life is."

Timon's shaking increased. He struggled to breathe. He sat on the floor, broken. He could not look her in the eye. He tried to speak. A trembling, grief-stricken falsetto came out, not a word, just the hesitation of a word. Perhaps he was trying to say he was sorry.

Silbrey continued. "From this day forward, you are dead to your god. Do you understand? Your small god will no longer listen to your prayers. Instead, I want you to pray to my husband's spirit. Forget the grain. I want you to light candles in honor of my children. They are your gods now because they are the sole reason why you are still alive at this moment."

Silbrey walked out the front of the temple. As she left, she brought her staff down upon the sacred floor. The boom echoed off the high ceiling of the temple. The staff split the floor of the entryway.

* * *

From Gydan's explanation of what had happened, Silbrey knew which alley it was. Penderyn might feel like a maze to visitors, but every twist and turn had its logical destination. Every alley was wide enough for a horse cart, with an opening at both ends—except one atypical alley, closer to the docks, which dead-ended into a millinery with no back door. It was a perfect spot for an ambush. An archer on the rooftop across the street would have a clear shot.

Silbrey did not walk far until she saw a gaggle of children near this location. The children saw her. Their instincts took over as they scattered. However, Silbrey grabbed one boy by the collar. She tripped him with her staff and sent him to the ground. She pinned the boy with such determination that it startled him.

"A steady journey, little one."

"Aye! Whaddaya want?" the boy hollered.

"A boy. About your age. He's missing half his left ear. What's his name and where does he stay?"

For a moment, Silbrey's hostage looked like he would try to

be tough and not snitch on a fellow scamp, but they both knew how this worked.

"I know the one. What's in it for me?"

"Two silver."

The boy stopped struggling. He looked confused. The going rate for this kind of information was a few coppers. But for two silver, this was a much more serious situation.

"Is it about the dead man, yeah, from a few days ago?"

"Maybe so."

"He didn't kill him. He was to lead him into the alley. He didn't know."

"I want the boy's name and where he stays." Silbrey gave him another shove to remind him who was in control.

"His name's Kaleb. You can find him over at the south-end dock stables. He and his sister sleep there at night. They get paid to keep watch over the horses."

Silbrey let off of the boy and tossed him two silver. It all felt familiar—getting into it with the other street kids. She had to remind herself she was more than twice his size and a mother. She wanted to hit the boy for no reason at all, but she resisted. The boy saw this urge in her face, and he ran.

The smell of salty sea air wafted throughout Penderyn, but at the docks, the foulness of fish hit like a sucker punch. To the nobles, it was unbearable. To the residents, it was familiar. But to the fishermen, it was the smell of a good haul and honest work. By this time Silbrey arrived, many of the boats had cast their sails. A single ferryboat from Rhyll was at port, adding to the Bren rumors buzzing throughout the city. As Silbrey walked to the south end of the docks, she heard the name

"Bren Caius" no less than ten times. The consensus was that she and her soldiers were camped outside the city, and she was on her way. Silbrey saw no evidence of this during her ride last night. If her visit was a secret, it was a poorly kept one.

Silbrey walked to the side of the stables and the conjoining hayloft.

She regretted her conspicuous appearance. She had a shield strapped to her back. She was wearing a breastplate and carrying her staff. Silbrey looked like someone ready for a fight. She knew once Kaleb saw her, he would run. The stable had ample space all around the bottom for a child to crawl under and a wide gate in the front for horses and carriages. Kaleb had chosen a good place to stay if he needed to escape.

Silbrey looked through a space in the boards. She could see the boy, wild hair, and half an ear missing—possibly from a street fight or punishment from Dahlia. Silbrey snuck around to the front and rushed at the boy. It took him a moment to register what was happening, but before he had a chance to react, Silbrey grabbed him.

The boy flailed about, his hands reaching for her face to claw at it. He hissed and spit. Silbrey held him tighter, but he did not give up. He kicked with his heel against her shin, which hurt, but she would not let go.

"I'm not here for you, Kaleb." Saying his name seemed to calm him. "Kaleb, I need to confirm who gave the order. Who told you to lead my husband into the alley?"

Kaleb struggled against Silbrey.

"Say her name."

Sounds came from the boy, but Silbrey could not make out what he was trying to say. She eased off on her hold, and he spoke again.

"Shirin!"

Silbrey was baffled. "Who?"

"Shirin! Shirin! My sister."

Silbrey heard the thump of a bowstring. She could hear the whistle of an arrow, but she did not have time to react. The arrow went through the shield on her back, and hit against the plate armor. Now she was thankful for her conspicuous armor.

Still holding Kaleb, Silbrey turned around to see a girl standing on the hayloft of the stable. This girl carried a shortbow, designed specifically for children due to its lighter draw weight. This bow was useful in the confines of a city where range wasn't a concern.

Silbrey saw herself in this girl. Silbrey had darker hair, bluer eyes, and was much skinnier at that age, but she recognized a soldier of Dahlia Tulan. The girl's eyes did not waver from her target as she nocked another arrow. The girl aimed at Silbrey again.

Silbrey held Kaleb in front of her. She remembered the advice of her fighting instructor, Keote the Goatslayer: *Keep your shield up.* Right now, the shield was this boy, but he would have to do.

Kaleb brought his head back, hitting her in the face. Blood poured from her nose. She recoiled and cursed. Kaleb squirmed away and ran to the back of the building. The hit dazed Silbrey. She could not see, but she heard the bowstring thump again. She moved her staff in front of her, guided by instinct. The arrow struck the staff instead of hitting her throat. She spun the staff around and caught a second arrow with it. Silbrey surprised herself with this move. Shirin must have been surprised, too. She dropped her bow.

"Shirin, you killed my husband," said Silbrey. "Callis was a good man. He was gentle. He was loving. He was a good father to our children."

Shirin's face trembled, but her stern expression remained. She was angry. She stomped her foot to summon her brother out from the back of the stables. She moved her right hand to her chest with an articulated gesture and then touched the side of her forehead. She was speaking with hand signs. Kaleb spoke for her. "I know."

"I'm not here to kill you," said Silbrey. She took a moment to wipe the blood from her nose. "I need you to tell me, was Dahlia the one who gave the order? Was it Dahlia?"

Shirin nodded, but Silbrey wanted more.

"I need the words, child," Silbrey commanded.

"Dahlia gave me the order to kill Callis," Shirin signed.

"She said it?"

"She said the words," Shirin signed fast, but Kaleb kept up without any trouble. "She said there was a shepherd in the market with a green cart. He was there with his daughter, who is a little younger than me. I was instructed to kill both of them. My brother led the man into the alley. I shot him three times. I then waited on the rooftop for the girl to find him. It wasn't a good plan, but I was afraid of being seen in the market. Several hours later, the girl arrived. She reached down and grabbed the apple Kaleb had left behind. She cut the apple and saved the seeds. And I don't know why, but I couldn't do it. I wanted to, but I couldn't."

Silbrey's throat tightened at this news. It never occurred to her how close Gydan had come to death.

Kaleb spoke again as Shirin continued to sign. "When Dahlia found out I did not kill them both . . ." Shirin pulled her hair back to reveal several bruises up and down her neck.

Silbrey looked at the two kids. She hated them as she hated her own past. She hated how they took her husband, but she also knew how terrifying Dahlia could be.

"I want you to leave Penderyn," Silbrey said. "I want you to change your names and travel far from this place. Leave the bay and go west. There are other cities, safer places for you to live. If you stay here, when you come of age, I cannot promise what I will do. Do you understand?"

Shirin signed an acknowledgment and included some harsh words which Silbrey had seen before on the street. It was time to leave.

* * *

For the second time in Silbrey's life, she climbed the gate onto Dahlia Tulan's estate. It was easier when she was younger. Last time, she wasn't wearing her armor and carrying a staff. She landed on the other side with a heavy grunt. Like before, none of the guards were around to stop her, and like before, she could smell the garden, the largest and most well-tended in the city. More than any other place, it smelled like home.

Silbrey took the shield off her back and adjusted the straps tight across her forearm.

She walked through the garden to the front door, which was always unlocked. Who would dare break into Dahlia's home? She opened the door and looked inside. The foyer was empty. Every room in this house was beautiful, but the foyer was decorated to intimidate, showing off Dahlia's hunting trophies—two bear pelts on the far wall and next to them, three stag skulls with antlers intact, and over the archway to the right was a taxidermied wildcat.

The manor was silent. Every echoing step upon the stone floor felt like a public greeting: presenting Silbrey of Penderyn, formerly known as Piper the Tiresome Street Urchin, former ward of Guildmaster Dahlia Tulan, widow of Callis the Shepherd, and soon to turn her children into orphans. She walked toward the parlor where guests were received. A tea set and almond cakes were laid out, awaiting company. Her favorite flowers were cut and arranged in a vase. For a confused moment, Silbrey wondered if Dahlia had prepared it, expecting her return. Then at the opposite end of the room, Keote the Goatslayer entered, taking up the entire doorway. The goliath held a sword, unsheathed and ready. She had forgotten how tall he was. His substantial reach would make all the benefits of her staff a moot point.

"Hello, Silbrey," Keote said. His deep, gentle voice pained her. "I was hoping I would never see you again. Dahlia gave me specific orders if you ever returned."

Silbrey gestured to the food. "You were to throw me a party?"

"Apparently, Bren Caius is coming to Penderyn. Dahlia sent scouts in every direction to find the high general and invite her for tea. Twice a day, the servants fan the room and prepare this," Keote pointed to the tea and cakes, "in hopes that it'll be ready, if and when, Bren Caius makes an appearance."

Keote looked out the window, as though he expected to see the high general. This distracted moment was Silbrey's opportunity to strike. She had been trained well by Keote.

She swung her staff at a silver ewer, filled with water, on a serving table. Water went everywhere. The ewer hit Keote. He flinched. Silbrey took advantage of the moment. She jumped over the smaller table with its teacups and carefully arranged almond cakes and struck at Keote with her staff. He brought his sword up to deflect the attack, and then pushed forward, sending Silbrey stumbling over the table and falling to the ground. The tea set shattered. Cakes went flying.

An almond cake was on the floor next to her. She grabbed it and took a full bite. It had been so long since she had one. These were good, still warm. And now, Keote was charging at her with his sword over his head.

She jabbed with her staff, hitting Keote in the chest. This gave her just enough time to scramble back to her feet.

Silbrey finished chewing and swallowing. She turned to examine the mess that was the parlor.

"Mother is going to be upset."

"She's in the vault," Keote said. "She'll be here soon enough. There's still time for you to escape. If you go, I won't pursue."

"But I just got here." Silbrey gave her most charming smile. The dried blood from her nose offset the effect.

Keote shook his head. "My blade is sharp, little one. We're not sparring."

"There was a time, Goatslayer, when you wouldn't harm any innocent creature."

Now Keote smiled. "You're not innocent."

Silbrey spun her staff, which thudded against his chest. Keote labored to catch his breath. With one hand, he grabbed at her shield, and with his considerable strength, forced it in front of her face. He swung with his sword, hitting her on the side of her breastplate. The blow dented the armor inward. She could feel it pushing at her side.

Silbrey and Keote stepped into a familiar dance of strikes and parries, counterstrikes and blocks. Neither one could land a hit. But Silbrey was out of practice. She was a half second too slow with each move. And although it did not seem possible, Keote had become a better fighter with age. He could anticipate Silbrey's peculiar approach to combat, and Silbrey's airy confidence deflated against Keote's ability and experience.

Silbrey swung at Keote's head, but he blocked with his sword. The two weapons locked in. Keote overpowered Silbrey and punched her face with the pommel of his sword. The hit rocked her. Her knees buckled. She took a series of wild swings at Keote, which bought her time to regain her senses and orientation. She looked at Keote, but Keote was looking over her shoulder. It was a miniscule shift of his eyes, but it said everything to Silbrey. She pivoted, and blocked Dahlia's rapier, which would have gone right through her throat.

"Mother. With my back turned?"

"Win the fight. That's all that ma—"

While Dahlia spoke, Silbrey swung her staff hard at Dahlia's forearm causing her to drop the rapier—another jab to knock her back a few steps, and then Silbrey turned to deflect an attack from Keote who tried to take advantage of Silbrey having an opponent in front and behind her. Silbrey moved to the other side of the room. She kept both Dahlia and Keote in view.

Dahlia had more gray hair, some wrinkles around her eyes, but Silbrey also noted how beautiful Dahlia was. Like a spider dancing across the web, Dahlia had a symmetry and grace that was terrifying to watch and difficult to turn from. Dahlia's even expression showed no sentimentality, no affection or warmth, no love for the girl who grew up in her house. Silbrey was hoping she might be wrong and that maybe Dahlia did feel something. If so, it was not revealed.

Dahlia reached down for her sword.

"I told you to never return. You, more than anyone, should know I don't waste time with idle threats."

Silbrey was a fool. She could defeat Dahlia in one-on-one combat. But Keote? She might have a chance against the Goat-slayer on her best day and his worst. But the two of them together? She was going to lose.

"I'm here because you ordered the death of my husband."

Dahlia raised an eyebrow. "Did I now? That was your husband in the market?" For a moment, Silbrey believed her, but this was naïve thinking.

"You know it was him."

"Since you've been gone, I've pushed for control of the open market. Your husband should have known better. And you should have stayed home with your children. I've heard your farm is idyllic. I should visit."

Silbrey felt the weight of her staff, the staff she found in the grip of a horned fey statue, a statue that did not exist. The staff was real, though. It was wood. The wood was once a tree. The tree had roots, a trunk, branches, and leaves that extended into the world. The tree took it all in—the decay of soil, the moisture of rain from above and far off oceans, the light from the sun. It was all connected, and she was going to use it to bring some serious hurt to Dahlia Tulan.

Silbrey moved forward and swung her staff. There was a loud pop from the speed of her strike. Dahlia tried to react, but one might have a better chance reacting to a lightning bolt. Silbrey hit Dahlia across her torso. With the crack and crunch of ribs and sternum, Dahlia fell to the floor. This was the last good hit Silbrey would get. She left herself open to Keote's attack. He hit her in the chest with his sword. The strike would have been fatal, if not for the armor, but the pain still spread through Silbrey's body. It was difficult to breathe and stay conscious.

Dahlia found the strength to stand again. She thrust with the sword. It pierced through the plate and into Silbrey's side. The pain burned. Silbrey tried to counter, but Dahlia was able to move back. Again Keote came at Silbrey with his sword. She was able to block with her shield, but with the second strike, she felt something give in her shoulder.

The pain was part of the tree, too. The tree was cut down, carved into the staff, denied its leaves and its roots. That was what it was like to lose Callis. She felt like every part of her that connected to her surroundings and found nourishment was violently removed. She was isolated, and she wanted to be part of creation again.

More synchronized attacks from Keote and Dahlia.

In autumn, the leaves would fall from the tree.

Silbrey tried her best to protect herself with the staff and the shield, but they were too fast. The attacks kept coming.

In winter, the tree slept.

Silbrey could hold up her shield to protect her head, but the shield itself was splintering from the hits.

The tree, like all of creation, also slept.

She tried to keep Dahlia back with her staff, but Dahlia moved from side to side to find her opportunities. Throughout the melee, Dahlia's face remained blank.

The tree was dormant, waiting for spring, new warmth and new growth, a sleeping child in the night.

Silbrey, beaten and defeated, felt a voice speak to her. She could sense ancient wisdom in its chipped voice, the voice of a woodland spirit. "You are not a child of Dahlia Tulan. You are a child of the forest."

Rays of shimmering blue danced and swayed around the room. This light felt familiar, but Silbrey could not recall from where or from when. Keote the Goatslayer and Dahlia Tulan both dropped their weapons. Their eyes rolled back, and they collapsed, asleep!

Silbrey exhaled in shock and relief, but there was little time to ponder what had happened. Dahlia was unconscious on the ground. Silbrey could kill her now. She could crack her skull open with her staff. She could break her neck. She could take Dahlia's own sword and stab her through the heart. Penderyn would be a safer place, a better place without her. How many lives would be saved with this one act? Dahlia knew where Silbrey's home was. Silbrey would never be safe if she let Dahlia live.

Silbrey held the staff over her head. She was poised for a fatal blow. Then it would all be over, and she could return to her children.

But she could not.

Dahlia—cruel, spiteful Dahlia—was the woman who had raised her. She was the only mother Silbrey had. Let someone else kill the guildmaster. She couldn't do it.

Silbrey saw another woman standing at the archway amid the parlor wreckage. It was Bren Caius, the Northern Light. She wore a white gown with gold trim. Her sword, the sword she used to defeat Kret at Pynne's Field, was sheathed at her hip. She was aged, but not old. Vitality undiminished; she was a goddess in human form. An owl flew past and landed on the ground to pick at the almond cakes. Silbrey knew that owl. It was stamped on every coin in Amon.

Bren Caius looked at a stunned Silbrey.

Silbrey instinctively knelt before the great high general to show her fealty. Bren could hardly contain her amusement. "If I were you, I would've put them to sleep at the beginning of the fight."

Silbrey muttered what felt like an apology. "I've never done that before."

"But you think you could do it again?"

"Possibly. I don't know. Maybe."

"I know an arcanist at Sage Hall who could help. There is more to you than you realize."

"With all respect, your grace, your excellence—" Silbrey wasn't sure how to address the Hero of Eloe Vale.

"Call me 'Bren.' I also like 'Bren the Beloved.'" Bren placed a hand on Silbrey's bruised cheek. The warm touch startled Silbrey. It felt like flirting. Silbrey wondered if the traveling actors were right about Bren and her numerous lovers. "People call me 'the Northern Light,' which is a strange glow in the sky over the Ringaré Sea, but my sigil is a sun. It makes no sense."

"With all respect, Bren, why are you here?"

Bren righted a chair that had been knocked over. She sat down.

"Word got back to me that the people of Penderyn were expecting the High General Bren Caius. I knew nothing about this visit, but it's possible someone forgot to tell me. I haven't visited the city in a while. I took a few of my guard—" Silbrey noticed movement in the hallway behind Bren and saw the legendary Oren of Angnavir coming into the room "—and we traveled this way. Dahlia's scout found us and said the guildmaster wanted to meet, so I came here."

Silbrey had no strength to stand or sit. She stayed kneeling on the ground.

"Do you know Dahlia Tulan?"

"Everyone knows who Dahlia Tulan is."

The answer did not satisfy Silbrey. Bren continued.

"I've done many great things, but I am not proud of the vast amounts of coin I've spent. It forces me to indenture my government to the nobility of the region, and no one has more gold than what Dahlia has in that vault below us—or weapons in that tower."

Those last words hinted at a more extensive alliance. Silbrey stood up, even though it was painful to make any move, and stumbled toward Bren. Oren of Angnavir moved forward, but Bren waved him off.

"What deals have you made, Bren?" Silbrey asked.

"Dahlia enjoys her autonomy in Penderyn because she pays for it, not because we haven't noticed her butchery. But I do not need to go over those details with you."

"Why not kill her and take her gold? What you are doing is an offense to the gods."

Silbrey was not aware of the rising anger inside her, but she swung her staff at Bren, a fast and deadly attack. Bren held up her hand and stopped the staff with her open palm—like it was nothing at all. Her palm glowed with a faint blue light. Bren's voice lowered to a whisper. "The gods are big, but so are we."

Silbrey turned around to see several of Bren's guards had moved into the room with weapons drawn, ready for Bren to give the word.

"Oren, guards," Bren spoke casually. "While you are here, take Dahlia and her goliath to their respective beds. I don't want them waking on the stone floor. And do not let them leave their rooms until my business with this woman is done."

Bren turned back to Silbrey. "You never told me your name."

"I'm called Silbrey."

"Beautiful flower in Volir? Not a name, but lovely. Silbrey, what can I do for you?"

The question sounded mundane enough, but there was subtext in the cadence, which hinted an exchange. I will do something for you. You will ignore my dealings with the guild-master of Penderyn.

"You can't help me," Silbrey asked. "My family will never be safe, not as long as Dahlia Tulan is alive."

Bren Caius considered Silbrey's problem. "I own land throughout Amon. Some of the farmland in the family's name has remained untouched, unworked. I can deliver a sealed scroll, a writ granting you a modest acreage with an unoccu-pied house. I'll send it to you within a day, giving you and your family time to pack. Do not tell anyone where you are going."

"Where is this land?"

"I'll include a map with the scroll."

Silbrey barely had the strength to stand, let alone argue with Bren Caius. She simply nodded her head to accept the terms, both spoken and unspoken.

*  *  *

Silbrey walked down the crowded streets. Her hair was matted with blood, her right eye swollen nearly shut—but she kept her head raised. The people moved to either side, allowing her to pass undisturbed. A hush fell. Word had spread through

Penderyn about the return of Dahlia Tulan's prized soldier. They watched Silbrey, abandoning the impulse to hurry in the opposite direction. A small dog followed along, curious about her and the smell of blood.

She continued her slow parade from the gated upper district to the temple near the east gate. Sweat and blood blurred the vision in her left eye. She was nearly blind, but the streets were familiar enough in this section of the city. Many of the merchants under Dahlia's authority worked here.

The main street bent to the left and then another block to reach the front doors. Silbrey could make out the dome silhouette of the temple against the red sky and the glare of the setting sun.

In the merchant row, she could smell the warm yeast of the bakery. She knew this smell. Silbrey had often visited this bakery while running errands. The baker would always offer her an almond cake with dried fruit. The baker would smile and tell her, "Sweet flour for the beautiful flower," amusing herself with the play on words with Silbrey's name. Today, the baker and her family stood at the entrance of the shop. The baker had the grim expression of a funeral or perhaps a public execution. Her children were similarly uncharitable. They watched as Silbrey walked past.

More blurred ghostly forms came out of their shops and homes. They stood shoulder to shoulder, lining the street in solidarity against the wounded monster walking. Everyone was silent.

The small dog lost interest in Silbrey, barking twice as a polite farewell before leaving.

Silbrey had been trained to view everyone as a threat—a lion with hungry jaws wide open—and to stay out of everyone's view. With these merchants and their families all watching her, it overloaded those instincts. Through her obscured vision, she could not identify the faces in the crowd. This created a gut-instinct fear. Who had a sword? Who had a crossbow? Was anyone about to rush at her? With whatever strength she had remaining, she gripped her staff tighter.

Silbrey could hear her own footsteps on the cobblestone. She could hear her rasping breath and her heart beating. The city had never been so quiet. Even at night, people toiled and conversed. The drunks and the displaced kept the city alive while everyone else slept. Now, everything paused. The whole city stood vigil in hushed observation of the wounded monster.

The temple wasn't far now. She had walked past the last of the shops, the apothecary. Before her was the wide gravel path, lined with larger smooth stones. A woman stood between her and the entrance to the temple.

The woman had the distinctive braided hair of someone from Raustfweg. She dressed as an indentured farmer. She had never seen this person before, but she knew who it must be. When Silbrey murdered the immigrant family on the Welton estate, apparently, she had missed one.

"You killed my family. My mother, my father, my brother—"

"I know."

The woman's face contorted with rage, sadness, pity. So much was happening on her twisted countenance, wilted like dried fruit. The woman raised her fist.

Silbrey handed the woman her staff.

"Use this."

The woman held Silbrey's staff in both her hands. This was justice. Silbrey had thought she had gone to the temple for protection, but fate had decided otherwise. She was here to pay for her crimes.

Silbrey made her confession.

"I am Silbrey of Penderyn, widow of Callis the Shepherd, mother of two children. I murdered your family at the Welton estate, your mother, your father, your brother, your sister. And the only crime your family committed was that they saved enough coin to buy their own farm. Dahlia told me where to find you, but I did the rest. That was me. That was my choice."

The woman looked sick. Silbrey could see so many emotions moving across her face. It settled into a general disgust for everything that came out of Silbrey's mouth. Then the woman could bear no more.

"Choice?" The woman landed on this word. "Choice?"

Her tears started to flow, which caused Silbrey to cry as well. She didn't cry for the loss of her husband or for herself. She saw the pain she had caused this woman, the lives she had taken, and she felt deep remorse for everything she had done. Nothing would ever make it right, not a lifetime of charity and penance, not even her own death. The guilty feelings, which had eluded Silbrey, came as a torrent of deep sobs.

The woman dropped the staff to the ground and gave Silbrey a hug, a strong and unguarded hug. She held Silbrey like a dear and distant cousin, coming home at last. The hug confused Silbrey, but she accepted it. After a long moment, the woman pulled back. Their faces could not have been more than a hand's width apart.

"You were a child when that happened. A child," the woman said, struggling to hold back her sobs. "By the gods, we're the same age! And I can barely remember the details of that horrible day. What you did was wretched, but you are also a victim."

This mercy was more than Silbrey could stand. It felt wrong. It felt unearned. Silbrey could take abuse—she had taken it for much of her childhood—and she could endure the hits, but to be absolved? She would rather die than be pardoned.

The woman placed her hands on Silbrey's shoulders.

"I am Olstel of Penderyn, wife of Katreen the Fishmonger, mother of four children. And I forgive you."

Silbrey mouthed the words "thank you." It felt too hard to give them a voice.

"I've been waiting my whole life to say that to you."

"I thought you wanted to hit me."

Olstel smiled. "That too. I figured we'd start with forgiveness."

Silbrey had no more strength. No more steps she could take. No more fight left in her. Finally, at long last, Silbrey lost consciousness.

When she woke, she was lying on a cot in the temple's guest quarters. Her wounds were honeyed and bandaged. Four candles were lit, representing each domain of the twelve named gods. There were acorns, dried leaves, and a few pebbles scattered on the table, which Silbrey assumed was Timon's joking tribute to the unnamed gods. Her staff leaned against the wall —next to her breastplate and shield on the floor. She would need a new shield and a blacksmith to repair the armor.

Silbrey felt warm breath on her neck and heard a low snort. She looked over to see Feste, her horse, crowded in the room with her. He was ready to leave.

\* \* \*

Maricel had been tasked with spying on Silbrey. That was why she purchased the land from Callis farm in the first place and became her neighbor. That was why she had to invent the elaborate story of a former life in Aberton. One lie after another covered a series of truths. In truth, Maricel had been watching Silbrey and taking notes on every interaction.

Maricel knew she should have kept a closer watch on Silbrey after the funeral. But she did not expect her to leave in the middle of the night on horseback. According to Gydan, her mother had gone to Penderyn. Maricel was at a loss for what to do. Stay and hope she returned? Chase after her? By the time she sent a message, it would be too late. She decided to wait.

After the second day of waiting, Maricel's anxiety got the best of her, and she made plans to load the cart and head to Penderyn. If she ran into Silbrey, she could always do it under the pretense of a concerned friend checking on her. As fate would have it, the moment Maricel opened the door to go, Silbrey was already standing there.

The details came in a flurry. A horse in the temple. Urchins skilled in archery. A tea party. A forgiving fishmonger's wife. With some coaxing, the crucial detail surfaced. The guildmaster of Penderyn wanted her dead. Silbrey could not stay at the farm. They would be found, and they would be killed. Silbrey was waiting for a scroll, which would arrive within the day, granting her land far away where she and her children could live. Most surprising, Silbrey wanted Maricel to join them. The promised land was sufficient, but she could not work it alone. She did not want to raise her children alone. Silbrey fumbled with her words, but Maricel put a hand on her shoulder and just said, "Yes." She had no ties to this area. Wherever Silbrey was going, she would follow.

Maricel packed what few things she owned. She helped Silbrey and the children load their possessions into the cart.

As Silbrey predicted, later that day, a rider delivered a wooden case that included a wax-sealed letter, which Silbrey did not let anyone else see, and a writ granting the land. In the case was also a map of the location, indicating the territory. It was about twice the size of the current farm. The rider was a strong, older man. He had seen combat in his life. He looked a lot like Oren of Angnavir. Maricel wanted to mention it to Gydan, who was an expert on everything related to the War of the Hounds, but the man left while Gydan was still in the house tending to some final details.

With the documents in their possession, there was no reason to stay and every reason to leave.

Igvan and Wardi were bewildered, then enraged. From their perspective, Silbrey was overreacting. Silbrey was tearing the family apart. Silbrey must hate them and want to hurt them. They had lost a son. Now they were losing a daughter and two grandchildren.

Silbrey pleaded with them to come along. She tried to explain that no one was safe at the farm. Dahlia would have her revenge. But Igvan and Wardi would not listen, and no amount of evidence would persuade them. The children made tearful goodbyes to their grandparents. Silbrey's last words to them were to trust no one.

Maricel hitched her draft horse to the cart. Slow but strong, he was good for the task. Silbrey would ride alongside them on Feste. By the day's end, they were well on their way, taking the long road to avoid Penderyn.

Maricel would be able to keep a closer eye on Silbrey now.

\* \* \*

Silbrey read Bren's letter again.

Over the past month, she had read the letter so many times she could recite it from memory. She could tell by the sloppy penmanship that it had been written in Bren's own hand, and not the work of a scribe. This detail made the letter even more precious, but she could not hold on to it. She had promised to keep the high general's secret in exchange for a new life.

She placed the paper in the fireplace. The flames consumed the message and sent the ash up the chimney of their new home near Barcombe, far from Penderyn and far from Dahlia Tulan.

Silbrey whispered to herself, "The gods are big, but so are we."

The children were asleep in their room. Maricel was tending to the horses in the stable. The house was quiet, and Silbrey could enjoy a moment of peace.

Snow covered the fallow fields outside. The harvest time had long passed. Soon, the family would gather close to endure the winter—thinking of spring, a new planting season, and the treasures hidden below the surface.

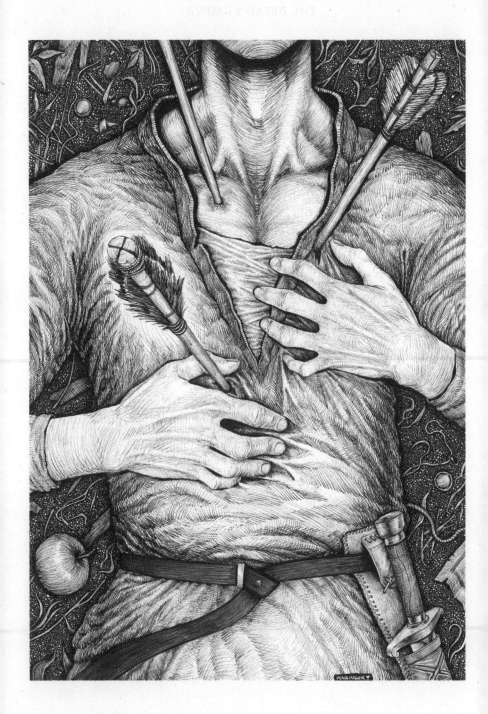

# II

AUSDRE LOST THE FEY CHILD. She screamed and clawed at the ground of the muddy riverbank. She screamed until her voice gave out. All that remained were deep involuntary inhalations, and then she gagged on the mucus gathering in the back of her throat.

Ausdre and the others were chosen to find the child because they were special, they had power—and they were wiped out by an ambush of gnoll raiders. She had sensed the danger; they all had. They should have been prepared. But the druids did nothing of consequence to save themselves or the child. They panicked and scattered like field mice before a swooping owl. Ausdre had a lifetime of training, but it was a sheltered education without trial and thus, without value. She had never known what it was like to fear for her life. The battle-tested gnolls rushed at them, full of fury and violence. Ausdre's companions fell. She grabbed the child and ran. It might have been the right instinct, but it did not save them.

The child was gone. Her companions were gone. Ausdre had no path forward. She was alone on the other side of the Great Thayl'em Sea, far from her village. Without the child, she could not return.

Ausdre dug her fingers into the mud. She wanted to crawl inside the earth and rest like the four titans: Raustfweg, Amon, Lunthal, and Karkasse, covered by the primordial earth of Terron. She wanted to feel the earth around her, ever consuming, breaking her down, decomposing her, and pulsing with life. A feast for worms.

Around midnight, the sounds of the forest roused Ausdre. She got up from the ground, stiff and unsteady. The tragedy of the day left her hollowed out, but her sense of fatalism had subsided. She stood there, covered in dried mud, which she could feel cracking on her face as she contorted her features. She pulled a stick from her tangled hair and tossed it into the river.

Ausdre decided to see where the river would lead.

A day later, she walked into a farming community. Four families worked this shared land—never three. Three was a cursed number. The four families welcomed her, and according to the customs of hospitality, served her tea and a meal before asking for her name. Ausdre could not hide the runic patterns tattooed on her face or her strong accent. Her presence was a boon for the community. She was a druid with gifts to enrich the farmland. She had a natural sense for farming and the seasons. So, she stayed.

She worked hard. She had to be coaxed away from the field at the end of the day. And as she worked, she thought about the gnolls, the river, and the fey child.

She would tell the families about her life in Raustfweg—

how their customs differed, how they worshipped the same gods but with different names, and how specific braids and knots had significance—but she could not tell them about the fey child she lost in the river.

As part of this community, Ausdre came to a deeper understanding of a concept from her old homeland, *dumeil*. No word existed for it in Amon, and there was no easy way to explain this idea. The most literal translation might be a "good measurement" or perhaps a "good return." *Dumeil* was love, but a love that doesn't feel like soft charity and flippant affection. It was a worthy love, an earned love, one that increased the worth of both parties.

In contrast, the love of a parent is unearned. No matter what foolish thing a child does, the parent will love them. While it's a powerful love, it doesn't say anything about the true worthiness of the child. Unearned love can also be the unrequited yearnings of a fool who presses the object of their affection. This is a cheap and distorted love. It hurts and complicates.

But Ausdre felt *dumeil* in this community. She brought something to them, and they gave her something in return. This exchange, which began out of a necessity for survival in a strange land, grew into genuine love for the families who welcomed her.

After a long year working in the fields, Ausdre went to bed in the guest room and woke up no longer a guest. A crown wreath of white flowers hung on a hook in her room—a gesture of adoption from her host family. Ausdre could not return to Raustfweg, and these kind people were offering her a new home.

Then, there was Rue.

Rue lived in the house on the other side of the pasture. He was gentle and sensible, which everyone recognized as virtue. Before Ausdre arrived, he had planned to leave the community in search of a spouse. When Ausdre arrived, all conversation of him leaving had ended, and he stayed. A sensible choice, since Ausdre loved him, and he loved her.

By the end of the following year, Ausdre was pregnant.

\* \* \*

Silbrey had been dreaming of Callis again. This time, they were naked at the base of the menhir near the farmhouse, before Callis brought her home as his wife, before she met his parents. An awkward introduction. She and Callis were both flushed and unkempt. It was obvious what they had been up to. She remembered that day and that moment at the menhir as being the innocent fumbling of two young lovers. Passionate and desperate, but tentative. This dream was different. In the dream, all modesty was abandoned. She used her strength and took her pleasure—each pushing against the other, in aggressive rhythmic thrusts. They were both covered in sweat. Muscles strained. She moaned as she could feel the mounting energy rising and rising.

And then, before she could reach completion, she woke up. She was out of breath and alone in her new bed, far from the menhir and the place she once called home. Her legs were wrapped around the quilt blanket, which served as a proxy for her husband while she was dreaming.

Silbrey was wide awake. She felt jittery. She sat up to regain her sense of place. This home near Barcombe was given to them by High General Bren Caius—a detail that Silbrey kept from Maricel and the children. They had lived here a few months. Now winter neared its end. The snow was melting, yielding to the wet chill of early spring.

Silbrey got up from her bed and walked into Maricel's room. Sometimes, when Silbrey had trouble sleeping, Maricel would let her stay in her room. Silbrey pulled back the blanket and lay next to her. Silbrey's breathing was unsteady. She could tell Maricel was also awake. Silbrey nuzzled closer to her. She dared a kiss on the back of Maricel's neck, who exhaled in contentment. Maricel rolled over and kissed Silbrey. It was gentle, almost friendly, but as Silbrey kissed back, it escalated into a fuller use of lips and tongue and mouth to explore each other's bodies. Nightgowns were pulled off and thrown to the floor.

Maricel moaned. Silbrey had to shush her as a reminder that the children were in the house. This was a common ritual for Silbrey and Maricel. They believed the children were unaware of what went on at night.

Besides one being a man and one being a woman, the differences between Callis and Maricel were profound. Callis was larger and heavier—which also meant he was more careful in bed, always asking how she was and what he should do. He was attentive and forthcoming, which was ideal for any partner. Maricel, however, acted with intuitive confidence, a sense of what felt good and what was wanted. This was also a good thing. The Callis in her dream was also Maricel. The sex was hers. Silbrey did not think anyone could take Callis' place. But her unconscious mind was replacing him.

In the early morning hours, half-asleep, her body could

seek satisfaction in Maricel. But in the lucidity of daylight, could she love Maricel as she loved Callis? Silbrey didn't know.

Afterward, Silbrey rested next to Maricel.

Silbrey had dark hair, short and messy. Maricel had long blonde hair that fanned out perfectly across the mattress. Maricel had lighter skin, almost snowy white. She was taller than Silbrey with slimmer features, long arms, long legs. Silbrey had joked once that Maricel could act as a scarecrow for the farm. It was a thoughtless thing to say. Maricel did not like to be made fun of, at least, not by Silbrey and not about her height or skinny frame. Maricel could tease all day, but she did not like to be on the receiving end. Silbrey had to apologize later. Callis was not like this. It was an adjustment for Silbrey. If something bothered Callis, he spoke about it. He wanted to talk about everything. The first time Silbrey was naked in front of Callis, he couldn't help but ask about her scars, the marks of her abuse as a child, which she lied about. Maricel noticed them too, but she never inquired.

Silbrey wasn't sure if she was ready to tell the truth. Silbrey had confessed to more than she had intended on that day when she asked Maricel to flee with them. But she withheld information about her past as the ward and trained enforcer of the Dahlia Tulan—how she was a gifted warrior with her staff, a staff she received under bizarre circumstances and to which she felt a mystical connection. Silbrey also omitted the detail about how, during her fight with Dahlia, her staff conjured a blue light that put her former master to sleep. Silbrey did not tell Maricel how, ever since that day, she'd been driving herself mad trying to replicate the effect. A few times, she attempted to work this magic from her staff onto her children when they wouldn't go to bed. No such luck.

Silbrey had her secrets. Farther from Penderyn, farther from Dahlia Tulan, Silbrey could hold on to her hidden past a bit longer.

Silbrey watched Maricel sleep. She was beautiful. Not that it mattered, but Silbrey decided Maricel was much more delicate and lovely than Silbrey could ever hope to be—long and fair, like a maiden in one of those bard songs. Silbrey was scarred and muscular. Silbrey's face was boyish, her hair disheveled. Silbrey had never been aware of it when she was with Callis. But Maricel's presence made Silbrey scrutinize herself. How could both Callis and Maricel, such comely creatures, desire her? Would they if they knew about her monstrous past?

Silbrey crept out of the room and back into her bed for another hour before the sun rose.

Gydan was already in the barn feeding the sheep. The routine was familiar. For as long as she could remember, her dad had woken her up to tend to the chores before breakfast and often before Yurig was awake. During that dark hour, she had her father all to herself. It was wonderful. Now, even without her dad and without much cause, she woke to the dawn chorus of morning birds. Gydan was already dressed when she heard her mother sneak back into her own room. Houses held few secrets. Every creak of the floorboards proclaimed truths, while the people remained silent.

Gydan fed grateful sheep. They crowded around the girl, nuzzling against each other for a prime spot in front.

The barn housed the livestock during these cold months with two stalls to stable the horses. Barely more than a shed, it was warm with the huddled farm animals. A gap in the barn's paneling would send a cold reminder of the weather outside.

Gydan wondered why they even bothered raising these few sheep. Her mother had purchased them on their way to the new farm. She had no interest in breeding or raising the sheep for market. She barely checked on them. Gydan was the one who fed them and let them in and out to pasture. Soon the spring grass would return, and they could graze. Gydan cared for them as best she could, but all this effort felt like an act to create the appearance of a farm. Nothing they did was enough for the market or to make a livelihood. To Gydan, it felt like a ruse.

And what of her mother and Maricel? Was that another deception? Maricel never complained. She never wavered in her support of Silbrey. While the family grieved the loss of a husband and father, Maricel was patient. She gave space when space was needed. She was close whenever someone needed a hug or a word of comfort. She never tried to take the place of Callis, but she felt like part of the family.

Gydan did not know what to make of her mother's relationship with Maricel. Gydan was too young to understand the complexities of love, but she did notice the playful demeanor Maricel had around Silbrey. The unnecessary touches with every exchange. They were living in a house that was not their house. They were pretending at farming and raising sheep. Perhaps her mother and Maricel were pretending at courtship? When trying to make sense of it all, Gydan decided it was better not to. She preferred the company of sheep.

*Who are you, human-child?*

Gydan dropped the wicker basket she used to feed the

sheep. Her knees buckled. Her eyes crossed. She fell to the straw-covered ground. A wave of voices filled her head, speaking in a language not her own, but which did not need to be decoded. Purest thought, purest communication.

*Who are you, human-child?*

She tried to scream, but her quivering mouth prevented her. All that came out was a warble of unguarded distress. The wave spoke within her mind again.

*You do not need to fear us. We are the one in a cage.*

Rolling to her side and curling up, Gydan whispered a reply.

"I'm Gydan, a shepherd, daughter of Silbrey and Callis."

Gydan's two front teeth were still growing in, thin white marks breaking through the gum line. A lisp could be heard on her parent's nearly symmetrical names, Silbrey and Callis.

*A shepherd? You protect small creatures.*

"Sometimes."

*Will you protect us?*

"Who are you?"

*We are in a cage. We will reach out again.*

Gydan wiped tears from her eyes. Her breath returned to her, and the wave was gone. The voices had been overwhelming, surprising, but not painful. Curiosity filled the emptiness left by the voices. She wished they would speak again.


Gydan had been in the barn longer than usual. The morning meal had already been prepared—beans, eggs, brown bread, and tea. Yurig was already finished, and Gydan's seat remained empty. Silbrey was about to send Yurig to look for his sister, when Gydan entered through the back door. Gydan was dirty and covered in straw.

Yurig saw her and snorted in amusement.

"You were supposed to feed the sheep, not live among them."

"Shut up. I fell down."

"How many times?"

Gydan raised her hand to give Yurig a good wallop, but Silbrey interceded, grabbing Gydan's arm. Normally, she would let her children fight it out. She wasn't obligated to be the peacemaker, and at times, their squabbles were entertaining. But in this instance, Yurig had a point.

"Gydan, you're a mess. Go to the washroom and clean up. There's some water in the basin from last night."

"That water is freezing."

Silbrey gave her daughter a look that said, this is not a problem to be solved.

Gydan rolled her eyes and made her way to the washroom on the other side of the kitchen. Maricel, who had been observing, spoke up.

"I can heat the water over the hearth."

Silbrey looked at Maricel. Once again, Maricel was challenging Silbrey's authority with benevolence. Maricel did it often without realizing. She wasn't a parent. She never had to discipline a child or let them face any consequences. Maricel was trying to solve a problem, but Silbrey was trying to get Gydan to do better. And every time Maricel offered to help, it made the children more resistant to Silbrey the next time she had to punish them. They would plead and sigh and bellyache, all the while waiting for Maricel to act as their protector.

Silbrey could feel her anger rising, and that anger took the form of a single statement in her mind: Callis would never do this.

Silbrey's expression revealed nothing, which was common for her. Many years living under the cruel care of Dahlia Tulan had taught her to keep everything well hidden. An unintended eye roll could be another beating. A downturned corner of her mouth could incite further discipline. Silbrey knew how to keep her reactions in check.

Maricel stoked the hearth fire while Silbrey fumed.

\* \* \*

Yurig balanced on a fallen log as he and his sister walked through the forest.

"I don't understand. Why would Mom want you to wash up and then send us both out to collect spring water? You're going to get dirty again. The well is closer."

"Mom wants us out of the house. It's a fey errand."

Gydan swung the empty bucket as a way to show how trivial the task was. But no matter how pointless their journey, because she was the oldest, she got to hold the bucket.

"A what?" Yurig teetered on the log.

"A fey errand. It's a pointless task to get us out of the house. Remember when I told you a unicorn was stuck in the brambles near the menhir?"

"I remember." Yurig held lingering resentment.

"That was a fey errand."

This forest on the west end of the bay was different from the forest to the east, where they had lived. This forest was denser, darker, and smelled of decay. The ground felt spongy underneath their feet. They were always climbing in or out of small gullies, worn from flooding. The eastern forest had oak and birch trees, which grew a comfortable distance from each other. Gydan and Yurig could run and chase, carefree. But in this forest—with misshapen boxelder, cottonwood, and black-thorn—the trees crowded in on each other. Gydan and Yurig couldn't take a step without tripping over a fallen tree limb, slipping on a patch of moss, or being slapped in the face by low-hanging branches. It was a forest for hiding in or getting lost. It was a forest for things that crept and crawled and slith-ered, for snakes and spiders and monsters.

When they first came to the strange house in the strange woods, Yurig and Gydan were not able to explore much. Only recently had they been able to leave their burrow to journey past the grazing land, past the tree line, and into the forest. The children knew about the spring water because their mom had showed it to them, but the rest of the area was a mystery to explore. And for children, there was no greater impulse than exploration.

*"Sah'le vuk!"* Yurig cursed.

Her brother's exclamation annoyed Gydan. She had been lost in her thoughts about the wave of voices. The more she considered that intrusion, the less real it felt. Gydan thought about talking to her mom or Maricel about it, but now it felt like nothing. A dream.

"Yurig! What is it?"

But she was already in front of the object which had star-tled her brother. She jumped when she noticed it.

Small bundles of hay were wrapped to form an effigy, which hung from a tree and dangled a few inches off the ground. Gyden pushed at it. The hay figure had some heft, yielding only a little to her effort.

"Don't touch it!" Yurig was afraid.

Gydan placed her arm around the straw figure's waist as if they were old acquaintances. "Why are you afraid of my friend? This is Lord Strawbottom. He and his family rule over this forest. If you knew your manners, you would bow and apologize."

Yurig eyed Lord Strawbottom with suspicion. "I'm not bowing. You bow."

Gydan obliged. She faced the effigy and gave a sweeping bow, exaggerated to an extent only seen from bards before their audience or priests before their gods.

"Lord Strawbottom. Good Strawbottom, please forgive my brother. He is stupid. And he did not know this forest belongs to you. We are a shepherding family, new to this region and your ways. As a token of our appreciation, I would like to offer you five of our best sheep and my brother's head. Although it is hollow, it hasn't been used much and—"

"Stop it!" Yurig gave his sister a shove. She slipped on the wet ground and fell over, laughing the whole way down. Lord Strawbottom turned as Gydan lost her grip on it, moving back and forth, sharing in the laughter. Gydan rolled on the ground. As Yurig prophesied, his sister got dirty all over again.

Gydan looked up at her brother. He wanted to go home, with or without the spring water. Gydan's laughter settled, tempered by a pang of sympathy.

"It's a straw dummy, nothing more," said Gydan. "Someone must have hung it in the forest as a joke."

She held out her hands to regard the effigy as harmless. At that moment, the wave of voices returned.

*Human-child, human-child, you are close. Come save us.*

Gydan cursed.

When they first arrived at the new house, Maricel found a heavy plow in the barn. She had used a similar plow on her parents' farm and wanted to give it a try, but the soil was too cold and wet to till.

Maricel was eager to put her draft horse to work, a large beast she ironically named "Mustardseed." Today, she walked Mustardseed, back and forth, across the field with a bridle to get him familiar with the task. Meanwhile, Silbrey's horse Feste ran in wide, haphazard laps, bucking and flaunting his freedom.

Silbrey walked with Maricel. Other chores needed to be done, but Silbrey was uninterested. She broke the silence with a statement, seemingly out of nowhere.

"The children are safe here. We're fine."

Even as she said these words, Silbrey didn't believe them. It was true once; Dahlia Tulan's grasp only extended as far as the city. They were safe at the old farm. But when Callis returned to Penderyn, the agreement had been broken—by Silbrey's foolishness. She doubted anywhere was safe. She knew Dahlia would send her agents to look for them.

Maricel reached out to hold Silbrey's hand, but Silbrey moved it away.

"What are you trying to say, Sil?"

"Gydan and Yurig don't need another mother. They have one."

"Oh," Maricel looked like she had been punched in the stomach. "This is all because I wanted to heat the water?"

"It's not that. You're constantly protecting them and mothering them."

"Someone should."

Silbrey thought about her staff. She thought of how much easier it was to spar with weapons than words. If Maricel were a goliath like Keote, she would have knocked her to the ground for those words. Instead, not knowing how to respond, she cocked her head to one side and grunted.

Maricel spoke again, "When we got here—to a house I still don't know how you acquired—you stayed in your bed for almost a month, mourning your loss. The children lost a father, but they also lost their mother to her grief. Who do you think fed them and cared for them during that time? Who told them stories before the evening candle was extinguished? I came to be with you. You have me, but you must allow me to be in their lives as well."

"I lost a husband to Dahlia Tulan. Now I lose my children to you?"

"I'm not taking them from you."

"You are!" Silbrey raised her voice without intending. Mustardseed stopped at the outburst. Maricel clicked her tongue and gave his bridle a slight tug to urge him onward. Silbrey continued. "Every time you contradict me, you are furthering the wedge between me and them. Who will they go to? Not me. Not when Maricel acts as their servant."

"That's not true." Maricel shifted the topic. "What are we? I wait for you at night, and you come to me. But your affections are gone with the morning. You think the children are confused. I'm confused. Am I your lover? Am I your partner?"

"My husband died not long ago."

"And yet?"

"And yet," Silbrey agreed. She paused and gave her response some thought. She looked at Feste, who was ready to race, far and fast from here, but stayed in the pasture. With Callis, her feelings had been so clear. A young love. But with Maricel, her feelings were complex—a mature affection that wasn't fooled by the realities of life. And yet, it created new paths, new possibilities. "I don't know."

Maricel wasn't satisfied with this answer. Neither was Silbrey.

"Who am I to you?"

Silbrey thought about saying "a friend," which for Silbrey —who had no friends—was the highest compliment. But she knew it would not be well received by Maricel.

"I don't know," Silbrey repeated.

"Then who are you?" Maricel's question was plain. No other meaning was intended. It was a fair question, the kind of question a hurt lover might ask. Silbrey knew so little about herself. Bren Caius had told her an arcanist at Sage Hall might have answers—her past, her powers, her connection with the natural world. Maricel wondered about none of this, but these were the true questions that needed answers.

"I don't know," Silbrey said a third time.

They both walked the wet field, unsure what to say next.

"I'm sorry." Maricel's voice cracked as she held back her tears. "I'm trying, but—" She composed herself. "It is hard to love you. I do love you, but I don't know if you love me back. I want to be part of your life. I want to be part of Gydan and Yurig's lives. But you pretend like our nights together mean nothing, and it hurts."

Silbrey wanted to say something to comfort her. Before she could respond, Maricel spoke again.

"I need to go to the market in Barcombe to get some supplies for the spring planting. I'll leave tomorrow morning. The trip won't take long. During that time, maybe you can think a bit more about your answers?"

"You can take Feste," said Silbrey.

"I prefer my horse."

Yurig and Gydan were nowhere near the spring. They had gone off the path as soon as Gydan told Yurig about the voices she was hearing. These voices directed her elsewhere. A sibling accepted such revelations with aplomb while parents and other adults would only have more questions. A sibling knew when to believe and embrace the inexplicable. Gydan said it, and Yurig followed.

As they traversed the underbrush, Gydan realized she had forgotten the bucket. She looked behind in hope, but it was nowhere to be seen. The bucket was somewhere between Lord Strawbottom and their current location. Mom would be furious.

*Human-child, not much farther. Be careful that Speck does not see you. Enter quietly, and free us.*

The voices became more focused.

"Who is Speck?" Gydan asked.

"What?" Yurig responded.

"Not you. The voices."

*Speck keeps us in cages. He is fearsome and terrible. He is the nightmare we see every time we open our eyes. Be careful, human-child. A little further and follow the badger path.*

Gydan followed the directions, and they came upon a gnarled tree. Bird skulls hung from the branches, tied with twine. The skulls were larger with short, hooked beaks. Each skull had a different rune carved into it and a dark chalk rubbed on it so the marking would be noticeable.

"These are arcane runes," Yurig whispered. "Witchcraft."

Gydan, who had never heard her brother say anything halfway intelligent, turned around surprised. "How do you know?"

"Oma Igvan," Yurig shrugged. "She liked to study these things."

"I didn't know."

"You weren't her favorite," Yurig said without a hint of malice. He then pointed to one of the skulls. "This one. It means 'warlord.' The rest are different monstrous folk—gnolls, ogres, goblins, trolls."

"What did you and Oma talk about?"

"If you live away from the city, you need to know about such creatures. A gnoll raid could wipe out an entire village."

"Not since Bren Caius won the War of the Hounds," Gydan countered.

The tree was situated so the ground was much higher on one side and sloped down on the other, exposing a tangle of roots. At the base was a cave, which went underneath the tree and continued farther into the earth. She saw a faint light coming from deep within the cave, and she could hear tiny chirping noises.

"We need to leave," said Yurig. His voice trembled. Her brother was shaking all over.

Gydan wanted to venture into the cave and help the voices that had called to her, but she couldn't force Yurig to take another step. It would be too cruel.

She nodded and promised the voices that she would return,

but there was no response. Gydan and Yurig turned around and left the gnarled tree. Retracing their steps, they were able to find the way back home.

\* \* \*

The children returned to the house much later than expected, dirtier than before, and without the water bucket. Silbrey did not make a fuss about the washroom this time, but she scolded Gydan for losing the bucket. It was even more infuriating because Gydan's excuse amounted to little more than "I forgot it."

Unless they planned to cup their hands to transport the well water, Maricel would need to buy a new bucket at the market.

The house had a large hearth; copper warming pans for each of the beds; a box filled with honeycomb candles; three butter churns—why anyone needed so many was anyone's guess; an assortment of furs and woolen blankets; enough utensils, cookware, and serving ware for a large family; an embarrassing supply of decorative chamber pots; but only one water bucket. The house felt like it was stocked by nobles who had no sense of what was required to run a house, except they feared walking outside to use a privy in the middle of the night. Since Bren Caius had provided the house, Silbrey assumed the High General was responsible.

After dinner, Silbrey sent the children to bed. As usual, they asked Maricel—not Silbrey—to tell them a story. Maricel looked to Silbrey for permission. Silbrey waved them on.

Silbrey, as she often did, crept close to the bedroom door to listen as Maricel told her story.

When Silbrey was a child, Timon would tell her stories—
but they were often short, didactic narratives. Parables were the
best she could get from him. And with Dahlia Tulan, there
were no stories. In those days, Silbrey would train until she
collapsed, and sleep came easily. When Silbrey's children
started requesting stories, she had no knack for it. But Maricel
was a masterful storyteller. Silbrey loved to listen in, sitting in
the dark hallway outside their room.

Maricel began with a quiet, low voice.

"As you know, in the beginning was darkness. No one
could see anything. The unnamed gods and the titans all
wandered in the darkness, bumping into each other. Then, one
day unlike any other, a raven, as he was flying, saw a darkness,
more terrifying than the surrounding darkness. But the raven
was not afraid. He recognized this was an unnamed god."

Maricel placed dramatic emphasis on all the right words to
pull her audience into the darkness.

"And since the raven was clever, he had an idea. 'I will land
upon the unnamed god,' said the raven, 'and then I can rest my
wings.' Then, along came a wise owl. She saw the resting raven,
and she said, 'The raven has a good idea. I will join him.'"

Maricel had unique voices for the two birds. The children
laughed at how raven-like the raven sounded, how owl-like the
owl was. Silbrey's face brightened at their laughter.

"Next came the crane. The crane saw the owl and the
raven. As a cautious creature, he decided it was better to follow
their lead. After all, the raven and the owl must know what
they're doing. Finally, along came the eagle. The eagle saw
these birds and scoffed. The eagle was the strongest of the
birds and did not need to rest. But the other three birds
mocked the eagle. And since the eagle was a proud creature,

she relented and also landed on the darkness to avoid further insult."

Maricel flapped her arms and made disgruntled faces, acting out the arrogance of the eagle.

Silbrey knew she was fortunate to have Maricel. She wished she were able to articulate her feelings. It should be easy, but every time she tried, it came out wrong.

"The four birds stayed upon the unnamed god for so long they forgot how to fly. Each of the birds began to worry. The crane began to cry. 'We cannot fly. What will happen to us? We thought we were clever, wise, cautious, and strong, but we were ignorant, foolish, reckless, and weak.'"

Maricel delivered her lines, overflowing with melodrama. All was lost. Hope was gone. But every child knew this story and what happened next.

"Then Ignasi, the primordial fire, heard the crane and took pity on the four birds. Ignasi formed a greater light, the sun, to journey around the unnamed god to keep the birds warm. Aylo, the primordial water, showed compassion, and gave the birds water to drink, which became the many seas. But Cael, the primordial air, was ashamed of the birds' foolishness. As punishment, it gave them the wind—a reminder of flight and how they gave up the sky. Against Cael, the four birds suffered."

Silbrey understood why Cael acted that way. Birds were meant to fly. It was an insult to the wind for them to stay on the ground. She wondered if Dahlia Tulan felt the same way, seeing Silbrey—her gifted warrior—leave Penderyn, get married, and have children.

"But Terron, the primordial earth, showed mercy. It lulled the raven, owl, crane, and eagle into a deep sleep, and then covered them, to keep them safe from the taunting of the primordial air."

Maricel ended the story as she began it with a quiet, low voice to let them know the tale had come to its end, and like all good children's stories—it ended with a not-so-subtle reminder to go to bed.

"These four birds became the four continents known as 'Efre Ousel.' The raven became Raustfweg. The owl became Amon, where we live. The crane became Karkasse. And the eagle became Lunthal. All four of them slept. And while sleeping, they dreamed of flight. That is why, from time to time, the world shakes under our feet as an earthquake."

Silbrey could sense Maricel moving along the wooden floor. Not the creaking sound—although that was present— but she could sense the actual touch of another person upon the wood. So natural was this sense, she never thought about how abnormal it actually was. Things that are hard to put into words also elude our thoughts. But she knew Maricel was walking to their beds to kiss the children goodnight. Then she heard her son.

"I wish you were our mom."

Silbrey felt a pit form in her stomach.

Sometimes sadness crept. Sometimes it approached with long strides, or it crashed into the room. However it choose to move, one could never escape. It must be faced and fought. But Silbrey was not ready. Obviously, Maricel was the more desirable mother. Maricel was kind and loving. Maricel was patient and wise. Silbrey was not a caretaker or a provider.

These were not revelations. More than anything, Silbrey felt she had betrayed her late husband. In his absence, she failed their children. Silbrey was so blinded by these dark thoughts it never occurred to her the meaning of the statement could be "I wish you were our mom, too."

Silbrey needed to get out of the house. She was in no position to be anyone for anybody at this moment. She walked into her room, grabbed her staff, and left the house.


Once Maricel was no longer in the room, Gydan waited a moment before also sneaking out of the house. Her brother tried to stop her, but Gydan was determined to discover what was in the cave and to recover the missing bucket. Because Yurig felt guilty about his cowardice, and because he was also curious about what she would find, he relented and swore to not tell anyone. He wished her a clear path on her journey and that he hoped she wouldn't die. Then, as soon she was out the window, he fell asleep without a care. In this way, brothers could be peculiar.

Gydan retraced her steps, which seemed like a sound strategy when trying to recover lost items, but it wasn't as effective in practice. She stumbled through the forest on this moonless night. She did not take a lantern because she assumed her eyes would adjust, but the ever-changing terrain thwarted any attempt to navigate it. Then, she saw a flicker of a blue light and heard a deep, repeating noise, a thud—like the sound of a full bag of grain being tossed to the ground. With each thud, she could feel the vibration in her chest and stomach. Gydan crawled upon the ground and hid behind a tree.

She looked around to see the silhouette of a woman with a staff. This woman spun the staff around and around in one hand, then she hit the hanging straw effigy, another thud. Poor Lord Strawbottom. A blue light rippled across the staff. It momentarily illuminated the living shadow to reveal Gydan's mother.

Gydan put her hand to her mouth, holding back the exclamations she felt inside. She knew her mother was strong, but she had never seen her like this. Silbrey's muscles across her body were taut and well defined. She looked like she could wrestle a giant, subdue a dragon, or defeat an army. Gydan's mind went to all the stories she had heard about brave warriors who were the unknowing avatar of a god, performing spectacular feats of violence. Gydan saw her mother, and she was afraid.

Silbrey struck the effigy so quickly it didn't even look as if she had moved. Her position changed, but the in-between was nothing, a snap, a blink, a flash. And what of the blue flickering light across the staff? The light was not unlike the static on Gydan's wool blanket on a cold, dry night, when she shifted underneath it. But here, something supernatural was at work. The trees around her mother leaned closer with each strike of the staff, peering with curiosity at this display of might.

Gydan did not know her mother, not as daughters should. Her mother was a mystery. But as she watched this warrior practice her craft, she felt the strangeness every child feels seeing their parents out of context. She saw Silbrey for who she was. Much did not make sense, and many questions would come later. Such a fighter should be employed by the high general, or part of a militia to protect wealthy fiefdoms, or perhaps acting as an elite assassin—not a mercenary, not a thug bullying for spare coin, or a roadside robber. What Gydan saw was something only her bedtime imagination would conjure. Her mother, who had no skill with children and even less skill with raising sheep, was something else. She was a force, glorious, devastating, ageless, miraculous.

When Silbrey was done, nothing about the effigy looked human. What remained was crumpled mush tied to a rope, tethered to a tree branch.

She felt a presence against a nearby tree—as she often had a sense for such things in the forest—but when she walked over to check, it had already left and was scurrying away deeper into the dark.

Silbrey often retreated into the forest. She told Maricel about needing the outdoors to clear her mind, which was true. She felt more like herself in the forest. She grew up in the city and then lived much of her adult life on the farm. But she had not spent much time among the trees until now. Despite the cold winter, she would walk through the sleeping forest, which stirred and bloomed with each footstep—as if she was willing springtime into existence. Silbrey felt a restless twinge as the plants budded, breaking free again. The forest's growth was her growth, and her growth was part of the forest.

She always took her staff on these walks. It also served as an opportunity to train in solitude. And despite her isolation, she never felt alone in this forest. There was something else within the earth.

She was out of practice when she faced Dahlia and Keote. She had been lucky to survive, lucky Bren Caius arrived when she did. She would need to be ready for the next time. The staff had placed an enchantment upon Dahlia and Keote to lull them unconscious. The magic within the staff needed to be harnessed. She would not make these discoveries on the farm. Such insight belonged to the forest.

Gydan moved clumsily through the dark, away from her mother and toward that cave. With a vague notion guiding her, she strained to find the badger path leading to the gnarled tree.

*You returned, human-child. We knew you would not abandon us.*

Gydan had become more comfortable with the voices in her head.

"I don't know what I can do. Why haven't you called to my mom? She's the—" Gydan wasn't sure how to describe her mom anymore, not in concise terms. "The one training for a war?"

*We don't want another soldier. We need a shepherd, you who protects the small creatures.*

Gydan tripped over a tree root. She fell to the ground, landing on her elbows and knees. She grunted her annoyance. "Falling down" was a theme for this long day. She hated this forest. She hated this farm. She hated this new life without her dad. Nothing felt right, and stumbling was the only way she could move forward. When she looked up, there was the tree. The runes from dangling skulls glowed and formed its constellations. The light from within the cave was brighter and framed in darkness. She heard again the chirping noises. Gydan picked herself up and, without any reasonable hesitation, she walked in.

The cave went much farther down than she expected. The incline was so steep in places she had to place her hand on the ground to steady herself as she found her footing. The cave did not branch off or take any drastic turns. The direction was consistent—downward and onward. The cave opened to a cavern. The ceiling looked as if it were melting onto the floor. Everything sagged. Roots from the trees above the ground broke through.

Light emitted from a series of runes painted upon stalagmites. It cast shadows across the distorted landscape. In a recess just beyond the cavern amidst scattered leaves were four small cages, two on the ground and two stacked haphazardly on top. Each cage contained a small, winged dragon—the size of a farm cat. The dragons shifted as best they could in their prisons and chirped. Four living dragons. Each dragon had vibrantly colored scales with accenting patterns along the wings and snout—green with silver, blue with silver, red with gold, and white with gold.

Gydan had never seen a dragon before, and she had never met anyone who had seen a dragon. A person wouldn't keep such a thing private, but would share almost upon introduction—hello, I'm Gydan, and I've seen a dragon. The woodcuts and tapestries depicted dragons as mountainous, able to flatten a village with the beating of their wings. They were, after all, the descendants of celestial titans. Gydan did not expect to see them so diminished, so humbled.

The red one looked at Gydan, who stood at the other side of the cavern. Their eyes met, and she heard the wave of voices again.

*You found us, human-child. Please free us.*

"You're a dragon?" Gydan whispered.

*We are. If you can call us that when we have never stretched our wings or—*

The dragon's eyes closed, sensing something beyond the limits of vision.

*Speck returns. Hide.*

Gydan heard footsteps coming from the cave's entrance. She took cover behind a rocky mound near the recess. She peered over the top and saw the creature named "Speck" pad his way across the cavern.

Gydan had also never seen a goblin before, and here was one. A hideous thing. The way she had heard them described, she imagined goblins to be oddly adorable, like newborn piglets. Instead, Speck was a monster in every sense. His skin was pale green, covered with warts and boils, and his eyes, milky white. His facial features were jagged, exaggerated, and sinister. His disorderly teeth protruded like the splinters from a broken board. Across the cavern, he walked bowlegged, hunched over, in jerky movements. Two dead rats were tied to his waist, and as he moved, they danced like some deranged puppet show. Gydan could not tell if the rats were kept as food for the dragons, food for himself, or for his amusement.

Speck carried a stick with a flint blade tied to the end. In his other hand, he carried the bucket, Gydan's bucket.

"That bastard," Gydan whispered without even realizing it. Speck stopped. His ears perked up.

"I heard that," he said. Gydan closed her eyes in frustration. "Do you think these enormous ears are decorative and serve no natural purpose? I live in a cave, my dear. I depend on my hearing. I can hear the droplets of condensation hitting the floor with a plink, plink, plink." While he looked hideous, the goblin spoke like a scholar with grace and sophistication. "I hear the lightest scratching of any living wretch that enters. I heard you scramble to hide from me. I could hear you and your brother tramping through my forest—and your inane conversations. Yesterday, I heard you drop your bucket, no more than 50 paces from the entrance of my home. Your family moved here and seemed to think you had no neighbors. Entitled and idiotic. I heard you arrive. I hear everything. When I served in Kret's legion, I could put my ear to the ground and hear the villagers on the other side of a hill before they even knew we were coming."

The mention of Kret caught Gydan off guard and curious.

"You knew Kret Bonebreaker?" Against all common sense, Gydan stood up from behind the mound. Speck acknowledged her presence and bravery with a nod.

"I was his war mage. In every battle, I fought by his side."

"So, you were there at Pynne's Field?"

Everyone wanted to know about the last battle between Bren Caius and Kret Bonebreaker.

"It was—" Speck paused to find the right words. "For as long as I live, I will never forget it. Two great warriors facing off in single combat, ready to sacrifice everything for the chance to kill their rival. Kret hated Bren Caius for disrupting his mission. Bren Caius hated Kret for the carnage he caused. But through it all, Bren Caius respected Kret. She did. Maybe even admired what he was trying to do."

"What was he trying to do?"

"Devour the world."

When Speck said this, Gydan took a few steps back.

His gentle voice had lulled her into letting down her guard. She looked over at the red dragon in the cage, hoping to receive a word of wisdom. The dragon was silent. The wisdom had been to hide, which Gydan ignored. The dragons pitied her, aware that this would not end well.

"That's my bucket," Gydan stammered as she pointed to the bucket in his hand. Speck threw the bucket to the ground. The clattering noise echoed throughout the cavern. Speck grabbed his spear in both hands and hobbled toward Gydan.

"Lost things in the forest belong to nobody, my dear. The bucket is now mine, as are you."

Speck bared his teeth in a wicked grin. His white eyes glowed.

\* \* \*

In the morning, Silbrey walked into Maricel's room, hoping to find her in bed, but she was already gone. Silbrey stood in the doorway for a long time, looking at the empty bed. She had never been in the room without her. Everything was quiet. Silbrey could faintly hear the sheep bleating in the barn behind the house. She replayed yesterday's conversation in her head, and how she could have said everything differently. It would not be so terrible to love again, even while grieving a husband's death. It would not be so terrible to be happy.

Silbrey wondered if she had ruined everything with the wrong words. In combat, the wrong move could mean a person's life. In love, was a misspoken word as unforgiving? Maricel had said Silbrey needed to think more about her answers. Silbrey considered the three questions. What are we? Who am I to you? Who are you? Whatever the answers would be, she knew she couldn't respond with, "I don't know."

The room was small with few personal effects. Maricel had a bed, a writing desk, and a chair. Her window had a view of the cart path, which connected to the main road.

Silbrey leaned on the windowsill as she looked to the forest that enveloped the path. As she leaned, she felt a slight give in the ledge and noticed the board was not nailed down. Silbrey lifted the board and saw a bundle of wrapped cloth in a hollowed space within the wall underneath the board. She set the bundle upon the desk and unrolled it to reveal four leather-bound books.

Silbrey opened the first book and saw a series of dates from when Maricel first bought land from Callis. Next to each date were notes about Silbrey, mundane details about the day. With great precision and commitment, every day was logged into the journal with a few words about what the author had observed of Silbrey from afar.

*Silbrey left the house in the afternoon.*
*Silbrey herded the sheep from the knoll at the*
*south end of their land.*
*Silbrey appears to be of a serious mind during*
*an evening stroll.*

Page after page, the books recorded her life as observed from her once neighbor, now lover. Maricel wrote down her plans to visit their house, to ingratiate herself with the family. Whenever she did visit for dinner or some other occasion, pages were devoted to her many observations within the house. There was even a hand-drawn map of the old house's interior. Special care was given in the journals to any time Silbrey traveled from the farm and where she went.

The few gaps in the journals were when Maricel had to leave. But it was clear Maricel was not selling herbs at the markets along Tu'enya Bay. She abandoned her vigil only to deliver reports to the person who hired her.

With shaking hands, Silbrey wrapped the journals in the cloth and returned them to the hidden space within the window ledge. Silbrey was devastated. She was heartbroken. She was not entirely surprised. It made sense Dahlia Tulan would find someone to keep an eye on her former ward. Was this where Maricel was right now, giving information to one of Dahlia's agents in Barcombe to then deliver to the guildmaster?

The sheep continued their bleating, which distracted Silbrey from her dark thoughts. Something was not right with the sheep.

Silbrey hurried out of the house toward the barn. In her rush, Silbrey had not bothered to put on her boots. Her feet pressed upon the grass, wet with the morning frost. Yurig was also walking toward the barn. He turned around and jumped, startled when he saw his mother approaching.

"I forgot to the feed the sheep," Yurig said. "They're hungry."

"Isn't that Gydan's job?"

Yurig took a second too long to find the right response. "She asked me to do it."

"Yurig."

Every child knows there are a hundred ways a parent can say their name, and each inflection carries a different meaning. This one said, don't lie to me.

"I lost a bet. I have to feed the sheep." He sounded even less confident.

"Yurig."

This time, the inflection said, I'm giving you one last chance to tell the truth.

Her son acquiesced. "She snuck out last night to find the bucket but never returned."

Silbrey looked to the sky and spoke a mother's prayer to the named goddess Yoon, asking what to do with a child like hers. Maricel's journals became a distant thought as she considered all the horrible fates that could have prevented her daughter from returning home.

"Yurig, feed the sheep. Then you're going to show me where you and your sister went while in the forest."

Silbrey went back into the house for her staff.

Silbrey, still barefoot, stood with her son in front of the cave opening underneath the gnarled tree.

"I wish you would have told me the part about you and your sister discovering a mysterious cave surrounded by arcane runes."

"Sorry."

Silbrey held her staff in one hand, and she took her son's hand in the other.

"Let's go."

They descended into the cave, both into the darkness and also closer to the dim light farther within. They took each step with care, not wanting to slip and tumble down the steep incline. In some places, the ceiling was so low Silbrey had to crouch to fit through.

Silbrey and Yurig entered the cavern with its unnatural light. Silbrey saw the bucket on the ground, the dragons in their cages, and Gydan in another cage next to them. Her daughter looked livid, but alive and unharmed.

"Your daughter came to me," a voice reverberated across

the cavern. "And now you're bringing me your son? Are you anxious to be free of your children? You don't have to tell me in front of them, but I am curious."

Speck walked out from the darkest depths of the cave to reveal himself, spear in hand. His white eyes pierced through the darkness even before the rest of his form could be seen.

"They are a pain, but I would like to keep them," Silbrey said. "They've grown on me." Silbrey moved Yurig behind her. "Let's skip tea and customs. I am Silbrey, a shepherd, widow of Callis. Who are you?"

"I am Speck, a war mage of Kret Bonebreaker, and this is my cave. And it is my forest that surrounds your farmhouse. In keeping with the traditions of your people, perhaps you should call me Lord Speck. Have you come to pay tribute?"

"That farmhouse and the land was given to me by High General Bren Caius."

Gydan looked at her mother in utter confusion, as if none of those words made any sense.

Speck laughed, shrill and sinister.

"If that is the case, Bren Caius is either woefully unlucky or cruel, maybe both?"

"I have a special writ granting the land, marked with Bren's seal," Silbrey said. "If you have a complaint about my rights, you can take it up with the Northern Light in Rhyll."

Speck disregarded the suggestion with a hand wave.

"Your daughter is the matter. She tried to steal my dragons. Promise me you will never again set foot in my forest except for the cart path and the main road, and she can go."

"This is fair," Silbrey said. Her jaw clenched. Her neck strained. There was no comfort in negotiating her family's safety.

"Mother!" Gydan yelped. "We have to save the dragons!"

Speck kicked the side of the cage to shut her up.

Silbrey moved on Speck. She spun her staff around, pinning the goblin to the ground.

"Do that again," Silbrey said, "and I will crack your skull open."

Speck struggled to speak with his face pressed against the wet earth.

"The children may go. You must stay for a while longer."

With a shallow exhalation, Speck's breath appeared as luminous smoke. He disappeared from his prone position on the floor to reappear on his feet and farther from Silbrey. With the goblin no longer under her staff, Silbrey fell forward but regained her balance. Yurig and Gydan gasped in amazement at Speck's magic.

Mages were rare—one in a thousand, one in a thousand of thousands. One might think they didn't exist and were more a product of stagecraft and exaggeration. But everyone had a story they couldn't dismiss as trickery—the distant cousin who turned into a bear, the gourd containing an unlimited supply of fresh water, or the day every tavern in town erupted in flames, except the one that served the mage's favorite ale. Just because something is rare does not mean it is to be doubted.

When Silbrey was young, Dahlia Tulan had introduced her to a mage from Sage Hall. He was the only mage from Sage Hall. His name was Aubec Skarsol. He had brown skin and blue eyes. His hair was braided in rope-like strands and tied back. He wore a dramatic red cape that swished from side to side as he walked. Silbrey loved that cape. Dahlia had attempted and failed to buy his services. Aubec was too proud. He stood before them with such rakish confidence that Silbrey thought he was the head of an old noble family or a military general. Only later did she realize all the teachers from Sage Hall walked around with this air of superiority. Unlike the other teachers, though, he was a mage—which was not an education one could pursue on a whim. The knowledge was complicated, esoteric. To the most gifted scholars at Sage Hall, even the simplest spell confounded the learned and made a mockery of their intellect. That is, except Aubec. He carried his spellbook with him at all times. He studied at all times. Spells were among the first written records because the information could never stay within anyone's memory. Arcane knowledge was so slippery a mage could lose all they had gained if they took even a day off from their practice.

Remembering Aubec's spellbook, Silbrey looked for Speck's. She saw it near the cages, warped and tattered from years of meeting the demands of its impish owner.

Here was a magical goblin in a magical cave. Here also were caged dragons. One could easily become lost in the wonder of it all, but Silbrey just wanted to hit Speck with her staff as hard as she could. The goblin had her daughter in a cage, and that eclipsed everything else.

"Why must I stay?" asked Silbrey.

"Because you lied to me when you introduced yourself."

"I told you my name is—"

Speck pointed his spear at her. "You said you were a shepherd. You are many things, but nothing so mundane as a shepherd."

Silbrey walked to the cage that contained her daughter, but kept her eyes on the goblin. With a single strike, she broke the latch and out tumbled Gydan.

"Gydan, Yurig. Go home. I won't be long." That last part carried the hint of a threat.

"But Mom, the dragons!" Silbrey's heart ached at Gydan's pleading tone. Normally, her daughter could do little to persuade Silbrey, but the pain in her voice couldn't be ignored.

"Gydan, take your brother and leave."

Gydan held out her hand to the dragons to let them know she did not want to leave. She went to where the bucket was and grabbed it out of spite. Gydan looked at Speck. With the back of her hand to him, she extended three fingers and waved them. The gesture was a malediction, a threat, and a sure way to start a brawl at any tavern.

After the children made their way back to the surface, Silbrey spoke again.

"You have dragons. How do you have dragons?"

"I breed them," Speck said. "None of these dragons have seen the light of day, much less the outside of their cage. The original miniatures I plundered from a noble during the war. They are easy to breed. They can reproduce within their own bloodline, and they are sexless except when they are in heat. They change from male to female, female to male, depending on what is needed."

Speck examined his dragons, walking around the cages in admiration.

"Miniatures?"

"The cages stunt their growth," Speck explained, happy to share his hobby. "It makes them easier to sell. I can't detain a full-size dragon. Can I? It would kill me without hesitation. Which is why I also remove the glands that produce their fire breath." Speck held up his spear and pantomimed the crude surgery. "A noble will pay a fortune for such a fabled beast. One sale and you can live comfortably without ever working again."

Silbrey looked around his squalid cavern.

"This does not look like comfort."

"My needs are simple. Humans, elves, dwarves, halflings, their kind require so many comforts to be comfortable, so many needs must be met before they are no longer needy. I'm saving my coin for when Kret returns. Wars are expensive. Weapons are expensive, even though Dahlia Tulan is selling to me at a discount."

He said Dahlia's name with a smirk—hoping to get a reaction from Silbrey. The goblin knew Silbrey had once worked for Dahlia Tulan, but so what? All of Penderyn knew Silbrey once worked for Dahlia Tulan. And Silbrey knew Dahlia Tulan was selling weapons to Bren Caius. It was no surprise the guildmaster would deal with both sides—another reason why Silbrey should have killed her.

"Why are you sharing this?"

"In the spirit of an open dialogue, neighbor to neighbor, I felt I should tell you."

"There's a reason, and you're not telling me why."

Speck sneered, "And who will believe you? Your family is in hiding. Do you even exist?"

"You said *when* Kret returns. Kret is dead. He died in Pynne's Field."

"Did he? I served with him during the War of the Hounds. After Pynne's Field, those left behind spread across Amon. Lost veterans of an old war. Many of us went into hiding, but we didn't disappear from existence just because you ceased to think about us."

Speck walked about the cave in his irregular, halting

manner. Silbrey listened, but the two dead rats tied to his waist distracted her. The sounds of the dragons chirping in pleading tones distracted her. Her desire to hurt Speck distracted her. She was in no mind to hear old war stories. She changed the subject.

"You're a mage. What can you tell me about this staff?" She held it in front of him to examine, but she did not let go of it. "I've had it most of my life. A blue light will radiate from it, but only sometimes. I don't know how it works. It has some sort of sleep magic. Tell me about the staff, and I won't hit you with it."

Speck looked at the staff. "You don't know anything about yourself, do you? The staff is interesting, but not magical. The power comes from you. You could pick any stick off the ground and achieve similar fantastic results."

Silbrey thought about the connection she felt to nature, that intimate and essential sense. She held her secret close, hidden within herself. So deeply, she rarely thought about it, but she always felt it. And here, this goblin was in on the secret. "I don't believe you."

At this, Speck laughed. A grating cackle. "This? This is the thing you find unbelievable? Look at your feet! Look at them." Silbrey looked down at her bare feet. Where she stood, there was a patch of grass and budding flowers. "Nothing grows down here, nothing except mushrooms and moss. Since you've been here, that flora grew underneath you. I'm sure if I allowed you to live here, we'd have a lush garden in this cave by the end of the fifth day.

"You came here barefooted. The snow has barely melted, but you don't seem to mind. I'm sure you could've walked here naked as a mewling newborn and wouldn't have noticed how cold it is. In the old days, your kind would often frolic through the woods without a stitch of clothing on. I'm sure that's why the poets and painters loved you."

"My kind?" She did not like his smugness.

"All that time in the city was not good for you," Speck tapped the side of his head to indicate a deficiency on her part. "Not that the farm was much better. You need the untamed wilds where life does not grow in rows across level fields. Is it any wonder as a child you sought the one place in the city with the most greenery? The garden at Dahlia Tulan's estate. That's where you chose to live."

"Did Dahlia tell you all this?" The conversation bewildered Silbrey.

"It's been a while since I've seen the guildmaster, but she told me some things. It's hard to keep secrets from me. But just as I told your daughter, these enormous ears do not merely exist to charm you."

"Your ears?"

"The better to hear you with, my dear. You are a noisy neighbor. I've been listening to you for months. I know more about you than I would like to know. What was it you said yesterday? 'Gydan and Yurig don't need another mother. They have one?' What sort of melodrama are you throwing at this woman?"

"You heard that conversation?"

Speck laughed. "I couldn't avoid it. Your sad relationship was echoing across the forest."

Silbrey should have been furious, but instead she smiled. She knew something Speck did not. "You pay such close attention to me and my disastrous life, perhaps you should focus more on your surroundings."

Silbrey nodded in the direction adjacent to the cages. Speck's tattered spellbook was gone.


"Yurig! You can read the book when we get to the house. Come on!"

Yurig and Gydan staggered through the forest. They were almost to the house. They would have been there sooner, but Yurig kept stopping to flip through the book he stole from the cave.

He was lost in another world, distracted by the possibilities within these pages. "It's his spellbook! You would think he'd have some sort of ward protecting it, or—"

"Whatever it is. It's yours now, and you can look at it later."

"You were making such a performance over the bucket. I'm surprised he didn't know you were distracting him."

Gydan gave him a wink. She could be quite the trickster.

"Maybe you aren't so stupid." This was the closest Gydan could get to a compliment.

"Maybe." Yurig was partially listening as he flipped through the book. The runic marks, the smattering of Volir, symbols for measuring space overlapping it all. At first glance, it made no sense, but patterns emerge for people willing to look for them. Truth found in the nonsense. Yurig could not look away.

"Speck knows we stole the spellbook," Gydan said. "And he's angry."

"How do you know that?"

"The red dragon is speaking to me. Remember, the voices."

"Many voices," Yurig pondered, "but it's the one dragon speaking?"

"I believe so. Dragons don't think the way we do."

"Now you're an expert on dragons?"

"I know more than you do." Gydan flashed an agitated look. He wondered if she was going to breathe fire. Yurig risked another question.

"How was the dragon able to direct you to the cave or contact you in the first place?"

Gydan was about to give an answer, but paused, stumped by this one. Then, after a moment, she responded. "The dragon says they can see out into the surrounding area with their mind. A second sight. Many dragons will remain hidden away for centuries while still observing the world around them. And—"

Gydan heard a high-pitched whistle. A panicked expression formed on her face. She grabbed onto her brother's wrist.

"We need to go!"

"Why?"

"There are others in this forest."

They heard the sounds growing louder behind them, yipping noises and the rustle of footsteps.

As soon as Speck noticed the spellbook was missing, he threw a spectacular tantrum.

Like all parents, Silbrey did her best to ignore it. "Tell me. How do I use the magic? It's not my staff. You said the power comes from me. That enchanting sleep. I want to do it again. You tell me, and I will return your book."

"I can get the book myself."

"My children will hold your book over a fire in exchange

for the dragons. I can return the book in one piece, but you must tell me how my magic works."

"Is this Sage Hall? Am I your teacher? Am I expected to explain Al'taru to you?"

"Al'taru? There are the four elements—Ignasi, Aylo, Cael, and Terron—and Al'taru weaves them all together."

Speck groaned at Silbrey's rote response. "My dear, people think the unnamed gods were the primary cause for order in the world, but it was Al'taru. Al'taru distinguishes the elements from each other. Fire is fire, and not water. Air is not earth. But it's more complicated than that. It always is. Everything is connected. All the elements exist within each other as well. There is warmth in the earth. Fire. There is water and air in the soil. Fire needs air to breathe. It needs fuel to burn, which is the earth. Al'taru connects it all, the spine."

"So what?"

"Answer this for me: Can anyone control the elements—not entirely, but to some degree?"

Silbrey considered the question. "Yes. I can dig up the earth, till the soil. I can route water for irrigation. I can set fires to cook meals. And I fan the kitchen to clear any floating dust before I prepare a meal."

"One can also control Al'taru. Mages do it through study and by putting a bit of themselves into each spell. It's not only about the four humors—blood, yellow bile, black bile, and phlegm. It's about the air we breathe and the sounds we make, about movement, the space we occupy, and the time within it. Mages develop the arithmetic to manipulate this in-between force. Druids—more common to Raustfweg—their craft depends on old blunt practices, more ancient than my studies. But the premise is similar. They use berries, acorns, leaves, or a pinch of soil to beg nature for a moment of its time. They shift things around and then return them to normal. However, you are different. You are neither mage nor druid. You are fey, which makes you able to manipulate Al'taru without ritual or research."

Silbrey laughed, so unrestrained and spontaneous that it startled Speck.

"Fey?" Silbrey asked while stifling her laughter. "Like in the stories? And where are my fairy wings and my magical dust? Did I forget my riddles? Or how to spin golden thread?"

"Not all fey creatures are the same," Speck continued, "nor are they like the stories you've heard. But they do exist. You see these dragons. You've seen the power I can work. This world is full of terrifying wonders. Undoubtedly, you've seen the signs throughout your life, and you've dismissed them like a fool. Don't be willfully ignorant. You want to work your magic, then you need to better understand yourself."

Apparently, everyone—from Timon to Bren, Maricel to this goblin—wanted her to become an ascetic. She had heard of a community to the south, Maynor Settlement, where idle folk spent their days wandering the wilderness trying to better understand why they were idle. This approach did not feel like the way to unleash the magical blue light. She needed something she could see and touch.

Silbrey spun her staff around casually. "For someone who hates to teach, you do talk a lot."

"For someone who asks a lot of questions, you remain unschooled." Speck took a step back.

"You want your spellbook. I'll get it."

"Ah, I never agreed to those terms." Speck wagged his finger. "I told you I can retrieve my book—as easily as I can strike down your children. Your existence offends me. I want repayment for the insult to my dignity."

"And the payment?" Silbrey dared to ask.

"I want your heart torn out of your chest and placed in a box."

The lesson was done. The chatter was over. Only one of them was leaving the cavern. From Speck's mouth, as before, came the luminous smoke, which he manipulated with his boney fingers. Silbrey jabbed at him with her staff, but the staff went through him as if he were an ethereal mist. The mist dissipated, and he was gone.

Silbrey looked at the caged dragons. She jutted her head forward slightly, indicating a little help would be nice. The red dragon, seeming to understand what was being asked, gestured to the left. Silbrey swung and connected against Speck, who grunted as he reappeared. At close range, he threw his spear at Silbrey, but she knocked the spear away with a whirl of her staff that had more flourish than necessary.

Speck held up his hands, palms out. Silbrey knew she should be worried, but did not know what to expect. A shockwave boomed. The blast knocked Silbrey across the cavern and against the far wall. The cages scattered. Crumbling bits of the ceiling fell to the floor.

"If I were you," Silbrey rubbed her head, disoriented. "I would've done that at the beginning of the fight."

The blast cracked the ceiling. The tree roots that protruded above them held larger chunks in place.

The dragons crawled out of the broken cages, stretching their wings. Without hesitation, three of them took flight and escaped the cavern. They flew fast, like arrows shot from a bow.

One remained. The white dragon lay dead. Debris from the ceiling had crushed it.

Silbrey was injured. Her side was bleeding. She should have repaired her breastplate and shield from the fight with Dahlia and Keote. It would've helped. She made a silent promise that if she survived today, she would never be without either. She would go to bed with her breastplate and shield. She would walk around the house with her breastplate and shield. Everyone would think she had lost her mind, but she would be ready for the next time something horrible disrupted her attempt at a life.

She saw Speck bent over, holding his stomach. Silbrey ran toward him, staff braced across her inner forearm, poised for another strike. He disappeared. Silbrey swung in every direction, hoping she might find him.

He appeared again at the tunnel, which led back to the surface. He spoke in gasps and groans, but his arrogance remained unhindered.

"I have dragons to retrieve, a book to recover, children to punish. Time to call on the old troops."

Speck cupped his hands together and blew in the gap between his thumbs. It created a high-pitched whistle. After he finished, he then held up his hands toward the cavern ceiling, palms out and upward.

"No! No, no, no!" Silbrey ran to Speck, but the distance was too far to cover. Another shockwave and the cavern collapsed onto Silbrey.

Speck's whistle called the others from their burrows. A remnant of Kret's legion surfaced and marched through the dark forest. The gnolls, mangy and merciless, padded along as a pack. The goblins, diminutive and full of mischief, hurried in their hunched fashion. The trolls, gaunt and nightmarish, seemed to glide with each long step across the uneven terrain. And a single ogre, tall as a goliath and twice as thick, stomped straight through, knocking back the trees as he went. All of them predators to the common folk. These creatures did not farm or build or make treaties. They only knew to raid and scavenge. Violence was their trade.

Long ago, before the age of giants and dragons, the twelve named gods had banished the demons and devils who once dwelled on the continents. But their heirs took the form of these monstrosities. And Kret Bonebreaker was able to organize them under a single banner, his own. In the years since the war, unlucky communities have encountered the surviving soldiers of Kret's legion. And here within this forest, several resurfaced to answer the summons of Kret's old war mage.

Gydan and Yurig traveled as fast as they could, but the tangled forest halted their efforts with every step. The branches and brambles whipped at their faces as they forced their way through. Gydan and Yurig would slide down one side of a gully and then grasp at the ground to crawl back up the other side. Stumbling was a clumsy manner of progress. And every time they looked back, the creatures of the forest were gaining on them.

"They've been in the forest this whole time?" Gydan shouted to her brother, who was ahead of her. "I'm never leaving the house ever again!"

"We can make it. I see the barn!"

They passed the tree line and were back in the open field. They sprinted through the mud as best they could—Yurig holding onto the book, Gydan holding onto the bucket. Yurig veered off to the house, but Gydan stopped him.

"Go to the barn."

"But what if Maricel is back?"

"Go to the barn!"

Gydan had not thought of Maricel's return. She dismissed it as wishful thinking. Even if Maricel didn't stay long in Barcombe, she wouldn't return until later. No, the barn was better. If these creatures wanted to fill their bellies, then the sheep and the horse might be a substitute while they hid. Gydan loved the sheep, but she would sacrifice them in a heart-beat if it saved her brother.

They ran to the barn and shut the door, just as the first gnolls made it to the field. Gydan and Yurig crept past the sheep. The sheep bleated, wondering if dinnertime had come early. Feste could sense something was wrong. He snorted and moved around in his stall. Gydan thought about hiding in the stables, but the stalls were clean and uncluttered. They could be spotted through the slats. Instead, Gydan and Yurig squatted behind the plow in the corner of the barn.

Yurig trembled. His pants were soaked at the crotch. Gydan could smell the urine.

"I'm sorry," Yurig said as the tears came.

"It's okay. Please. Be quiet."

"I don't want to die."

"They will have to go through me first."

Gydan had always wanted to be the hero like Bren Caius, but her words did not feel heroic. They would kill her first, and then they would go after her brother, and there wasn't much she could do to stop them.

Both children jumped as they heard a pounding at the barn

door. Once, twice, and then with a third hit, the ogre smashed through the door and into the barn. The ogre had arms like tree trunks with hands that dragged along the ground. He had a distorted, crumpled face with tusks protruding from his lower jaw. Light streamed into the barn through the massive hole he made. The ogre roared. The sound shook Gydan's insides.

She hoped her death would be quick.


An unbroken stalagmite halted some of the collapsing earth and created a pocket of space, where Silbrey had sought cover. She was able to get halfway underneath. The stony cascade crushed everything from her waist down. Her body mangled. The pain twisted through her like a hundred knives, stabbing in different directions. Each one, agony. Each one, a flame. She pushed against the rock, but she could not move. And even if she could, there was nowhere to go. She was entombed under the earth. She could taste blood filling her mouth. Her breathing came in gasps. She could not bring in enough air.

Her thoughts were addled. She struggled to stay conscious.

The phosphorescence from a rune on the stalagmite provided light. From that faint glow, she could see how hopeless it all was. She was enclosed on all sides.

She had her staff.

She tapped it against the rock. A hairline crack spread up the deteriorating shelter. This rock served as the levee holding back the flood of rock above her. One more strike, and she could bring everything down upon her and end it.

She did not think of her husband, whom she loved and missed. She did not think of her children, whom she cherished, but was never able to show it. The love she felt took the form of a fear that could never resolve itself. She feared for their safety. She feared for their happiness. She feared for their future. She feared for everything she could not control. The world and fate itself that conspired against a mother's ease. But her thoughts were not with them. Instead, she thought of Maricel and the three questions. What are we? Who am I to you? Who are you?

She thought of the deceit she found in those journals, and she could only laugh. What did it matter now? She thought of Maricel's beautiful face, her perfect face. She thought of her long blonde hair that fanned out across the mattress. She wished she could kiss Maricel one last time, and say she was sorry for not having better answers to the important questions.

Despite the pain, Silbrey decided to hold off on that final strike, and instead, stay with those thoughts of Maricel a while longer. She looked up and saw the roots, which had broken through the cave ceiling, and were now a few inches above her. She reached up and took hold.

The ogre tore through the terrified sheep. He made a meal of them. Blood and raw meat spread across the barn. Gydan and Yurig had nowhere to run that wouldn't attract the attention of the ogre. Feste, in his stable, also appeared ready to escape, but had no easy path. Gydan had never ridden him without a saddle. It was unlikely she and her brother could stay on at a full gallop. But if she had a chance, she would open the stable door. Gydan looked at her brother, who had receded into a catatonic state, holding to the spellbook—just as Gydan maintained her grip on the bucket. She had gone through too much to leave it behind. Perhaps if she ran in one direction and if he ran the other way, the ogre would only get one of them? She nudged him, but he was somewhere else.

"Yurig," she whispered, as quiet as a gentle breeze. "Yurig. Please." She paused. "Hey stupid." At this, he looked at her. "Yurig, I love you. I need you to run."

"I can't," Yurig pleaded.

"If you don't," said Gydan, "we'll both die."

The ogre stopped his carnage. All was silent. He sniffed at the air and took a step toward the plow.

Yurig ran out from behind the plow. The ogre turned to follow him. But then, Gydan ran in the other direction. The ogre considered his options and reached out to Gydan. He swiped at her, but she ducked. She ran to the stables, undid the latch, and threw the stall door open. Feste bolted from the stall, straight toward the gaping hole where the barn door had once been. Any hope of riding away went out with the colt.

The ogre reached again for Gydan. This time, he was able to grab her and lift her into the air. Her head nearly hit the top of the barn. The ogre roared as he squeezed Gydan tighter. Gydan was no longer afraid. Her thoughts were elsewhere:

*Bren Caius climbed a mountain to save a baby owl.*
*Bren Caius fought a pack of wolves to save her family.*
*Bren Caius wrestled a stag to the ground.*
*Bren Caius defeated Oren of Angnavir while blindfolded.*
*Bren Caius won the War of the Hounds at Pynne's Field.*

Gydan used the only weapon she had. She swung the bucket around and hit the ogre upside the head. It was a good hit. The ogre roared and dropped Gydan to the ground. She ran toward the opening to join Feste and her brother outside, but the ogre recovered, blocking her escape. He raised both fists in the air, ready to bring them down and crush her. Gydan held up the bucket as a poor excuse for a shield. Then she heard a wave of voices in her head.

*Human-child, we are here.*

Three dragons—a green one, a blue one, and a red one—shot into the barn, faster than Gydan imagined possible, faster than any bird of prey, more like a bolt of lightning in the night sky. The dragons' wings did not seem to provide any driving momentum in flight. Instead, they only adjusted to change course, which the dragons did effortlessly and often. The dragons were able to stop in midair, hover, and then redirect.

The ogre was confused as the dragons pinwheeled around him. The red dragon landed onto the ogre's face. The dragon bared their fangs. With the foreleg talons, the dragon grabbed onto the ogre's right eye and yanked it out. The eyeball dangled from the socket, hanging by the tendons. Gydan winced at the sight.

The ogre screamed and punched at the dragons, but they were too fast.

*It is time to go.*

Gydan took a wide route around the flailing ogre.

As they exited the barn, Gydan saw the monstrous soldiers occupying the farm. Some were spread out across the open field. Many had rushed into the house. Gydan looked frantically for her brother. Any of these creatures could have killed Yurig. She expected to see her brother lying in the mud with three arrows stuck in his chest, just as she had found her father. She would lose both within months of each other. She could not endure it again, not again, but she had to find him. Then she saw Yurig in the distance. He was alive and riding Feste. They were heading down the main road—not toward Barcombe, but in the other direction to the docks farther away. Gydan shouted in triumph and punched at the air.

Perhaps it was fate or luck or a miracle. As the saying goes, "even fortune will smile upon the foolish." But Feste had enough sense to stay behind and wait. Yurig was able to climb on, and they navigated the treacherous obstacles to safety. The world was large enough for miracles. Gydan was thankful to see her brother would make it out.

Gydan looked to the far tree line in the direction Feste was traveling, on the opposite side from where Speck's cave was. If she could cut through and make it to the road, then she would have a chance. She began to run. The three dragons flew around her, protecting her as she ran. The goblin soldiers ran after her and threw their spears. But the dragons were so fast, they were able to catch the spears in midair and then drop them to the ground. Gydan did not see this. She kept her eyes on the tree line.

A grinning goblin jumped in front of Gydan with a pike in his hands.

The blue dragon flew at him, grabbed the goblin by his loincloth. The grin left the goblin's face. The dragon shot several feet into the air, taking the goblin along. The goblin yelped in surprise. Then the dragon let him go. The goblin hit the ground and did not get up again. The green dragon followed blue's lead and flew at the other goblins. They were light enough to launch into the air and drop.

The red dragon did not leave Gydan's side.

To Gydan's relief, the trolls appeared disinterested in pursuit. They glided across the open fields, back and forth, holding their ground and waiting. The gnolls were focused on ransacking the house and setting it on fire.

Gydan and the dragons reached the forest line.

*Speck is nearby. Stay close.*

A path led from this point and connected with the main road farther down. Gydan had pushed herself as hard as she could but needed to stop to gather her breath. It was at this moment Speck stepped onto the path. The dragons flew at him, but with a wave of his hands, he blinked away and reappeared a few feet over. They flew at him again and again, but he was able to avoid each pass with his magic.

"Where is your brother?" Speck asked. "Where's my book?"

Gydan didn't like to lie. She was mischievous through and through, but lying always felt like surrendering to a guilty conscience. Her father was honest. For this reason, among many, she enshrined her father's memory with respect and awe. However, if she were to lie, she would do it masterfully, a performance for the ages.

Gydan wept the theatrical tears of a child. As she sobbed, she pointed back to the barn that was on fire. Thanks to the gnolls.

Speck's eyes grew large, imagining his book in flames. If Gydan was lying, it wasn't a gamble he was willing to take.

To further sell the lie, the ogre stumbled out of the barn. His eyeball dangled from its socket. He was covered in sheep's blood—not the blood of a boy—but how would Speck know the difference?

Speck held out his palms. He was casting another spell.

The dragons latched their talons into Gydan's shoulders, piercing her skin. They lifted her high into the air as Speck's shockwave failed to hit its target. Speck hobbled toward the barn to find his book. The rats tied to his waist danced as he moved.

Gydan shrieked, but she wasn't about to ask the dragons to let her go now that they were so high in the air. The pain in her shoulders burned, but it could be endured. Anything could be endured.

*We don't mean to hurt you.*

"I know," Gydan said through gritted teeth. "You saved me."

*You saved us.*

From this great height, Gydan could see Feste and her brother racing along the road.

"Do you see them? Can you fly me to them?"

The dragons set Gydan upon the road as Feste approached. They released their grip, and Gydan exhaled. Her shoulders were numb and raw.

Yurig jumped off Feste as the colt came to a stop. Yurig ran to his sister and wrapped his arms around her.

"I was so afraid," Yurig said.

But Gydan wasn't having it. She took her brother's face in her hands. She looked him in the eyes, so he would never forget what she said. "You don't have to be brave. I'll be the brave one. Together, we'll make it through."

"What about Mom?" Yurig dared to ask.

Gydan shook her head. "I don't know. No matter what, we can't stay here, and we can't head back that way to Barcombe. We should go to the docks and wait for a day. Those boats sail to Rhyll, which means they will be well guarded by the High General's troops. From there, let's sail to Rhyll and then back to Penderyn. We can walk to the old farm. Oma and Opa will be there."

"How can we afford the trip?" Yurig asked. Gydan pointed to the book, but Yurig held it close. "I'm not selling it."

"We don't have to sell it, but let's tell the ship captain we're taking it to Sage Hall and that the teachers have agreed to pay our fare. Once we're there, we can loan them the book to copy it in exchange for passage across to Penderyn. That's something sages do, yes?"

"How do you know they'll want it?"

"It's a book of spells. They would give us Silva's goat for a chance to look at it."

Yurig smirked at the mention of this story. Their father often warned them to not be like Silva and Guldur.

Silva and Guldur were sibling giants who fought endlessly over their inheritance until they realized it was a goat. But Silva discovered she could reach into the goat's mouth and pull out gold coins. She offered to buy the inheritance from Guldur for a hundred bushels of wheat. Guldur accepted, and Silva hid the goat's secret from her brother.

Gydan, Yurig, Feste, and the three dragons continued down the road, away from the farmhouse, engulfed in flames.

* * *

Silbrey held onto the root above her. She remembered Speck's words. The power came from her. She could pick any stick off the ground, and it would work like her staff.

The power came from her.

In her delirium, she whispered to herself.

"I am Silbrey, a shepherd, widow of Callis. I am Silbrey, the mother of Gydan and Yurig. I am the ward of Dahlia Tulan. I am Piper, a street urchin under the care of Timon, a priest of

Taraki."

She coughed up more blood.

"I am dying."

No, this wasn't true. None of this was true. A tree without leaves isn't dead. A tree without branches isn't dead. The roots are what matter. A tree can survive as long as it is connected to the earth. Where there is water and sunlight, where there is soil, hope remains. The tree can be reborn.

Silbrey held more tightly to the root.

"I'm not dying down here. I am a seed buried within the earth."

The root curled around Silbrey's hand and then around her arm. A blue light shimmered across her body. More roots broke through the earth and reached out to Silbrey, wrapping around her head, her neck, her torso. Even though she could not see her legs trapped under the rocks, she could feel roots there as well. A prickly sensation returned to her lower body. The roots tightened and then pulled her upward into the earth. Silbrey did not fight it.

The whole forest bent to her will.

The tree above the collapsed cavern started to glow a brilliant blue. Motes of light glinted around the tree. The light magnified in brilliance until the tree could no longer be seen. Everything radiated. A human form stepped out from the light, out from the tree itself. Silbrey was whole again. What was broken had been restored. When her bare feet touched the ground, the light faded.

She stood once again in the forest. Every inch of her body tingled. Her skin was smooth, but hard as hickory. She was stronger than ever, more focused, more aware of her domain. In her right hand, she held her staff. In her left hand, she held a wooden shield that bore the intricate rings of a tree's cross-section. Silbrey did not enter the forest with a shield, but she wished for one, and the forest provided.

She heard the creatures at the farm. She could feel the vibrations of their footsteps across the field, and she sensed the fire. She looked in that direction, and the trees had already shifted to create a direct path.

The ground rose to make the way level. The branches formed a canopy like drawn weapons raised high to announce the arrival of their leader. Silbrey sprinted down the track. Speck's cave was so close when the way was clear and smooth. He had been here the whole time, listening in on everything.

Silbrey's thoughts narrowed as she saw the burning barn and farmhouse and the summoned creatures positioned across the field. Her face flushed with rage. The farmhouse was supposed to be a second chance, a safe place. Bren Caius said so. And, in a single day, she had lost Maricel; she had lost their home, and she had almost lost her daughter to Kret Bonebreak-er's war mage. Silbrey knew her children were in danger. Though she didn't know how, Silbrey could sense they were still alive.

The rage she felt was good. The rage gave her something to feel beyond the numbness, which always had the potential to swallow her whole. Rage reasserted the self. She was alive. She had power. She did not fear these monsters.

Silbrey burst from the forest line, jumping between two gnolls. She extended her staff to the right, hitting the creature across the neck. Then she brought her staff to the left side, hitting the gnoll in the head. The two hounds dropped to the ground.

She ran to the center of the field, closer to the barn and

farmhouse. A few gnolls threw their spears, but she deflected them with her staff and her shield. Another gnoll ran at her with an axe poised to strike. Silbrey stepped forward, hitting the gnoll with her shield. The creature tried to scramble away, but she brought her staff down on him, once and then twice.

More gnolls tentatively moved toward her, each one wanting the other to make the first move. Silbrey felt an energy emanating from her. Rays of shimmering blue danced outward to the gnolls.

"Finally," Silbrey said. The magic returned. She paid attention this time to what was happening and how she felt. If this enchantment was hers, then it was hers to control, and she could make it happen again. The gnolls dropped their weapons and slumped to the ground, asleep.

The unaffected trolls approached with long strides.

While the gnolls and goblins carried weapons, the trolls relied on their long claws upon spindly fingers, each one like the tip of a scythe. The troll closest to Silbrey opened its large mouth and hissed. The troll's breath smelled like mold and decay. The monster took a swipe at Silbrey. The attack looked like it was moving slowly, but Silbrey found it difficult to move out of its path. The trolls were able to lull her into an idle state. She stepped back as one of the claws grazed against her cheek and drew blood. Though the cut was superficial, it burned.

The trolls were much closer to her. They surrounded her. Silbrey was distracted, her thoughts cloudy. Even though she was fighting for her life, she had trouble concentrating. Another troll swiped at her, hitting her raised shield—and sending her tumbling end over end across the field. Farther from them, her focus returned. The trolls all turned their heads toward her. Some of their heads rotated with the sound of grinding bone. Whatever effect they had on her, she knew she needed to keep her distance. Silbrey got to her feet and ran toward the barn, which was in flames. The trolls moved closer but kept away from the fire.

As she ran, she stumbled over a dead goblin lying in the field. She saw a few more scattered between the barn and the far end of the field near the path that lead to the road. She couldn't imagine Gydan and Yurig would have been able to fight them. It might have been fighting among the monstrous folk. Silbrey wouldn't be surprised if the goblins, except for Speck, were at the bottom of the hierarchy.

Silbrey neared the barn. She could hear a creature howling in pain. An ogre came around the corner of the barn. One of his eyes hung out of its socket. The ogre was covered in blood. Had the ogre gotten to her children? No, they were alive.

Silbrey leapt toward the ogre and jabbed her staff into his other eye. The ogre dropped to his knees, hands to his face.

The heat from the barn was intense. Silbrey moved from the fire and the ogre. She looked into the barn and saw the carnage of the sheep. She also saw Speck pacing within the barn, searching. He looked up and saw her, and then disappeared.

Silbrey knew better this time. Without looking, she swung her staff behind her and connected with Speck, who had reappeared there. She heard the goblin grunting in pain. The ogre reacted to the noise. Silbrey took this as an opportunity.

"Good sir, ogre! I'm right here! Follow my—"

The blinded ogre ran toward Silbrey, swinging his arms, hoping to pulverize her.

She held her ground, shield raised, and then just as he was about to plow through her, Silbrey took a flying leap to avoid the charge. She hit the ground and rolled over to see Speck crushed by the rampaging ogre. The ogre continued running until he was back in the forest.

Silbrey stood over Speck. He was broken as Silbrey had been broken under the earth, a fair and just fate. He gasped, trying to form words.

"The Ancient Beast will see . . . you . . . in . . . Aberton."

Silbrey considered a killing blow, but he once again disappeared. Wherever he reappeared, Silbrey didn't know.

With the absence of their leader, the trolls drifted back into the forest. Silbrey thanked Olar, the named god of war, for this mercy. The few remaining gnolls and goblins followed.

The fire continued to burn the farmhouse. All their remaining possessions and all those decorative chamber pots were consumed in the fire. Everything was gone. Maricel's journals were gone too, which was comforting in a way. Silbrey needed to find her children, but for this moment, she thought about how yesterday she had argued with Maricel about how safe they were here. The roof crumbled into the house, and the flames rose as more air from the outside rushed in.

Silbrey appreciated a grim sense of humor, but even this was a little much.

Grass grew around where she stood barefoot, and she felt the shimmering energy return. Ever since she emerged from under the ground, it was easier to sense the presence of this natural magic, realizing how it had always been within her.

Silbrey was done pretending to be surprised by who she was or what she was capable of. Too much went ignored, too much had been denied, but it was always within her. She didn't understand it. She didn't know what to call it or always how to control it. She felt a connection to the natural world, and she could no longer hide from it.

"Spring has come. It's been holding back for too long."

Silbrey sensed a seedling, long dormant, underneath the house. It had been there before the house was built. Denied water, the sun, and room to grow, the seedling's progress was cut short, but it did not die. It waited. Silbrey admired its patience and felt the time had come.

Her thoughts reached out to the seedling, and it began to grow. The sapling broke through the floor of the house, right where Maricel's bed was, and extended upward past the hole in the ceiling and higher into the sky. Silbrey urged it on. The tree branches unfurled and green leaves sprouted along it. The tree was strong. Flames scorched the thick bark of the massive trunk, but the fire could not catch. The branches were too high up for even the flames to reach. The fire receded, as it had nothing left to feed upon.

Silbrey followed the main road to the docks. She had never seen traffic on this road, so it was easy to follow Feste's hoof prints along the soft ground. Further down the road, she saw a small set of footprints that appeared out of nowhere and then joined the procession. Silbrey was relieved at the possibility that this might be Gydan.

* * *

The road to the docks was busier once it connected with the other roads—one from Laust to the south, Aberton to the north, and a more direct route from Barcombe to the west. Gydan, Yurig, and the dragons were comforted by the extra traffic of merchants with their carts, robed students from

Sage Hall, and a few soldiers on horseback. If Speck was pursuing them, at least they were no longer alone. Most of the travelers took quiet notice of the three small dragons and gave them a wide berth. The students were curious. A group of students not much older than Gydan and Yurig chatted incessantly, floating along with the buoyancy of juvenile philosophers. Neither Gydan nor Yurig had the energy to answer the questions. At one point, a student reached toward the green dragon—wondering how the dragons maintained their flight with so little wing movement. The dragon snapped at them. The students jumped and decided to cease their inquiries.

The dock was small, a single pier that jutted into the bay. A ship ferried passengers from this harbor to the one near Sage Hall on the island of Rhyll. The journey would take one day. The ship was gone and wouldn't return until the next morning. The captain and crew would spend a few hours unloading cargo, then they would set sail again.

A vardo was positioned next to the stone path leading to the pier. The wagon was painted in vibrant, warm colors with elaborately carved patterns on the sides. The wheels were removed. The wagon rested on the ground, so it appeared to be a permanent feature of the harbor.

On the other side of the stone path was a campsite with a fire pit. People gathered while waiting for the ship's return. Two merchants played chess on a travel-size board, while others gathered around to watch. In a copse of trees at the far edge of the campsite, some travelers slept in hammocks. Next to the hammocks was a post for tethering horses. An old woman sat near the trees, tuning her lute. This musician wore a large floppy hat, which often indicated a professional. Gydan hoped for a performance that night. It had been so long since she heard music, and she needed the diversion.

The students explained to Gydan and Yurig that the captain's daughter lived in the vardo, and she sold the tickets for passage to Rhyll. The ferry had an arrangement with Sage Hall. All students could travel for free. Everyone else was charged one silver coin, stamped with the High General's owl, plus an additional bronze coin for any horse to be transported in the hull. A single coin was a fair price, but impossible for Gydan and Yurig, who had no coins on them.

*Human-child, your mother approaches.*

Gydan could not see anyone on the road. She waited a few moments, and then, far off in the distance, she saw a woman. The woman carried a staff and a shield. Gydan ran to her mother. Yurig followed. Silbrey dropped her staff and shield and ran to meet them. She embraced them in her arms. Their mom had a gentle smile, as though she was always sure of their safety and that they would be reunited. Gydan—who had no such confidence—was a mess of tears.

"Mom, where are your boots?"

"I forgot them."

Gydan couldn't resist. "That's much worse than forgetting a bucket."

"You're probably right," Silbrey admitted.

"Did you really get the farmhouse and the land from Bren Caius?"

"I did. I really did."

Of all the unbelievable things Gydan had witnessed of late, this was the one detail she had the hardest time accepting.

"Mom, are you and Bren Caius friends?"

"I wouldn't go that far."

"I have so many questions."

"I know," said Silbrey, as she went back to pick up her staff and shield. "But we're together. There's time enough to ask."

But that wasn't true. They weren't all together.

"Mom, should we go back to find Maricel?"

"No, we should travel to Rhyll." Silbrey's response was cold. "You made the right choice coming this way. We need to go to Rhyll and tell others about Speck and his warband in the woods."

Gydan pointed to the soldiers from Rhyll who wore the Northern Light sigil. "We could tell them."

"We need to go there in person. We can't trust anyone to carry this message for us."

Gydan was about to challenge this reasoning, but thought better of it. Whoever her mother was, Gydan had to trust that she knew what to do.


As Gydan predicted, showing the spellbook to the captain's daughter was sufficient to earn them a trip to Sage Hall with an understanding that the teachers there would cover the cost. Silbrey mentioned one of the teachers by name, Aubec Skarsol. The captain's daughter knew this man to be highly respected.

Once their fare was settled, they walked to the campsite where Feste and the dragons waited.

Two of the dragons, blue and green, took flight. They were pinpricks against the gray sky. They flew north.

Gydan looked at the red dragon, who—since they reunited —had not left her side.

"Where are they going?"

*We decided they should search for other dragons, much*

*larger dragons, ones who had not been enslaved by the goblin mage. Perhaps they would like to know about Speck and his activities. They might want to visit him.*

"I would like to see that."

*No, you would not.*

The wave of voices came only from the red dragon. Gydan understood now. Dragons do not think in terms of an individual self. Their minds operated in the collective, not like a hive, but as an internal council, governing all their decisions. A dragon was one and many.

"What do I call you?" Gydan asked. "Do you have a name?"

*We spent our entire life in that cave. Names weren't something we used among ourselves. We were simply us.*

Gydan thought for a moment. Bren Caius named her owl "Ruth" after the goddess of the hunt, Cyruth the All-Seeing— a fitting name since Ruth scouted on behalf of Bren's army. The dragons also possessed a sight beyond what could be seen.

"How about Cyru?"

*If that is the name you wish to use, then use it.*

Gydan also learned that dragons were not sentimental creatures. Dragons were not pets. The way dragons perceived their surroundings, the way they communicated, altered the way they think. They were rational and disconnected from many of the concerns that define relationships, but the red dragon allowing Gydan to choose a name was a promise of friendship, a bond Cyru would never break.

Gydan tried to pat Cyru on the head, but the dragon moved away from her touch. The relationship wasn't there yet.

* * *

After sailing through the night and much of the next day, Gydan found the courage to ask her mother more questions. Silbrey was surprisingly candid. In hushed tones, she told her daughter more about herself than she had ever told Callis or Maricel.

She told Gydan about being raised as an orphan by the Taraki priest and how he joked about her being a fish. She told Gydan about Dahlia Tulan, and how she was abused and trained to kill people. She even told her daughter about how she allowed Callis and Gydan to go the Penderyn market. She thought they would be safe, but she was horribly wrong. She told her daughter about how she returned to Penderyn to seek revenge, but couldn't go through with it, and how she met the High General there. And finally, she told Gydan about how Speck believed she was fey. Gydan did not find this as outlandish as Silbrey did.

Silbrey did not tell Gydan about Maricel's journals or how Silbrey believed she was a spy for Dahlia Tulan. Gydan had lost enough. At least, she could hold on to Maricel as she remembered her.

Through it all, Gydan did not judge. She only listened, asking questions about small details here and there.

Gydan was most curious about the staff. "Can I see it?"

Silbrey handed it to her, and Gydan examined it with more care than Speck did.

"And can I see your shield? The one given to you in the forest."

Silbrey handed it to her as well. Gydan looked it over thoroughly. "Mom, the shield and the staff are made of the same wood."

Silbrey had not noticed it before. "So they are."

Gydan and Silbrey sat in silence, contemplating what it might mean.

The captain's son called out from the crow's nest that he could see Rhyll. It was one of the few moments when Yurig looked up from his book. Gydan and Silbrey stood close to each other at the railing. Neither could see anything yet. Cyru took to the sky to see the shore. The red dragon was free and found every reason throughout the journey to fly and explore.

The old woman with the floppy hat, whose name was Ilset, was indeed a professional minstrel and even performed for the High General. She set her lute upon her lap. She plucked a slow, swaying song. She sang with a lovely, low voice. The sailors, the students, and others who often sailed this course joined in singing.

> *When the waves no longer beat on the shore,*
> *When my sweetest lover regards me no more,*
> *When Amon stirs from her slumbering rest,*
> *Still a place in Rhyll where I count myself*
> > *blessed.*
>
> *When the wars have taken my home from me,*
> *When Olar and Golwin are all that I see,*
> *When my mead's all gone and spilled on the*
> > *floor,*
> *Still a place in Rhyll will pour me some more.*
>
> *When food at my table is but a mere dream,*
> *When friends and shipmates are not what they*
> > *seem,*
> *When every port's closed, every which way I steer,*

*Bren the Beloved still welcomes me here.*

*But woe to the days when my ship won't sail,*
*And woe to the nights when my course will fail,*
*Woe to the red moon, Aegir's anger I've crossed.*
*If I can't find Rhyll, then truly I'm lost.*

\* \* \*

Maricel returned to the farmhouse with Mustardseed pulling the cart. The cart was filled with supplies for the spring planting. She had even bought a few extra water buckets since they only had the one. While she was still a long way from home, Maricel could smell the smoke. Fear overtook her as she thought about Silbrey and the children. Before the house came into view, she could see black smoke wafting over the tree line. As she turned the corner, the burnt wreckage of the house came into view.

A massive tree—one that was not there when she left— protruded from the house. It was three times the size of any other tree in the surrounding forest. The branches extended far past the house itself. The muddy field where she and Silbrey had their argument the day before was lush with green grass and wildflowers, swaths of blue and violet and deep red.

Maricel walked through the remains of the house. The charred ruins emanated considerable heat. She knew the journals would have been destroyed in the fire. She was relieved to find no bodies. She would need to find them, Silbrey and the children. Maricel saw Silbrey's breastplate, which had melted in the fire, the one Dahlia had given to her as a gift. Silbrey had kept it hidden underneath her bed, which was completely incinerated. Although warped from the heat, the armor was unmistakably custom built for Silbrey's frame.

As Maricel explored the ruins, she couldn't help but look up to where the roof had once been. She looked at the tree, which had burst through the house, through her bedroom, and towered over its surroundings. She admired its strength and beauty.

"I should let Mother know."

# III

AUSDRE'S DAUGHTER was fair and kind. She had an idyllic life in the farming community. Everyone doted on her. For the first few years of life, her feet rarely touched the ground. She was always being passed among the kinfolk. She loved the attention, and it did not spoil her. Instead, she was compassionate and of a gentle disposition.

Ausdre could only shake her head. This was not how children were raised in Raustfweg. They were seen and not heard. They were put to work and not coddled. They were taught to be tough, not tender. But to quote a Raustfweg saying, "You stay on the horse you're riding." Ausdre lived in this Amon community; she would follow their ways.

Ausdre had one regret. Her daughter did not possess any skill in the druidic arts.

Ausdre tried her best. She explained to her daughter how with the right materials and the proper incantation one could trick the natural world. A druid could use a mushroom to ensnare an enemy, a sprig of mistletoe to heal wounds, a pomegranate seed to walk on the air, a honeycomb to distract a foe, and wolfsbane to stun them. A druid could spread sulfur and bloodroot powder upon fallow fields to yield a plentiful harvest. Powerful druids were able to use wormwood and juniper incense to transform into animals. All these spells were temporary. A druid could only confuse the natural world for a time before order would be restored.

Mostly, druids were taught to listen. The primordial elements were speaking. Sages joked that the primordials never shut up. A gentle breeze under certain circumstances might mean danger is near, or it might just be a gentle breeze. A druid knew the difference. A sudden vibration along the earth, a hum from the trees, an unexpected chill, or even a peculiar taste of dewdrop could be a message about nearby events.

Everything was connected. The slaughtered stag decomposed and returned to the earth. In its belly were the digested nutrients of another field, where the sun warmed the plants. The light from the sun was a message about time and space, of great distances traveled. For this reason, Verin—the named god of travel and messages—had rainbow-colored wings, a reminder of the light that spoke to all creation.

While this magic might amaze the outsider, the practitioner understood their humble place. A druid befuddles. A wizard manipulates. The fey alone have authority to command nature without the use of potions and powders. Druids and wizards were tricksters. What the fey do, they do by right.

Thoughts about the druidic ways led Ausdre to thoughts about the fey child she lost all those years ago. So Ausdre did not push her daughter too hard to learn druid magic because it was too painful a reminder of how Ausdre had failed.

Ausdre's daughter, though fair and kind, heard no messages from the wind or the earth or dewdrops. She could not ensnare someone with a mushroom or distract someone with a honeycomb. When she spread sulfur on a field, she was more likely to kill the crops or loosen the bowels of grazing farm animals. And while it provided manure to fertilize a field, this was more coincidental than magical.

Ausdre's daughter loved the farm and the people of the community. But her daughter was too trusting. She was once bit by a raccoon, which she tried to befriend. The mischievous bastard only wanted the baked treats being used as an offering of friendship.

With tears in her eyes, the little girl held out her hand to show the betrayal. The bite, which was more of a warning, did not even break the skin. Ausdre laughed. "My sweet *Owlet*, even the druids of Raustfweg do not have magic to turn a raccoon into a prince. Keep your distance. They'll only break your heart."

One day, Ausdre saw her daughter sitting in a clearing in the woods. Ausdre approached from behind. She half-expected to see furry creatures all sitting politely in a circle for an afternoon tea. If anyone could prove Ausdre wrong and tame the wild beasts, it would be her daughter. But something was not right. Her daughter did not turn around as Ausdre approached. She called her daughter's name, but her daughter did not respond.

Ausdre stepped in front and gasped.

Her daughter's eyes were rolled back. The whites shone. Her daughter was quivering. The muscles in her neck strained. She took short, rapid breaths. Ausdre shook her and shouted her name again, but her daughter did not respond. Ausdre picked her up and carried her back to the house. She called for help. Rue, who was in a nearby field, came running.

For the rest of the day, the community waited outside the house for any word of a change in the young girl's condition. As the sun set, the girl's eyes returned to normal. Her breathing slowed down. Awareness returned. She looked to her mother, who had never left her side.

Ausdre's daughter spoke in a quiet, weak voice. "Mama, I saw her."

"Who did you see?"

"The little girl. The girl who turned into a fish."

"What?" A chill went down Ausdre's spine.

"The girl who turned into a fish. She's still alive. An old man caught her and took her to a priest. I saw it all. The priest lost her to the guildmaster. This girl. She is slippery." Ausdre did not expect these words from her daughter. A girl who had no gift for the druidic arts had seen a prophetic vision. Like Verin, she had a message to share. "We need to find her."

Gydan wasn't sure what she should have expected when the ship docked at Sage Hall. After everything that had happened, waiting on the dock for permission to enter Sage Hall was tedious.

The ship had already offloaded its passengers and ship-ments, including Feste, who was handed over to the hostler and taken to the stables. Even their horse was allowed into Sage Hall before them.

Silbrey gave her name to the steward who welcomed everyone onto the island. The steward was a nervous and implacable rule-follower. He was skinny. Gydan assumed his only nourishment came from feasting off the disappointment of others, a meal that always left him hungry for more. At least five times, he interrupted Silbrey to say, "I don't see your name in the book." Silbrey asked to meet with Aubec Skarsol, a professor and former war mage to Bren Caius. Silbrey had met Aubec briefly in her former life as the ward of Dahlia Tulan. Dahlia's name could open almost any gate, but Gydan's mom would not use it. Instead, she showed the steward her children: Yurig, who carried a spellbook, and Gydan, who was accompanied by a small dragon. These guests were sufficiently peculiar. The steward agreed to check with Professor Skarsol.

Now they waited alone on the dock for the steward to return.

"Mom, I'm bored." Gydan groaned.

"You weren't bored when the gnolls were chasing you."

"Why would you say that?"

"Sometimes, bored is better. That's all."

Gydan gave a tiny grunt.

The steward finally came back. He apologized as if reading from a script, and then he escorted them to Sage Hall. Every few steps, he would turn around to get a look at them, as if he feared the family would run away.

Gydan saw her mother drop an acorn to the ground. There was a flash of blue light. Immediately, the acorn sunk into the soft earth and began to sprout. Silbrey smiled at her daughter and put a finger to her lips. Gydan did not know what that was about, but she enjoyed this mischievous side of her mother. They kept walking.

The steward directed Silbrey to the common room of the dormitory where Aubec was. He then introduced the children to Professor Cherrycheeks, a halfling, who offered to give them a tour of Sage Hall.

What Gydan knew about halflings came from her father. Most halflings lived in villages to the west of Tu'enya Bay in the hill region. Her father had worked with them at the open markets when he was younger. He said if someone befriended a halfling, they would have a friend for life. Halflings never forgot a name, and they would never betray a person's trust. They were honest folk—peaceful, never ambitious nor prone to overworking. As their name suggested, they were half the height of a human and shorter than dwarves. A halfling usually had a full rosy face, curly hair, and a round belly. Professor Cherrycheeks was no exception.

Gydan was disappointed to see Professor Cherrycheeks wearing shoes. She had gotten it into her head that halflings walked everywhere barefoot. But Professor Cherrycheeks wore a pair of soft leather shoes. The shoes came to a sharp point and were tied at the sides.

The professors had no standard uniform. Each dressed to their preference, which was uniformly ostentatious. They had a pretense of affluence. The students were the ones who had to wear drab robes. The robes never fit properly and looked uncomfortable. The irony was not missed on Gydan. From talking with the students on the way to the docks, she knew they were all from the wealthiest families. This dress code was one way the professors could extend power over their benefactors, the students, much to the students' annoyance.

However, Professor Cherrycheeks was admired by all the students of Sage Hall, and Gydan could see why. As he gave Gydan and Yurig a tour of Sage Hall, he peppered his lecture with fascinating observations, humorous asides, and word play.

He asked Gydan and Yurig questions that showed interest in their thoughts. What could have been a boring stroll, pointing at ivy-covered, red-bricked buildings, became a lesson on Amon and how everything on this small island of Rhyll reflected larger themes of the entire continent. Like all great teachers, Cherrycheeks made the world more interesting and worthy of discovery.

Cherrycheeks led them up a spiral staircase in the tower of the main hall. Yurig and Gydan had never been up so high before—even when the dragons flew Gydan to safety. At the top, Yurig and Gydan could feel the tower sway uneasily in the breeze.

Cyru soared in the distance, occasionally swooping past the tower to check on Gydan. Some of the students had probably seen miniature dragons before, but always in captivity. To witness such a creature in flight was to see their true nature. Everyone far below stopped to watch. Gydan wondered if the students ever considered the cruelty of those cages where they saw dragons on display.

From the tower, Gydan could see much of the island. Rhyll was in the middle of Tu'enya Bay, the heart of northeastern Amon. Cherrycheeks explained that while each Amon city managed its own affairs, every year, the northern cities convened in Rhyll for matters affecting them all.

"But why Tu'enya Bay?" Cherrycheeks asked Gydan. "Why not a city near Nengwë Bay to the south?"

"Because there are more people in the north?"

"And more coin," Cherrycheeks agreed. "What else?"

"Rhyll is safe. It's not connected to the mainland. After the War of the Hounds, they wanted a place that felt safe."

"True! Kret Bonebreaker had many things, but he didn't have boats."

The island was a rolling green countryside—with three communities along the coastline, the stately Sage Hall on the west shore, the pastoral Thistle on the north shore, and the sprawling city of Rhyll, the island's namesake, on the south shore.

"Yurig, what do you know about Thistle?"

Yurig thought for a moment.

"I know, 'before you praise the wonders of Rhyll, give a nod to Thistle.'" Yurig quoted the popular saying about this town. "Thistle is a farming and fishing town. Without them, Rhyll doesn't eat."

Cherrycheeks laughed. "That is true. Let's think about the War of the Hounds again. It changed everything. Kret targeted the farms for a reason. They weren't well defended. These easy victories made Kret appear unstoppable, and it hurt everyone. We lost almost as many people to famine as we did to the raids."

Cherrycheeks pointed to the south. The city of Rhyll was somewhere beyond the horizon. Rhyll became the military and government center of the region. It was the home of High General Bren Caius.

"Did you know the city was originally an elven settlement?" Cherrycheeks asked coyly.

Gydan's eyes widened. Cherrycheeks spoke as if this were a precious secret only halfling scholars possessed, and he was sharing it with them because he knew they could be trusted.

"I'm sure you and your mother will head there next—after she is done meeting with Professor Skarsol. When you're there, look at the buildings. Any with white limestone are from the elven city that stood before. The high general's palace is a beautiful example of elven architecture, entirely intact. Those buildings date back hundreds of years before the Great Firestorm."

"How is that possible?" Yurig asked.

A valid question, but Cherrycheeks shrugged. He turned his attention to Sage Hall itself, gesturing to the surroundings below with a sweeping motion.

"And what of Sage Hall? How did the bloody war affect this sanguine institution?"

The professor's use of the word "sanguine" confused Gydan. It meant "hopeful," which might describe a school, if one believed in the value of such places. The word also meant "red," so perhaps he was referring to the bricks. Gydan also remembered the word being used in the epics to describe someone who was "bloodthirsty." The school taught soldiers. Gydan supposed "bloodthirsty" worked too. Maybe Cherrycheeks intended all three meanings.

Neither Gydan nor Yurig had an answer to the professor's question. Cherrycheeks waited longer than they were comfortable, holding out for last-minute inspiration that was not coming, before he gave his answer.

"Many of these buildings are what we like to call 'instant relic.' Only that building over there," the professor pointed to a longhouse that hugged the coastal cliff, "and a few of the houses were here before the war. Everything was built by order of Bren Caius within her first year as high general. She requested everything look as if it had been around for generations, old and grand. The school was a priority after the war because she was tired of being the most knowledgeable person looking at the map. As high general, she's not only the military leader. She's also expected to put forward goals and plans for the region. And she's the deciding opinion on controversial issues—regardless of the vote tally. That's a big responsibility. Our job is to educate leaders, so that when she's gone, we have capable people to take her place."

"That's very wise," Gydan said.

"And very naïve," Cherrycheeks countered.

"How so?"

"That presumes the most capable person will ascend to their rightful place. I'm a historian, and I know how this goes. People come to power for many reasons. It's rarely because they deserve it. While I am grateful for my vocation, I haven't seen the next high general—"

Cherrycheeks caught himself slipping into uncharacteristic pessimism and stopped. "Then again, what do I know? Maybe I've met Bren the Beloved's successor without realizing it. Maybe they are standing right in front of me."

Yurig pointed to a cluster of shacks along the bottom of the hill.

"What about that place? It's not Thistle, Sage Hall, or Rhyll."

"How observant you are." Cherrycheeks looked to where Yurig pointed. "I have students about to graduate who still haven't realized that the people cooking their meals, cleaning their rooms, and keeping the grounds need a place to live. We call that humble hamlet 'Two Lanes,' but the cartographers throw it in with Sage Hall."

"I see one lane." Gydan noted the small path, which winded from the back of the main hall down to the shacks.

"You go up the lane, and you go down the lane. That's one and two." Cherrycheeks was clearly amused by the intentional misnomer. "Come, let's visit the grove planted in honor of the named god Fen. Halflings and heights do not go well together. I prefer being on the ground."

Professor Cherrycheeks led the children down the spiral staircase. Cyru rejoined them, hovering near Gydan's shoulder. Cherrycheeks took each step carefully, as though afraid to awaken the tower with heavy tromping. Gydan thought to ask about his leather shoes and if halflings preferred to be shoeless, but she decided it might be rude to lump a group of people in such a way. She had no way of knowing if this was a delicate issue and had the sense to hold her tongue. She would meet more halflings in her life, and she would figure out the shoe situation on her own.

Silbrey sat across from Aubec Skarsol in the common room of the dormitory. The walls were covered from floor to ceiling with framed woodcut prints. In most homes, such prints would depict the lives of farmers and artisans. At Sage Hall, however, the prints illustrated famous battles dating back to *Eto Cora Aspru'eir*, before the Age of Many Kingdoms. Silbrey assumed these images were used as teaching aids. She wondered how a skirmish between dragons and giants at the dawn of time had any application to soldiers facing a shield wall of gnolls. But here it was, the violent history of Efre Ousel, on display for the students.

Aubec did not look like how one might imagine a mage. He wasn't crumpled and gray with a wiry beard and foul disposition. Instead, Aubec was the ideal of grace and sophistication. He was confidently attractive and perfectly dashing with his red cape, his dark locs of hair tied in the back.

Silbrey remained unaware of how she appeared. Her bare

feet rested on the chair cushion as she slurped her tea. A dribble of the drink rolled down her chin, which she wiped with the back of her hand. She set the teacup down on the table beside her and let out a satisfied "ah" to indicate she approved.

They looked at each other, waiting for one of them to break the silence. Silbrey could tell that Aubec was not about to deviate from tradition. Silbrey was the guest. She must be served tea before Aubec could ask her what she was doing here. Silbrey, once the ward of Dahlia Tulan, arrived at Sage Hall with her two children—one with an invaluable spellbook in his possession, the other with a small dragon. Aubec likely had too many questions. Silbrey, with her bare feet on the cushion, maintained her eye contact with Aubec. She smacked her lips.

"You still have your cape," she said. "It looks nice."

Aubec couldn't stand it anymore. "Damn the gods. Where are your shoes?"

"Oh. Huh." Silbrey acted surprised. "I forgot my boots at the farmhouse, which was burned to the ground by a warband of gnolls, goblins, and trolls. Then I fled to the docks with my children, and now we have nothing, which includes my boots."

After he fought in the War of the Hounds, Aubec had left the battlefield to become a teacher at Sage Hall. He had taught many students. Most likely, they all worshipped him. Silbrey refused to be charmed. Instead, she was like the incorrigible student who got satisfaction from annoying the teacher with wild statements.

Aubec whistled in surprise. "If what you say is true, we need to talk with Bren Caius."

"And one ogre."

"What?"

"In the warband. Sorry. I forgot to mention the ogre."

Aubec tried to suppress a smile. "First time we met, you were a little girl under the care of Penderyn's guildmaster. I refused your boss's offer to work for her. Knowing how she operates, I thought the next time I'd see you—you'd be tasked with beating me with that staff."

"That was a long time ago," Silbrey said. Her voice wavered. Her confidence disappeared at the thought of Dahlia Tulan. "She had my husband murdered. My children and I went into hiding. But we hid in a hornet's nest without realizing it, or maybe they knew where we were all along. I don't know. I have no coin. I have no allies. All I have is information —and my children."

"Children are an investment in the future."

Silbrey rolled her eyes at this uninspired response. "You sound like someone who has never worked on a farm. Why wait for the future? You can put them to work when they're young. And I would've had more children if it weren't for two stillbirths." She shook her head. This small confession crept up from nowhere. "Why am I telling you this?"

"Because you want me to understand your pain."

He said these words with such compassion. When Silbrey looked at Aubec, she didn't see a teacher. She saw a warrior, much like herself, trying to fit into a world that didn't need another war. Could she trust him? She thought she could trust Maricel. And where was Maricel right now? Did she return to the farmhouse to see the house burnt to the ground and everyone gone? Did she think they were dead? Silbrey wanted to write her a note, send word that they were okay. But if Maricel were an agent of Dahlia, rumors of their death might give them a chance at a new life. The children could live in the sheltered safety of Sage Hall. Silbrey hated Maricel for the deception, but she could not forget what they shared. Her face flushed just thinking of her. Silbrey took her feet off the cushion, set them on the ground, and leaned toward Aubec.

"I can't drag my children all over Amon. But I can keep them here, and they would be safe."

"Your son—"

"Yurig."

"He has a spellbook."

"It belonged to Speck, Kret's war mage. You served in a similar position for Bren Caius. You can look at the book yourself. Do whatever arcanists do with such books."

"Does Yurig understand what he's looking at when he flips through the pages?"

"I think so," Silbrey replied.

"This is not a school for mages," Aubec said. "It's a place to educate the spoiled children of wealthy families. And you just told me you have no coin. That's not a great place to start negotiating." Aubec shook his head. He did not appear to like his options or the obligation. "But I'm the only mage here, and I need an apprentice. With your permission, he can work for me and enroll for the general coursework. I'll test his understanding to see if he's capable of becoming a mage. If he does in fact understand the text, I might be able to find a place for him long term. I can't take your daughter."

This offer, while generous from Aubec's perspective, was almost worse. Silbrey didn't know if her children could stand to be separated.

"What if Gydan worked here?"

"Then she'd put one of the other workers out of a job. I can't do that."

Silbrey did not take these words as a "no," merely a "not

yet."

"Thank you," said Silbrey. "Yurig will stay here. I will return later with Gydan."

"Yurig will stay here. Gydan will not."

"We'll see."

Yurig would be safe within Sage Hall. Silbrey would find a way to enroll Gydan as well and keep them together. Silbrey would bring it up once she met with the high general. Right after they discussed how Bren Caius almost got them killed at the farmhouse.

"I will travel with you to the city of Rhyll," said Aubec, "so we can talk with Bren Caius about what you have seen. Yurig will stay here to get acclimated. He's already behind on the spring semester. Is there anything else?"

Silbrey pointed to the set of windows.

Aubec sat up and looked out. He saw a group of amazed students gathering around a fully grown oak tree that was not there this morning. A few climbed the tree to belittle the phenomenon. Others plucked leaves from the branches as souvenirs. Being students, they debated the meaning and origins and significance of the tree. Between this and the dragon, it was a memorable day at Sage Hall.

Aubec stared out the window. He laughed.

"That is no mage spell," Aubec said. "I would say you were a druid, but no druid spell would last so long. That means—"

Aubec kept his eyes on the tree. He was shaken by the realization.

"Fey," Silbrey responded. "So I've been told. By Speck. I think it's also why I've preferred to go shoeless lately. My connection, this power, is stronger when I can feel the grass and soil."

"An actual fey. And you're only now realizing it?"

Silbrey had been thinking about this question herself.

"The dragons we found in Speck's cave, they were caged—and it stunted their growth. Dragons were meant for the open sky. Likewise, I spent much of my life in the city and then on a farm. I was meant for the wilderness. Maybe I am stunted as well. Bren Caius said an arcanist at Sage Hall would be able to tell me more. That's you."

One of the students climbing the tree fell and landed on another student bent over examining the trunk of the tree. The students laughed. They should have been in class, but no one cared. They would talk about this strange tree for years to come. It would become part of the school's lore.

"There are many kinds of fey," Aubec answered. "You're not of this world, but you are also not alone. Like you, they may not realize it—or they may be in hiding."

"Hiding from what?"

"The fey stories are dark and beautiful, but they don't provide easy answers."

"And what of this other world?"

"That, you already know." Aubec stepped away from the window and returned to his chair. "A court for each season, ruled by a different monarch. Four kingdoms. These tales have been told and retold for generations. Our worlds exist to each other as fables. But, at times, we take on some of their orphans as they take some of ours. And maybe the borders between the two worlds are less rigid in some places—enchanted groves, sacred springs—or during rare celestial events, when the world is more open to wonder."

Silbrey had heard the stories about miscarriages and still-births being the result of fey stealing a child's spirit. The fey would give them new flesh and raise them as one of their own. Silbrey thought of these stories as a way to comfort grieving parents or to give them something to blame. Maybe there was truth behind these fictions.

"Tomorrow we should leave for the city to see the good Bren Caius," said Aubec.

If their conversation did anything, it confirmed what she already knew. Aubec was honorable, and he was eager to fight for a worthy cause. Her son would learn much from him. Yurig would be safe here.

Silbrey took another long sip of her tea. It was quite good. She added a slurping noise at the end because she knew it annoyed Aubec. Ever since Silbrey was under the care of Timon, she had taken pleasure in poking at people in authority. This predilection might get her in trouble someday.

* * *

Aubec Skarsol offered the family one of the guest houses for the night. Gydan was in a panic because Yurig had not returned since dinner. The last time they were separated, they had nearly died. She was especially irritated that her mother didn't feel any urgency to search for him.

"Mom, what if Speck followed us here? Or what if Yurig climbed the tower and fell? He could be dead. And you wouldn't even know."

"I'm sure I would find out eventually." Silbrey closed her eyes, took a deep breath. Motes of blue light sparkled around her. "He's not in any danger."

Cyru, who claimed a cozy floor pillow, chirped.

*I see him. He's in the library. The south wing of the main hall.*

Gydan groaned. "Am I the only one in this family who doesn't have some magical third eye?"

"It seems so," said Silbrey.

*Yes, you might want to work on that.*

Gydan left the guest house. She tried to slam the door, but it wouldn't shut without the latch, so the door clattered and swung back at her.

Gydan walked across the field to the main hall. She noticed more students were out at night than in the afternoon. Each student carried a lantern to guide them. She saw clusters of lantern light at Fen's grove. During the tour, earlier that day, she had remarked about a pipe and spent sweet leaf at the base of Fen's statue. Professor Cherrycheeks feigned innocence said the faculty and the student body needed their private assemblages. Gydan thought about her brother's new life at the school, his new life away from her. A lantern-wielding student ran past her, playfully chasing after another student. The students fell upon the ground, giggling and rolling in the grass. Gydan wanted to kick them. Instead, she walked around.

The library was smaller than Gydan expected, even though it was the first library she had ever seen. She had heard stories about how these libraries contained a maze of shelves, tomes stacked high, rows upon rows. She had pictured a cavernous temple, but instead it was only a single altar, a shelf with no more than twenty books upon it. Each one was chained to a bar below the shelf, so the books could not be taken from the room without the chief scribe's permission. The books were all handwritten texts. Even this small collection was a treasure. No one could handle these books without gloves and a blunt blade used specifically for turning the pages.

Gydan found her brother huddled over his spellbook, surrounded by several candles burning low. Yurig was given access to the library after hours. Judging from the melted wax, which dripped down the tapered sides and gathered on the table, Yurig had been at the library for a while. Yurig was not here for those chained books. He came for the candles and the quiet.

"Yurig," said Gydan, but her brother did not look up from his book. "Yurig!" She called again, louder this time. He looked up in a daze.

"Hi," he replied, and then returned his attention to the book.

"Yurig!" Gydan sat across from him. "Mom and I are leaving tomorrow. You're staying here. I don't know when I'll see you again."

Yurig did not respond. He turned a page in his book. Gydan reached out to stop him, but Yurig glared at her. She had never seen her brother like this before.

"If I take a break from my studies," Yurig's voice was steady and unsympathetic, "I risk losing everything I've learned."

"You'll remember it."

"That's not how it works. This knowledge is different. Watch."

Yurig raised his hands. He chanted a series of words from an unfamiliar language.

The candles floated in the air. They circled Yurig and Gydan. The flames grew brighter and rose higher. As the candles revolved around the children, long shadows against the walls moved as well. The wax dripped upon the table and the floor. Yurig then lowered his hands, and the candles returned to their original place next to the book.

The candlelight illuminated Yurig's face from underneath, creating a ghastly visage.

"That spell required a full day of study," Yurig said. "Imagine what else I could do if I had more time?"

Gydan reached out again to take Yurig's hand. He pulled away. "Please, Yurig, you don't have to do this. Leave the book here. Come with us to the city. We're going to meet Bren Caius. Can you believe it? The Northern Light."

"No, I have to do this."

Gydan sat for a moment and looked at him. Her brother was somewhere else. And wherever he was, she could not rescue him. She tried to say goodbye, but the words lodged in her throat.

* * *

Silbrey, Gydan, Cyru, and Aubec left in the morning. The sun, a thin line on the horizon, painted the clouds above with a purple and orange glow. Silbrey rode Feste, while Aubec and Gydan traveled in an uncovered carriage drawn by two horses. Cyru flew overhead.

At the bottom of the hill along the road was a menhir. The students would leave baubles and coins at the base of the menhir to beseech the unnamed gods, most often before exams. There were no named gods to look out for the interests of students, so they came here for small blessings and wishful thinking. The servants who lived at the bottom of the hill would gather the coins, which supplemented their meager salaries. In this way, the students were blessed by the gods. The servants were blessed by the students. And the gods were fine without the coin—as they often are.

Silbrey rode past the menhir. The standing stone was about her height. She felt no pulse of energy from it. Silbrey called to Aubec. "That's a fake."

"The scholars at Sage Hall have a term for it. 'Instant relic,'" replied Aubec. "We teach history at Sage Hall. It's always good to have some on display."

"Even if it's a lie?"

"History is a story told by the people privileged to tell it. History isn't uncovered. It's created. Ask your friend Bren Caius about that."

Silbrey had never sat in a classroom, but Aubec's words felt like they were from a first-day lecture. When Keote taught Silbrey how to fight, he enjoyed sharing his wartime wisdom. He would say, "Your training isn't any good once you get hit. All wisdom and confidence abandon you. You need to train so hard that you act on instinct." Keote would go on about how terrible war was, and then reminisce about how much he missed it. Silbrey decided teachers were the loneliest people in the world—so eager for someone to care about what they knew.

Aubec continued to share with them his thoughts on how history wasn't a study of the past, but a study of how we understand the past—and why that was so important. Gydan wasn't listening. She was in a foul mood. But Silbrey felt good about the decision to leave Yurig here, and she would get Gydan enrolled as well. The children were safer away from her, Silbrey decided. Gydan, on the other hand, looked like she wanted to burn Sage Hall to the ground. That's how it was with Silbrey and Gydan. If one of them was feeling good, then the other felt bad. They could never agree on how they should respond to anything.

Silbrey didn't have the chance to say goodbye to her husband. At least with her son, she knew she would see him again. The night before, Silbrey had gone to the library and found her son asleep. His head rested on the spellbook. Each candle flame clung to life in a puddle of hot wax. Silbrey picked up her son, along with his book, and carried him across the yard to the guest house. Yurig muttered incantations in his sleep, and Silbrey wondered if any mages could cast spells while unconscious. Silbrey heard teasing voices from the grove— students, up past curfew, who would probably pick on Yurig for having his mother carry him to bed. It was the sort of cruelty young people were known for. Back in the guest house, Silbrey laid him down on the cot next to his sister. Both were sound asleep.

As they rode away, Silbrey looked back at Sage Hall, high on the hill overlooking the bay. In the tower, she saw Yurig. He waved goodbye. Silbrey guessed Professor Cherrycheeks—who was a kind and thoughtful person—woke up Yurig and forced him to climb the stairs to wave goodbye to his family. Silbrey waved back. Gydan turned around to see him as well. Gydan held her hand up, a diffident farewell.

"Soon, I will have both of you at the school," Silbrey said it so Aubec could hear. He pursed his lips and kept his eyes on the road ahead.

"I don't want to go to Sage Hall," said Gydan. "I want to stay with you."

"You'll be safer at the school."

"I have a dragon and a fey mother. I'll be safe anywhere I go."

At this, Aubec laughed and said, "I would draw the exact opposite conclusion."

The trip took most of the day. They traveled on a well-padded dirt road, a view of the grassy plains on the left and the ocean on the right. Every few miles, there was an outpost with an oversized bukkehorn on top. The horn was used to send coded messages from one end of the island to the other, passed along from outpost to outpost. Each guard waved to Aubec, and the teacher waved back. They were all former students, now in service to Amon and the Northern Light.

The island was beautiful, but the trip was dull, more and more of the same, one outpost after another, until they reached the city.

* * *

Cyru saw the city first. At Gydan's urging, the dragon flew ahead to scout and send messages back to her. The messages were not helpful.

*We see several buildings.*

"Yes, Cyru, that is true of any city."

*We see people, lots of people walking in the streets.*

"Again, you're describing every city."

*What kind of information do you want?*

"Can you describe the buildings? Do any of them look like a palace, which could belong to the high general?"

*The buildings are made from wood and stone. The buildings are sized to contain people, and one of those persons could be a general.*

"Cyru, why don't you fly back to us? And we'll enter the city together."

Gydan's frustrations with her brother faded as her excitement about meeting Bren Caius grew. Her mother said she had met Bren Caius in Penderyn and that they would be able to meet her now. The high general would want to know about Speck and the other creatures near Barcombe. She would want to know about Speck's dealings with Dahlia Tulan to help Kret Bonebreaker's former soldiers and how Speck believed Kret was returning. Her mother would also tell Bren Caius about Speck's last words to her, "The Ancient Beast will see you in Aberton."

Gydan had only seen Bren Caius depicted in woodcut prints and in the marginalia art found in maps. The Aylers—a network of traveling actors—had described Bren Caius to her in detail, and her mother confirmed that Bren Caius lived up to her reputation. She was strong. She was beautiful. She was like a living god. This came from her mother—her mother who sought to lower expectations at every opportunity. Bren Caius was a legend, and on this day, Gydan would meet her.

Unlike Penderyn, no wall surrounded the city of Rhyll, and no gate with guards positioned at the threshold. Small shacks with small gardens littered the open fields. Farther down the road, the homes increased in size and were built closer together. The transformation from field to city was gradual. The market, the street vendors, the military patrols occupying the web of streets, the city noises and smells created a confounding crescendo. Professor Cherrycheeks was right. Some of the buildings were made of white limestone, but in portions. A house might have a corner of limestone, and then the rest of the building would be built of stone and mortar more common to the region. Gydan thought about the elven kingdom that once occupied this island. What enlightenment did they possess? What magic did they keep from the primeval world?

Rhyll—built upon the ruins of something greater—existed to serve the needs of the region, catering to visitors and outsiders. Gydan could identify the people they rode past as belonging to one of three groups.

First, diplomats from across Amon wore fine clothes that represented their hometowns. For example, the man with the tulip-print gambeson was from Ilden, which was known for its flowers. The woman with the bronze chain necklace, which hung well past her waist, was from Caesting—a famous mining town in the south. And every person dressed as a pirate king or queen was from Fel Harbor, since nearly every pirate called Fel Harbor home.

Second, soldiers could be easily identified. They were the ones carrying weapons—most often a spear or sword—and wearing Bren's red sun sigil. The city surrounded the garrison, which housed most of the soldiers in Amon. From Rhyll, they could set sail for wherever they were needed. Each soldier was deputized to keep the peace in the city where they were stationed, which made Rhyll one of the safest places to live. Criminals did not last long when most of the city could arrest them.

Third, there were the merchants who profited off the other two groups. A merchant could not conduct business in Rhyll unless they had a writ with the high general's seal. They could fix prices and often charge rates twice as high as anywhere else. It had the intended effect of ensuring diplomats did not over-stay their time in Rhyll. They couldn't afford it.

Within the groups, Gydan noticed more halflings, all wearing soft leather shoes. The shoes came to a sharp point with a stylish upward curl. The stories of barefooted halflings appeared to be a lie. She also saw a pair of elven and dwarven diplomats, each with a retinue of advisors. The coalitions mingled. Dwarves had always been great admirers of the elven kingdoms. They were eager to learn what they could. Gydan tried to hear their conversation, but they were speaking in Volir, which Gydan did not know. If she were forced to attend Sage Hall, it would be the first thing she would have to learn.

Not far from the garrison, the clutter of the city yielded to a green lawn, upon which was the white stone palace of Bren Caius. Soldiers patrolled the road connecting the garrison and the palace. The garrison hid behind a wall of wooden posts, driven into the ground, tied together, and covered in pitch. Aubec told Gydan that the garrison was nothing special. But the palace—their destination—was miraculous, a work of sublime beauty. Delicate columns spiraled along the outside and in between the curved archways. Balconies jutted from the upper floors, extending far into the open air. The spires twisted skyward. The palace was warped and impossibly stunning. This building did not belong to this age. It was a reminder that other civilizations achieved much greater things with the time they were given. The architects and engineers of this generation were still struggling to build something sturdy, let alone dare to create a structure so nonsensical. Only the great Bren Caius could occupy this palace and call it home. Gydan looked at each window, hoping she might see Bren Caius standing there.

A grizzled beast of a man walked out from the palace and greeted them. It was Oren of Angnavir, Bren's loyal confidant. He had a thick neck, broad shoulders, and a broad chest. He was an imposing stone wall. His muscular build contrasted with the signs of his age—bald head, long gray beard, deep crow's feet. The wall was imposing, but ancient and scarred.

It was happening. Gydan would meet Bren Caius.

Oren hugged Aubec. Gydan remembered the debonair professor was once a war veteran. He had fought by Oren's side. She could hear Aubec grunt in pain from Oren's strong embrace.

Oren spoke in a low voice to Aubec. Gydan strained to hear.

"*Yakost.* I'm glad you're here, my brother. Bren is not well."

"What happened?" Aubec whispered.

"She was poisoned, and she's fighting it as best she can."

Gydan's heart sunk at this news.

Oren led Aubec and Silbrey into the palace. Gydan and Cyru followed. Gydan felt invisible to the adults and their concerns. They rushed down a hall, past a large aviary containing a white barn owl. Trophies from Bren's exploits hung from the walls—a broken shield, various tapestries and banners, a wooden owl mask gilded with gold paint, a letter of admiration signed by the previous high general. Kret Bonebreaker's axe was prominently displayed. It was the largest weapon Gydan had ever seen. She doubted any normal person could lift it. Gydan could not walk straight as she kept turning around to take in every artifact on display. Guards and servants were stationed at every corner. They all had sullen looks on their faces.

Oren took his guests up a small flight of stairs, then another, until they were at a set of double doors, wide open. The room was dimly lit. All the curtains were half closed, allowing a few shafts of light through each of the open windows. A steady breeze blew in. The curtains billowed and appeared alive. Shadows from this movement rippled across the far wall. A canopy bed was positioned in the center of the room. Honeysuckle vines wrapped around the posts of the bed. Bees dutifully worked the flowers, flying in and out of the window to wherever their hive was.

The old woman in the bed did not look like how Silbrey had described Bren Caius. If this were the Northern Light, she would have a fire in her eye and a confident smile. She would be ageless, unblemished, and vital. Instead, the woman appeared frail, sick, and tired. Gydan did not know how to react to this person who was supposed to be the Bren Caius of legend, Bren the Beloved, the Hero of Eloe Vale. Gydan could not see that person. She did not want to be dismissive or disrespectful, but the reality did not line up with the expectation. A bee crawled up the old woman's arm. Both appeared oblivious to the other's existence.

Bren's eyes fluttered open, and she looked at Silbrey. She held her hand out to her. Silbrey took it, and out of respect, knelt.

"Last time I saw you, you bent the knee," the woman said. "I'm not a queen. You'll put ideas in people's heads."

Silbrey stood up again and nodded. "It's good to see you."

"Is it?" The woman looked over at Aubec and smiled. "What are you doing here? Aren't you supposed to be teaching young nobles about all my great victories?"

"My lecture is simple." Aubec threw his cape over his shoulder. "I tell them you had an amazing war mage."

The woman laughed at this comment, then she winced and started coughing.

Gydan screwed up her courage. If this was Bren, she needed to say something. Gydan stepped forward and spoke out of turn while Aubec was explaining the reason for their visit.

"High General Caius," Gydan blurted out, cutting Aubec

short. "I know all your stories by heart. I am honored to meet you and—"

"Who is this?" Bren asked, annoyed.

"I'm sorry," Silbrey said, placing a hand on Gydan's shoulder. "This is my daughter, and she came with—"

"High General Caius," Gydan interrupted again, but Bren Caius refused to acknowledge her.

"I do not hold court with children. Escort her out of my chambers."

Before Gydan knew what had happened, she was on the other side of closed doors.

She was not sure what to do next, so she sat down on the stairs.

Cyru nestled next to her. It was the most affection the dragon had ever shown.

*I hope you're okay.*

Cyru's words loosened something in her. Her cheeks flushed with embarrassment. The tears came up. She cried because she felt like a fool and she missed her brother. She thought about Bren Caius and the menhir near Sage Hall, a bit of history on display, but ultimately, a fake.

* * *

Behind the closed doors, Silbrey told Bren Caius everything she had learned from Speck during their encounter. Bren shook off her fatigue as she listened. The poison afflicting her was not as strong as her sense of purpose. If Bren was needed, she could be powerful. One more time, at least.

Bren's first response was to send soldiers to the woods near Barcombe to root out any creatures still hiding there and to find Speck himself. Bren ordered soldiers to Aberton as a precaution against whatever Speck had planned. While Kret never raided Aberton during the war, the city was important to the region. It was located on the isthmus that connected the wealthy bay cities to the east and the rest of Amon to the west. Bren also sent troops to Penderyn to apprehend Dahlia Tulan. By the next day, almost every soldier in Rhyll would be on a ship, either heading west to Barcombe, north to Aberton, or east to Penderyn.

After the meeting, Bren asked Silbrey to stay behind to talk further. Aubec was shown the guest rooms at the other end of the palace, where they would stay for the next few days.

Silbrey did not know what else Bren wanted to discuss. She had already told her, as candidly as she could, everything she knew. The palace staff lit several candles for them. They also brought dinner and a pitcher of warm, dark ale.

Every time Silbrey tried to discuss matters of importance, Bren would nod her head and veer toward more casual conversation. When they first met, Silbrey had been beaten nearly to death, and Bren had confessed to conspiring with Dahlia. It was a strained introduction. Now Bren acted as if they were old friends, and Silbrey was unsure how to navigate this new role. The ale helped. After a few rounds—Bren drank twice as much as Silbrey—the conversation rolled much later into the evening. Silbrey knew this couldn't be good for Bren's recovery. Silbrey stood up to leave.

"You must be tired."

"Please stay. A bit longer."

Bren looked at Silbrey and winked. Silbrey remembered in Penderyn when Bren had stroked her cheek. It was an innocent, if not overly familiar, gesture. She wondered if Bren, despite her ill health, was flirting with Silbrey.

"Why are you keeping me here?"

Bren's face grew serious. She leaned forward in bed and spoke as if the fate of the world rested on these next few words. "There's an ancient prophecy—"

"No, there's not." Silbrey laughed.

"There's no prophecy." Bren leaned back again, conceding the ruse. "But you wouldn't believe how effective that line is."

"Is that the secret to your fame?"

"It's all an illusion. That's what made me a legend. The story grows, while I diminish."

"You're an ass. That's what you are. You gave me a farm-house next to your old enemies—"

"*That* was an accident."

"For you, maybe. Speck knew what he was doing. He knew who owned that land. He was hoping you'd be there."

"Maybe so. I am an ass."

"While I would agree, my daughter thinks the world of you. You were harsh with her."

Bren nodded. "I'll make it up to her before you leave. Does she need an owl?"

Silbrey laughed again. The drink was strong. "She has a dragon! A damn dragon. What does she need with your lousy owl?"

Bren tried to laugh, but she grabbed at her chest in pain. The humor of the moment evaporated.

Quiet reflection filled the void.

"Bren, why are you sick?"

"In life, I never denied myself any food, drink, or lover that I wanted. I have secrets that would make priests blush and old men faint. I slept little and drove myself hard every day. I lived with the constant burden of caring for the people of Amon." Bren raised both hands to indicate her innocence. "I have no idea why I am in ill health."

"Are you being ironic?"

"Yes. I'm being ironic." Bren was amused that Silbrey even had to ask. "In truth, I think my son, my only son, Mendal, is trying to become king, and it'll be the death of me."

"There are no monarchs in Amon. Nobles, yes. But no monarchs. There haven't been any for centuries."

"And I have no interest in starting that vile tradition. However, when I die, my son will try to crown me posthumously and then take on the mantle as rightful heir. The little bastard."

"Where is he now?"

"He went into hiding after I was poisoned." Bren's eyes welled up. "He's somewhere in the city. I don't know where."

"Have you told anyone else what he did?"

"I told Oren. I told his other parents, Corrinae and Halsten. But there's not much I can do about Mendal."

"Why is that?"

"Because I love my son. Am I supposed to lock him away for conspiracy against the high general? Never." As she spoke, Bren watched the bees fly about the honeysuckles. The bees toiled, oblivious to the burdens of Bren Caius. "The joke's on him, though. He spent his entire life with me as his adoptive mother, and he forgot something everyone else knows."

"Which is?"

"It's really, really hard to kill me."

Everything that Bren Caius said sounded so confident. Silbrey believed Bren was invincible, even while she sat in bed, sick from a poison that nearly killed her and still might. Silbrey believed Bren was honorable, even while she ordered troops after Dahlia Tulan, a person Bren herself dealt with for weapons and bribes. Bren had a power over people—or maybe it was the ale.

Silbrey gestured to the sword hanging on the wall. It was a question that needed no words.

"Yes," Bren answered. "That is the sword. The one that killed Kret at Pynne's Field. It doesn't sing. It doesn't dance. It's just my sword, and it's served me well."

"Your power doesn't come from your weapon. It comes from you."

Bren considered these words. "Isn't that true of every warrior?"

"Perhaps." Silbrey thought about what Speck said, about the source of her power. "Are you fey? In Penderyn, I saw a blue light from your hand when you blocked my strike. You said the gods are big, but—"

"So are we," Bren completed the phrase as if it were a mantra. "I remember. I was there. Am I fey? Maybe. It would explain a lot. I don't look anything like my family. Maybe the summer queen of the Fey Court traded me for my mother's true born daughter. I know the stories. That's something they do."

"You've seen what I can do," Silbrey said. "I have a super-natural sense of my surroundings, but not in this palace."

"The white walls. Ancient elven magic. It keeps mages from spying on me."

"So, Aubec?"

"Other mages exist. You met Speck. They're rare, but they exist."

"And I command plants, make them grow." It was her favorite trick.

To illustrate, Silbrey lifted an index finger. The honeysuckle blooms opened wider, and the vines twisted more densely around the posts. The sweet floral aroma wafted in the space between Bren and Silbrey.

"I can't do anything like that. I can see through the eyes of animals. I sense what they sense, and they serve me. Mostly, I use my power to keep an eye on the palace and the city."

"Your owl, Ruth?"

"There have been several Ruths. I've lost count. Those owls live for about four years. And I can't tell you how many times Kret's archers shot down my birds during the war."

The more Silbrey listened, the more she understood what Aubec meant when he said history was something created by the people privileged to tell it. Bren Caius was great, but her legendary status was both well-deserved and well-constructed. It was a better story to have one faithful owl, which accompanied the high general everywhere she went, than to see the owls as fodder for the war.

They continued to talk through the night. Silbrey could tell Bren wanted to tell her something. With every lull in the conversation, Bren hesitated. Words needed to be said. Silbrey was, by nature, a quiet person. She didn't feel the need to fill every space with chatter. Bren was holding back. It looked so uncomfortable for her. Silbrey did not push for disclosure. In her experience, it never went well. But curiosity got the best of her.

"Northern Light. Illuminate me. What's on your mind?"

"Speck is telling the truth," Bren said in a flat voice. "Kret lives."

"Kret died at Pynne's Field," Silbrey insisted.

"I was there. And he didn't."

"Are you—?" Silbrey was shocked. "Where is he?"

"Let me show you." Bren took Silbrey's hand. She closed her eyes. Through Bren's touch, Silbrey was able to share in her power.

Silbrey saw through the eyes of a creature, low to the ground. Her vision was blurry and did not extend far. The color range was limited as well, gradations of lightness and darkness. The immediate surroundings were mostly experienced through a twitch of her cheeks. Whiskers? Her senses of smell and hearing compensated for the vision. She could pick up the scent of water, fresh spring water, thick with minerals. She could smell the urine of a single creature. No other animals. She could smell various wines and spoiled food—potatoes, cabbage, and corned beef. She picked up the scent of salt and fat. So complete was the sensory experience that Silbrey almost forgot she was still sitting in Bren's room.

"Well?" Bren needed some reaction from Silbrey.

"Am I a rat?" Silbrey asked.

"You are sensing what the rat senses."

The rat scampered along a mossy stone floor. It appeared as if the rat was at the bottom of a deep cylindrical sink hole. A staircase made of the same white stones as the palace's exterior extended from the curved wall, up past the rat's range of sight. At the bottom of the pit was a dome steel cage, the size of a small house. Inside the cage were many comforts for a hospitable captivity. A bed, a writing desk with maps and charts scattered about, a dining table with wine bottles stacked upon it, and a hammer dulcimer. The only item that spoke to any inconvenience was the latrine bucket on the other side.

Contained within the cage was a large, shadowy figure. The rat's poor eyesight could not distinguish any features. The figure was a silhouette against candlelight. Silbrey could feel the fear in the rat. Bren's power held it in place.

"That ain't you, is it, Bren?" The creature spoke in a gruff voice, loud with a crackle, like a rotten tree collapsing in the forest. He said, "Bren" in a casual, abbreviated way, so it came out more like "Br'n."

This was Kret Bonebreaker.

He leaned against the bars and spoke again. "Oh, I know you. I smelled you before. When you first entered the palace. I can always smell the fey. Is Bren letting you have a peek at the big, bad monster? Is that it?"

Silbrey wished she could see his canine face. Were gnolls the inspiration for the Wolf who appeared in so many fey tales? Was it Kret? Did Kret follow the lost girl to the cottage? Did Kret use honey and flour to trick the seven goats into letting him in? Was Kret the one we were warned to stay away from?

"You've come to see the monster. Is that it?" Kret shouted his question again and grabbed at the bars. His voice echoed throughout the pit. The rat was afraid. Silbrey was afraid too. "Here I am! Come down! Come down and introduce yourself proper-like. I want to see you."

He kept shouting "I want to see you" over and over again —each time louder and more terrible—until the phrase was nothing but a maniacal howl.

Bren let go of Silbrey's hand. Silbrey's senses left the rat and returned to the room. She had been squeezing Bren's hand tightly.

"Kret's been in a mood lately," Bren said as she rubbed her sore hand. "He misses me."

"You visit him?" Silbrey was amazed. "Where is he?"

"He's imprisoned beneath the palace. It was a dragon pit from back when the elves lived on this island. I haven't gone down there since I've been confined to my bed."

"Aren't you afraid of him getting out?"

"Those bars are made of adamantine steel. He can't break them, but he's tried."

"But why is he still alive?" Silbrey could not imagine what possible reason Bren would have to allow that beast to live. Silbrey could not kill Dahlia Tulan when she had the chance, but Dahlia was a just another guildmaster obsessed with power. Kret was legendary for the destruction he caused.

"After the war, everyone expected me to rule northeast Amon," said Bren. "I was good with a sword, but I don't know how to govern. The previous high general allowed minters to use less silver and gold in their coinage. It drove prices up in the south. How was I supposed to resolve that? I kept Kret imprisoned and used him as an advisor. No one else knows he's here, but there is value in his counsel. His mind. It's astounding. His ideas, not mine, brought prosperity to this region."

"The same prosperity that put you in debt and beholden to guildmasters like Dahlia Tulan?" Silbrey's voice rose. She could feel her face warm with anger. "Why would he advise you unless it was to his advantage? Think about it. His guidance made the guildmasters more powerful than you, and he leveraged one of them to rebuild his army."

"He is a clever one."

"What about Aubec? What about Oren? You trust them. Do they know? You were their commanding officer."

"I'm still their commanding officer," Bren said with indignation. "It's better to limit Kret's contact with the outside world. Dark forces guide Kret. He listens to them."

"And you listened to Kret."

"I was never his puppet." Bren's words sounded hollow, as she tried to convince herself of this point.

* * *

The next few days, Gydan and Cyru wandered the palace. They became a familiar presence to the palace staff—as Gydan and Cyru wended through the kitchen, the storage rooms, the guard's chambers, and the back hallways. They met Bren's long-time partners, Corrinae Yol and Halsten Elytor, who lived on the opposite end of the palace. Gydan and Cyru discovered secret passageways that allowed for discreet exits, and they found a stairwell leading to a locked cellar door. It was here that Cyru learned their sight was limited within the palace. The dragon did not like it. Cyru had always known what was around every corner.

Gydan's favorite part of the palace was the courtyard menagerie in the middle of the palace. Each enclosure had exotic animals from across Amon and beyond. Cyru was less impressed or possibly jealous. Gydan was fascinated with the strange creatures. On more than one occasion, the groundskeeper had to remind her to keep her distance from the tiger's cage.

No one had to tell Gydan to keep her distance from Bren's private chambers. She avoided it for fear of further embarrassment. However, Gydan followed every bit of news that came from behind those doors. Bren's condition remained unchanged. She was tired, with periodic sharp pains in her chest. Her body was discolored, and her features sunken. She labored to breathe. For a few hours each day, she would be awake and alert. During that time, there would be a flurry of activity, decrees, updates, and then back to resting.

Most remarkably, the news of Bren's failing health did not leave the palace. The people in Bren's inner circle showed an amazing degree of discretion, or they were in denial that her condition might be fatal.

On the last day before they were to leave, Gydan was served a delicious dinner of roasted duck, nuts, dates, and goat cheese. She ate in the kitchen with the chef and the waitstaff. It was part of her routine in avoiding Bren Caius. She also took the opportunity to extract stories about Bren from the staff. People in the kitchen were hospitable and welcomed Gydan's company. They had a few innocuous stories, mildly entertaining but hardly worth telling. They gave each other knowing nods and secretive smiles. When Gydan couldn't get anything further from them, Gydan and Cyru retired to the aviary to observe Ruth as they did most nights.

Ruth was more active at this time. Gydan sat on a bench next to the aviary and watched the owl. Cyru flew in circles, cartwheeling through the air—hoping to upstage the modest owl. Gydan's mind soared through all the stories she had heard, all the adventures Bren and Ruth had together before the war and after. It was hard to imagine Ruth anywhere but upon Bren's shoulder. The owl, on this night, appeared more aware of Gydan's presence. They watched each other. Gydan tilted her head to the side, and Ruth did likewise. The owl's head shifted to look past her. Gydan turned to see Oren of Angnavir standing there, large enough to block out everything behind him.

"The high general requests your presence this evening. May I walk you to her quarters?"

Gydan reacted by coughing and choking. All the air had left her. She saw the twinge of a smile at the corner of Oren's mouth. "Am I in trouble?" Gydan asked. Bren had made her bias clear. Her words forever burned into Gydan's memory: *I do not hold court with children.*

Oren wasn't going to ease Gydan's fear. "I cannot presume to know the high general's mind."

*That's not an answer.*

Gydan had come to appreciate the blunt honesty of dragons.

Like before, the double doors were wide open. When Gydan stepped in, she gasped. Bren Caius was seated in a chair with a quilt blanket over her lap. She still looked tired, but she appeared pleased to see Gydan. An empty chair was positioned next to Bren Caius. She invited Gydan to sit. Across from the two chairs was a draped white curtain, illuminated with several lanterns behind it, the only light in the room. Three young entertainers, dressed in the bombastic clothing of their craft, stood at attention. They were holding cut figurines on sticks. Shadow puppets. An old woman with a floppy hat sat at the side of the makeshift stage with her lute. It was Ilset, the minstrel from their ferry to Rhyll. She gave Gydan a nod of acknowledgment.

"*Yakost,*" Oren said. "I present Gydan, menace to ogres, daughter of Silbrey."

This title shook Gydan. How did he know about the ogre?

"That's quite a title," Bren said.

"Bren, I think you have enough titles," Oren responded. "It's time for new stories."

"You don't like the old ones?" Bren teased.

"My legacy will be that you defeated me in single combat while blindfolded. If I had known you were to become Bren the Beloved, I would've tried harder."

Gydan could not believe she was there, listening to them banter. Oren and Bren!

"Your loss, my friend."

"Oh, I am aware." Oren bowed and left the room.

Bren smiled at Gydan and again offered her the empty chair. Gydan felt weak and suppressed her stomach's rumblings —the roasted duck, nuts, dates, and goat cheese.

"Please, Gydan, join me."

*Gydan, do not retch and expel your dinner.*

"High General Caius," Gydan stammered. "I am sorry about before, when I spoke out of turn. I didn't mean it. And you were busy—"

"Gydan, I need to apologize to you. I was rude. Simple as that. I'm not a monarch. I do not sit above people. I'm a servant, and I did not act as I should. I'm sorry." Bren spoke with poise, but her failing health weighed down the words. "Your mother has been a friend to me these past few days, and she told me about what happened in the woods and at the farmhouse. You were very brave."

Gydan's stomach tightened. Her mind went to Yurig, hiding with her behind the plow, how he wet himself. The pungent smell. The sheep slaughtered in the barn.

"I don't think I was."

Gydan's eyes shifted to honeysuckles wrapped around the bedpost. A few bees were working late.

"It seldom feels like that in the moment," Bren responded with sympathy. "But your actions have led to us sending troops into the forest to finish them off, which will save many more lives. It's worthy of honor—" Bren coughed. She was in pain but regained herself. "No speeches. It's a bad habit from a life in politics. To the point, I commissioned a ballad to immortalize your bravery."

Ilset plucked her lute and sang. None of this made any sense to Gydan. Why would anyone think it was a good idea to write a song, a ballad no less, about children hiding from an ogre and then fleeing for their lives? One might as well write a song about a sailor drowning or a hunter being mauled by a bear.

On the luminous curtain, a scene was set in silhouette, rising from below, a castle along with monstrous trees. A princess bounded out from the castle.

Bren leaned over to Gydan and whispered, "There are always princesses in these types of stories. But that's you." Bren pointed to the princess.

Ilset sang about the dark, evil forest that surrounded the castle, but Gydan was hardly listening to the words. She focused on the dancing shadows.

The princess was accompanied by a miner's son, a clear stand-in for Yurig. The scene changed. Gydan heard the puppeteers behind the curtain scramble as they traded out the forest-and-castle vignette for a cave with stalactites and stalagmites—like sharp teeth, a gaping maw. Together, the princess and the miner's son descended into a cave where they met a goblin. No dragons mentioned, which Cyru disapproved of. With this omission from the story, it was unclear why the princess and the miner decided to go into the cave. The story made no sense. The princess, the miner's son, and the goblin danced as the lute played. Gydan did not know what the dancing was about, except that afterward the two children escaped. The goblin then called for the other monsters of the forest to chase after the children.

The chase moved from the forest into the palace. The puppeteer hurried to switch out the forest vignette for the interior of the castle. But Gydan was not thinking about the princess or the palace; her mind went to mutilated sheep, the look on her brother's face.

The ogre pursued. The princess grabbed a bucket from her nurse, a character shown in the opening but soon forgotten and now reintroduced. The miner's son was gone, probably because the puppeteers did not have enough hands for more than three characters at a time.

Gydan watched the play unfold. She was feeling everything all over again, the certainty she was going to die in the barn. ("Yurig, I love you. I need you to run that way, while I run the other way. If you don't, we'll both die.") And she almost had, if it weren't for Cyru and the other dragons. Gydan's jaw trembled. She bit at her knuckles. It was a nervous habit she had developed. She felt a pounding in her ears. Everything was too close and too loud.

*Gydan, we can leave at any time. You don't owe these humans anything.*

The puppet ogre picked up the puppet princess, waving her wildly in the air—not sure of what to do with her now that he had her. Gydan remembered being squeezed by the ogre. In fact, she still had the bruises on her body. The puppet princess swung her bucket and bopped the ogre on the head. And the ogre fell on his back, dead. But that's not what happened. That wasn't it.

Gydan didn't notice the puppeteers had stopped performing. Ilset had stopped playing her lute. Everyone was looking at Gydan. Concern showed on their faces. Gydan didn't realize she had screamed when the ogre fell over.

The deluge of significant events since that moment had pushed back the darker thoughts. It was easier to forget, to pretend everything was okay—until it was performed in front of her.

Bren Caius gave a sympathetic frown. She was embarrassed for Gydan, which was worse than having the high general chastise her when they first met.

"The play was wonderful," Gydan said. "I'm sorry." She ran out of the room. Cyru followed.

* * *

"Within one week, my son has tried to kill me—and I sent your daughter out of this room on the verge of tears, twice," Bren sighed.

The puppeteers and minstrel had taken their coin and cleared out. Silbrey arrived later to help Bren back into the bed. Bren wasn't strong enough to walk on her own. A serving boy brought in a pitcher of ale for Bren and Silbrey. It had become their evening ritual. The conversation often went to Kret. Bren wanted to talk of old battles. Silbrey wanted to know what Bren planned to do with him. But for tonight, they talked about their children.

"Should I send guards to look for Gydan?" Bren asked.

"She'll come back." This response made Silbrey look negligent, but Gydan was raised on a farm where it was common for children to wander off and return only when they were tired or hungry. "She needs space right now."

Silbrey knew about the commissioned play. She had thought it was a good idea. Gydan had always loved the traveling actors. Her father had been hospitable to a theatre company once—just once—offering lodging and a place to perform for the families in the area, and like a dog, they kept showing up, year after year, waiting to be fed. Callis was too kind to refuse. Thus, Gydan and Yurig had a childhood filled with entertainment.

"You should give your daughter a sword," Bren said. "With her tragic childhood, she'll grow up to be a great warrior."

"Staff." Silbrey held up her gnarled staff. "It's a better weapon."

They had already spoken about how—once Bren's health returned—they would need to have a sparring match. However, with Bren's health not improving, it seemed unlikely they would have a chance to settle the debate.

"*Sah'le vuk.* You'd give your daughter a stick?" Bren laughed. "I guess I am the better parent."

Another voice came from the doorway. "The better parent. Are you sure about that, Mother?"

A young man stood there, dressed in a fine, black, silk tunic, all puffs and frills. His outfit boldly announced his privilege, something the son of a high general might wear. He had dark hair with thick curls. Handsome features, with the exception of his eyes. His bloodshot eyes were sunken. The skin under his eyes was discolored and drooping. Such eyes belonged to a tormented person who did not sleep.

"Mendal." Bren said his name, but there was so much in how she said it—pain and disappointment, dashed hopes, the severed connection. Not every child grows up to be like their parents. Despite being loved and having every comfort, some children are born cruel. They cannot come back. Mendal was such a child. Silbrey was thankful her own children had their father's kindness.

Mendal took a few steps forward. Silbrey moved in front of Bren, ready to strike with her staff. But Bren put a hand on Silbrey's arm, asking her to stand back.

Mendal ignored Silbrey. "Mother, I'm glad to see you're feeling well."

"You are?"

"I am your son." Mendal acted wounded by her question. "The only thing I care about is your wellbeing."

"Where have you been this past week?"

"At the temple, Mother, praying for your recovery."

Bren laughed at this obvious lie. Mendal's mouth formed a smile, but the rest of his face remained morose. "It's not that I love you less—but I love Amon more."

"So, you admit it?" Bren took this as a confession.

"I will unite this continent and create a golden age like the elves had long ago."

"Do what you must, but don't release Kret," Bren said, almost pleading.

The mention of Kret stopped Mendal. His blank expression turned into a sneer turned into a smile. "You figured it all out."

"Kret is manipulative, a real charmer." Bren put all the pieces together. "You must be the one coordinating with Dahlia and Speck on his behalf."

"*Tem gol'naran jut il idon lete'feer,*" Mendal said in Volir as he unsheathed a dagger he had hidden behind his back.

Silbrey hit him with her staff no less than three times before he even took a step toward Bren—across his hand, forcing him to drop the dagger, in his stomach, doubling him over, and upon his back, driving him to the ground. Silbrey was not thinking. She reacted as she was trained. She brought her staff up for one more strike.

Bren shouted, "No!" The fear in her voice shook Silbrey. "He's my son."

Mendal retrieved his dagger and ran out of the room.

"He's releasing Kret from his cage, isn't he?" Silbrey asked.

"Please do what I couldn't do. Kill Kret."

It was a familiar job. Silbrey grabbed her shield and chased after Mendal.

Gydan and Cyru left the palace. She needed to get away for a moment. Gydan knew it wasn't a good idea to be away from the palace in an unfamiliar city, but she felt safe with Cyru.

They worked their way through the crowded city. After all that time secluded in the palace, Gydan felt a rush being surrounded by people. There was a certain joy to being young and small—and able to navigate a busy street. She moved twice as fast. The path was hers to exploit.

Gydan turned a corner into an open area—a small market, emptied of daytime commerce, transformed into an outdoor tavern. Soldiers clustered. They drank and conversed, laughing and staggering into each other. Across the way, Gydan saw a tall woman in a hooded cloak, wisps of blonde hair protruded. She was fair and slender. It was Maricel.

Maricel did not see Gydan, who ducked back around the corner. She dared a second look. It was her. Gydan resisted the urge to run up and throw her arms around her.

*Who are we hiding from?* Cyru asked. Everyone who

walked past them did a double take at the miniature dragon hovering in the air.

"Maricel. She lived with us at the farmhouse."

Maricel had a desperate look on her face. Silbrey had never explained why they didn't go back for Maricel or leave a message for her. Her mother had told her much on their trip to Rhyll, but the silence about Maricel spoke loudly. Instead, Silbrey had only said they made the right decision by avoiding her.

Gydan walked back down the street, away from the open market, unsure what to do with her discovery. Then Gydan felt a hand grab her arm.

"I've been looking for you!" Maricel was behind her, wide-eyed and full of questions. "Where is your mother? Where's Yurig? And—is that a dragon?"

*Do you want me to destroy her?*

Gydan waved off Cyru. No point in escaping Maricel.

"How did you know we were in Rhyll?" Gydan asked.

"I didn't see you on the road to Barcombe, so I checked the dock. The woman in the vardo told me you sailed to Rhyll."

Maricel was on the verge of tears as she recounted the experience. Gydan remembered that, though her mother barely showed any emotion, Maricel always kept her feelings close to the surface. She cried often, but not in a way that felt manipulative or weak. Gydan appreciated this vulnerability from Maricel. It felt honest. Gydan grabbed her hand to reassure her. She knew her mom wouldn't approve, but she couldn't pretend Maricel wasn't part of her life.

"You didn't stop at Sage Hall first?" Gydan asked. "That's where Yurig is."

"I didn't stop to check. I assumed you were in the city, but I couldn't find you. Where have you been?"

"In the palace."

Maricel shuddered in astonishment. "The palace? How?"

"Mom is friends with Bren Caius."

Gydan saw the surprise on Maricel's face and knew she was sharing too much. Maricel grabbed both of Gydan's arms this time. Cyru hissed. Maricel's voice lowered, almost threatening.

"I need to see your mom. Can you go back into the palace and get her? Please? I only want to talk."

Gydan wanted to get away, and she knew agreeing to the request was her best chance.

"I'll do it."

Maricel loosened her grip.

"Tell your mom. I'll be waiting at the docks. It's important."

Gydan barely heard a word that Maricel said. She only wanted to get away. She no longer felt safe outside. Gydan and Cyru retraced their path back to the palace, unaware of the danger within.

Silbrey stood at the wide-open cellar door. Mendal had come this way to release Kret. Silbrey planned to use her enchantment to put them both to sleep. Then she would kill Kret. A strike to the head should do it. It wasn't an honorable way to fight, but she had no history with him—no need to get sentimental. She didn't need any ballads to be written. For Mendal, she would bind him, and let Bren deal with her son.

The cellar door led to a storage room. The cellar was unremarkable. Wooden crates lined the walls. Several coils of rope were at the far end. No Mendal. Next to the rope, a portion of the wall was pushed back, revealing another staircase leading into the dragon pit. Silbrey looked into the dark depths and decided after today she wouldn't set foot in any more caves. Nothing good ever came from descending into the earth.

The dragon pit looked different from when she had experienced it through the rat. She noticed more details, deep scratches along the walls—belonging to dragons, much larger than Cyru, no longer in captivity—and swirling flourishes carved into the stairs. The pit was more colorful. A single ray of light from above reflected onto the walls and caused flakes of the stone to sparkle with an opal sheen. The spring water, which dominated the rat's senses, was barely a trickle along the curved wall at the bottom. Silbrey wondered if those borrowed animal senses felt more normal for Bren. Silbrey was convinced they were both fey, and yet wholly different. Silbrey didn't know if she believed in fate or the will of the gods, but she couldn't deny the path that had led her here.

A rat followed Silbrey at a distance down the stairs. The high general was keeping watch. Silbrey showed the rat the back of her hand, three fingers extended, a crude hand gesture. She hadn't forgiven Bren for putting her in this situation.

As Silbrey descended the stairs, she noticed the door to the cage was open. Blood was smeared around the lock where a key had been inserted. Kret was gone. In his place, behind the bed, a body was torn in two.

Silbrey walked into the cage to look at the body. It wasn't Mendal. He looked like one of the palace guards. A gruesome sight. Torn below the rib cage from end to end. The entrails and blood trailed across the floor. The body had been dragged here.

Silbrey heard a voice behind her.

"That guard—I forgot his name—was stationed in the cellar as part of an ongoing rotation," Mendal said in a cool, even voice. "They had no idea what they were guarding, the greatness beneath them. Sometimes my mother would excuse them of their duties so she could visit."

Silbrey cursed herself for not seeing him sooner. She must have walked right past him. Where did he hide? She dropped everything and sprinted for the gate. Mendal smiled and closed the gate before Silbrey could get there. He locked it with the key and took a few steps back as Silbrey collided into the bars.

"Mendal, let me out!"

"No," he laughed. He was enjoying this. "This is the hour we've been waiting for. The beast is loose."

"Let me out!" Silbrey grabbed the bars of the gate and shook them. "Where is Kret? Where is he?"

"He escaped before I ever entered Mother's room. Do you think I'm dumb enough to take a chance on you or her stopping me?"

"He will kill everyone in the palace."

"I hope so." Mendal rolled up his sleeves. "I showed the guard the secret entrance to the pit. Curiosity got the best of him, and he made a terrible mistake."

"Which was?"

Mendal pulled out his dagger and stabbed at Silbrey.

"Never stand close to the cage."

At least two guards always stood at the front of the palace, but tonight, there was no one. Gydan and Cyru approached without anyone to stop them. Gydan opened the doors.

The palace was dark and empty. Usually, Cyru would flit about like a hummingbird. But now, Cyru flew slow and steady in front of her.

She held her hands out in front of her and worked her way along the halls by memory. She then heard cries from the back of the palace, near the kitchen. Cyru chirped in response. She heard a series of footsteps and shouts. The guards were back there. Gydan didn't know what was going on, but it sounded like someone had broken in—someone who didn't belong here. Gydan heard a crash and more shouts. She needed to find her mother. Silbrey would be with Bren in her room. She and Cyru hurried past the aviary. Ruth —Bren's famous owl—flapped her wings, trying to escape the cage.

*At the farmhouse, we knew what was coming after us.*

"I did not need you to say that," Gydan whispered through clinched teeth.

*I was trying to be encouraging.*

"How is that encouraging?"

*There's a possibility this is not worse than what we've faced before.*

Gydan ran up the stairs to Bren's bedroom. The doors were open. The moonlight shone through the windows. She could see Bren Caius was awake and lying in bed. Something dreadful was loose in the palace, but Bren maintained her repose.

"Where's my mom?" Gydan asked.

"I sent her on a little errand."

Gydan jumped at the sound of more screams from downstairs. "What happened?"

"Kret is still alive," Bren said, as if it were nothing. "I kept him prisoner beneath the palace. I believe my homicidal

son has released him." Bren closed her eyes. A blue light
shimmered briefly. "And I am certain Kret is coming this
way."

Gydan had heard the rumors that Kret was still alive. It was
harmless gossip among the Aylers, the traveling actors who
passed their spare time speculating on such things. When
Gydan first heard it, she even believed it was true. But now that
the rumor was confirmed by Bren herself, Gydan was in
disbelief.

"Kret died at Pynne's Field," Gydan said.

"I was there, and he didn't," Bren said.

Gydan remembered the barn, she and her brother hiding
from the ogre. She did not want to hide again. She wanted to
take the high general and run away. Gydan had faced too much.
These experiences made her braver, but less daring. She could
walk the dark hallway, but she wouldn't stay to face whatever
lurked in the shadows.


Silbrey stepped away from Mendal's attack and grabbed his
arm. Braced against the adamantine bar, she pulled his arm
back. A cracking noise. Mendal screamed. He dropped the
dagger. Silbrey kicked the weapon across the floor, away from
him. Mendal slapped at Silbrey with his free hand, trying to get
her to let go. She was undeterred. She undid her belt and then
grabbed his other arm. She used her belt to wrap his forearms
together, and then knotted the belt, a constrictor knot she
learned from the dock workers of Penderyn. Mendal pulled
back but could not free himself. All he could do was cuss and
spit.

As he struggled against his bindings, Silbrey walked back to pick up her staff and shield. "You poisoned your mother?" Silbrey asked.

"I tried to," Mendal grunted. The struggling made the knot tighter. "That poison should have killed a giant. I couldn't make it any stronger without it burning a hole through the cup it was placed in."

"And then you freed Kret to do what the poison couldn't?"

"Freeing Kret was always part of the plan. I studied my history. A great crisis requires a strong leader. The people will beg for Bren's heir to take a crown once Kret's legion returns in strength."

"You have it all figured out," Silbrey said, mocking him.

"Kret is ageless," Mendal said. "Before he ever took a physical form, his spirit raged across Efre Ousel. He saw fire rain from the sky upon the earth. And he will awaken the sleeping titans and watch the world break once more."

Mendal sounded like a fanatic. Kret had used Mendal to coordinate his efforts with Speck and Dahlia. And Mendal had confused this role with being important.

Rays of blue light swirled around Silbrey and reached out to Mendal. He fell to the ground in an enchanted sleep. She noted how much Mendal—and Speck too—loved to hear themselves talk, desperate for validation.

Silbrey reached through the bars to grab the key, and she let herself out. She untied Mendal and moved him into the enclosure. She then locked him in. Mendal, the aspiring tyrant, could use his time in captivity to consider all the ways he had been manipulated by the gnoll warlord.

Silbrey wondered about this beast who could obtain mercy from the high general and convince a son to murder his mother —calculating, but also capable of tearing a soldier apart with his bare hands. She imagined he must be a talker, too. Silbrey would make sure to strike the moment he opened his mouth. She was tired of talk.

Silbrey climbed the stairs out of the dragon pit, ready to face him. In the palace, the axe that once hung in the hall was missing. Kret had left a trail of bodies. Silbrey's daughter was not among them. Silbrey thanked the gods. Gydan had run away after the shadow puppet performance. It probably saved her life.

Silbrey followed the trail of blood.


Bren and Gydan heard the screams throughout the palace. They echoed off the stone walls, accompanying the percussion of thuds and crashes, a horrific symphony to announce the return of Kret Bonebreaker. Cyru chirped their unease. The dragon stretched their wings, preparing for a fight. Gydan looked at Bren for guidance. Bren's eyes were watery, filled with a lifetime of sadness. But her overall countenance was one of resolution.

"Gydan, help me up."

Gydan pulled Bren up to a seated position on the bed. Gydan then moved Bren's legs around to touch the floor. Bren gritted her teeth in pain. She placed her hand on the bed to steady herself. The poison, which had devastated her body, made every move agony.

"Hand me my sword."

Gydan was confounded by this request. Bren wouldn't be able to fight Kret. She barely had enough strength to sit up, let alone hold a sword.

"My sword, child."

Gydan obeyed. She took the sword hanging on the wall and handed it to Bren. The sword was a reminder to all who visited of what she had accomplished in life. It was a myth built on a lie. Bren hadn't killed Kret. The legend of Pynne's Field was a convenient tale on which to build her reign as high general. Now the truth was coming for them both.

Bren unsheathed her sword and tossed the scabbard to the ground. The once-great warrior held the sword, but her hand shook. The sword wavered. Bren kept her eyes on the open doors leading into darkness and the screams echoing beyond.

"Help me stand up."

"But—"

"Help me stand up."

Gydan wrapped her arms around Bren and struggled to lift her up. Gydan didn't have the height or strength to be much use, but Bren placed her elbows on Gydan's shoulders and with a few grunts was able to stand. Bren wobbled and then found her balance. She stared at the open doors.

For the rest of her life, Gydan would tell people it was the bravest thing she had ever seen.

"Gydan," Bren said, "You've endured things no child should have to endure. Kret is coming for me. You shouldn't be here. Take my signet ring—it's in a box on the other side of the bed—and go out the open window. The supporting columns are easy to climb down. Go to the guard tower at the center of the city. Hand them the ring and tell them to blow the horn— one long, one short, one long blast. Then, I want you to get on a boat in the harbor. Any boat. No one is safe on this island. You will not wait for your mother. Go."

Gydan did as she was told. She took the ring out of the box and climbed out the window, glancing at Bren one last time.

Bren gestured to the open door and the darkness beyond. "What's taking so long?" Bren smiled. Tears were in Bren's eyes, and her voice faltered as she spoke. "Goodbye, Gydan."

Gydan descended the column, and she ran across the lawn. Cyru flew by her side. She did not look back, but she imagined what happened next. Kret would emerge from the darkness of the hallway. The gnoll, as large as a brown bear, would roar at his old adversary. He would be terrifying, truly terrifying, covered in blood. This was it, the final battle between Bren Caius and Kret Bonebreaker. He would say how he wanted to get his revenge, and then she would respond with something clever. Kret would raise his massive axe. And Bren would find an inner strength, a final boon from the named god Olar. Bren's shaky hands would steady, and she would point her sword at Kret. He would run at her, but she would dodge every attack. And she would stab her sword through his heart. He would howl, and then collapse to the floor. Bren would have her victory at last.

This was how Gydan imagined it, even though she knew this was not how it would go. Aubec said history is a story told by the people privileged to tell it. A final piece of Bren's story now belonged to Gydan.

Silbrey ran through the halls, calling for Bren, calling for her daughter—hoping neither was here to respond. Motes of blue light illuminated her path.

She ran to Bren's room. A deep groove was cut into the floor, where Kret had dragged his axe, leading to the open doorway.

When Silbrey arrived, Bren had already been defeated.

Kret had hacked her apart with his axe. He then cast the axe aside and further disfigured Bren with his claws. Silbrey thought she had seen violence—the body opened up, blood pouring out—but this mutilation was something different. Beyond cruel, it was an absolute desecration. What stunned Silbrey even more was that Bren was still alive. She was still standing. Their eyes met, and Silbrey could see the fear.

Bren brought her sword down on Kret and cut into his shoulder. If Kret felt the hit, he did not give Bren the pleasure of reacting. It would be Bren's last time to wield her sword. Kret grabbed her hand, and with a twist, broke her forearm. The sword was his now. He moved behind her, so that he was facing Silbrey and had Bren's own blade at her throat.

Silbrey was finally able to get a good look at Kret. He stood as tall as a goliath—but bestial, like a rabid dog, snarling with thick yellow scum dripping from his jaws. His muzzle was flaked with gray. One ear had a deep cut that had healed over so that it folded unnaturally. His eyes were dark pits, an abyss. Kret's eyes hinted at some ancient and godlike spirit that preceded his current form. This was a creature who had seen fire rain from the sky and wanted to watch the world break once more.

"No." It was all Silbrey could say.

"You're here," Kret's gruff voice startled Silbrey. "It's the little mouse. I can always smell the fey. Didn't I tell you? Hey, little mouse, watch this."

When Silbrey was a child, her fighting instructor Keote had told her that training wasn't any good once someone got hit. All wisdom and confidence would abandon them. At this moment, Silbrey understood. She was so horrified. She could not move. She could barely breathe. Instead, the blue light of her fey powers extended toward Kret and Bren. The light had no effect on Kret, but that was not Silbrey's focus. She placed Bren in a deep, enchanted sleep, a painless and peaceful sleep. Silbrey did not want Bren to suffer any longer.

Kret used Bren's own sword and cut deep into her neck. Blood spilled out. He cut deeper and deeper, sawing at Bren's throat, until her head fell to the ground. Her body collapsed in a mangled heap. Kret then dropped her sword to the floor.

"There," Kret said. "The death I always promised her. I feel a sense of achievement, you know? And I'm glad you were here to see it. I truly am." Kret reached for his cut shoulder, finally acknowledging the blow. "But I have places to be. We will save our dance for another time. Perhaps, in Aberton?"

Kret picked up his axe and, with a few steps, was already across the room. He leapt through the open window and landed without a sound.

Silbrey could only hear the ringing in her ears and the bees buzzing. She could feel her heart beating. Kret was gone. She knew she should follow him, but she couldn't leave Bren's body unattended.

She placed her staff on the chair where she usually sat. A curious bee explored Bren's lifeless face. Silbrey waved it away. Silbrey set the head—as well as the sword—next to the body. It felt wrong. Grotesque. She felt an urge to cover the body. Nobody should have to see this. Silbrey pulled the blanket off the bed and over Bren.

It was all too much. Silbrey shouted and shouted again.

She grabbed her staff and swung it at the air, wanting to hit something, but there was nothing. She felt a divine urge, a holy wrath, to purge and smite. Bren had told Silbrey: "Do what I couldn't. Kill Kret." Silbrey's purpose was clear. She would find Kret, and she would kill him. It had been a long time since someone had commanded her to kill, but she would fully accept this final command from Bren.

Silbrey heard the bukkehorn blasts. One long, one short, one long. It came from the tower at the center of the city. Then she heard the horn blasts repeated, more faintly, farther from the city, at one of the outposts. The blasts would be sent from outpost to outpost, passed on to Sage Hall and also to Thistle.

A quiet moment passed, then Aubec and Oren entered the room. They were unscathed, and that made Silbrey even angrier, if it were possible. The two stopped, fixated on the mound under the blanket on the floor.

"Is that her?" Aubec asked.

Oren fell to his knees.

Silbrey walked up to Aubec. He smelled of rum.

"Where have you been?" Silbrey got in Aubec's face. The stench was overwhelming.

"It's the fifth night," Aubec fumbled over his words. "We always meet up with . . . old friends from the war to . . . drink and tell stories on the fifth night."

Perhaps this was why Mendal had chosen tonight to free Kret. He knew Aubec and Oren would be away from the palace.

Aubec continued to ramble. "We saw no guards at the entrance, came here first, and—"

Silbrey shoved Aubec. He stumbled backwards.

"What's the point of a mage if you aren't able to protect the high general?"

"We saw the palace was dark."

Oren stared at the mound. He sang a dirge from his Raust-fweg homeland. His voice shook, but it grew in strength.

*Albjorn, lead me to battle and to my reward.*
*I will follow the gods until my steps fail me.*
*His ravens watch over all. Our honor restored.*
*If I fail you, hang me upon the cursed tree.*

*The enemy is great. He adds to my sorrows.*
*All are blinded in death, and lo, they cannot see.*
*When I lose in the light, I fight in the shadows.*
*If I fail you, hang me upon the cursed tree.*

*I hold my iron axe, and I hold my wood shield.*
*Death is a door, and my blood-stained weapon,*
*    the key.*
*Side by side, we form a strong wall. We shall not*
*    yield.*
*If I fail you, hang me upon the cursed tree.*

*I kill without shame because I respect my foe.*
*I fight for my family, and I fight to be free.*
*I march without fear because for honor, I go.*
*If I fail you, hang me upon the cursed tree.*

*Every raven warrior eventually will fall.*
*Our victory belongs to the farmer and king.*
*I pour my short life out, and then answer death's*
*    call.*
*But we shall meet again to fight, drink, and to*
*    sing.*

The song ended. It was an ode to Albjorn, the Raustfweg
name for Olar, the god who claimed lives lost in battle. Like

with so many soldiers, people try to simplify Olar. They see him as a warrior with a weapon and nothing more. But Timon had once told Silbrey that Olar was in love with Taraki, the male and female god of agriculture. A love doomed to fail. Since Taraki was complete in himself and herself, Taraki had no need of Olar. Timon saw it as a divine message about the futility of violence. Olar waged war to find a reason for Taraki to love him—more territory, protection of borders.

Silbrey saw it differently. Every great warrior was motivated by something larger than themself—a great love. Silbrey looked at the blanket, under which lay Bren Caius. She wondered what had motivated Bren. What great love?

Silbrey, Aubec, and Oren paused for a moment longer. No matter who was at fault, no matter what must be done next, they paused in mute realization. Before them was the body of Bren Caius. Yesterday, she could have moved all of Amon with a word. Now, she lay there—not upon a battlefield, but at the foot of her bed with a blanket covering her because the sight was too gruesome.

"We need to go after Kret," Silbrey said.

At his name, they both looked at her.

"That's impossible." Aubec joined Oren on the ground, kneeling in his grief and devotion to Bren. "I saw Kret die at Pynne's Field."

"Bren was the one wielding the sword," Silbrey replied, "and she said he didn't die."

"That explains the three horn blasts," said Aubec. "Bren must have sent word to the tower."

"What do the horn blasts mean?" Silbrey asked.

"One long, one short, one long, it's a crisis signal," Aubec explained. "In the event of a great threat facing Rhyll, all boats are to leave harbor and not return. Any boats that do not leave Rhyll's shore—even the smallest fishing boat—will be burned. This signal has never been used before. The purpose is to isolate the island from the rest of Amon—or, in this case, to keep Kret on the island."

Finally, Oren spoke. "The entire island is a prison cell. That must be why Bren kept so many soldiers here. Without knowing it, we were Kret's guards. Now he's loose, and we're trapped on this island with him."

"It's too quiet out there," Silbrey observed. "He's hiding or trying to get out of the city, but how does a gnoll of that size escape into the city unnoticed?" Silbrey pointed to the open window.

"I tried to understand Kret's motives during the war," Aubec said. "He was cunning, strategic, and yet, his end goal was to increase suffering. It wasn't an uprising. It wasn't a move for territory or power. No banner or new ideology to defend. Just carnage. And now, you're telling me he's still alive?" Aubec paused to consider the impossibility of it, and then his thoughts lead to another. "Silbrey, where is your daughter?"

*  *  *

Gydan and Cyru made it to the docks as the horns blasted. Every sailor knew the horn signals. Panic prevailed. Captains commanded their crews to load what they could and disembark. The larger ships blocked the way of some smaller ships. Vessels could not leave until the ones anchored near the port sailed farther out. The ship crews yelled at each other to hurry up. Gydan moved through the trammels of the crowd. She dodged the sailors running this way and that, and then she bumped into Maricel once again.

"Gydan, where is your mother? You said you'd get her."

More ships left the docks. She had no time to fill Maricel in on the details.

"Maricel, no one is safe on Rhyll. We need to get on a boat."

"I'm not leaving without your mother."

"And I can't stay," Gydan said. "I promised Bren."

Maricel reached into her belt pouch and handed some coin to Gydan.

"Take this and go to the boat on the end." Maricel pointed it out. "The *Elona*. They will sail for Penderyn. There's a farming community east of Penderyn but west of the Hazelef Forest. My mother lives there. She's from Raustfweg. Stay with her, and we'll come find you. Ask for Ausdre."

"Ausdre." Gydan repeated the name to make sure she wouldn't forget.

"My mother came to Amon to find your mother."

It felt like a betrayal to trust Maricel, but she needed the coin. She needed the boat. She needed a plan. Gydan decided to trust her, but only one step at a time. First, she would take the coin. Then she would board the boat. From there, she would see what was east of Penderyn and west of the Hazelef Forest.

Maricel gave Gydan a hug before she left. It was such an earnest embrace that Gydan did not know how to respond. She gave a reluctant smile, and then Maricel was gone in search of Silbrey.

The captain of the *Elona* accepted Gydan's coin. And before Gydan even set both feet upon the deck of the ship, they were already moving from the dock. No more passengers would be taken, even as desperate sailors in search of their families were left behind.

Gydan and Cyru found a place at the stern along with some merchants who knew the significance of the three horn blasts and had hurriedly paid their way onto the ship. They huddled close to be inconspicuous, to let the sailors sail. A halfling sailor with red cheeks and fuzzy brown hair was tying down a crate they weren't able to offload. The halfling was barefoot upon the ship. Despite everything Gydan had been through, when she saw this, she smiled.

Maricel waited until Gydan was safe upon the ship, then she turned back toward the palace. Maricel had been in the city of Rhyll for a few days. After talking with the woman in the vardo, she knew Silbrey would be here. Maricel asked around, but no one in the city had seen her—and according to Gydan, for good reason. They were in the palace. Silbrey had never told Maricel about Bren, but knowing this, it made sense Silbrey would travel to Rhyll to report on what had happened. Maricel knew what she saw, but she couldn't construct why it happened. The house and the barn had burned to the ground. Several dead goblins and gnolls were in the field, and a massive tree had grown through the middle of what remained of the house. A lot needed to be explained.

Why did Silbrey run away from her?

Was it because they were in the middle of an argument? Maricel regretted leaving. She couldn't put Silbrey on the spot and expect the answer she wanted to hear. That wasn't how

Silbrey worked. It was unfair to expect Silbrey to love her when she hadn't been honest.

Maricel saw Silbrey leave the palace and head in her direction. Silbrey had the savage expression of a mother searching for her daughter, but she hadn't noticed Maricel yet. Maricel looked at Silbrey long and steadily, and she was afraid. Was this the woman who snuck into her bed throughout the winter? So broken and beautiful. Silbrey walked at a hurried pace, holding her shield, her staff. This was the Silbrey that Maricel knew existed but had never seen. Silbrey was a warrior, and she was terrifying—something about how her soft, gentle face could harden with such resolution. The transformation was profound. Maricel thought about letting Silbrey pass by her without saying anything. But then her senses returned to her. She remembered Gydan. Silbrey needed to know where her daughter was. So much of Maricel's life had been devoted to finding and following Silbrey. She couldn't let her go now. With a moment of courage, she tried to say Silbrey's name, but nothing came out. And yet, Silbrey turned to look right at her.

"Maricel."

*Don't hate me,* that was the thought in Maricel's head. Maricel took a step toward her, and Silbrey took a step back. The world around them was chaos. All the ships had left the harbor. Soldiers were fanning out through the city. The common folk were left wondering what it all meant, peering from their windows and cracked doors. But for Maricel and Silbrey, there was only each other.

"Maricel, where's my daughter?"

"I put her on a ship, the *Elona.*" Maricel noticed the relief on Silbrey's face. "The ship's heading to Penderyn." And then Silbrey's expression hardened once again.

"To Penderyn? You're sending her to Dahlia?"

"No, I would never. Why would I do that?"

Silbrey tightened her grip on the staff. Was she going to attack her? Did Maricel need to get away?

"You've been spying on me."

That explained it. A pit formed in Maricel's stomach. Silbrey had found the journals. And then Maricel realized the misunderstanding.

"No! I wasn't spying on you for Dahlia—"

"You're a liar." Silbrey's face was chiseled stone.

A blue light came surrounded Maricel, and then she blacked out.

* * *

When the *Elona* had sailed far enough that the coastline vanished, Gydan learned the halfling's name was Roby Roundtree. She also learned that halflings only go barefoot in their hometown. For Roby, the island and the ship were the closest things she had to a home. Gydan thought of her mother, who now preferred to go without boots wherever she went. At first, it embarrassed Gydan, but she reconsidered it with a halfling's logic. Roby asked Gydan why she was in Rhyll and why she traveled with no family, except the dragon. The dragon's presence led the sailors to speculate that Gydan was of a noble family. Possessing a magical beast was sometimes an eccentric affectation of wealth.

Gydan told her story to Roby Roundtree. Her ears perked when Gydan mentioned Bren Caius.

"You've met the Northern Light? What's she like?"

Gydan could tell Roby the truth. She could tell her Bren

was old and weak; she was rude and boastful and overly confident; she was a drunk and a glutton. Bren Caius was not the wise and noble hero from the stories and was in many ways a disappointment. But she also thought of Bren Caius attempting to apologize with the grand gesture of commissioning a play. Gydan thought of the old woman struggling to stand and hold her sword, facing down a nightmare, all because she wanted to spare Gydan from what was approaching.

In the end, Gydan told Roby the story everyone had already heard about Bren the Beloved. She was brave and honorable. Gydan told Roby that she was every bit the living legend and more until the very end.

\* \* \*

The soldiers could not find Kret after searching the city. So they spread throughout the countryside, looking for the giant gnoll warlord. A horn signal came from Sage Hall, indicating all was well there. However, no signals came from Thistle. Silbrey loaned Feste to one of the scouts who rode to the town.

The idea that Kret had returned from the dead was met with mixed opinions. For some, it confirmed a vast conspiracy. For others, it was a lie and part of a wholly different set of conspiracies. No one outside the palace had seen Kret, but everyone knew the horn signals were to be taken seriously. Clearing the harbor threw the city into disarray. Families were separated. Merchants—who depended on the ships that sailed between Rhyll and the cities along the coastline—were left unmoored. Everyone had a story of how it inconvenienced them.

The next day, the city was quiet. Few people walked the

streets. The remaining guards continued their patrol. When the immediacy of the threat faded in people's minds, they joked that the guards were hoping to find Kret hiding under a bushel basket or tucked away in the washroom of some peasant's home. Maybe Kret was hiding among the chickens. This dark humor distracted them from the other impossible news that made its way across Rhyll: Bren Caius had died. The Northern Light had gone dim. Few could remember what the world was like before her arrival, and no one was ready to imagine what a world would be like without her. The possibility of Kret's return was horrible, but the truth of Bren Caius's death was too cruel to consider.

The palace was quiet as well. Bren Caius wasn't the only life lost on that night.

Mendal was kept as a prisoner in the dragon pit, while Maricel was detained in Ruth's aviary. Oren had his soldiers lock up Maricel before Silbrey had a chance to speak with her again. Maricel slept through the night and well into the next day until she regained consciousness.

Maricel could have been transferred to the holding cells at the garrison, but Silbrey wanted to keep her in the palace until she knew more about Kret's plans. If Maricel worked for Dahlia, and Mendal worked for Kret, then both should have useful information. Silbrey also wanted to know about the journals. It may not matter to Oren or Aubec, but Silbrey felt she deserved to hear it from Maricel. She wanted to talk with her before anyone else had the chance, but first Silbrey waited for the scout to return from Thistle.

Oren coordinated the efforts to find Kret. Aubec worked with some of the other generals to prepare for a new war with Kret and to understand how this had slipped past them. Silbrey thought of the fight ahead and the precariousness of her situation.

Until they found Kret, they would not be able to leave the island. That meant her son at Sage Hall was also trapped on the island with the most dangerous creature in Amon's history on the loose—and it was Silbrey who had let the gnoll warlord escape. While trapped on the island, Silbrey also could not go after Gydan, who was on a ship heading to Penderyn and presumably to Dahlia Tulan. Every effort Silbrey made to protect her children had only further endangered them.

Later in the day, Feste and the scout returned, much sooner than expected, and without a horn signaling "all is well" from Thistle. From the scout's haggard expression, Silbrey knew he had seen something dreadful.

"What's the news from Thistle?" Silbrey asked.

The scout burst into tears. He buried his face in his hands.

"Thistle is gone," he whimpered.

"What do you mean?"

"Everyone in the town is . . . they're dead. All of them, horribly, horribly—not a single person was left alive. I could have searched the fields, but I knew to come back."

"Were the boats still in the harbor?"

"No, it appears the sailors got the signal and left before he could arrive."

Other soldiers arrived to hear the news. Many of them knew people in Thistle. They were overwhelmed with grief. Wailing filled the quiet city.

Silbrey thought about the boats. Unless Kret decided to swim Tu'enya Bay, he was still on the island. And if he was on the island, Silbrey could fulfill Bren's last request.

# IV

AUSDRE SPENT the morning sowing the fields with cabbage seeds. The community had its midsummer harvest, and the weather was right to plant fall crops. It had been a quiet, peaceful morning, which made Ausdre pause. The parents of sick children learn to interpret silences. Her daughter had been singing earlier. Now there was no sound coming from the house.

Ausdre dropped her bag of seeds and ran into the house. She saw Maricel on the ground, her body contorted, her beautiful face twisted in expressions of pain and wonder. Her eyes were rolled back. She was having another vision. Ausdre held her daughter until it passed.

"What did you see this time?"

"The girl was training with her staff. She was sparring with that goliath."

"She's always fighting the goliath. Are you sure it's not the same vision?"

"No, it's different," Maricel said weakly. "She spends most days fighting. She's not eating. Her stepmother denies her food if the girl doesn't train to her satisfaction."

"And beats her?" Ausdre asked.

"Always."

The visions had become more frequent, and many in the community wondered if Maricel had the falling sickness. After each bout, with sweat on her brow and a deathlike pallor, Maricel would beg her mother, "We need to save her. Let me bring her back to the farm. She can live with us." But Ausdre knew about the guildmaster Maricel kept seeing in the visions. If the fey child was under the care of Dahlia Tulan, it wouldn't be so simple to take her. A price would be paid—one they couldn't afford.

Ausdre didn't know if a fey child raised in the city would even be able to use her powers. The fey were creatures of the forest. The boundaries between the worlds were more delicate in the wild. Could an uprooted plant survive? Could it grow without sunlight or water? Was the fey child a lost cause? Ausdre had been sent to Amon to bring the fey child back to Raustfweg. After losing her, Ausdre had given up and started a new life in this new land. Maricel now carried that original sense of purpose that once belonged to her mother. Each vision and convulsion was a reminder of the mission Ausdre had abandoned.

Druids believe the unnamed gods punished people who refused their calling. The visions would kill Maricel if she wasn't sent to save the fey child.

Ausdre took her concerns to the elders of the farming community. They were too old to work the fields—but they had wisdom, and they had compassion to solve problems too burdensome to carry alone. The elders listened to everything she had to say—every fear bound in the fragile circumstances of an immigrant from Raustfweg.

But Ausdre was family. And for the elders, that was enough. At first, they thought to send Ausdre, but Maricel, now a young adult, insisted it should be her. The visions belonged to Maricel, not her mother. She wanted to go. The community gathered its resources together to send Maricel to Penderyn. The plan was that Maricel would observe the fey child at a distance. Maricel would keep notes of everything she saw and send it back to Ausdre, who could then provide the insight and direction that might hopefully satisfy the calling she refused.

After Maricel left, she didn't return for a year. Ausdre was beside herself with worry. Maricel had never lived outside the farm. She would have to survive on her own. She would need to avoid the watchful eye of the guildmaster. And at Ausdre's insistence, Maricel would not take any actions until she shared with Ausdre what she had seen. Many times, Rue had to talk Ausdre down from traveling to Penderyn to spy on their daughter, who was spying on the fey.

Then one snowy evening, Ausdre heard a knock at her door. Maricel stood at the stone slab in front of their cottage. She was bundled in a wool jacket and wore an oversized fur cap that reminded Ausdre of the fashions in northern Raustfweg. Ausdre invited her daughter inside. When Maricel took off her cap and jacket, she appeared much older and even more beautiful. Ausdre cried and embraced her daughter.

"Where have you been?"

"Penderyn," Maricel responded to this obvious question with the most obvious answer. She was doing what she had been sent to do. She reached into her pack and pulled out a leather-bound book wrapped in cloth. "I filled this one. When I return, I will buy more journals. You may read through it now, but I'd like to keep it with me. When writing, it's helpful to compare with previous notes."

"You're going back?" Ausdre ached. She assumed once Maricel had gone into the city, she would find what she needed and return. Maricel's violent visions would end, and she could put it all behind her. But Ausdre should have expected this. Maricel had not returned with the fey, and nothing short of that would satisfy her daughter. There was a look in Maricel's eyes that Ausdre knew well in Raustfweg, the myopia of a sacred calling. Maricel had buried deep within herself the purpose of Ausdre's original mission—to sail to Amon, find the child born from a tree, and bring that child to Raustfweg.

"We can save her," Maricel said. "She's lived a cruel life. She has the heart of a killer, but she can change. *We* can change her—"

Ausdre knew what Maricel was about to suggest. "No, it's not right."

"The druidic spell would be temporary. It would open her heart and help her realize what she's missing. She can leave Penderyn and start a new life."

"I use that spell to help the livestock breed, not on a person. It wouldn't be love, not if a druid's behind it. I don't even know how such a spell would work on fey."

"Mother, I had a vision. Her heart changes. She falls in love."

"With whom?"

"With me."

Ausdre's daughter was filled with the pangs of young love.

Maricel had grown up on the farm—a small community where everyone was like a parent or a sibling. After a year in the city, she had become fixated on this person whom she watched at a distance. The person had a pitiable life that pulled at Maricel's sympathetic nature. The fey even had played a pivotal role in Maricel's own life, bringing her mother to Amon. How could Maricel not become enamored?

"That's not how the spell works," said Ausdre. "Don't ask me again."

Maricel stayed home through the remaining winter months. Ausdre hoped the time away would allow her daughter's head to clear and her heart to heal. Instead, the visions returned. They were painful, causing Maricel to thrash about; her muscles would go rigid, leaving her sore and exhausted.

But when Maricel returned to Penderyn in the spring, Silbrey was already gone.

Thistle was a quaint town. Just as Sage Hall was built to look like a venerable institution that went back generations, and just as the city of Rhyll was built to look like a thriving center of government, Thistle's quaintness was intentional. The whole island was Bren Caius's argument for the Amon way of things. Sage Hall represented intellectual rigor. The city of Rhyll represented efficiency and power. Thistle represented the idyllic beauty of agricultural life, complete with a windmill at the far end of town. But anyone who worked on a typical farm knew Thistle's quaintness rang false. There was seldom time for intricately carved trim along the roof line or a fresh coat of cherry red paint at the beginning of spring. No one had lace curtains. Who could afford lace by selling parsnips and fennel? And the plots were never distributed in perfect rectangles. Instead, there would be a fight over whether the stone marker or the creek indicated the true border of a property. In Thistle, everything gleamed like it was coated in syrup. The high general paid for artisans to maintain the appearance of Thistle. All that was expected of the citizens was to keep farming and don't raise a fuss over a slow season. They would be compensated for any losses.

Now there were no citizens left in Thistle. No one left to compensate. They were all slaughtered by Kret.

The town was a baked pastry crushed and thrown to the floor. The filling smeared across the ground. Nothing could be saved or put back into its original sweet state.

Soldiers dragged the mangled bodies to the town's center, where they were burned in a heap. The smell of smoldering flesh penetrated the air. The dead of Thistle were not given the solemnity Bren Caius would receive at her funeral, but families would be told that all dignity and ceremony was provided—even though the only priests on the island were among the dead. The priests had been servants of the named god Taraki and worked alongside the farmers. They also died alongside them.

Aubec, Oren, and Silbrey walked through the town to see the devastation for themselves. They had become an insepa-rable triumvirate. Three was a cursed number, but after the murder of Bren, it was a cursed time. They felt a connection, a mutual respect, a completeness in each other's council. Aubec and Oren had known each other for years, but Silbrey fit well within the group. The three stayed close, knowing if Kret was to be found they would need each other.

Oren nodded to the soldiers. They all bowed in deep reverence to the old warrior. And Aubec knew many of these soldiers by name, as they were once his students. Silbrey was the stranger among them. Even though the soldiers knew little about her, they respected any requests she made. After all, Silbrey had Bren's blessing, and Aubec and Oren often deferred to her. This point was not missed by the soldiers, who circulated rumors as if they were a currency, weighty as gold, insubstantial as air.

To the soldiers, Silbrey was an oddity. She walked everywhere barefoot. She carried a wooden staff and a shield that looked like the cross section of a tree. Some soldiers even claimed they saw flowers bloom and grass grow around her, as if she was a woodland witch. Despite her strangeness, soldiers would accept anyone willing to fight and die. They might not be friends in any other situation, but once someone enlisted—they were kindred. So it was with Silbrey. She was an outsider, but with Bren's blessing, she was *their* outsider.

Estrid, an armorer from the garrison, even made a new breastplate for Silbrey. The gift had been commissioned by Bren when Silbrey first arrived. Bren had heard that Silbrey never fixed her previous breastplate after the fight with Dahlia and Keote, and then the armor was lost in the farmhouse fire. Bren sent a letter to her favorite armorer and commissioned this new breastplate. It would be a surprise gift. Normally, it'd take her about two weeks or more to finish a piece of this quality, but Estrid worked as though possessed by Wedril, the named god of craft. She finished in half the time. Toward the end, when the work was mostly fine-detail embossing, she labored through the night. Bren had been murdered. The horns had sounded. Estrid wanted Silbrey to have this breast-plate before Bren's funeral.

The breastplate was her finest work. Estrid the Armorer infused adamantine steel into the plate, a skill she spent years honing but only achieved perfection while working on this commission, this gift from Bren. The story of Bren's request to the armorer spread throughout the ranks. So, when the soldiers saw the shining breastplate on Silbrey, they viewed it as a sign of succession. The northern cities would convene in time to elect a new high general. Until then, Silbrey would be a stand-in for Bren the Beloved.

Silbrey would have preferred to be off the island, looking for Gydan, but the boats had all left. A signal fire would bring them back. Oren refused to give the order until he was certain Kret was nowhere on the island. Although Silbrey didn't show it, she ached thinking about Gydan alone in Penderyn. Silbrey tried to push those thoughts aside and focus on Kret, because as long as he was alive, no one was safe.

Aubec broke the silence of their stroll.

"Is Tom still on the island?"

"Marcus Tom?" Oren looked incredulous. "That bastard is in Laew, writing poetry, last I heard."

"No, not him."

"Tom the Fletcher?" Oren tried again.

"No, Tom the Barber," Aubec corrected. "I always get a shave from him when I visit the city. I haven't seen him. He travels back and forth between the city and Thistle. I didn't know if—" Aubec pointed to the bodies.

"Ah, Tom was sent to Aberton with the soldiers that Bren deployed," Oren explained. "He's been working for the Northern Army as a surgeon."

"Pity."

"A pity that he's not dead?" Oren was confused by Aubec's response.

"No, I need a shave." Aubec rubbed his neck, regretting the stubble.

"We know where Tom the Barber is," said Silbrey, shifting to the matter at hand. "But we still don't know where Kret is. Even though he butchered an entire town?"

"You need to remember this about Kret," Aubec said. "He doesn't take unnecessary risks. It makes sense he would go after the people of Thistle. He left the city of Rhyll as quickly as possible. The garrison is there—all those soldiers. And he wouldn't attack Sage Hall. Almost every student there is an eager soldier. *Almost* every student." Aubec looked at Silbrey when he said it, alluding to Yurig. "Kret went after the easy win: the farmers. It's the same reason he killed Bren only when she was near death from the poisoning—and why he didn't fight Silbrey. He would have won that fight, but why risk it?"

"Thanks," Silbrey responded grimly.

"He might still get injured," Aubec said. "That would spoil any future plans. During the War of the Hounds, Bren's battle with him at Pynne's Field was significant because we forced his hand. We gave him no other option. And he lost. He won't make that mistake again."

"Then why did Kret and Speck both mention Aberton?" Silbrey asked. "It's the most well-defended city in Amon."

This question stumped Aubec, and it wasn't the first time Silbrey had posed it. Aubec gave the same response as before. "It's possible Aberton is Kret's endgame. Maybe if we hadn't stopped him at Pynne's Field, he would've made his way to Aberton."

"What's in Aberton?" Silbrey asked again. Their conversation was going in circles. It had been this way for several days.

"I don't know."

"We don't even know if he's on this island anymore." Another refrain from Silbrey.

"Kret Bonebreaker had many things during the war," Aubec recited, "but he didn't have boats."

A new realization came to Silbrey. "The guildmaster of Penderyn has boats. *Sah'le vuk.* The guildmaster has boats. We are flourishing in our ignorance! We deserve whatever misfortune comes our way. That's how Kret got off the island. One of Dahlia's boats must have been waiting for him near Thistle on the north coast."

"Why would she help that monster kill her own people?" Oren asked.

"Remember, the war," Aubec spoke as though lecturing a classroom of students, "the six ruling families of Gandryll helped fund Kret's army in exchange for regional control after the war ended. Dahlia could have made a similar deal. It's possible. What's more likely, that Kret is hiding in a ditch somewhere waiting for us to give up our search?"

The silence among them confirmed it. They had stumbled upon something crucial, and they should have realized it on the night he disappeared. The coordination between Kret and Dahlia may have been more intricate than they first presumed.

"We need to return to the city," Oren said. "I'll light the signal upon Bren's pyre."

Before leaving Thistle, Oren ordered that the students of Sage Hall take over the farmlands and work the fields until suitable farmers from the mainland could be found to replace them. They were to leave the school and help where they could. It was planting season. Without Thistle, the residents of the island— Sage Hall included—would not last long.

"You want to turn my students into farmers?" Aubec was amused.

"They'll figure it out." Oren muttered. "It'll be good for them to do actual work."

If Callis were still alive, he would laugh about Oren's mandate. High-born children tilling soil and sowing seeds. Their son Yurig had grown up on a farm. Yurig came to Sage Hall to leave that behind. And here he was, returning to the farm. Yurig wouldn't want to be known as the farmer among his courtly peers. Despite his youth, he had more farming experience than all of them, including the teachers.

Silbrey, Oren, and Aubec rode through the night to the city of Rhyll. The island was mostly grassy hills separating the three communities. While riding Feste, Silbrey looked out on the countryside, softly glowing in the moonlight and cloudless starry sky. In this light, the grass rippled like the gentle waters of Tu'enya Bay. No one spoke during this ride, even during their short breaks to rest the horses. They returned to the city in the morning. The silence of the evening had followed them into daybreak. The city was slow to rouse. With the port closed, the residents had little reason to wake up early.

Silbrey, Aubec, and Oren returned to find that the pyre had been built. Bren's remains were wrapped and lying in the palace, waiting to be moved. Oren requested the funeral be performed immediately. Afterward, they would summon the boats to return.

* * *

The *Elona* sailed into Penderyn's harbor. Roby Roundtree and the others were preparing to dock. They didn't notice the bodies hanging from wooden beams along the coastline, but Gydan and Cyru did. The beams were raised several feet in the air by posts driven into the ground at regular intervals. The beams extended almost the length of the city's coastline. The dock workers, as they went about their business, had to walk in between the dead bodies—swinging from nooses.

Each discolored, bloated body wore the padded armor and kettle helmet typical of a soldier in Bren's Northern Army. These were the soldiers Bren Caius had sent to apprehend Dahlia Tulan. The words *"Sune peneir sot Penderyn"* were painted in white along a portion of the beam. The phrase was a mystery to Gydan.

Gydan looked to the captain. He stayed focused, sailing the ship to the area reserved for ships coming from Rhyll. The captain must have noticed the bodies. He was choosing to ignore them. At second glance, the other sailors had a similar demeanor—as though they had been warned of what would be waiting in Penderyn and to pay it no mind.

Gydan found Roby clearing the deck.

"Roby!" Gydan called to her in a loud whisper. Roby tried to ignore Gydan as though she were among the dead. Gydan would not be deterred. "Roby!"

Roby walked to her, not looking at the bodies that lined the coast. "What is it?" She asked through gritted teeth.

"Who owns this ship?"

This question surprised her, as if it had the most obvious

answer. "Dahlia Tulan. Most captains who sail between Rhyll and Penderyn work for her."

Cyru reached out to Gydan's mind. Hovering near her, Cyru scratched at Gydan's shoulder. *This is a trap. We need to leave this ship.*

Gydan took a few steps away from Roby. "*Sune peneir sot Penderyn.* What does that mean?"

"It means 'No royalty in Penderyn.' When Bren Caius announced she wanted to be queen, she sent soldiers to remove the guildmasters from each of the cities. Dahlia rallied the people against them."

"That's not true." Gydan was shaken by the injustice of this lie. Her voice quivered. "Bren never wanted to be queen."

Roby looked around, hoping no one was listening. "It doesn't matter what's true. It's what's believed that counts. But you'll be safe. I swear it."

"If there's something the last few months have taught me," Gydan said, "no one can promise my safety."

A group of sailors, each holding a pair of manacles, approached the passengers. They did not appear menacing or cruel. They walked with a disinterested sense of duty, a mechanical task needing to be performed. One merchant interposed himself between the sailors and the other passengers. A sailor backhanded the merchant, and the would-be hero dropped to the floor. With this act, the sailors rushed at the passengers to bind them in the manacles. The remaining passengers were too scared and confused to act.

Gydan ran from Roby toward the railing of the ship. Roby went after her, but Cyru swooped past and clawed at the halfling's face. Roby cried out as blood poured from her flayed cheek. The other sailors wisely kept their distance. Gydan climbed the railing, swung her legs over the edge, and jumped. Gydan disappeared into the dark water below. Cyru flew over the side, keeping watch.

*Wait. Stay under. You will hit your head if you resurface now.*

The ship passed. Gydan came up for a gulp of air. Gydan had difficulty swimming in the choppy waters of the harbor. Her layered clothes were drenched and took on more weight. Cyru grabbed her sleeve and pulled her toward the shore. The dock, farther down the coastline, was much busier. No one appeared to notice the girl and her dragon going overboard.

Once Gydan could feel the muddy bottom with her feet, she waded through the water and stumbled onto land, falling to her knees. They were far enough away from the docks to avoid attention. The grass was high. The shore sloped up to a gravel road that led to a cobbled road that led into the heart of the city. Gydan couldn't stop staring at the bodies that hung from nooses. Now that Gydan was closer, she noticed the flies and maggots that infested each corpse. She was kneeling before several dead priests, dangling alongside the dead soldiers.

"Cyru, I thought Roby Roundtree was good," Gydan said. "I thought I could trust her. My dad said if you befriend a halfling, you will have a friend for life. They're honest people."

*Good sees goodness where there is none. Perhaps Roby was a good simpleton and trusted her captain too much. Good? I'd rather be friends with someone wise.*

Gydan pointed to the dead priests. "They're wise. Look what happened to them."

*Maybe it's better to not be anything in Penderyn.*

. . .

Gydan walked through Penderyn with Cyru flying nearby. Everyone stopped to look at them. Cyru attracted attention, which Gydan did not like, but she also knew no one would dare interpose themselves between her and Cyru. The dragon was small, but ready to pounce. Cyru's presence had the same effect as if Gydan had dragged a loaded ballista down the cobbled street.

Gydan thought of the last time she was in Penderyn, when she had found her father's body in an alley, his chest punctured with arrows. Gydan wondered if the mare or the green cart she had left behind were still in the market, but she didn't dare revisit that place. Instead, she took a long path around.

The shop windows Gydan walked past had the same Volir phrase painted on them. *"Sune peneir sot Penderyn."* No royalty in Penderyn. Some windows had the abbreviation S.P.S.P. A few stores did not have this marking. Those stores had their windows smashed in. The doors were broken off the hinges, looted bare and burnt from within. Failure to join the revolution had consequences.

The revolution was counterfeit. Gydan had witnessed the truth. Her mother had knelt before Bren Caius, and Bren had told her, "I'm not a queen." Bren disapproved of such posturing. Bren Caius was arrogant, but she wasn't ambitious. The common person wouldn't know that. It would be easy enough for Dahlia Tulan to twist the arrival of Bren's troops into something else, an attack on the autonomy of the city. Last fall, Penderyn buzzed with excitement over a possible visit by Bren the Beloved. Now she was their enemy. They didn't even know about her death. The *Elona* would be the first ship to deliver that news, but they didn't know either. The ship had left the harbor in response to the crisis signal. Only Gydan knew.

Gydan made her way to the temple. Her mother had told her about the priest, Timon. Gydan decided that before she went to the farming community in search of Maricel's mother, she needed to see if the old man was able to help. That is, if he wasn't among those priests she saw hanging from the beam.

Gydan came to a wide gravel path with smooth stones lining both sides. Before her was the cylindrical tower of the temple. The white limestone was scorched black and partially collapsed to where Gydan could see inside. The interior was incinerated. The wooden dome roof had fallen into the sacred space, scorched but still intact. Everything around it was soot and ash. The flames had died out days ago, but Gydan could still smell the burnt wood. The smell reminded her of her father's funeral pyre.

Gydan was not a devout person. She acknowledged the named gods when they were needed. She thanked them when they delivered on a request. But when Gydan saw one of the altars, which had been consumed by the fire—a charred dragon effigy and glass bottles warped in the heat, most likely the altar of Tian—it stirred something in her. She uttered a curse upon whoever was responsible. No hollow sentiment to satiate her anger. It was a call for the gods to act.

"Whoever did this does not think the gods can hurt them," Gydan whispered. "They do not fear you. If you won't deliver justice, how can anyone respect you?"

Then Gydan heard a voice behind her.

"*Yakost!* You sound like a prophet. If the gods ever listen, I'm sure they can hear you."

Gydan turned to see a bald, bearded man with a large belly. He walked with a cane. He dressed like any peasant, but his smile and tired eyes belonged to a priest.

"*Ya.* Are you Timon?" She asked the question but knew the answer.

His smile faded. He tilted his head to one side and then the other.

"By the gods, you look just like your mother when she was your age."

Gydan had no response. His comment meant nothing to her.

Timon's attention turned to Cyru, who flew around the priest, carefully observing him. "Your mother never had a pet dragon."

"Cyru is no one's pet," Gydan said. "Cyru is my friend."

*He wouldn't call me a pet if we were able to reach our true size. We could lay this entire city to cinder and ash.*

Gydan smiled at Cyru's draconic zeal. Timon, who could not hear their psychic communications, assumed the smile meant she was warming to him.

"Cyru," Timon considered the name. "As in, Cyruth the All-Seeing? I've never known of a dragon bonding to a human before, even in the old stories. They're an imprisoned show-piece for the elite, or they're burning cities to the ground."

*I told you.*

Timon reached his hand out to Cyru and then thought better of it.

Gydan surveyed the area around the temple. "Are we safe here?"

"I've lost many friends this week. Every time I think I have no more tears left, I surprise myself with more." He smiled and wiped his eyes. Gydan knew some people were like this when faced with grief. They broke down and smiled, fully aware of the absurdity. "When Bren's soldiers arrived, Dahlia Tulan was nowhere to be found. The soldiers were treated as heroes, driving out the despot. They were given food and drink, fine lodging in Dahlia's estate, but it was all a pretense.

"Dahlia's mercenaries came in the night and slaughtered them all. Anyone in the city who did not speak out against Bren Caius was killed. She rooted out the disloyal. More people joined her militia, in some instances, to spare family members who were known supporters of the high general. The militia marched out yesterday morning to Aberton."

Timon gestured to the destroyed temple. "Even the gods and those who serve them are not beyond Dahlia's scorn. But you asked, 'are we safe here?'" He shook his head. "Her supporters are everywhere. They are quick to spread rumors. It would be best if we left. A granary's nearby. It belongs to a family of brewers I know. We'll be safe, and we can talk further. Walk with me."

Gydan once heard an Ayler say that priests befriend brewers like bears befriend beekeepers. Gydan thought it was a funny phrase, but it appeared that truth hid in the Ayler's jests. As a custom, Taraki priests received the best grain—more than they could ever use—and the brewers were convenient buyers. The granary's proximity to the temple was no accident.

She could smell the musty, sweet grain before they even turned the corner. Outside the granary, a woman led a yoked ox in a circle, which turned a wheel. The wheel rotated a shaft. The shaft was attached to the brake wheel and wallower, which Gydan could see through the open doors. Two men with rakes shifted and leveled the grain under the millstone. Gydan was familiar with the mechanics involved. Near her grandparents' farm, another family operated a watermill, which operated under a similar premise.

The woman with the ox waved to Timon.

"You're back soon," she said cheerfully.

"I was curious what news the ship from Rhyll might bring," said Timon, "and the messenger came to me."

"Aye," the woman nodded to Gydan. "Verin must be in a gracious mood."

"The god of messages loves wanderers," Timon responded.

"Seems like a wanderer would make a terrible messenger," Gydan observed. "They'd get lost before they ever get where they need to go."

"You look like your mother, *and* you sound like her," Timon laughed. "The most important messages rarely travel in a straight line. Life takes strange turns."

Timon and Gydan walked into the granary. At the back of the storage area, the grain sacks were piled up to form four walls with an entryway, wheat sheaves were layered on top as a roof. In effect, it was a small fort, a child's hideout. The inside was a bedroll, a broom, a coin pouch, and not much else.

"Welcome to my safe house," Timon said. "You can stay here. There's a comfortable pile of hay on the other side of the granary for me."

"I don't understand."

"You and your dragon, Cyru, you sailed in from Rhyll. The rumor was that ships would be arriving soon—loyalists from Rhyll—who would be apprehended at the docks. You made it to the temple, looking for sanctuary, yes? Bren the Beloved will come to take back the city."

At the mention of Bren, Gydan shifted uneasily. "The high general died in her palace at the hands of Kret Bonebreaker—or, at least, I think she died. I fled on a boat with others evacuating the city."

Gydan thought of those last moments with Bren. She did not actually see Bren die. There was a chance she was still alive. Gydan wanted to believe she survived.

Cyru chirped. *Gydan, don't give yourself false hope. We know what happened.*

Gydan corrected herself. "No, Bren is dead. The saviors of Penderyn are hanging at the docks. There is no one else."

Timon lowered himself to the floor, lost in this revelation. The priest started breathing fast and then, aware of his reaction, consciously worked to take deeper, more controlled breaths. Once he felt his peace return, he looked at Gydan. "I won't accept that. There is us, and we have a dragon. Sit down and tell your story from the beginning. As you feel comfortable, spare no detail. I want to know how fares Piper and her family."

Gydan told him everything from when they arrived at the farmhouse to when they fled and their week at Bren's palace—to this day, with Gydan fleeing once more, only trusting each step as she took it. So much had happened, and Gydan was exhausted.

After a moment, Timon spoke.

"I will help you find Ausdre. I know of that farming community, but we need to be careful. Even though Dahlia and her mercenaries march to Aberton, her people patrol the roads."

"Why is Dahlia Tulan doing this?" The politics baffled Gydan. "The guildmasters owe so much to Bren Caius."

"Dahlia Tulan was always a tyrant, but the guildmasters' power expanded after the War of the Hounds. Since Bren Caius had no interest in commerce and trade, she let the guildmasters do as they pleased. Now, Dahlia Tulan proclaims 'no royalty' while crowning herself."

"Does she want to be queen?"

"No, not in the traditional sense, but this conspiracy with Kret and Mendal is an opportunity. She's turning mercenaries into soldiers. A mercenary fights for coin and little else, but soldiers fight for a cause—and with that kind of loyalty, there's no end to what you can achieve."

Gydan decided that she liked the priest. He was a good man, perhaps a bit lost in his own ideas, but it was a common fault among the religious. When her mother talked about Timon, Gydan could tell how he might annoy her with his pious veneer. Gydan did not mind. There were worse aspirations than that of a priest. Her mother's irritation and Gydan's amiability marked the difference between seeing someone as a father and seeing someone as a grandfather.

Timon continued with his thoughts. "Two kinds of people wear the crown, those who want to serve and those who want to be served. And when an heir is born, we never know which kind of monarch we're going to get. After too many corrupt leaders, the people rose up and did away with the whole mess. But the tyrants are still with us. They always will be. Now they rule with their wealth and not their lineage. Dahlia Tulan has always been power hungry, but it looks like now she's grasping for more. Bren had an army, and now Dahlia wants to see how an army can serve her."

\* \* \*

A small group gathered around the pyre outside Bren's palace. Had Kret's return not thrown everything in disarray, such a

funeral would have been held off for a week or longer allowing
the whole region to converge upon the island to grieve the loss
of the Northern Light. An entire year of ceremonial mourning
would follow. Instead, only a few were on hand to return Bren
to the elements. Corrinae Yol and Halsten Elytor were there,
cloaked in black and huddled close. Bren had many lovers in
her life, but these two were her true partners, never formalized
with a marriage ceremony, but everyone viewed them as a
union. Corrinae and Halsten did not hold the same sway as
Bren Caius, but their proximity to the legendary Bren was
power enough. They had her ear and her heart. The three of
them adopted Mendal and raised him together. Mendal was
also there, with two guards on either side of him. His wrists
were bound in shackles, but his arm was in a sling from when
Silbrey broke it in the dragon pit. His black tunic was dirty and
tattered. His dark, curly hair clung to his unwashed face.
Mendal did not look at the body of his mother being laid upon
the pyre. Instead, he stared at Silbrey with his sunken red eyes.
He smiled whenever she dared to return his gaze. The impish
expression said, *Look what I did*. He was Bren's son. He had to
be there, but his cruel presence was felt by all. The great
betrayal, a son orchestrating the poisoning and death of his
mother.

Aubec stepped forward to begin the ceremony. He looked
to Silbrey as the witness to Bren Caius's death.

"Silbrey the Shepherd, which god claims this death?"

The question was a formality. Aubec and Silbrey had
already discussed what she would say.

"Kret disarmed Bren during battle and slayed her with
her own sword. To die at the hands of another, without a
weapon, that death would belong to Cyruth the Hunter.

But before that, she did strike at Kret, dealing a wound to his shoulder. To injure your attacker, that death would belong to Olar the Warrior. And lastly, I placed Bren under an enchanted sleep to spare her any further pain. To die while sleeping, such a death would belong to Golwin the Fated."

"Are you saying all three gods of death would claim her?"

"I am, yes." Silbrey replied.

Several people murmured their approval. It was a wise to avoid talk of Bren's death being anything less than legendary. This idea of all three gods claiming her positioned the death as something worthy of the high general's mythic status—Cyruth, Olar, and Golwin all wanted her, and circumstance found a way to appease them.

Mendal trembled with laughter. It rose from a soft tittering and transformed into a shrill cackle. The aberrant sound of his laughter cut with a serrated edge. One of the guards gave him a shake, but Mendal laughed harder. Tears rolled down his cheeks.

Aubec tried his best to ignore Mendal. He handed a torch to Corrinae and another torch to Halsten. With an incantation and wave of his hands, Aubec cast a spell, which set the torches ablaze. Corrinae and Halsten walked around the pyre's base, lighting all sides.

Aubec's voice rose to speak over Mendal's laughter, but the solemnity was spoiled.

"Bren Caius, in this year, *Cora Aspru'eir* 776, we return you to the elements, Ignasi, Aylo, Cael, and Terron, as well as Al'taru, which weaves them together. You have been claimed by the named god Golwin, the named god Cyruth, and the named god Olar—and we release you now to their care."

As the flames grew, Aubec recited a poem, which competed with Mendal's rending disruption.

> *When lesser lights do shine upon the earth,*
> *Creatures keen silently hunt in the glen.*
> *What mysteries, what portent of worth,*
> *Happens when they discern the fallen wren?*
>
> *With wounded wing, ne'er a chance to escape,*
> *As foxes, as wolves consider their prey,*
> *The bird curses the light on its frail shape,*
> *Begs darkness and Cyruth, damning the day.*
>
> *Wherefore curses have strength, forming a*
>    *shield,*
> *If wings not mended, no wind can dare lift?*
> *Golwin intercedes where Cyruth does yield.*
> *The wren discovers a fortunate gift:*
>
> *War upon war, the virgin vale stained red,*
> *Creatures competing—fools fated, now dead.*

The sonnet was old, often recited at funerals. The poem described the interrelation between the three gods of death. While Olar was not named in the poem, the "war upon war" line was seen as a reference to him. At this point, Mendal was winded from his laughter, hyperventilating, gasping for air, and unable or unwilling to shake off his hysterics.

Aubec turned to Oren. Oren was to throw the signal powder into the fire, so the ships would know to return. They felt it would be an appropriate way to honor Bren, to include her in the summoning, since it was her command to send the ships away. But now, Silbrey wondered if it would have been better to handle the signal elsewhere, away from this disaster of a funeral.

Oren marched over to Mendal and grabbed him by his frilly collar—with his other hand, he grabbed Mendal's throat. Oren's arms were as thick as tree limbs. His muscles bulged as he tightened his grip. Oren pulled Mendal away from the guards. A collective gasp came from the gathering. Oren dragged Mendal to the pyre. Mendal tried to resist, but Oren was unyielding in his strength. It took a moment for everyone to realize what was happening. When it registered, Corrinae screamed.

Oren held Mendal close to the flames. At first, Mendal shook with discomfort. Soon, though, he started to spasm.

"Not laughing now, are you?" Oren said through gritted teeth. Oren's hand trembled as he, too, felt the heat of the pyre. "Tell me, son, and it will all be over. Did Dahlia send a ship to the north shore to rescue Kret?"

Mendal's hair sizzled while his skin boiled and peeled. Silbrey could see his eyes softening in the intense heat.

"Tell me, son," Oren said again, but Mendal was in too much pain to respond.

The cries from Mendal's parents shook Silbrey into action. She jabbed her staff behind Oren's knee, causing him to stumble, then she swung around the staff to knock him back from the pyre.

"Your violence dishonors the high general," Silbrey seethed.

"Then you didn't know Bren Caius." Oren stood and tried to clench his fist, but his hand had blistered from holding Mendal over the fire.

Mendal fell to the ground. He could not speak, just made a rasping sound. He nodded his head to confirm what Oren asked. Corrinae and Halsten ran to their son, placing themselves between him and Oren. They were too afraid to touch his damaged body and cause further pain. If they had druids, some magical healing with a sprig of mistletoe could be applied, but such people were so rare as to be almost mythical. Otherwise, an apothecary in Rhyll might have potions and salves to ease the suffering.

Oren was unfazed by his own savagery. He took out a pouch. From the pouch, he poured fine purple sand into his unburnt hand. It was an elvish concoction discovered in the palace by some of the first humans to occupy the island. Oren tossed the sand on the fire. The flames shot up twice as high, a bright column of purple light, but it did not give off any additional heat. This light was the signal for the ships to return. Then Oren walked back into the palace.

Within the light, Silbrey could see the silhouette of Bren's body consumed by the fire. It hurt Silbrey's eyes to look into the light for too long. She and the others had to turn away.

The chambermaids who served the Caius House tended to Mendal. They placed a linen cloth underneath the young man and used it to carry him, not to the palace, but to his private lodging. Corrinae and Halsten followed. The guards were unsure if they should let Mendal go. After a hushed exchange between them, they walked behind at a distance.

Once they were gone, a silence—more solemn than the ceremony—fell over those who remained, silence like an invocation. Silbrey understood this silence in her bones. Growing up around Timon, she had heard his philosophies and lectures and insights, the liturgy of his restless mind. Yet he never seemed wiser than when he was quiet, lost in an unspoken moment.

Silbrey stood near the illuminated pyre of Bren Caius, and she knew not everything needed to be put into words. She could be silent with her grief. Another loss.

The column of light brought people out of their homes. After a while, a larger crowd gathered in reverence. They shielded their eyes against the light. Everyone reflected in silence upon the significance of Bren Caius, the end of one age and the beginning of the next.

Silbrey felt a rumbling deep under the surface of the earth.

She looked around, but no one else noticed. Was this part of her fey sense, a warning for what was to come? The rumbling stretched across the deep earthen plate upon which the island was a part, miles in every direction. Small earthquakes were a common enough occurrence, but this felt different.

The story of the four birds described how Efre Ousel was formed. Raustfweg the Raven, Amon the Owl, Karkasse the Crane, and Lunthal the Eagle all lost the ability to fly and were buried under the earth where they slept. The story explained these tremors as moments when the birds dreamed of flight. The small earthquakes were often ignored, barely warranting a reaction, something to talk about if conversation about the weather wore thin. What Silbrey felt was no small tremor. Whatever was about to hit would be very bad.

Silbrey looked at the crowd assembled. She yelled at the people standing near shops and homes across from the palace. "Get away from the buildings!"

They looked at her as if she were mad. Silbrey waved her arms in warning. Aubec's eyes narrowed, and he began to chant, moving his hands back and forth.

A massive jolt and a deafening boom tore through the city. The earth cleaved open. Web-like cracks spread in all directions. In some places, the ground rose up. In other places, it dropped. To Silbrey, the shock felt like she had been hit by a battering ram. Pressure built up in Silbrey's ears and started ringing. All other sounds were muted. The earth continued to shake. Buildings collapsed.

Only a few seconds ago, the path to the docks had been obscured by city structures. Now, with everything flattened, Silbrey could see plainly to the bay. White-capped waves crashed against each other.

The solid ground rippled as if floating on a rising tide. The wooden beams of the fallen houses creaked as they broke against each other in the stubborn current of the earthquake. The breaking wood murmured dreadfully, a thousand disapproving voices.

Silbrey looked to the crowd she had tried to warn and was relieved that Aubec's spell, a protective ward, had been effectively cast. A flickering wall of translucent force blocked the debris from falling on the people. Not everyone in the city was spared, but Silbrey knew if they hadn't come out of their homes to see the light from the pyre, they would've been buried alive. A bittersweet mercy, but a mercy nonetheless.

The palace was unharmed. The ancient building swayed as the earth shook, but it didn't crack or collapse—less a miracle and more a feat of elvish engineering.

Bren's pyre and her remains were gone. They had fallen into one of the larger cracks. Not only was Bren claimed by all three gods of death, but she was also burned for the named gods and buried for the unnamed gods. Silbrey thought of Timon. She imagined he would find this fascinating. This profound moment reduced to a pithy anecdote, which could prove his theology. Timon annoyed her, but she needed him. Would fate be so kind to have Gydan cross his path before she crossed Dahlia's? And what about Yurig in Sage Hall? Was he safe in those buildings? No, the students had been called to Thistle. Another mercy.

The rumbling continued, but without the same force as before. The worst was over. Silbrey's ears were ringing. She sensed the earth underneath her. The limestone bedrock, which formed the walls of the dragon pit, was prevalent from here to the coastline. It slowed erosion, which made for a good harbor, but not so for farming. With her fey sense, Silbrey reached farther into the earth. She wanted to connect with stirring titans but found nothing.

A quiet confusion fell over the crowd. It took a moment to realize what had happened. An earthquake, unlike anything they had ever experienced, had shaken Rhyll and perhaps far beyond it. Panic spread as scared parents called for their children, and scared children called for their parents. People ran back to their homes to see what remained. Others fell to their knees in awe of the transcendence they witnessed at Bren's funeral.

"If she wasn't a legend before," Aubec said as he walked next to Silbrey, "Bren's practically a god now. I don't know how she does it. The Aylers are going to love this. The final ballad of Bren Caius, the Northern Light, Bren the Beloved, the Hero of Eloe Vale—what began as a mundane and humble funeral is marked with violence and magic and earthquakes, a moment that will be talked about for generations to come."

"This is what you do?" Silbrey grimaced at Aubec's levity. "Whenever we're surrounded by death and tragedy, you make light of the gravity. You did it in Thistle and now here."

"You'll get used to me."

"And you don't think this is the result of some greater force?" Silbrey surveyed the damage in Rhyll. "In the dragon pit, Mendal said Kret would awaken the sleeping titans and watch the world break once more."

Aubec walked to the edge of the crevasse where Bren's pyre had collapsed. "Greater forces. Do I think giant birds are napping underneath the earth? No, absolutely not."

"You're quite convinced for someone who can do the impossible." Silbrey waved her hand about, mimicking Aubec's spell casting motions.

"Everything I do requires careful study and practice. The world I manipulate makes sense, even if few can see it as I do."

"Are all mages this arrogant?"

Aubec paused and gave the question real consideration. "Every mage I've met is a complete bastard."

"And you're training my son to become one." Silbrey rubbed her forehead. "If the earthquake doesn't bother you, what are you most worried about?"

"The earthquake was bad, but it has happened, and it has passed," Aubec said. "Right now, we need to get to Aberton— and find Kret."

"I agree. As long as Kret lives, no one is safe."

"One more thing. I'm worried the Caius House will be set against us. Corrinae and Halsten do not see their son as some monster who conspired to have Bren killed. No, they will see a victim who was tortured by Oren—at his own mother's funeral, no less."

"Mendal is stark mad. Surely, they can see that."

"Or they dismiss it as the eccentric nature that often accompanies greatness," Aubec said. "If he survives his wounds, those scars may rally people more than repulse them. He will be the next high general, and if he had his way, a future king. Bren resisted the crown. Mendal will accept it on her behalf."

"That may be a concern for another day." Silbrey saw the captain of the palace guard. She waved him over. He navigated the cracks and rubble and waited for her command. "Sir, can you go to the garrison? See that all soldiers are put to good use. We need to rescue the trapped, restore the injured, recover the dead."

The captain took to the task.

Aubec raised his eyebrows. "You could be the next high general."

Silbrey looked over the edge of the crevasse. "I'd rather be thrown off a cliff."

"That's not a 'no.'"

"Oren should be the next high general," she said it in a hushed voice, even though she knew no one was listening.

"Oren is from Angnavir in Raustfweg." Aubec also lowered his voice. "He may be a war hero, but he'll always be seen as an outsider. He'll never get elected by the convening leaders to become the next high general."

"And I'm *not* an outsider? Farmer, foundling, fey-born—I don't even know if I'm from this world."

"Farmer, foundling, fey-born, and friend of Bren," Aubec countered. "Word has spread about you, the woman who was with Bren Caius during her last week and was there when she died. Your name is Volir in origin. Can you speak the language?"

"Dahlia taught me when I was young. I'm not eloquent."

"Few are." Aubec walked back to the palace. "If you speak Volir, you can manage the politics and the aristocrats—"

"Since you think I'd be such a great leader, I'll start by saying I didn't dismiss you." Silbrey's voice took a sly turn, more maternal than monarchical. "Until the ships arrive, we have work to do. I told the captain that all available soldiers are helping with recovery efforts. You're still part of Bren's army."

Aubec stopped. Those words meant something to him. He bowed obediently, as though chastened, and joined Silbrey, tending to what was broken.

* * *

The palace was designed so that, no matter the time of day, the windows always caught the sunlight, which illuminated the soft white walls. The common areas in the center of the palace had vaulted ceilings open to the sky, which brought in even more light. The aviary was one of the few areas where the light was dappled and dim.

Silbrey approached the aviary and saw Maricel sitting inside it. Her head rested against the iron cage. Maricel shared the enclosure with Ruth. It was an unsteady arrangement. They kept their distance from each other. Maricel was the intruder, but appeared mostly harmless to the owl.

Maricel's face was covered in grime and sweat. A great exhaustion weighed on every part of her. Maricel had braided her hair in the Raustfweg style. Silbrey had never seen Maricel with braids before. It was a sloppy, solitary attempt. As a tradition, Raustfweg family members would help each other with the braiding. Maricel was alone.

Silbrey stood outside the aviary. Maricel had no smile for her, just weariness.

"The palace shook but did not break," Maricel said.

"I've never felt an earthquake so powerful." What Silbrey saw in the wrecked city would stay with her. Surrounded by the dead, she retreated within herself, a blank state that allowed her to keep moving—if not for her sake, then for her lost daughter, who needed her to survive. "We spent the day digging out people. There's still a lot of work left to do, but I must go to Aberton. And then, I can rescue Gydan."

Mentioning Gydan prompted Maricel to speak. She needed to explain her actions at the dock and in the journals. "Sil, I wasn't spying for Dahlia. I wasn't sending Gydan to Dahlia."

"Stop lying—"

Maricel raised her voice to speak over Silbrey's accusation. "You won't give me a chance to explain myself. You leave me in here, and I'm left wondering when I will see you again. You know me. I'm not the enemy."

"I saw the journals," said Silbrey. "You've been dishonest from the beginning. You've been spying on me."

"Before the children were born, before you were married, I spent a year in Penderyn, following you, and I wrote everything down. What started as a way to record my observations became a habit and turned into a compulsion."

"Why?"

"I wasn't doing it for Dahlia. I was doing it for my mother, Ausdre."

Silbrey did not expect this response. The sincerity shook her.

Maricel grunted as she stood up to look at Silbrey, eye to eye.

"My mother is a druid from Raustfweg. She and others of her kind were sent to Amon in search of a child born from a tree, a true fey. They found a baby in the Hazelef Forest, being cared for by a woman. The woman had not yet weaned her other child, and she nursed that baby with her own milk. The druids took that child, but they were attacked by gnolls. Everyone was killed, except my mother and the child. They survived by crossing the river. But the baby turned into a fish and slipped out of my mother's hands and into the river."

Silbrey gasped. Some of her first memories were of Timon's silly bedtime stories about how a farmer caught a fish that turned into a little girl. The farmer took the girl to the temple, and Timon raised her in devotion to Taraki. He had named her Piper, then Dahlia Tulan renamed her Silbrey.

Timon had said to her, *I make space for a few miracles, and maybe you're one of them.* How could Maricel have known this prologue to Timon's story unless it was true?

Silbrey unlocked the aviary gate.

Flecks of sunlight rolled across the gate as it opened. Maricel stepped out of the aviary and into the light. Ruth gave a relieved hoot. Finally, the owl would have some peace.

"How did you find me in Penderyn?" Silbrey asked softly.

"Ever since I was a child, I was afflicted with visions. They were all about you." Maricel moved toward Silbrey to kiss her, but Silbrey backed up.

"No," Silbrey said. "You should have been honest with me from the start. It would've changed things."

"You wouldn't have believed me."

"It's not your responsibility to decide when I'm ready to hear the truth. This is my life. I needed your honesty from the beginning."

"Like you were honest with Callis?" After Maricel spoke, her face twisted apologetically. She didn't mean for her words to have such venom.

"Are you saying that because you want to hurt me?" If the words did hurt, Silbrey refused to give any indication. She kept her voice even, her face as carved stone. She could hide her pain when necessary—

"You left me in a cage for days!"

—while Maricel expressed every tender feeling plainly on her face.

Silbrey nodded. Maricel had every right to strike back.

Silbrey, lacking any reply, returned to what needed to be done. "I'm heading to Aberton to settle a matter with Kret. I need you to sail to Penderyn to find Gydan."

"She won't be there," said Maricel. "If you had listened before you knocked me out, you'd know that."

"Where is she?"

"She should be with my mother at the farming community east of Penderyn, west of the Hazelef Forest. My mom will care for Gydan and protect her."

Silbrey thought for a moment, and then said, "Go to the farm and to Gydan. Let her know where I am and that I will meet both of you there—east of Penderyn, west of the Hazelef Forest. If I don't arrive in a month's time, assume that I died in battle. And if so, when it's safe, return to this island with Gydan. Take her to Sage Hall. Aubec owes my children, *both* my children, a place at Sage Hall."

Silbrey could see Maricel hadn't even thought about the possibility of Silbrey dying. Maricel's face twisted at the mention of death. However, Silbrey had seen Kret. She saw his form and his speed, his malice. Silbrey wouldn't stand much of a chance against him, but it had to be done.

"But what about you?" Maricel asked. "If you survive the battle, where will you go once your children are safe at Sage Hall?"

The question confused Silbrey. Maricel hadn't considered death, but Silbrey hadn't considered life. What did a world of possibility look like? She didn't know.

"Maybe I'll live in a cottage in the woods, next to a large tree," Silbrey said. "I'll grow old, and I'll scare the children in the nearby village who wander too far from home. They'll tell stories about me."

"You want to be a crone?" Maricel said, stifling a laugh. Silbrey was pleased to see that Maricel had picked up on her dry humor. "Are you going to eat the children if they break into your house?"

"Probably. I'll turn the children into pigs first and then eat them."

"That is horrifying." Maricel shook her head while smiling. "You will make a great crone."

Silbrey and Maricel shared a comfortable silence, just looking at each other. Almost imperceptibly, Maricel leaned toward her. Silbrey gestured for Maricel to wait. Silbrey rushed down the hall. Then she returned with a sword in its scabbard.

"Is that—?"

"The sword of Bren Caius? Yes." Silbrey turned the sword around and handed it hilt-first to Maricel "How did you know? The sword looks like any other."

"It's how you hold it. Also," Maricel pointed to the scabbard. The sword was beautiful, but the scabbard's leather tooling patterns, which integrated the Northern Light sigil, were distinctive.

Maricel pulled the sword halfway out of its scabbard. The blood had not been completely cleaned from the blade. Maricel slid the sword back in.

"When you see Gydan, give her this sword." Silbrey said. "Bren would want her to have it. Keep it wrapped in your cloak. Don't let anyone see."

Without Silbrey's intervention, the sword would go to Mendal. But if Aubec was correct, the last thing they needed was that demented man waving around his mother's legacy, pretending he had her blessing.

Silbrey looked at Maricel holding the sword. She knew Maricel wanted to be worthy of trust. And a part of Silbrey wanted to rebuild whatever they had before, but it wouldn't come easy.

"Also, take Feste," said Silbrey. "I'm not a calvary soldier, and where I'm going, I don't want to get him killed."

Silbrey thought Maricel would once again refuse her offer of the horse, but Maricel suppressed a weak laugh, which formed into a smile.

"I love you," Maricel said the words. It felt like an apology and a plea for reciprocation.

"I don't even know you." Silbrey placed her hand on the back of Maricel's neck, and then gave her a strong, slow kiss. When Silbrey finished, their eyes locked. Maricel's mouth was slightly open, not ready for the kiss to be over. Maricel kissed her back. Nothing about this day made sense. At least they could part ways with hope.

* * *

Gydan rested at the granary. She could not remember a time when she had ever slept in so late. Her father would not have approved. But she reminded herself that there were no sheep to feed.

The brewers were established enough within the city to have a surname. They were the Cobb family. The husbands were Elias and Loren. The wife was Minare. They had four sons who were elsewhere in the city—as this granary was part of a much larger operation. Gydan helped where she could. She filled and tied sacks of grain, and she loaded them onto carts. She fanned the granary to prevent mill dust from getting too thick in the air, a fire hazard. She swept and cleaned the mill-stone at the end of each day. After she finished, Minare Cobb waited for Gydan with warm cider. Minare felt each workday should end with a kind word and something sweet. Gydan had spent a week at the palace of Bren Caius, and yet the Cobb family's humble hospitality outshone the extravagance of Rhyll.

Cyru did not want to help with chores, but Gydan convinced Cyru that a dragon of their size would make an ideal ratter. Cyru was reluctant at first, but a large pile of dead rodents lay outside the granary by the time Gydan was done sweeping.

Gydan was eager to leave Penderyn and look for Ausdre, but Timon wanted to stay longer to see if any more news about Bren Caius would reach the city. They knew Rhyll had sent its ships from the harbor, and the island was cut off from the rest of Amon. Later, they heard that Dahlia's troops were close to Aberton. A siege appeared inevitable.

Timon agreed they would leave Penderyn and head east to the farming community.

Neither Timon nor Gydan had much to pack for their trip. Gydan had lost everything in the fire at the farmhouse. Timon had lost all his possessions when the temple was burned down. Timon jokingly referred to it as a fiery conspiracy and suggested they carry a bucket of water with them wherever they go. Minare Cobb did not give them a bucket, but she did provide the two with sealed jugs of water and hardtack rations. She gave them two bedrolls and two tents in case the journey took longer than they expected. Everything was neatly folded and placed in a haversack. On top was a small sack of grain, only a handful. This was a common gesture among brewers to say the guests had an open invitation to return.

They weren't but a few yards outside the gates of Penderyn when the earthquake hit. The booming force knocked Gydan and Timon both to the ground. The shockwaves even pushed back Cyru, who tumbled midair head over tail. The earth shook violently. Buildings swayed and toppled into each other, crashing down—including what remained of the temple. They saw portions of the city wall collapse.

*Destruction follows you wherever you go.*

Gydan ignored Cyru. She couldn't believe what she was seeing. In places, the earth itself had cracked open. She could feel pressure build in her ears.

All was quiet. For a port city that bustled as it did, such silence was unsettling. First, they heard a child's cry, followed by distant screams within the city. More voices joined them— people buried alive in need of rescue; people searching for loved ones, consumed by the collapsing buildings; people horrified by the wreckage around them. The people of Penderyn called for each other. No immediate replies, only more screams.

Timon got to his feet. He brushed himself off and walked back to the city.

"Where are you going?" Gydan called.

"People in there, they need my help."

At that point, Gydan understood her mother's frustration. When a priest is the surrogate father, there will always be a greater need, a higher power, a larger injustice that requires attention. Timon saw the entire city of Penderyn as his responsibility, his flock. How could anyone compete with that?

"I need you." Gydan tried not to cry, which made her choked words even more pitiful. Timon stopped. "The gods never asked you to save Penderyn. They wanted you to take care of my mother, and you didn't. Now you have a second chance to help me, her daughter. You can't save Penderyn. We must find Ausdre."

Gydan thought of the Cobb family, such good people. Was their granary still standing? Gydan was asking Timon to neglect them and countless others to favor her.

The ground continued to shake with smaller tremors.

Timon considered Gydan's rebuke. "Are you sure you're not a prophet?"

Gydan coughed as the breeze carried dust and ash from the city. Her eyes watered. She felt so frail. "Maybe I'm a god."

\* \* \*

Silbrey, Oren, and Aubec stood on the bow of the ship. They leaned against the railing, and each held to the knotted line running along it. Most of the soldiers remained under the deck.

Some with sailing experience managed as best they could to keep the ship on course. Since the earthquake, the waves were much higher and more temperamental, though the winds were calm. Everyone on the deck was soaked. This ship had a similar build as the seafaring cogs, but not as large. It wasn't made for sailing on these erratic waters. Silbrey wondered what it would take for the ship to roll and capsize.

The ship had carried them across the bay to Aberton. This city occupied an isthmus, which connected the trade cities of the east, such as Penderyn, to the larger territory of the west. Anyone with a map could see Aberton's strategic importance, which is why it had always been well fortified. The walls surrounding the city were twice as thick as any castle wall. The ditches surrounding the walls were twice as deep. The guards were twice as vigilant. The west and east gates always had a winding line of travelers waiting to get in. The walls extended along the north and south coasts at the shoreline, so no one could walk around the city. The walls kept Aberton safe and profitable. City officials collected a toll from everyone who passed through. For this reason, the docks were also outside the city walls, or at least, they were supposed to be there.

The docks had been burned down by Dahlia Tulan's army, one of two armies—Kret's gnoll soldiers at the west wall and Dahlia's mercenaries at the east wall.

Dahlia Tulan's army stood a good distance from the wall. Catapults and trebuchets were lined up, lobbing flaming balls of tar into the city. The mercenaries had set camp and were settling in for a long siege. Aberton expected it. Large timbers were driven deep into the ground near the wall to discourage undermining.

To the west, the situation was different. It was a full-scale attack. The earthquake had cracked the wall, leaving a ten-foot gap. Thousands of gnolls, a dark mass—like the waves crashing against the shoreline—moved against the west wall, trying to gain control over the compromised section and break into the city.

"It makes little sense," Aubec observed. "They aren't even bothering to signal the other side, not by any means I can see. They couldn't have planned this assault. Kret's side is taking advantage of that breach in the wall. Dahlia's side is barely active."

Somehow, both armies were part of the same war. These divergent tactics would never be taught at Sage Hall, even Silbrey knew that. If the plan was to drive the citizens eastward, retreating like rats from a burning barn into the waiting arms of Dahlia's mercenaries—why bother with a siege, unless it was to further harry the city's resolve? The mercenaries did not appear as though they were expecting anyone to retreat in their direction. Possibly Dahlia's army was unaware of what was happening on the west wall. The distance between the two points and the waves from both coastlines muffled all noise.

"I'm less worried about their strategy," Silbrey said as she brushed her wet hair from her face, "and more worried about what we're going to do. Where do we dock? I don't like the idea of swimming ashore."

Silbrey had her staff, her shield, and her new adamantine breastplate. She was never a strong swimmer—and liked the idea even less while carrying weapons and wearing armor.

"The waves are choppy," agreed Oren. A statement so obvious, it was unnecessary. There had been no reprieve from the abuse of the violent waters. Not only did it take a toll physically —stirred and swayed over the course of a day-long journey—

but it also affected the demeanor of the people onboard. Everyone withdrew into their worst nature. Oren was sullen. Aubec was moody.

Silbrey was flippant. "I never told you this, but I was once a fish." Oren and Aubec looked at her, confused. "I don't remember it. I was too young. But clearly, the gods favored me with fins. If we must swim to shore, maybe the gods will turn me into a fish again. I can't make any promises the gods will do the same for you."

Silbrey got a laugh out of Aubec. He shook his head. Silbrey playfully punched him in the shoulder. Oren ignored her odd confession.

"The hounds to the west or Dahlia's mercenaries to the east? Either would be waiting for us right at the water's edge. It would be a short battle or a watery death."

"We could sail farther down the coast and march in," Silbrey suggested. "There's no need to land right where the enemy is."

"A good point," Oren replied. "We're still facing a much larger force on open terrain."

"We would still be outnumbered, but Dahlia's army is smaller," Silbrey pointed to the eastern front. "The mercenaries look bored and unready. To me, it's an easy choice. East. Because meanwhile," Silbrey pointed to the western front, "*that* army looks like a kicked ant mound. More gnolls than what I encountered near Barcombe."

"My guess is the hounds were dispersed throughout the forest from Asher to Aberton," Oren said, "waiting for their warlord to return."

Aubec stroked his chin. "West or east, neither option works. And if we wait for more troops, firstly, we risk losing

Aberton. That breach needs to be secured. Secondly, where are our reinforcements coming from? Perhaps the cities to the west? Silva and Guldur? They allied with us during the War of the Hounds. One of Bren's last commands scattered her army across the region."

"Not the whole region. Bren deployed troops to Barcombe and Penderyn," said Oren. He defended Bren Caius with an emphatic tone, but he deflated as he considered the result. "With the hounds coming from the west and Dahlia Tulan's mercenaries from the east, we should assume both of our groups failed. The dead may be littered along the two paths to Aberton. If so, we're all that's left, a single ship and the souls within it. We can hope for Silva and Guldur, but there's no oath binding them to us."

The triumvirate reflected on the impossible situation. The ship crashed into the waves, sending a spray of water across the bow. Silbrey again had to brush her hair from her face.

Silbrey thought of the seedling she had forced to grow straight through the farmhouse and then the oak tree she willed to maturity at Sage Hall. "If you get me to the breach, I can seal it. All I need are a few acorns."

"I have a spell," Aubec said, "which might provide us safe passage to the breach if we move quickly. It's an impenetrable translucent wall. Same one I cast during the earthquake. It's temporary, and we'd have to get close, which means we'd need to run the ship aground."

Oren waved off the idea.

Silbrey teased Aubec, "If you can do that, why can't you rain fire down on the entire gnoll army and . . . ?" Silbrey made an exploding gesture, fanning out her fingers and moving her hands away to demonstrate the devastation.

"Why can't you use your fey magic and enchant the gnoll army?" Aubec countered. "Make them all go to sleep."

Silbrey had never considered it a possibility before. She opened her mouth. Closed it. And then settled on an answer. "There's too many. I couldn't enchant but a fraction of them."

"And if I could rain fire and destroy an entire army, do you think the War of the Hounds would have even happened?"

Silbrey looked at the armies to the west and then to the east and the massive walled city that separated the two. When Silbrey served Dahlia, she engaged on her terms, in a place of her choosing, her timing and benefit. She fought one on one, a duel, never in the vanguard on a battlefield.

Oren weighed their ideas before making up his mind.

"We do the hard thing, because it's the only way forward. The eastern side gives us an easier fight but with nowhere to go. Instead, we land this boat on the western side. Aubec, as you said, we run her aground. Use your spell to create a path to the breach. Silbrey, use your fey magic, and say goodnight to as many hounds as possible. The rest of us, we get behind the walls and join the others—and then we fight to keep the hounds back. We do the hard thing. For Bren Caius, for our families, and for Olar—"

Several soldiers stood on the deck, facing Silbrey, Aubec, and Oren. Silbrey noted how some of them trembled and how all of them had one hand on the pommel of their sheathed swords. Their kettle helmets were already strapped on.

"What's this?" Oren barked. He appeared ready for a fight, even if it was against his own soldiers. His eagerness worried Silbrey. She worried for these poor soldiers. "Are you here to discuss combat strategy with your commanding officer?

Sergeant," Oren said, pointing to one of the soldiers who flinched when called out, "what say you?"

"We believe, sir," the sergeant fumbled over his words, a timid attempt at mutiny, "the fight in Aberton is a lost cause. We're outnumbered. Let us be discharged from service, if you must. We'll return to our families. But you can't make us fight this battle."

"You seem to forget how an army works." Oren pulled out his massive sword. The hand, which he had burned in the pyre, was unable to tightly grip the hilt. "You can either fight those damn hounds with me by your side—or you can fight me right now. Either way, you're not leaving my side until I dismiss you. This isn't about us. We fight for those who can't. Our victory belongs to the people of Aberton."

Oren took a step toward them. The soldiers all took a step back.

Silbrey held her shield up and readied her staff. Aubec, who did not have a weapon, sighed and straightened his cape.

"I have a spell," said Aubec. "We can get through the breach unharmed."

Aubec's words did little to resolve the standoff. The soldiers were committed to turning the ship around.

The disobedience outraged Oren. He wanted to test their mettle, appealing to the glories of war, the bonds of soldiers, and the honor of dying for kith and kin. But this was not the War of the Hounds—no matter how much he wanted it to be —and these soldiers didn't enlist to save their land or their people. Most were the second and third born of wealthy families. No inheritance, but with all the privilege and leisure. Oren wanted to break them and rebuild them. He believed his responsibility was to make the soldiers more afraid of him than they were of the gnolls. Silbrey knew this approach. Dahlia Tulan had renamed Silbrey, given her a new life, and then spent years terrifying her, so that Silbrey could be fearless everywhere else in life. It worked on an orphan girl with few choices and no understanding of her options. It would not work on these soldiers.

"Did you forget your oath?" Oren yelled at them. "I know mine. I will gladly die for the honor of killing hounds!"

The rough waters forced the ship's bow to dip with a lurch. The soldiers closest to Oren tumbled forward. The soldiers in the back misinterpreted this movement as an attack against Oren. They drew their swords and rushed at him, but the ship rocked back in the other direction—throwing everyone off balance. A soldier slid across the deck, over the edge, and into the waters.

The remaining soldiers steadied themselves and rushed again, but they slammed into an invisible barrier.

"I told you," Aubec said. "I have a spell."

Aubec resumed chanting his arcanic words, less than a whisper, a breath, to manipulate Al'taru and maintain the protection. Silbrey could feel the humming of this power around them. They were safe from the soldiers, and the soldiers were safe from Oren.

The ship lurched again, more aggressively. Silbrey looked to the stern of the ship. No one was at the whipstaff. The lever was cocked to one side. The rudder turned the ship in a circle.

"Who's supposed to steer the damn ship?" Silbrey shouted.

Oren pointed to where the soldier had gone overboard. Everyone paused to consider the horrible fate. Then the ship pivoted with enthusiasm, possessed by restless waters and a willful rudder.

"Someone, take the whip!" Silbrey did not feel this needed to be said, but she said it anyway.

With another incantation, Aubec disappeared from Silbrey's side and reappeared next to the whipstaff. He grabbed onto it and pulled hard to the other side, but Tu'enya Bay did not want to yield control to the mage. Two soldiers joined Aubec to right the ship. It didn't matter. The spinning caused the sail to catch the wind all wrong, and they were moving backward. The water piled up against the stern. A wave crashed onto the ship and held it down. The ship's aftercastle and cabins took on water, raising the bow into the air.

Every soldier slid toward the stern and then into the waters. Silbrey held on to the knotted line.

The ship was sinking, and Silbrey did not think she could make the swim to shore. The eastern side of Aberton was farther from the ship. The waters swirled and roared. It would be a much harder swim to the east. If anyone survived, they could throw themselves at the mercy of Dahlia. The western side was closer, but Kret's army would be waiting.

Silbrey let go. She plunged into the water. When she surfaced, she chose to swim to the west and take her chances on the battlefield. Oren and a few of the soldiers were already swimming in that direction. Silbrey could not see Aubec anywhere.

"Aubec!" Silbrey called his name again and then again. She heard nothing in response.

She looked at the soldiers swimming to the east. Many of them were already struggling. Then she spotted it, Aubec's red cape floating on the surface of the water.

Silbrey closed her eyes and called upon her fey senses. Motes of blue light flickered. She focused her thoughts—

thoughts like an incantation. *When she held her wooden staff, she held the whole tree. The roots dug into the earth and absorbed the water. The water rained from the sky. It pooled into springs. The spring water traveled like rivers into the ocean. Tu'enya Bay was connected to the ocean, which encircled the whole world.* She was connected to it all, and she could feel Aubec deep in the waters—trapped under the sinking ship, tangled in the netting along the hull. He was struggling to vocalize a spell that could teleport him to the surface. He could not make the necessary sounds under the water. He could not breathe. He could not concentrate. All the while, as the ship sank, it pulled him farther down.

Then Silbrey could no longer sense him. He was gone, abandoned to the depths.

Silbrey had not known Aubec for long, but she felt a twinge in her chest. She had met him once when she was younger and then again when she arrived at Sage Hall. Aubec was one of the few people who knew her when she had served Dahlia. He had no reason to trust her, and yet he showed her compassion and hospitality. She could repay him by surviving.

Silbrey opened her eyes and knew what needed to be done. She would have to swim to the shore and fight like hell to get through the breach and protect Aberton.

Swimming required every bit of strength she had. Silbrey considered her earlier wisecrack about the gods turning her into a fish. She wished they would do her the courtesy again, but no miracles came.

Silbrey kicked in the waters and was thankful she wasn't wearing boots. She had decided it was easier, more comfortable, to summon her powers while barefoot. Swimming barefoot was also easier. However, holding her staff and shield while paddling made everything worse. Silbrey tried placing the shield underneath her stomach as she swam, hoping it would provide some buoyancy. It worked to a degree. If she put her full weight on it, she sank a little. Her strokes were like that of a newborn foal trying to find its legs: wobbling, stumbling, and afraid of being left behind. But she wasn't about to fight the gnolls empty handed, so she held onto her shield and staff.

The waters were stubborn. Even though the currents moved toward the shore, it was a back-and-forth journey of its own pace. No amount of flailing and kicking could get her closer without the current's consent. Once Silbrey reached the shore, she would have little energy to fight an army.

Her wool clothes absorbed the water, and she became cognizant of the weight. She looked around to see if there was anything floating, larger than her shield, a barrel or pallet from the ship, which she could grab onto. Oren and his soldiers were farther ahead. She saw a floating object and made her way over to it. It was a soldier, still a young boy, who did not have the strength to continue. He was treading water, trying his best to stay afloat. Occasionally, he would go under and then reemerge in a panic. He saw Silbrey, and he paddled toward her.

"Help!" His voice was hoarse. He had gulped too much water. His eyes were bulging and bloodshot. "Please, please, help."

If Silbrey wasn't careful, he might drag her down in his struggles. She should swim around him and leave him to his fate. One drowning was better than two. But she thought of this young soldier's mother. She didn't mean to, but her mind wandered there and remained. If this were her son, if this were Yurig, she would risk everything to save him. She would find the strength. Silbrey sighed. Whoever this soldier's mother was,

Silbrey would honor her and try to bring him home, even though she knew this was a mistake.

"Do not swim any closer. I'll come to you," she yelled to the soldier, and he obeyed. "What is your name? Where are you from?" She did not ask this because it mattered, but she needed him to pause and calm down.

"I'm Sven from Guldur."

"Tell me your mother's name." Silbrey's hair was once again in her face.

"Annet. She works as a fortune teller in the market."

Silbrey resisted any bitter comments about how Annet's cards could have warned her son about this day, but she knew better than to mock a fortune teller.

"Sven from Guldur, I want you to grab the end of my staff." Silbrey held it out to him, and he took it. "I'm going to pull you to shore, but we're going to work together. I need you to kick with all your strength, and I will swim as well. Can you do that?"

Sven from Guldur nodded.

Silbrey started swimming to the shore. She was fighting the rough waters, enduring the weight of her wet wool clothes, keeping the shield under her, and pulling this boy behind her. She kept thinking, *I'm doing this for Annet.* Her heart pounded, and muscles contracted. Lungs tightened, twisting inside her. She had pushed herself as much as she could, but she kept going. There was no other option.

Silbrey found new strength. The current began working more in her favor, pushing with determination toward the shoreline—until she was so close her feet could touch the bottom. She waded through the water and stumbled onto land, falling to her knees. Sven from Guldur was still holding onto her staff.

The shore sloped up to a rocky field clogged with gnolls, pushing toward the west wall and the breach. Aberton's archers stood along the walls, greeting all who trudged through the complex series of ditches with a volley of arrows. The dying filled the ditches, writhing like maggots in mortal wounds. Oren and his soldiers were not far off, swords drawn. They were surrounded by gnolls, but they kept a tight formation. Any earlier thoughts of mutiny were gone. The soldiers depended on Oren and his two-handed sword.

Silbrey and Sven from Guldur needed to catch their breath. The gnolls hadn't noticed them at first. A brief mercy.

"Sven from Guldur, I need you to let go of my staff." And he did. "Stay close to me, and—" She noticed he did not have a weapon on him. Her tone changed, like a mother scolding a child for forgetting his morning ablutions. "Where is your weapon?"

Sven from Guldur looked out to where the ship had sunk. "There, ma'am."

Silbrey shook her head. "Do you prefer a spear, axe, or sword?"

"A spear."

Silbrey stood up and looked for a spear-wielding gnoll in the pack. Then she saw her target. Silbrey braced her staff against her forearm. She held her shield high. "When I kill that one, I want you to grab his weapon."

\* \* \*

The ship sailed past Penderyn and docked several miles north. The earthquake had ravaged the city, and no ship could sail into the damaged port.

Feste was offloaded from the hull. The horse had always been energetic and temperamental, but after sailing to Rhyll and sailing back again to the mainland, Feste hated ships. This voyage had been turbulent and unpleasant. The colt stomped as the reins were handed to Maricel. He was blaming her.

Maricel patted his neck and spoke plainly. "Don't look at me. Silbrey took you to that island. I promise, no more boats."

Feste snorted as though he understood and approved.

Maricel hand-walked Feste to stretch his muscles. She fed him and gave him water. Maricel then saddled him to begin the ride to her old home. She thought they would take a light trot, something gentle, before working up to a faster pace. But Feste was ready to gallop. He took off at a speed that startled Maricel. She decided this horse was more demon than equine. She knew he was fast and useless on a farm, but she had never ridden a beast that could move at this speed. It scared her as she held on.

Maricel had figured it would take about three days to get home. There was no clear path from here to there. She would need to ride to Penderyn and then go east. At Feste's breakneck pace, they could get there in half the time.

Gydan already had a head start of several days. Maricel was angry with herself for not traveling with Gydan. She should have. She absolutely should have. It was the right thing to do, and to do otherwise had cast suspicion on her in the eyes of Silbrey. Fortunately, Maricel had gotten an opportunity to explain herself. And she was given a chance, this chance, to regain a bit of Silbrey's trust. She was able to tell Silbrey that she loved her, and—that kiss—it made her weak thinking about it, playing it over in her head. Silbrey was giving her a second chance.

Feste and Maricel took a path around the outside of Penderyn. If Gydan was not at the farming community, Maricel would travel back here. The city was in chaos, and it had five times as many people as Rhyll. But if Gydan didn't want to be found, there was nothing Maricel could do.

The path around Penderyn connected with the main road that led to the Hazelef Forest. They had to move slowly. Large cracks in the earth stretched out from the city and across the road. Some of the deeper cracks were being used as mass graves. Several bodies were wrapped in a gray cloth, lined side by side and on top of each other. The burials were in keeping with the tradition of the unnamed gods. The people of Penderyn had opted for burial over mass burnings. Possibly the sight or the smell was too much for them to take.

Maricel and Feste continued for another hour until they reached a blockade of cut logs that crisscrossed the road. Two men and two women stood guard. One had a bow. The others were armed with pikes. They were not dressed as soldiers, not Bren's soldiers. Each one wore a scarf with S.P.S.P. embroidered on it.

The woman with the bow held out her hand. She had well-defined arm, back, and shoulder muscles. Whoever she was, she had the physique of an experienced archer. "That's close enough, maiden. Dismount, so we can talk."

"No." It was all Maricel could think to say.

The woman scowled. Was "no" even an option? She looked at her other three comrades. They huddled for a conference and then the woman spoke again. "Where are you traveling? You know Dahlia Tulan's instructions."

"Actually, I don't." Maricel then leaned on the lie she created long ago, when she lived next door to Silbrey and her family. "My wife and I live in Aberton, but I travel the coastal cities selling dried herbs to the markets along Tu'enya Bay. After the earthquake, I went to check on my storefront customers to see what help they might need."

"You're from Aberton?" another man spoke up.

"I am."

"And you just came here from Aberton?"

"I did." The more Maricel spoke, the more she regretted it.

The woman with the bow stayed back, but the other three moved closer to Maricel and Feste. Maricel followed their eyes. The one questioning her was looking at her side. Maricel followed her gaze and saw that a portion of Bren's sword was uncovered by her cloak, visible to the three approaching her. Maricel pursed her lips.

"That sword," said the other man as he walked past Maricel and stood behind Feste. The guards were encircling them. "It's a nice sword. Beautiful scabbard."

"Isn't it, though?" Maricel responded.

The guards talked among themselves.

"Is she—?"

"Couldn't be her."

"I've never seen her before."

"She has blonde hair. Didn't—" they left a pause instead of saying the high general's name, "also have blonde hair?"

"This maiden is too young to be her."

"I heard she is ageless. Magic preserves her beauty forever."

"I heard she's rallying loyalists."

"I heard she died in Rhyll at the hands of Oren, her closest ally."

DAVID HOPKINS

The guards were ready to believe many things, except that she was an herbalist from Aberton. The sword raised too many questions. She should've kept it better hidden—another mistake.

Sensing Maricel's discomfort, Feste grew skittish. He backed into the guard standing behind him. The guard reacted angrily, hitting Feste with the back end of his pike. It was a stupid thing to do. Feste kicked high with his hind legs and connected with the guard's head, caving it in with a crack and a pop. The dead guard fell to the ground.

Feste took off, jumping over the barricade with ease.

Maricel heard shouts behind her. She looked back to see the woman with her bow, nocking an arrow. Maricel stayed as low as she could, urging Feste to move faster. She heard the pluck of a loosed bow string and the whistle of an arrow in flight, zipping past her. Then, another pluck and whistle. This time, Maricel felt a pain in her side. The twinge of pain grew until it was unbearable. The punctured area registered every movement of the arrow as Feste galloped. Maricel reached back, and her hand was soaked with her warm blood. Another arrow pierced higher into her back. She felt the pain in her lungs. With each breath, it felt like she was being stabbed. Maricel tried to scream, but only a suffering whimper came out.

Maricel was given a chance to regain Silbrey's trust, to find Gydan. Before Maricel left, she was able to tell Silbrey that she loved her. Maricel was glad she had that chance. A final pluck and whistle. An arrow pierced her throat. That kiss.

\* \* \*

Sven from Guldur picked up the dead gnoll's spear.

"Will that work?" Silbrey's question was odd. Hundreds of gnolls stood between them and the breach. Sven from Guldur would be lucky if he made it five feet through the killing field. Silbrey had said it once already, but she repeated it, "Stay close to me."

Oren and his men were not far off. Many of the gnolls gave up on the breach and turned their attention to the fight with these soldiers. Oren's fury roused the feral nature of the gnolls. He fought the way they fought—filled with rage, his enemy's blood speckled across his face. Oren screamed and shouted and dared them on. He laughed at their deaths. Silbrey understood Oren as she had never understood him before. This part of him could not be diminished, and during times of peace, he ached for something to test his resolve. If this was how the people of Raustfweg fought, she was glad that an ocean separated the two continents.

Oren saw Silbrey through the crowd. He grinned. And then, he swung his sword and took off the head of a gnoll. Oren howled in triumph.

"Aaaaooooh! Kret Bonebreaker! Where are you? Oren of Angnavir is here! Your hounds bay and bite, but I heel them with my sword. They are flesh and fur and fatty meat and bone and blood." A gnoll ran at Oren. Rather than use his sword, Oren headbutted the creature. The gnoll fell to the ground, and Oren stomped on his head. "They can be cleaved as any creature can. I want to face down the one whose very name makes cowards of all creatures! And I will smite you!" Oren swung his sword in a wide arc and three more gnolls dropped. "I will smite not just your physical qualities, but at your name, at your legend. I will strike you down so thoroughly that our descendants will wonder why we were so afraid of Kret Bone-breaker." Oren grabbed one gnoll and bit his face. The gnoll whined. Oren hit him with the pommel of his sword, and the gnoll fell. "Kret Bonebreaker was nothing! An old man from Raustfweg with only one good hand defeated him on the bloody fields of Aberton. That is your future. Will you not face it? Be a coward then, but I will find you!"

Oren raged at the gnolls, tearing them down, left and right.

Silbrey liked her odds better if she could get closer to the wild man with the sword. She berated herself for not wearing a helmet. With so much going on, Silbrey would've opted for any additional protection. She thought of taking a helmet from a fallen soldier, but she didn't have time to scavenge for one.

Instead, she would need to rely on what she already had.

She held up her staff. Motes of light flickered. Rays of shimmering blue rippled through the gnoll army. Many of them, but not all, began to fall into an enchanted sleep. She focused her enchantment on the gnolls that separated Oren and his men from Silbrey and Sven. She had to be careful. She didn't want to accidentally enchant any of the men fighting on her side. Her power felt more like a gentle breeze than a tidal wave, but it was enough.

The archers on the wall saw what Silbrey had done. They cheered. She forgot they had an audience. Not sure how to respond, she waved with her shield arm.

Silbrey and Sven worked their way to Oren and the other soldiers, careful not to trip over the uneven ground or fall into the ditches. The gnolls who were still standing numbered in the hundreds. They moved against the soldiers with greater ferocity. They were eager to kill the strange woman with her magical blue light.

Silbrey stepped forward, thrusting her staff at the first approaching gnoll. She caught him in the chest and knocked him off balance. She stepped forward again, swinging her staff around, catching a second gnoll by the back of the neck, leading him forward and also off balance. She tripped a third. The three stumbling gnolls produced the effect she was hoping for—as the gnolls behind them rushed in, they tripped over the three and piled on top of each other. Two gnolls jumped over the mass, swords high over their heads, ready to strike. Silbrey batted them down with both ends of the staff, hitting one and then the other.

The battle was an odd dance, one where she wanted to keep her opponent out of sync and off balance. To an experienced fighter, the moves were anticipated. The options were limited, but if she could be stronger and faster, the technique was of little consequence. She moved faster than her opponent. Silbrey doubted they could see her strikes coming. She wasn't looking for a killing blow, not every time. She wanted to keep them down long enough so she could move closer to the breach and the safety behind the walls.

Silbrey saw movement in her periphery. One of the gnolls had slipped behind her. She turned but the gnoll already had the advantage. She could only hope the gnoll would stab at her breastplate or that she could deflect with her shield. Once again, a helmet would be nice. But the gnoll was already dead. A spear protruded from his chest. Sven from Guldur removed his spear, and the gnoll dropped to the ground. Sven looked as surprised as Silbrey.

"You said to stay close," Sven said between heaving breaths.

The moment of victory was brief as more gnolls approached, and Silbrey continued to fight them off. There were too many. Like Oren, Silbrey wondered where Kret was in this crowd. She thought he would be easy to spot, since he was about twice as tall as these other gnolls. She would have preferred to face Kret in single combat. Instead, she was facing down an army, and she couldn't fight them all. If they had any chance, it would be through her enchantments. She tried to use her fey powers again. The motes of light appeared, but soon flickered out. Silbrey was dizzy. She fell forward, but it felt as if the whole world tilted up to bring the ground to her. When she fell, her staff and shield skittered across the ground, out of her reach. Prostrate, she crawled toward her staff, but it was still too far away. The shield was even farther off. Darkness pushed in at the corners of her vision as she struggled to stay conscious.

Silbrey heard a tiny voice. The voice jingled with the musicality of wind chimes. "Ald'yovlet has drawn too much from the well, it seems."

The disembodied voice reminded her of the voice she heard in the parlor of Dahlia Tulan's estate, on that day when she fought against Keote and Dahlia. The voice was of a woodland spirit saying she was a child of the forest. Silbrey could not see the fey creature, but she heard the quiet buzz of flitting wings like that of a hummingbird.

"She is tired," the invisible fey mused. "She will die here. And then, we are lost. Can I help her? Is there anything I can do?"

Silbrey cried out, "Where are you?"

"Ald'yovlet addresses me," replied the tiny voice. "Ald'yovlet wants an audience. So honored, especially as she will die soon. If she could live, that would be better. The beast who wishes to break the world draws near. Can I help Ald'yovlet?"

Ald'yovlet. The word, like Silbrey's name, was Volir. The translation was "tree-born." That was her. She was Ald'yovlet.

Silbrey reached for her staff in vain. Oren's soldiers were outnumbered, but they fought with courage. It was a borrowed courage that belonged to their leader, but it was better than dying. The careful, vital formation had been lost. Each soldier fought their own battle. It was the worst type of war. No retreat. No clear path forward. Back to back with enemies and allies. The only option was to hold on to their weapons and keep swinging. Silbrey wondering if any of it mattered.

Then Silbrey heard a roar. She looked up to see Kret Bonebreaker, Kret as she remembered him from the dragon pit, an unassailable silhouette against the light.

"Hello, little mouse," his gruff voice was a nightmare, *the* nightmare, every monster in every bedtime story. "I told you once, I can always smell the fey. This place stinks of it, and I found you."

Silbrey inched closer and grabbed her staff.

"You found me," responded Silbrey. "And Oren will be so upset that I got to you first."

# V

"I LOVE HER."

Ausdre knew her daughter wanted to sound mature, but her declaration of love was the childish pleading of an agitated youth. Maricel wanted what she couldn't have. She equated love with possession.

"She doesn't know you," Ausdre responded coldly. "And she's married to that shepherd. He's a kind man, from what you tell me."

Maricel ran the comb through her mother's long hair. The comb was carved flat from an elk antler with the teeth cut into one side. It was one of the few things Ausdre still had from her homeland. Maricel combed her mother's hair until it fell in perfect straight lines, like a plowed field. Maricel would eventually set the comb aside and start braiding her mother's hair in the intricate fashion common to Raustfweg, but Maricel was lost in the ritual and took her time. Maricel had come home to visit and share what she knew. She was in no rush.

"It's not uncommon for partners to take a third into their marriage," Maricel said. "Your mother was married to two men."

"Yes, your grandmother had two husbands, six sons, and me, her only daughter. Our house was a battlefield, absolute chaos, but Oma loved her husbands. Could you be with a man to be with Silbrey?" Ausdre usually avoided saying her name, but for this conversation, it would sound strange to call her "the fey child."

"I have no interest in a man's bed." Maricel pulled playfully at Ausdre's hair to say this was not a conversation she wished to have with her mother. "But I could be a companion in all other senses." Maricel's tone turned solemn. "You know Silbrey had a second stillbirth. If she wanted children, I'd consider acting as a surrogate."

Ausdre thought of the pain Silbrey must have felt. She ached for her. "If she is a true fey, if she is the same infant I lost in the river, she'll never be able to have children with anyone of this world."

"Never?"

"It would be like a unicorn mating with a mule."

"That's crass." Maricel didn't approve of her mother's bluntness.

"I'm being honest. Our worlds are separate. Such creatures exist as stories and dreams. But occasionally, a servant from the Fey Court will come over and steal a child. Some believe this is why women have miscarriages and stillbirths. They've been robbed by the fey. And likewise, we receive a few of their lost children. If your Silbrey is a true fey, she won't be able to have children, not intended for this world, at least."

"The unborn never die. They're stolen away." Maricel's

hands paused as she pondered this idea. "That's sweet to imagine and also unthinkably cruel."

Ausdre put her hand on her daughter's, stopping her from combing any further. "Why don't you let me braid *your* hair? Like I used to when you were young."

Raustfweg braids told a story. Certain styles and patterns indicated familial connections and callings. A braid might tell two strangers if they were allies or enemies. It could signal a great accomplishment or a tragic past.

"Mom, you've said it yourself. I'm an owl. I'm from Amon. I'm not a raven like you. I would look strange with my hair braided that way. It would raise too many questions."

"Why would that matter?"

They often debated about hair. Ausdre didn't know why it mattered so much, but it made her happy to see her daughter with braids. The runic tattoos on Ausdre's face had faded. She wouldn't ask Maricel to consider a tattoo marking her birth month. Even though, that was common enough in Raustfweg. To Ausdre, braided hair was the consolation, but Maricel refused to follow any of her mother's customs.

"I purchased the land from Silbrey and Callis. I told them I'm from Aberton. It would be strange if I braided my hair like someone from Raustfweg."

"Your hair's color betrays you more than any braid. No one from Amon has hair as golden as yours. Everyone in Amon has different shades of dirt for hair color. Your hair is a field of wheat, of spun gold. You are a beauty with no equal, and Raustfweg is in your blood."

"I've seen other folk with blonde hair."

"And where do you think their parents were from?"

"It's not always that simple," Maricel said.

Ausdre knew the tone in her daughter's voice. In Maricel's heart, those words took on greater meaning. It's not always simple to deny the heart. "And sometimes, Maricel, it is that simple." Ausdre stood and switched places with Maricel, taking her daughter's golden hair in her hands.

Maricel said nothing, letting her mother have this moment —just this once.

As she combed and braided, Ausdre could tell her daughter's thoughts were drifting elsewhere, most likely to that of Silbrey. Her daughter was drawn to anything wild and untamed, like the forest animals Maricel had tried to befriend when she was younger. It was dangerous, but that only made Maricel more intent on approaching—cautiously, gently, with every movement and utterance, reassuring. "I mean you no harm. I'm a friend."

The next day, Maricel removed the braids.

\* \* \*

"I will cleave you in two, little mouse, and then I will deal with Oren." Kret Bonebreaker stood over Silbrey where she had fallen. Around them, the battle raged. Kret was darkness haloed in light, but Silbrey could see his jagged teeth. His lips were drawn back in a smile. "Watch this."

He raised his double-headed axe. Despite the size of the axe, he handled his weapon with ease. Silbrey could hear the swooshing of the axe as it moved through the air.

Kret swung the axe down. Silbrey blocked Kret's attack with her staff. The axe hit against it and recoiled. The peculiar staff—which she had owned since childhood—did not break. The axe was not even able to cut into it, nor was there even the slightest crack. The force of the hit drove the air out of Silbrey's lungs and made her hands twinge with pain.

"That's a large axe," Silbrey grunted. "You don't need an axe that size." She flipped her staff between Kret's legs and wrenched it to the side, throwing Kret off balance. She kept talking, trying to delay Kret, while she got a sense of his fighting style. He could fight with sophistication and finesse, but he opted for brute force—much like how he hid his vast intelligence behind an unstudied delivery. He wanted to be misjudged. "There are lighter weapons that get the job done."

Kret regained his footing and swung down again, but Silbrey was already on her feet and out of his range.

"This axe ain't just to chop down people," Kret said. "During the war, I also cut down trees. The fey love their trees. I heard about a fey baby inside of one. A baby in a tree. Ain't that something?" Kret said these words hoping it would pique Silbrey's curiosity. He knew more about her than she did.

"I don't remember that day," Silbrey responded, "but I've been told the story."

Kret swung his axe. A wide and slow swing, easy to antici-pate. Kret was not going for a killing blow. He was testing his opponent's fighting style as well. Rather than jumping back for fear of launching herself into another combatant behind her, Silbrey moved closer to block the axe shaft with her shield. The swing nearly caused Silbrey to fall over again. She jabbed the end of her staff toward Kret's throat. He dodged the attack, moving his head to the side, but Silbrey wasn't finished. With the staff near his head, she swept it around, hitting him across the face.

He paused to concede the hit, then he spoke in his low, rumbling voice. "The humans think the War of the Hounds was about them. No, oh no. I was hunting fey, the unwelcome children of that twilight world."

Silbrey sensed something approaching from behind. A gnoll readied to stab her in the back—a cheap shot, but there were no rules of honor on a battlefield. Without even looking, she thrust backward with her staff. She heard a grunt of pain, a cracking sound, and a thump as the gnoll fell.

Kret took advantage of this distraction. He stepped forward, dropping his shoulder and shoving Silbrey. She stumbled back and nearly tripped over the gnoll on the ground. Kret swung his axe, faster this time, with less of an arc to anticipate. Rather than blocking with her shield, Silbrey stepped to the side. She had trained against Keote, a true goliath, descended from giants. She knew how to fight against larger, stronger opponents. She knew how to counter strength with speed and footwork. But she also recognized the difference between sparring and actual combat. All familiar choreography was abandoned. Clever flourishes were set aside. One hit from Kret would kill her. Cleaved in two, as Kret said.

Silbrey heard the hummingbird vibration and the tiny fey voice from earlier. "Ald'yovlet decided to fight. This is good. But she's fighting the Ancient Beast. Not a wise decision to challenge an unbeatable foe."

The Ancient Beast. It made Kret Bonebreaker sound less like Bren's old adversary and more like a force of destruction or a god-killer. The appellation suited Kret. Silbrey felt his power, the darkness and the fury. Whatever he was, it went beyond his physical form. He was the predatory terror that shaped the world.

Silbrey raised her staff to keep him at bay, taking a moment to get a sense of the battle near her. She couldn't risk any more distractions. The other soldiers, both human and gnoll, had created space for the two combatants and Kret's wide swings. Oren's soldiers—the ones who had mutinied until the battle was thrust upon them—had made little progress toward the breach. The fatal weak point, if exploited, would leave the city sacked. The archers on the wall tried their best to cover the soldiers on the ground, but the battle had turned into a scrum with no clear formation. An archer was as likely to hit an ally, and so the archers instead focused on the waves of gnolls farther back to keep them from joining and overwhelming Oren's small band.

Silbrey took shorter swings at Kret. He raised his forearm to deflect the blows. These strikes would leave a normal person's arm broken, but not Kret.

"How did you escape from Rhyll?" Silbrey asked. "Did Dahlia Tulan send a boat?"

"You give my allies too much credit," Kret said. "We're aligned, but not coordinated. No boat waited for me."

"You couldn't swim Tu'enya Bay."

"I didn't need to, little mouse. I only needed to swim out to one of the smaller boats waiting off the coast. A fishing boat. I snapped the man's neck and sailed his boat to my army waiting outside Aberton."

"You make it sound like you could've escaped at any time."

"Not so," Kret considered this point while they fought. "Bren's dragon pit prison was impressive, especially the adamantine bars, but I earned my freedom by exploiting something much, much weaker."

"Mendal?" Silbrey ventured.

According to Bren, Kret had a great intellect, surpassing any scholar at Sage Hall. Other gnolls were barely more cognizant than wild beasts. They communicated with yips and barks and snarls. They were pack animals guided by smell and hunger, able to follow basic commands. Kret was a genius and a beast. Kret was both, and he was alone in his world.

"Yes, Mendal," Kret said, and then parodied his own gruff voice: "I says to him, 'Release me, and I'll kill Bren. I'll create an Amon desperate for a king and a king's army, and they'll crown you within the day.' That was all Mendal needed to hear. He has a narrow outlook and narrower aspirations."

"Why would he trust you?" Silbrey thrust with her staff. Kret parried with his axe.

"I bent his ear when he discovered the dragon pit as a boy. I spent more time with him than his parents ever did. During those visits, it was easy to shape his mind and convince him that Bren was the real monster."

Silbrey struck with her staff and was able to hit his shoulder in the place where Bren had cut him earlier. The wound hadn't healed, and Kret winced. He glared at Silbrey, adjusted his grip on his axe.

"Let's not worry about the future tyrant," Kret growled and gestured toward Aberton. "I'm here for the fey beyond that wall, but I'll start with you. The fey always find each other. Your lives entangle like weeds."

"Why the fey?" Silbrey asked.

Kret shook his head to signal he was done talking or that to answer this question would be to say too much.

Everything between Kret and Silbrey had been prelude. Now they stood across from each other—no more commentary, no circling and wild swings. This was the fight Silbrey had been dreading.

With her shield held high, Silbrey moved closer, daring

Kret to strike. When he did, she braced her shield against the hit and countered with a strike of her staff. Then the fight became a blur of attacks and deflections. Time slowed as Silbrey focused on each move, each step. The world reduced to this fight. Blue light flickered from her staff. A succession of thuds resounded as she connected with his abdomen.

Kret let go of his axe and grabbed the staff. Silbrey had not expected this move, even though it was the right one. She had overcommitted with her hits, leaving the staff within Kret's reach for too long. She tried to pull the staff from his grip, but there was no chance. He held on. She hit at his hand with her shield, hoping he would let go. He did not. He pulled her nearer. She could smell him, feel his hot breath on her face. Kret opened his wide jaw full of dagger-like teeth to bite her, a predatory instinct. She pivoted, and he bit at her shoulder. The breastplate protected Silbrey, his teeth grinding on steel. Kret tried to bite her face. His jaws snapped. She moved back before those teeth could clamp down. To do so, she let go of her staff. Kret grinned at his fortune. He picked up his axe and tossed her staff aside. He charged at Silbrey, who was armed only with her shield.

Silbrey braced for his attack, her heart thudding, knowing she had lost. She had trained for years with that staff, and without it, all she could do was deflect and defer. But she couldn't fight back.

Silbrey heard the fey's voice again, a whisper of a whisper, close to her ear.

"Ald'yovlet wanted help. So, I brought help."

Oren burst through and interposed himself between Silbrey and Kret. Kret stopped his charge, eyeing his new opponent.

"Silbrey, you fought well." Oren was holding his blood-stained sword and greedily staring down Kret. "But on the ship, you told me you could seal the breach. Is that still true?"

"It is," Silbrey spoke, regaining her breath and her life.

"Then seal that breach. This fight is mine."

"Is this what you want?" Silbrey asked.

"This is all I've ever wanted."

Oren had outlived Bren Caius, his commander and friend. Forever their stories would be told as one story—and Oren wanted to rejoin her in death. Silbrey could only step aside and oblige and hope her life was worthy of the sacrifice.

Silbrey looked for her staff and saw it was on the other side of Kret, closer to the shoreline. She would not get far with just a shield, but to circle around Kret to get her staff was even riskier, putting more distance between her and the breach.

"Fey, are you still there?" Silbrey hadn't imagined the fey voice. She was certain of the presence, even though she couldn't see them. She had hoped the invisible creature flitting about might be able to grab her staff, but she heard no reply. The staff would be left behind.

The wall was about a furlong away. With Kret's army pressing against Aberton, it might as well be a country mile. She exhaled, held her shield, and ran at the throng of gnolls, careful to avoid the series of ditches carved into the field. The deep trenches made for incredible defense against invading armies. It also made Silbrey's attempt to get inside Aberton much more harrowing.

She used her shield to bash in the face of the first gnoll that approached. The gnoll stabbed at her with his spear. And like Kret had done, Silbrey grabbed the shaft of his spear. She pulled it toward her. He moved forward and headlong into her shield. The gnoll loosened his grip, and she yanked the spear away.

The spear was heavier than her staff. The spear tip altered that familiar balance. The shaft was too smooth. The wood was all wrong, but it worked well enough. She had never used a spear before and had never stabbed anyone. The battlefield was no place to try a new weapon, so she held the spear with the blunt end forward, treating it like her staff. She braced the spear against her forearm and swung it around, hitting the gnoll upside the head, knocking him out.

She jabbed another gnoll in his kneecap, causing him to tumble over into a nearby ditch. Then she took out two more with a swing. As the gnolls ran at her, one at a time, two at a time, three at a time, she fought them with a ferocity that would've made Oren proud and with a skillful hand she wished Bren could've seen. After all these years, Silbrey was still Dahlia Tulan's protégé, the terror of Penderyn. She felt the eyes of the Aberton soldiers along the wall as they watched in awe.

Closer to the wall, more bodies pressed around her, some allies, some foes. The fight was less of a duel between combatants and more a struggle to avoid being trampled or crushed against the wall itself. The gnolls were at an advantage. Even in these confines, they had their sharp teeth and claws—whereas the soldiers were reduced to hitting with their fists or sword hilts. If anyone dropped to the ground, they would not be able to get up again. Silbrey and the soldiers were outnumbered with more gnolls flooding in. Sven from Guldur, the boy she had rescued from drowning, was not too far off. He was still alive and fighting. Their eyes met, and they both acknowledged how hopeless it had become.

Kret and Oren were still fighting nearer the shoreline.

Oren was bent over, shoulders slumped, and worn thin, while Kret was undiminished. But the old Raustfweg warrior would not retreat. Axe and sword clashed. Oren swung clumsily, without enough force. Kret blocked and pushed him back. Oren yelled his frustration at the gnoll warlord. Oren's teeth dripped with blood. His eyes were red. Every vein in his neck bulged. This is how Silbrey would remember Oren, all rage and intensity.

A rawboned gnoll soldier stumbled into the clearing made by the two duelists. The gnoll saw that Oren had his back to him. His lips curled into a silent snarl. The gnoll rushed at Oren with his spear and stabbed him repeatedly in the back. Oren pivoted to see the mortal blows. He was more confused than pained. Then the realization set in. He dropped his sword and began to tremble. Arms held out; Oren fell to his knees. The pose was an unspoken request for Kret to strike him down. Deliver the finishing blow. Kret denied him and walked away. Oren's body flopped to the ground—undignified, ungainly, unambiguous. More gnolls converged on Oren to further maim the great warrior from Angnavir.

It wasn't the death Oren had hoped for.

Silbrey had been well-acquainted with death. She knew how death snuck up on people and how death announced itself, sometimes with a whisper and sometimes a shout. People rarely yearned for it—not like Oren did—and no one got the death they wanted. But Oren was on the battlefield one last time. The War of the Hounds returned. He didn't die of sickness or old age. His only misstep was being surrounded by his enemies.

Silbrey tried again to use her enchanting sleep, but she was drained, and like before, nothing happened, except she felt dizzy. She was so close to the breach, but it seemed like a hundred gnolls stood between her and the city. The press of bodies kept her upright. She pushed back against the gnolls as they tried to rip her throat out.

The air became thick and rank.

Silbrey's hair stood up on the back of her neck.

Flames exploded next to her and along a line where the gnolls were concentrated, a blast of intense heat. The flames bloomed, rolling to the breach. The fire disappeared as soon as it appeared. Nothing remained but charred bodies, marking an open path to the breach, and Silbrey, who was spared. Smoke twisted from the scorched ground.

Aubec Skarsol emerged from Tu'enya Bay.

Aubec's wet garments clung to his muscular frame. His rope-like hair, usually tied back, hung down and fanned across his broad shoulders. He lowered his hands, having performed the spell that incinerated the gnolls. When he saw Silbrey, he smiled and called out to her.

"Silbrey, why didn't you wait for me?"

Silbrey cocked her head back in amusement. After so much death, this return felt like a resurrection. "You were trapped under the ship!"

"I can hold my breath for quite a while when my life depends on it."

The fire had cleared a path. This was their chance. Silbrey yelled to the soldiers, "To the breach!"

The soldiers, a scant remnant of those who first swam ashore, did not hesitate. They ran across the scorched ground to the breach, navigating the higher terrain around ditches. An Aberton commander on the wall shouted for the archers to focus their efforts to keep this blazed trail clear of gnolls.

Silbrey stood her ground to keep any gnolls from charging after the soldiers. She and Aubec would be the last ones through.

Aubec was still closer to the shore than the wall. A pack of gnolls ran at Aubec. He held up his hand. A flickering wall of force prevented them from getting closer. When one of the gnolls touched the wall, a shockwave sent him flying backward. Aubec reached down and picked up Silbrey's staff. He held it up so she could see it.

The wall formed into a half sphere and enveloped him. The protective wall moved with Aubec, keeping him safe as he made his way to reunite with Silbrey. More than a few gnolls tried to penetrate the sphere with a similar outcome as the previous gnoll—blasting them back.

Once Aubec reached Silbrey, the spell encircled them both. He handed the staff to her. It felt good in her hands.

"You left your staff."

"And you left your red cape in the bay."

Aubec glanced to his shoulders and frowned. He hadn't noticed it was gone.

"Is there a spell to retrieve it?" Silbrey asked.

"No, but there should be."

Silbrey pointed to the gnolls swarming the sphere. "We should get to the breach."

"The spell won't last for much longer—and I won't be able to cast it again until I've had time to study."

"More fire spells?"

"Not until I have more time—"

"—to study. Got it. Wizards love their books."

Silbrey and Aubec made it to the crack in the wall. The opening, created by the earthquake, was a space no larger than five feet across. The crack was a winding pathway through the thick wall that led into the city beyond. Dead gnolls were packed and piled high throughout the pathway. Silbrey and Aubec could not get through without walking on them.

As they entered the city through its newest gate, they were greeted by the surviving soldiers and a large company of Aberton guards, plus Bren's military, which she had sent days ago.

A man ran to Aubec and wrapped his arms around him in a hardy embrace. The man wore a bycocket hat with a feather in it. His features were handsome. His nose, chin, cheekbones, everything was at a sharp, mischievous angle. He had a thin mustache. Stiletto daggers were strapped to his waist and across his chest.

He leaned toward Silbrey and extended his hand.

"A steady journey. I'm Tom."

"And a clear path." She took his hand. "Tom the Barber? Aubec has missed you."

"That's no surprise," Tom said with confidence. "I have the keenest blades in Amon. For years, Bren trusted me to sharpen her sword. I'm also the best battlefield surgeon an army could hope for. I can mend, and I can rend." Tom drew his daggers with such speed, it startled Silbrey. He spun them around and sheathed them just as quickly.

"He also gives great shaves." Aubec scratched his jaw to show Tom he was overdue. "Skin close and never a nick."

"I'm an all-around useful person," Tom said.

Tom the Barber had an empty purple vial tied to his belt. An indication he had visited an alchemist. Whenever a person was born a boy or a girl—but was not meant to be how they were born—if they chose, they could visit a specialist in potions and elixirs. Treatments could be prescribed that would allow a person to have a more masculine or feminine presentation. Some people carried the alchemist's vial with them to pay tribute to their experience.

Tom saw Silbrey's eyes linger on the vial. He gave her a wink. "While it's great to have more allies on this side of the wall, we should worry about our enemies on the other side. Hm?"

The breach, which had been their best chance to get into the city, remained their greatest weakness in defending it. But this wasn't the only thing weighing on her heart. If she couldn't save the city, she might never be reunited with Maricel and her daughter. They were to reconvene at the farming community, farther east, a week's journey from here. Silbrey felt the pang of not knowing if Gydan was safe. She had to trust Maricel to find her. Also, Silbrey had made a promise to Bren Caius. She was fated to fight this battle for Bren. And she needed to know more about the invisible fey who called her "Ald'yovlet." This reprieve from the battle invited all the troubling thoughts she didn't have time to entertain. She looked back at the breach. How much longer could she have survived out there?

"I can close the breach," Silbrey said to Tom, "but I need some acorns."

The strangeness of the request amused him. "There's a grove of oak trees in the center of Aberton. The grove is older than the city itself."

Before Tom could say anything else, the captain of the guard stepped forward to speak with Aubec and Silbrey. He dressed more like a noble than a soldier. He spoke with such upbeat formality, Silbrey wondered if he understood that the fight wasn't over. "I saw Oren fall in battle. Was there any doubt the god of war would claim his death? Truly, he would've fought until the last hound. Where is Bren Caius? Is she coming with more soldiers?" And there it was. He didn't know the high general was dead. There were no reinforcements. They were alone in this fight.

Silbrey did not know how to respond, so she remained silent.

Aubec answered. "Bren was murdered by Kret Bonebreaker. There are no more soldiers. We're all that's left."

These words knocked the wind out of him. The captain looked at the remaining troops. There weren't enough to quell a tavern skirmish, let alone stop an army.

"*Sah'le vuk*," the captain responded, making no effort to put on a brave face for his subordinates. "We're all dead. Those monsters don't take prisoners. They don't negotiate. There will be no terms of surrender."

If Oren were still alive, he would have struck the captain for his cowardice. But Aubec instead patted the captain's shoulder. While Aubec was a veteran of the old war, he was also a scholar and a teacher. He approached this battle as a problem to be solved. He did not trust in the gods. He could only hope a winning strategy existed that would turn their fortunes. Something he could tell future students about.

"Take me to the top of the wall," Aubec instructed the captain. "I have more mayhem I can drop on those hounds before I'm spent of magic, and we're out of options."

"Can't you create that wall like you did out there?" The captain pleaded. "I saw it—"

"My magic is temporary. The protection spell I cast was intended to get us here. But Silbrey's magic is different," Aubec looked at her and spoke with confidence. "If she says she can close the breach, I believe her."

"The grove," Tom said. "Follow this road and you will find it."

Silbrey did not waste another moment. She ran into the city toward the grove. Even from the far end of Aberton, she could see the tangled treetops.

Aberton was an older city than Penderyn. The buildings were a mix of architecture from several eras, all crammed next to each other—from thatched wood to clay bricks. Old and new intermingled, painted in a spectrum of vivid colors. To Silbrey, the colors whirled like a kaleidoscope as she ran past. Her bare feet slapped upon the old cobblestones. The stones were worn smooth from generations of use.

On the voyage to Aberton, Aubec had told Silbrey she shouldn't presume a city under siege would be deathly quiet with citizens hiding in their homes, huddled and praying to whichever god pursued peace, if one existed. A city under siege was active. Silbrey saw it now as she ran, weaving in and out of the crowds. No one had time to cower. Some were carrying buckets of boiling water, which they had heated for the guards on the walls to pour on the hounds below. Others transported rocks and extra arrows.

Children were relaying reports to each other, which they spread throughout the city. Unlike idle gossip on a slower day, these reporters were accurate to the letter. No one wanted to make a mistake. If they gave the wrong name of a fallen soldier to the wrong family, then people suffered needlessly.

Silbrey heard the shouts of the children.

"The south end of the west wall needs more water!"

"All is quiet on the eastern wall!"

"Two guards died on the midsection of the west wall! No names given yet!"

"The barefoot woman needs acorns!"

This message was being shouted ahead of Silbrey down the street, and she had to laugh. The report was moving faster than she was. Then she heard another message.

"The Northern Light has fallen! No more soldiers are coming!"

"Bren Caius is dead!"

"Bren the Beloved died in Rhyll!"

"Kret killed Bren in single combat!"

All the other messages ceased. The activity of the city slowed to a halt as people took in this news. Silbrey continued to run. She had been there when it happened. The scene replayed often in her head—the way Kret taunted her before he murdered Bren. Silbrey was at the funeral when she watched as the world broke open and reclaimed Bren. Everyone would remember where they stood when they heard of the immortal Bren Caius' death. Silbrey rushed past the stunned citizens. One little girl—too young to grasp the full significance of Bren's death—pointed as Silbrey went by, "Look, it's the acorn woman."

Out of breath and half-delirious, Silbrey arrived at the grove. As Tom had said, the oak trees were old, centuries old, thick and slouching from the weight. The grove was not maintained by the city. No gardener tended it. The city had built itself around this wooded area and left it alone. Life hummed from every branch and every leaf. The roots dug deep and spread far. Silbrey wanted to stay here. She wanted to live here. However, she had to return to the breach.

Silbrey reached up to a low-hanging branch and grabbed a cluster of acorns. Then she heard a familiar tiny voice.

"Ald'yovlet lives. I spoke to the wild man named Oren, and he came to help Ald'yovlet."

"He died saving me."

"His life is not Ald'yovlet's life. We cannot lose another fey. Ald'yovlet survived an encounter with the Ancient Beast. I doubt Ald'yovlet can do that again."

Silbrey was surprised when she turned toward the voice and saw the fey was visible in the grove.

A single sprite sat on the branch of the nearest oak tree, among a cluster of leaves. The sprite was no larger than a chickadee and looked exactly how Silbrey imagined a sprite would look like from the stories she heard as a child. This sprite had large black eyes like polished onyx and wings like a dragonfly. The creature was uniquely beautiful and bizarre.

Silbrey bowed at the courtesy of the sprite's appearance. "You returned. It's good to meet you. And your name?"

"Our folk do not settle on names easily. For today, call me Thimbleberry Fig."

"Thimbleberry—?"

"Fig. Yes."

Silbrey looked beyond the sprite to see a hundred more hiding throughout the grove. All staring at her.

"Fig," Silbrey said, unsure of what to make of this audience. While she was glad Yurig and Gydan were not here in Aberton, she wished they could see this wonder. Actual sprites. "I have a breach that needs to be sealed, but we'll see each other again."

Silbrey started to leave, but Fig spoke again.

"Stay and hear why the Ancient Beast is at our door. It may benefit Ald'yovlet more than fixing a crack in a wall."

"Why?" Silbrey asked.

"Because more earthquakes are coming."

\* \* \*

The journey on foot to Maricel's farming community should have taken Gydan, Cyru, and Timon a day—or two, at most, since Timon relied on a cane and needed several breaks. However, the directions "east of Penderyn and west of Hazelef Forest" lacked precision—and increased the length of their trip. The main road ended a day's walk from Penderyn, opening to a grassy region well before the Hazelef Forest, and the road branched into numerous worn paths, each one leading to a different farming community. The paths went in several directions, so taking the "most straight one" as Timon kept pleading was not an easy call. None of the farming communities knew of Maricel or Ausdre. Worse yet, few of the people they met were able to agree on what constituted as the "Hazelef Forest." Among the locals, they distinguished the southern region as Pen's Forest, while the larger northern region was Hazelef Forest, but only technically so. The true Hazelef Forest was a patch much closer to the city of the same name. Every person contradicted the person prior to them, and on and on.

Each time, Gydan, Cyru, and Timon backtracked to the main road and tried again. Each time, they were a bit more irritable.

Timon would often mention how he'd never journeyed this far from the city, and this miserable experience traveling with him proved his point. He was a terrible companion on the path. He fussed and complained. Everything inconvenienced him and sent him into a litany of laments. During one of Gydan's weaker moments, she went into a tirade. She was astounded. An actual priest of the *god of agriculture* had never been to a farm. Her words wounded Timon's pride, and he stayed quiet, much to the guilt and relief of Gydan. Cyru—who was connected to Gydan's mind, but otherwise mute, except for small chirping noises—offered to kill Timon. It was a draconic way to deal with an annoyance. Gydan reminded Cyru that they needed Timon. And Cyru reminded Gydan that a dragon doesn't need anything or anybody.

*We are titans who have endured for untold ages. All other creatures cower before us.*

Gydan refrained from reminding Cyru that they, unlike other dragons, were about the size of a farm cat and not at all a titan.

Instead, Gydan broke her silence with the priest. "I'm sorry I made fun of you about the farms. I'm glad you're with us."

"Now, since this journey, I've been to several." Timon laughed at himself. "We've probably been to every farm east of Penderyn, except the one we need to find. You were right, though. Earlier, you said the gods never asked me to save Penderyn. They wanted me to take care of your mother. I failed her and the gods. I can't change the past, but I can help you get to this farm."

*I doubt his ability to get us to this farm.*

"Timon, the gods may not be done with you yet." Gydan gave Timon a playful shove. Timon scratched the back of his neck and smiled.

"We're here. Again," Timon gestured to where the main

road from Penderyn ended. "Should we try something farther north?"

Before Gydan could respond, Cyru darted about. Something terrible had happened.

*Gydan. Your mother's horse is nearby. I can sense him down the main road.*

"Feste?" Gydan asked.

"What is it?" Timon noticed Gydan's surprise.

"Cyru saw my mom's horse. We need to go back. Cyru, where is my mom?"

*I don't sense her anywhere.*

Gydan ran down the road. Cyru followed her. Timon struggled to keep up.

Near a cluster of trees with a growth of mistletoe surrounding it, Gydan saw Feste without a rider. Then she saw a streak of blood leading off behind the trees—as if a wounded animal had been dragged away.

"Mom?" A terrifying emptiness overwhelmed Gydan. She remembered her father dead in the alley, shot with arrows. She could not bear to also lose her mother. Silbrey must have come looking for her. Once again, it was Gydan's fault—her fault that her father died and her fault that her mother died. The edges of her vision darkened. Her stomach turned. She willed herself forward and followed the blood until she saw a body shot with arrows. Her mind flashed again to her father.

Gydan felt Timon's hand on her shoulder. She jumped.

Timon whispered in astonishment. "By the gods, how is she still alive?"

Gydan's focus returned. Her mother wasn't on the ground, nor her father. It was Maricel—an arrow in her side, another in her back, and one more arrow through her throat. She was drenched in her own blood. Her blonde hair was stained dark red. One leg was extended, kicking out in pain.

Gydan went to her.

Maricel groaned incoherently. The features on the right half of Maricel's face drooped as though afflicted with palsy. Maricel spoke again with her mouth hanging limp, her words came out slow and slurred. The arrow piercing her throat bobbed up and down as she tried to talk.

"Mistletoe . . . can be used in druidic healing spells. Finally . . . did it." Maricel waved a sprig of mistletoe, which she clutched in her fist.

"She's holding herself together with druidic magic," Timon knelt next to Maricel and Gydan. "The spell is temporary. We need to remove the arrows."

Maricel glared at Timon. Her breathing was deep and rasping as she struggled to speak, "Do what you need . . . to do." Her words were cut short as she coughed up blood.

Timon took Maricel's traveling cloak, which he had found lying on the ground near Feste, and handed it to the hovering Cyru. "When I pull the arrows out of her side and back, there will be a lot of bleeding. Cyru, we need to tear strips of cloth from this cloak to use as bandages." Cyru shredded the cloak into ribbons. "Gydan, hold this woman—"

"Her name is Maricel," Gydan responded.

"Hold Maricel while I try to remove the arrows. You need to keep her still."

Gydan couldn't believe what she was hearing. "I'm just a kid. How can I hold her?"

Timon thought about it and nodded in agreement.

"True. I'll hold her. You remove the arrows."

Gydan looked sick at the thought of it. Maricel met

Gydan's eyes. She was trembling, but her eyes said she was okay with whatever happened next.

Timon knotted one of the cloth strips and placed it in Maricel's mouth to bite down on. He braced one hand against her shoulder, and with the other, he held her side, angling her so her back faced Gydan. She grunted in pain at being moved. Already, Timon's hands were soaked in Maricel's blood.

"Gydan," Timon said her name, urging her to proceed. They couldn't wait any longer.

Gydan grabbed the arrow lodged in Maricel's side, directly above her hip. The arrow was sticky, covered in a greenish syrup. The arrow jostled a bit, and Maricel, muffled by the knotted cloth, cried out. The arrow was buried deep, but it hadn't come out the other side. Gydan took a breath and then pulled the arrow free. Maricel screamed, low and guttural, through the cloth. Blood sprayed as the arrow came out, speckling Gydan's face. Gydan tried to keep calm for Maricel. Timon went to work binding Maricel's wound with the cloth strips.

Gydan reached for the arrow higher in her back, on the right side. She expected Maricel to cry again in pain, but she did not react. Gydan looked at Timon in confusion.

Timon answered, "It looks like the arrows were coated with some sort of poison. I've heard of poachers who capture large game for menageries that use such a poison to paralyze their targets. I don't think your friend can feel anything on her right side. It may be a blessing in this situation."

Gydan noticed, for the first time, that any movement or thrashing about came from Maricel's left side—her left leg and left arm. It also explained the palsy appearance on the right side of her face.

Gydan pulled at the arrow in Maricel's back. It did not move. Blood poured from the wound.

"It's stuck," Gydan looked at Timon, unsure what to do.

Timon reached for the arrow. He pulled at it, then twisted and pulled it free—another spray of blood, but no reaction from Maricel.

"The arrowhead was behind one of her ribs."

Timon wrapped her with more cloth strips, which were already being soaked through. Maricel's whole body was going limp. She was losing so much blood.

Gydan looked at the last arrow, the one in Maricel's throat. If she pulled the arrowhead through, it would further damage her. If Gydan pulled in the other direction, the fletching would make it difficult to be removed. Cyru understood the dilemma and flew toward her. With the dragon's razor-sharp teeth, they bit down on the fletching end of the arrow, cleanly breaking it off.

"Thank you," Gydan whispered to Cyru.

Gydan grabbed onto this last arrow. Timon held Maricel down as a low whimpering noise came out of her, and she began to tremble. Maricel bit down harder on the cloth knot in her mouth. Gydan pulled the arrow out with a smooth deliberateness, a steady touch worthy of any seamstress. She did not know where this calm came from because inside, she was shaking. Her guts were twisted and aching. She wanted Maricel to live—and so she accepted the only option available.

Maybe that was it. Gydan had learned to accept how cruel life could be and take what was given. It was a miracle Maricel was even alive. The magic sustained her for a time, but the arrows had to come out. Gydan wondered, as she slowly pulled the arrow, if her father would still be alive had Maricel been there in the market instead of her. If such amazing magic was available to druids, why not share it with the world?

Maricel sobbed in pain as the arrow came out. Blood flowed from her neck. The rank scent of the body, the smell of mortality, of blood and urine and sweat, was strong.

Maricel squeezed the mistletoe in her fist. The cloth knot fell out of her mouth. Her eyes rolled into the back of her head, and Maricel uttered deep words in an unknown tongue. The words came out slurred, but they were powerful. The wind swirled around Maricel, and the wounds in her side, her back, and her neck closed. Then Maricel's grip loosened, and the mistletoe fell out of her hand. Her left eye closed in relief, but her right eye was still half-open.

Misfortune fell upon people with a vicious randomness. Gydan's father had died, but Maricel was going to live. The arrows were the same. The fate was different.

Maricel's breathing became steady again. Her face still had the drooping features of a paralytic.

"Why didn't the mistletoe heal—?" Gydan gestured to her own face.

"I'm no druid, but I believe this nerve damage may be beyond anything magic could repair. The magic is temporary. These consequences may be permanent. If you could take the reins of the horse, we can hoist Maricel into the saddle and lead her home."

With her remaining strength, Maricel lifted her arm and pointed in the direction of Feste, to a sword and scabbard on the ground. Gydan recognized the beautiful patterns on the scabbard with the Northern Light sigil. Bren's sword.

"Your mother . . . wanted you to have it."

Maricel tried to say more, but the words wouldn't come.

*  *  *

Thimbleberry Fig said more earthquakes were coming, and
Silbrey could not walk away from that. She looked at the sprite.
The black eyes of Fig were fixed on her. The world around
Silbrey and Fig grew dim and blurry. The trees within the grove
were illuminated with soft light, each leaf and acorn shined like
a star, including the cluster of acorns in Silbrey's hand. Time
had stopped. The boundaries between the world Silbrey knew
and the world of fey disappeared.

"Not every story is true, but there is truth in every story."
The tintinnabulation of Fig's voice was the only sound in this
void. "People tell a story about four sleeping titans that became
the four land masses known as Efre Ousel—Amon the owl,
Raustfweg the raven, Lunthal the eagle, and Karkasse the
crane. What the story omits is that Tian, the named god of luck
and misfortune, begged the Fey Court to send their kind to
Efre Ousel to help keep the titans asleep. A god begged.

"The terms of the agreement were made in secret, but Tian
got what she wanted. A world on the brink, but still a world.
Tian was wise to approach the Fey Court. She knew what the
fey could do. Some had wings. Some had horns. Some were
fast. Some turned invisible. Some could see through the eyes of
animals. And there were fey who lived in trees and could lull
other creatures into a deep slumber. The trees were a conduit
for their power, passing through the roots and into the earth.
These fey could keep the titans asleep through the trees. Tian
knew this."

Silbrey thought of when she was buried in the collapsed
cavern and how the roots wrapped around her, restored her,
empowered her, and pulled her up to the surface again. She had

a hard time believing it had ever happened, but Fig spoke truth. The trees were a conduit.

"These tree-born fey covered the four lands. Until the Ancient Beast began chopping down those trees and the fey within. He did this for centuries, before the War of the Hounds, before he was known as Kret." Fig stared deep into Silbrey's eyes. "Ald'yovlet may be the only one left. The earth is shuddering. The titans are dreaming those final dreams before waking."

Silbrey felt a hollowness in her chest as the implication sunk in. The earthquake that devastated Rhyll and the cities along Tu'enya Bay was a prelude to something much worse. Could anything survive Efre Ousel being upended? The chaos and violence would exceed anything that happened during the Great Firestorm centuries ago. It would please Kret to see the world end.

If Silbrey was the last of her kind, what hope was there? Eventually, she would die, and then there would be no one who could save the world from the waking titans. Kret would win eventually.

"Why is Kret trying to get into Aberton?" Silbrey asked. "Why not focus on killing me instead?"

"These particular trees belong to us," Fig flew around the oaks. Fig circled them, and the trees glowed brighter in response. "Many of the tree-born fey once lived here, before the city existed, and the magic is still strong in the roots. The Ancient Beast needs to chop down these trees if he hopes to wake up those titans and break the world, especially since Ald'yovlet alone may not be enough to keep the titans from waking."

"There's no hope."

Fig flitted from the trees to Silbrey, circling her now. "Hope is not an answer. It never has been." Fig floated in front of Silbrey. "Hope is the question every generation must ask and then seek out. I cannot say what will happen to Efre Ousel when all the fey are gone. Maybe the Fey Court will send more of its children here, but not while the Ancient Beast continues to slaughter us. Maybe more will come if he can be put down —if such a thing is even possible. One thing I do know, the druids of Raustfweg were sent to find Ald'yovlet as a babe. Their mission had great purpose, greater than even they understood. Hope might be found with the druids."

The trees lost their glow. The world faded back into the dim one she knew. It felt as though no time had passed, and maybe it hadn't.

Silbrey had to ask one more question. "Was Bren Caius fey?"

"Like Ald'yovlet, she was orphaned to this world. She was the summer queen's daughter—conceived there, born here, and sent with an unspoken purpose deep in her bones, to stop the Ancient Beast. She failed."

Silbrey felt an urge to defend Bren. But it was true. Bren failed. She had Kret in a cage. At any time, she could have gone down there with a company of archers—and ended Kret. She allowed him to live.

Kret's plan to elevate Dahlia Tulan and to corrupt Bren's son, to make them into his co-conspirators and to raise an army against Aberton, all while in captivity until it was time for an impossible escape, the plan was nonsensical, too elaborate. Had anything gone awry, he would still be in that cage or dead. Instead, everything went exactly how he had planned. Exactly. "Genius" was the wrong word. He was omniscient.

Silbrey shivered and shook her head. Fig looked at her curiously, head tilted, eyes wide open. The other sprites also stared at her, mirroring Fig's gestures. Silbrey knew so little about the fey or even her own abilities—except she knew what to do with the acorns in her hand.

She repeated what she had said before, "Fig, we will see each other again." She clenched her fist and ran back to the wall.

* * *

The gnolls were piled deep at the breach. They climbed the dead and tried to force their way into the city. They held shields over their heads. Arrows rained down from the archers on the wall. A few gnolls carried the dead on their backs, a makeshift shield as they hunched over and slogged forward.

Some gnolls broke through. The soldiers from Rhyll met them and fought to keep the hounds from spreading into the city.

Tom the Barber had a needle-like dagger in each hand. He danced between the gnolls, dodging their clumsy attacks, and would then slide the razor edge of his dagger across a gnoll's throat. The dagger would slice only in the most necessary place to cause the blood to pour. Tom would roll away and stab another in the chest. Whereas Silbrey fought to keep the enemy at a distance, Tom had the opposite approach. He embraced the intimate kill, to move in closer where he was most effective. A dangerous strategy, but Tom was—in his own words—the best battlefield surgeon an army could hope for.

When Silbrey arrived at the wall, she watched him operate.

As Tom worked, he sang a song, which he made up on the spot. It had a cheerful, swinging melody.

> *Slash and sever, rip and rend,*
> *The hounds will fall in the end.*
> *They come to storm the old stone wall.*
> *They come to kill us one and all.*
> *But Tom—that's me—cuts their kin,*
> *Once for his mom, twice for Bren.*
> *Slash and sever, rip and rend,*
> *Aberton's will does not bend.*

Tom took a wide step past a gnoll, placing his leg behind his opponent's. With a lunge, he sent the gnoll tumbling backward.

Tom paused from his singing. "Rhyming 'kin' and 'Bren' might be a bit forced." While considering a revision, he finished the prone gnoll with a few quick stabs.

"How about 'Tom' with 'Mom'? A more obvious rhyme. Too obvious?"

A gnoll thrust his spear at Tom, but Tom deftly shuffled sideways and grabbed the gnoll by the scruff of the neck, as if he were a pup. Instead of fighting the momentum, he guided the gnoll into another.

"I could change the line to: 'They get cut from the barber named Tom, once for Bren, twice for Mom.' What do you think?" Tom asked the soldier next to him. "Not my best work. It doesn't make much sense either way."

Silbrey watched Tom, thinking Dahlia Tulan would have loved him.

One gnoll close to Tom dropped to the ground, dead.

Silbrey didn't even see what happened. Tom was too fast. Tom spun around to see Silbrey.

"Finally! This whole time, I've been wondering what you're going to do with those acorns."

Silbrey and Tom fought their way to the cracked wall with the gnolls pressing through.

Silbrey whispered, "I am Ald'yovlet. I am a child of the forest." She conjured the blue dancing light, which was becoming more familiar to her. The light wrapped around the gnolls in the breach, and they fell asleep. Another wave of gnolls approached, so she had to be quick. She walked across the fallen, both dead and asleep, to the front of the wall that opened to the trenched field beyond. She could feel the matted fur of the gnolls between her toes, and it caused her skin to crawl.

She dropped an acorn to the ground. Silbrey then took a few steps back and dropped another acorn. She did this a couple more times until she was back at the city-side of the wall. Tom watched her with curiosity. Silbrey let her shield fall to the ground and held onto her staff with both hands. She thought of those acorns and, like she did at the farmhouse and again at Sage Hall, she coaxed the acorns to grow.

Asking the seeds to grow did not require as much from her as the sleep enchantment did. Growth was a simple request. The seed wanted to grow, and Silbrey gave it permission to proceed with haste. Silbrey felt stronger, renewed, whenever nature grew and flourished. The acorns were giving back to her more than she gave to them.

The acorns became seedlings and then saplings, and then young trees matured into larger, fuller oaks. The trees grew, and the bodies within the breach were pushed back—or were caught up in the unfurling branches and hanging like ripe fruit. The trees grew until they filled the breach, fortifying the once empty space.

"A miracle." Tom marveled at the trees. He reached out and placed his hand on the solid trunk. "I've always wanted to see a miracle."

The guards on the wall gathered around the trees, which extended over their heads and provided cover. One archer on the wall shouted in triumph. "The hounds have stopped their attack! They're leaving the wall!"

"They're retreating?" Silbrey called out to the archer. "Are they retreating?"

Another archer responded. "No, it looks like they are regrouping farther back. They're dragging the dead back with them."

Tom, along with the soldiers, looked at Silbrey expectantly. They were waiting for her command. Aubec was nowhere to be found. Oren was dead. Like it or not, they deferred to her. The widow of a humble shepherd, the ward of Penderyn's guildmaster, a street urchin under the care of a Taraki priest, and according to Thimbleberry Fig, the last of the fey who kept sleeping titans from destroying the world. Right now, she was the leader of a small army—the smallest of armies—besieged on all sides, with little hope of reinforcements to save them. She knew Bren Caius would be amused at the dire situation bequeathed to her.

The fearful and the battle-worn surrounded her, waiting for a response. She saw Sven from Guldur among them. He had survived. That gave her hope.

"Kret won't retreat," Silbrey stammered. She tried to imagine what Bren might say, but she had no idea. She spoke quietly, uncomfortable with the attention. Everyone leaned in to listen. "Retreat was never an option. If there's any hope of survival, it'll be because we hold them at this wall until there's not a single hound left to fight. We have no other option. We survived this last wave, and we were more than enough for them. And if we did it once, we can do it again. And we will." The soldiers nodded. She was not eloquent, but it was exactly what they needed to hear. "We're also going to take a moment to rest. Station a few sentries along the wall. Spread them out and rotate them throughout the night. The hounds could attack again at any time. Or maybe, like with Dahlia Tulan's mercenaries on the eastern wall—they'll wait us out."

Silbrey gave them the facts without any false hope or complications. The soldiers listened, knowing—if they survived—they would remember her words and share them with others. These were the words of Silbrey, the woman who made trees grow from the blood-soaked earth to fill the breach in the west wall, the woman who was friends with Bren Caius and was there when she died, the woman who faced Kret on the battlefield and lived—the woman with a wooden staff, a wooden shield, adamantine breastplate, and no boots. Silbrey's legend grew with each word, and she could do little to dissuade new myths. While she spoke, her thoughts strayed to the sleeping titans. Would this battle even matter if they awoke?

She felt a slight drop in the temperature and a heaviness in the air. A storm was coming once the air cooled further in the evening. Did this knowledge come from her fey senses or her experience working on a farm? She could not say. She did not look forward to fighting in the rain.

"When you eat and drink tonight, lift a pint for the fallen," Silbrey said. "We may join them soon enough."

\* \* \*

Silbrey opened the door to a supply room in the guard tower. The tower was one of two, built on either side of the main west gate. Among the provisions, she saw Aubec—sitting on the floor, crouched over his spellbook. A candle, melted to the base, illuminated the small room, casting shadows on the stone wall and the stone-faced mage. Aubec moved his fingers above the words, tracing his path as he read, but careful not to touch the page. He mumbled to himself, committing the words to memory. He looked like Yurig—as Silbrey remembered her son on the boat to Rhyll and at Sage Hall—lost in his studies, engrossed by whatever secrets that book held.

"There you are," Silbrey said.

Aubec held a finger up to indicate he needed a moment. He finished the line he was reading, and he looked at Silbrey with a sleepy expression on his face.

"Silbrey, you're alive."

"And so are you. When did you leave the fight?"

Aubec closed his spellbook and patted the cover.

"I cast what I could from the walls. After that, I was useless. I saw you returning, and it seemed like a good moment to excuse myself to study and regain my spells. I could pick up a sword, but it would be a disappointment, especially after seeing what I could do with magical fire."

"No, I understand," Silbrey responded. "You're worth more to us as a mage—and this," Silbrey gestured to the book, "is what mages do."

"When traveling, I keep my book in a dried calf's bladder. It's watertight, and I'm so thankful for it. If the book had been damaged when the ship sunk, my life's work would have been ruined. That will be my first lesson for your son: store your book with care."

"You were sinking to the bottom of Tu'enya Bay, and you were worried about your book? If you had lost it, so what? You have Yurig's book. Couldn't you transcribe those spells?"

Aubec blanched at the suggestion. "Every book is different and must be mastered on its own terms. The notations for similar effects may differ from book to book. It would be like learning a new language, divorced from any native speakers, written in a new script you've never seen before. Yurig took his book from Speck. In some ways, it will speed along his education. In other ways, it will be a hindrance."

Aubec stood up. The room was smaller now that they stood uncomfortably close, face to face. Aubec looked around her toward the door, but Silbrey wasn't ready to leave.

"The soldiers are looking at me like I'm the high general. With Oren gone, we need to designate a new leader. I'm not comfortable with it falling to me. You were a veteran of the War of the Hounds. You have the experience and the training. You're the obvious choice."

"You don't seem too upset about Oren's death," said Aubec.

"You saw him after Bren died. He died with her. Oren lost the trust of his soldiers because they were afraid he'd get them killed. Maybe a few more of them would've survived if they had followed someone like you."

Aubec shook his head. "For most of these soldiers, I was their teacher at Sage Hall. Once you've fallen asleep during my lecture on the elven empires, it's hard to see me as someone you'd follow into battle."

"Don't recast yourself as the stodgy, old academic."

Silbrey held her ground. "Once you see someone incinerate the enemy with well-placed words and a wave of their hands, yeah, you'd follow that person into battle." Aubec tried to protest, but Silbrey continued. "You may not be Bren the Beloved or have your pretty face minted on all the coins. But only one of us knows battle strategy. I was a street-level assassin when I was a child. I'm not the person you want leading the charge."

"And yet, you seem to find yourself leading the charge."

"Just promise me," Silbrey said, "you won't hide away again and leave me with the speeches."

"Neither one of us wants to command."

Aubec matched Silbrey's stubbornness with his own. If having an older brother was like this, then Silbrey was happy to be the last of her kind, the last of the tree-born fey.

"It's not a matter of 'want.' This is an office for someone from Rhyll. After the siege, if we survive, I cannot stay here to play politician."

"Is this about the 'larger forces' you mentioned at Bren's funeral?"

"Yes, and why Kret is trying to get into Aberton. The grove at the center of the city. They belong to the fey. Kret wants to cut them down."

"What do you mean?" Aubec rarely asked questions he didn't have the answer to, but this talk of fey confounded him.

"Certain fey, the tree-born, pacify the titans under the earth. It's how I can put people to sleep. It's all tied to my purpose, my role. The tree-born are now scarce. I may be the only one left. And the trees in this grove are special—they belong to the fey. Kret wants to cut them down to help wake the titans."

Aubec tried to make sense of it. "He makes a ruckus. Wakes titans. Destroys everything."

"He's the beast that breaks the world."

"And you are—?"

"I'm not a high general."

"You may be something greater." Aubec spoke in a soft voice. He gave her a sincere bow. Silbrey was touched. "Even though you are not the high general, may I advise you on the state of this siege?"

"I suppose," Silbrey said.

"We can wait it out. Aberton was built for withstanding sieges, but we don't have an army to rescue us. However, we can take advantage of the fact that Dahlia Tulan's eastern front and Kret Bonebreaker's western front are not communicating. Kret is rushing the wall. Dahlia is waiting."

"You think we should try to bust through Dahlia's army?"

"Look at you," Aubec said, pointing at her, impressed. "A street-level assassin, and you're thinking like a scholar of war strategy."

"It's common sense. The best shot to take is before the other person thinks the fight has started. Dahlia Tulan expects Kret to win the battle for them. She's holding her ground."

"That makes her a more appealing target—"

Faint thudding noises came from the outside. A pause. A few more dull, heavy sounds, and then the sounds increased in frequency. For a moment, it sounded like the rain, but the sound grew louder—too loud even to be hail—and then came the screams.

Silbrey rushed outside. She looked out to the bailey adjacent to the west wall. Dead bodies were falling from the night sky. Each time one hit the ground, there was a thud. The bodies were of the soldiers who had died earlier that day, twisting through the air and crashing to the ground. Oren's body was among the broken. Silbrey heard, beyond the walls, the snap of a release and a whoosh. Catapults. Kret was catapulting the dead into the city.

The townsfolk watched from open doorways and window shutters pushed open. More dead fell into the city, not soldiers this time, but farmers—men, women, and children—murdered in raids from the gnolls' approach to the city. It was the kind of cruelty that Kret was capable of.

"Why is he doing this?" Aubec asked.

Silbrey remembered the violence Kret wrecked upon Bren's body. She remembered the maimed corpses of the people from Thistle. For Kret, flesh was meant to be torn. Flesh was nothing to him. He knew how the mutilation affected the ones left behind. He cherished their pain.

The range of the catapults extended well into the heart of the city. The bodies were being flung and scattered across Aberton. Some bodies landed on the ground. Some crashed onto the rooftops of the densely packed buildings. Silbrey could see the treetops of the oak grove, farther into the city. That was Kret's goal. That was where he wanted to be. And then, Silbrey had a revelation.

"These bodies are a diversion. He's catapulted himself into the city, among the dead." Her words felt even more true once she uttered them. This was not a hunch. He was in Aberton. She knew it.

Silbrey ran across the bailey and into the city, trying her best to avoid the bodies littered upon the open spaces. Aubec ran after her, trying to keep up.

When they arrived at the grove, half the trees had already

been sundered by Kret's axe. Sprites hid among the trees, cowering. The bodies of a few braver sprites were crushed and scattered. Within the darkness of the grove was a greater darkness. The shadowy beast's massive back heaved as he took in his destruction. He stopped and sniffed. His breathing slowed. His shoulders relaxed. He did not turn around, but he addressed Silbrey and Aubec.

"I've done you a favor, I have. Did you know this city was infested with fairies? I killed a few of them buggers, and I ain't done. I think that—"

A fireball erupted where Kret stood. Silbrey jumped. She panicked at the thought of the grove in flames, but Aubec concentrated his spell just on Kret, sparing the flora.

"We didn't need to hear his whole speech," Aubec said.

The dark figure rushed out of the inferno. The flames shrouded Kret. A trail of the fire followed him, marking his path straight toward Aubec. Kret hit Aubec with the flat face of his axe. With a cracking sound, Aubec flew backward and fell to the ground, unconscious.

The flames on Kret died out and smoldered. The smell was atrocious.

"I'm gonna save him for later. Kill him slow-like. I never respected that mage. Soon, I'll tear his tongue out." Silbrey struck at Kret, but he parried with his axe. "But what about you? I respect you, little mouse. You've got a different outlook, a killer's heart. Even Bren was too soft when it came down to it. But you? You've seen people beg for their lives. I like that feeling." Silbrey tried again and then a third time to hit Kret, but he blocked each attempt. "I think you like that feeling too, but it's been too long."

Rather than strike again, Silbrey took a few steps back to

assess the monster in front of her. She looked for a weakness and saw none. "I'd like to make you beg for your life," Silbrey said.

Kret was not fooled by her bravado.

"You think that's how it would go down," Kret laughed. "Little mouse, you know better. I am as inevitable as the elements that make up this trash heap of a world. Kill me. I'll come back in a different form, with a different name. There's no end to me."

Silbrey held her shield high and spun her staff. Then she stopped the spin and held the staff behind her, bracing it and waiting for a charge. She smiled. She had an idea, and it was terrible.

Kret did not hesitate. He charged at Silbrey. Behind her back, she shifted her staff from her right hand to her left. Ever since Dahlia broke Silbrey's left arm, when she was a child, Silbrey never used her staff with this hand. She was weaker and unpracticed with it, but she knew Kret would not expect a strike from her shield arm. She figured any hit would be better than him blocking each attempt from her right side. The strike connected. She sent Kret off his path as she hit him across the face. Kret reached out and grabbed Silbrey, dragging her to the ground with him.

This fight was not well-choreographed, the kind Aylers describe in their ballads. This was a sloppy scuffle as Kret and Silbrey rolled on the ground. Each taking whatever blows were available to them.

No one would sing songs about it.

Silbrey pinned him, her knees on his injured shoulder. She put all her weight upon her shield, which she had at Kret's throat. He could not get a decent swing with his axe, so he

clawed at her back, tearing jagged wounds, wounds which radiated fiery agony. She kept the shield at his throat. She would
not yield until she was certain she had snapped his neck.

Through her pain, Silbrey felt focused. She knew how to
fight through the pain. Anyone else would relent, but Silbrey
kept pressing down on Kret's neck with her shield. He gagged
on his blood, and it pleased Silbrey. She indulged in the malice.
Something about the grove made her feel powerful. In this
moment, all forms were mists of energy, colors as expanding
light. Everything was alive, and everything was connected. She
could feel distant sounds as a vibration in the air. She could feel
tremors under the earth. Another quake—greater than the one
before—was coming soon.

She was going to kill Kret. She would savor the moment,
even if he was destined to return.

Kret stopped clawing at her back and grabbed her thigh.
He lifted her off him and threw her. She hit the ground hard.
The remaining sprites came to her aid, helping her back to her
feet.

Kret also rose to his feet. He tried to say something, but his
windpipe was crushed, and no sounds would come except a
strained wheezing.

Silbrey felt the vibrations from the trees, as if they were
calling out to be commanded. They yearned for vengeance. She
saw motes of blue light dancing about her fingertips, and she
knew what to do.

"For someone ageless and immortal, you should know
better than to fight me among the trees." Her voice did not
sound like her own, but darker and layered.

Large roots sprung up from the earth and wrapped around
Kret's legs. He tried to pull free, but the roots held; they pulled

him down with such force he slammed into the ground. The closest tree stirred and bent toward Kret with a loud creaking and popping.

Silbrey had heard about the Living Forest of Ioah. The trees and plants moved as a single unit slowly across the land, following the rivers and streams. There were stories about travelers resting in the forest, and then they'd wake up to find that the forest had moved on without them—leaving them baffled in the middle of a vast wasteland. Silbrey knew it wouldn't be possible to sleep through such a migration. The trees in the grove roared with the cracking of each movement.

The roots let go of Kret, while a thick branch wrapped around him. He chopped at it with his axe, but the tree whipped Kret back to the ground as a child might fling a poppet. The axe fell from Kret's hands. Another branch reached for Kret, entangling him and pulling him taut between the two trees. His arms and legs were stretched beyond breaking. His flesh was tearing at the axis points of his body.

Silbrey could tell the pain was immense, even for a being such as Kret. He snarled and growled at her. He had nothing left. She leaned forward and looked into his eyes. He was indeed ancient. His spirit had raged across Efre Ousel for untold centuries. He had seen the world when giants and dragons ruled it. He had been there when the elves migrated across the four continents. He had seen fire fall like rain upon the earth. And now, he was helpless before Silbrey. She noticed a blue light in his eyes. It was herself reflected in the darkness of his glare. She was glowing blue, illuminated in power. She was the only light in the grove.

Her awareness spread across Amon. The earthquake was imminent. Gydan and Maricel were safe. Yurig was studying his spellbook underneath the oak tree at Sage Hall. He had a lantern near him, so he could read at night. He sat by the tree because he missed his mother. "I'm sorry, Yurig. I miss you too," she whispered. He looked up from his book as if he had heard these words.

Silbrey returned her attention to Kret. The time had come. She leaned even closer. "Watch this."

With a wave of her hand, the branches binding Kret pulled and ripped him apart. He was torn in two. Blood and organs spilled out. His entrails steamed in the cool air. The trees released him, and his body slumped to the ground with a wet noise. The sprites looked at Silbrey in awe. She thought of Bren. *The gods are big, but so are we.* She knew what Bren had meant. Among the trees that had once belonged to her kind, she felt like a god.

She sensed that Aubec had regained consciousness. He had a blinding headache. He walked toward her on unsteady feet. His mind could not grasp the glowing form in front of him.

"Where's Silbrey?" Aubec asked in confusion. He reached out to her.

"Don't touch me. My power is too great."

Aubec held up his hand to shield his eyes against the light. His face was stricken with horror at the sight of Kret's remains. "What happened?"

"I am Ald'yovlet, born of the trees, rooted in the earth. I see everything. I sense everything. Would you have preferred a more humane death for the beast who murdered Bren and butchered everyone in Thistle?"

Aubec was silent. He understood power, but to an extent. He was limited by the hours in a day he could spend studying his spells. He could only cast what was written down. He followed the directions as a yeoman would. She gave the directions. She was beyond judgment.

Silbrey could feel Kret's raging spirit leave his body—filled with anger, and yet delighting in Silbrey's condemnation. His spirit descended into the earth, and Silbrey knew she had made a mistake. Whether Bren knew it or not, she was right to keep him alive and imprisoned. Even though Bren had changed her mind in the end, her first impulse was the right one. Kret was less dangerous while living.

The earthquake hit hard. Silbrey clenched her teeth. Her muscles tightened. She felt immense pain behind her eyes. Her nose bled from the shift in pressure. Her ears pounded and her head throbbed. The light surrounding her snuffed out as the earth shook. Her awareness dimmed. No longer a god. The sprites held onto the branches that swayed with the earth. Aubec knelt down. He cupped his hands over his ears. The pressure shift was overwhelming, and it would not pass for some time.

The first earthquake, during the funeral of Bren Caius, came with a rolling fury—rippling across the vulnerable land. With this second earthquake, everything all at once convulsed. The earthquake would be known as *Il Van Naran*, a Volir phrase meaning "the violent dream." It's a phrase used to describe the falling sensation, the sudden jolting reaction that happens when someone is almost asleep. Days after *Il Van Naran*, people described it as if Amon herself, the titan owl, had jumped awake and then resumed her fitful slumber.

The wild spasms of this earthquake continued for an unbearable span. Moment after terrifying moment, when it seemed the worst was over, the violent act intensified. Finally, the ground dropped several feet. Houses collapsed. Voices inside the houses screamed and then were silent.

The earthquake was over. But the horror that followed would haunt the survivors for the rest of their days.

Black waters surged into the city from Tu'enya Bay to the south and from the Ringaré Sea to the north. The water extended far into Aberton. The strong current flowed in and receded. It dragged hundreds of people into the open waters. The night was too dark for anyone to make sense of what was happening. They held onto whatever floating debris was available. This debris was both a lifeline and a noose. It kept them from sinking, but the dense mass made it impossible to swim back to land. Of the people pulled out by the sudden flooding, none returned. Their cries for help went unanswered and grew fainter as they drifted farther from shore.

The walls surrounding Aberton cracked and then fell in a series of large flakes until nothing was left. The walls had defined the city. Now they were gone. The proud walls reduced to pebbles. Rocky remains outlined the city along the east and the west, along the flooded north shore and the southern one. Aberton was exposed. Nothing stood between the city—its devastated buildings, the vulnerable people within—and two armies on either side. The earthquake had done its damage. The monsters and mercenaries could flood into the city and make the depredation complete.

The grove was at the center of Aberton, equidistant from the north and south shores. Silbrey and Aubec were safe from the invading waters. The rush of water was a low thrum. It shook

Silbrey's chest and stomach. Silbrey could also hear the far-off shouts of the gnoll army moving closer.

She caught the glance of a bewildered Aubec, still on the ground. Aubec looked in all directions, trying his best to assess the threats. They were too numerous. "Silbrey, what do you sense?"

Silbrey closed her eyes and placed her hands upon the earth. She took a deep breath. She felt a portion of the power return. She narrated her observations to Aubec.

"The gnolls are approaching the city. They will funnel toward the center. They're avoiding the flooded areas. Dahlia's army is in disarray from the earthquake, but they're mustering at the fallen east wall at the center point. They're ready to take the city as well. They—"

"I've got it!" Aubec shouted. The pure glee of his laugh startled Silbrey. He was crying. He was laughing. He crawled around on his hands and knees, gathering acorns. He held a pile of acorns to her. "Can you make them grow? Like you did before?"

"Yes, it doesn't drain me like—"

In his joy, Aubec dropped the acorns and hugged Silbrey. He was cackling in his manic delight. "It will work. I know it will." Aubec reached down and picked up the acorns again, handing them off to the sprites that gathered around the strange mage. "Get all the acorns you can carry!"

"What's the plan?" Silbrey asked, more confused than annoyed, but both feelings were there in fair measure.

"Isn't it amazing?" Aubec exclaimed, as if he hadn't even been listening to Silbrey.

"What?"

"Fey," Aubec gestured to the sprites flitting about him,

gathering acorns. "Fey *are* real! Like from the stories I heard as a child, they're real."

"You didn't believe me, back at Sage Hall, when I told you I was a fey?"

"I believed there was something to what you were saying," Aubec smiled, "but now, I see, and it's extraordinary."

Silbrey grabbed Aubec's shoulders. "You must tell me your plan."

"Aberton is more than a city. The isthmus that Aberton occupies makes it a gateway between the trade cities to the east and the rest of the continent. They collect a toll for everyone traveling the coast, and the thoroughfare between the east and west gates runs through the middle of Aberton. If those sprites can place the acorns along that road on either side, then you can grow those trees and form walls. We can herd the gnoll army through there and out the other end to Dahlia's army."

"We'll get them to fight each other," Silbrey realized. "The gnolls won't care that Dahlia is their ally, not with Kret gone."

The hummingbird flutter of sprites surrounded Silbrey and Aubec. Each one holding a pile of acorns, ready to carry out Silbrey's command.

"Go, quickly," Silbrey said to them. "Place the acorns two yards apart."

The sprites took off. Aubec and Silbrey followed.

Tom the Barber, along with Sven from Guldur and a few other soldiers, stood where the west gate had once been. The captain was not with them. Many of the archers and other guards had lived in the south section. When they went to take their rest from the battle, and the floods came, and they never returned.

A few drops of rain began to fall. Tentatively at first, but the rain increased with each passing moment.

The gnolls approached as a shadowy mass. Since there was no wall and no archers upon it to fire at them, there was no need to rush. They moved around the trenches, away from the flooded areas to the north and south.

The soldiers held out their weapons, waiting for the charge. All, except Tom, trembled. One soldier fainted. His eyes rolled in the back of his head, and he dropped into the mud. Tom helped him to his feet.

"This looks bad," Tom said, although his voice sounded as casual as if he was ordering a drink at the tavern. "But we're all going to die at some point. At least we know our end will not be boring. Eh? And remember the last time—"

"Tom, shut up," said one of the older soldiers.

"Hold on, I'm making my point," Tom rebuked him. "Remember the last time you thought you were going to die. What happened? Your old teacher from Sage Hall came out of the bay and rained fire on all these hounds. I bet you didn't—"

And then, like before, fire erupted upon the approaching hounds. The blast of fire lit up the night. That flash of light revealed the true size of the gnoll army. The soldier who had fainted earlier, his knees buckled, but Tom caught him. Tom gestured to the flaming gnolls, howling in pain. "See? Isn't that remarkable?"

"I can do that again, if you want," said a voice. The soldiers turned. Aubec and Silbrey stood there. Aubec finished the careful gestures of his fire spell. And behind them, dawn was breaking on the eastern sky. The stormy clouds were dark overhead, but they were a purple and red hue along the east.

Silbrey was heartened to see the soldiers were still willing to fight. In a way, she esteemed these soldiers above the great Oren of Angnavir. They were better soldiers, not because they were willing to die on the battlefield, but because they fought so others could live. The earthquake, the flood had claimed many lives, but there were survivors. There would always be survivors. These soldiers wanted to see them live. The soldiers were afraid—maybe even Tom, though he hid it well—and yet they stayed. The walls had fallen, but the soldiers stood tall.

Aubec explained the plan. He would use his spellcraft to hold back the gnoll army for as long as he could. Silbrey would grow the trees where the west wall had been and along the street that ran through the center of Aberton. It would be an arboreal barrier to protect the remaining citizens, keeping the gnolls from scattering into the city. The soldiers would then lure the gnolls along the street, fighting and retreating to guide them through toward Dahlia's army on the eastern front.

"Sit back and enjoy the chaos," Tom said. "I don't know if it's going to work, but I like it."

"I've already started," Silbrey said, as blue light sparkled around her. The sprites had worked quickly. She could sense the acorns breaking open, tiny roots searching the new world and digging deep. The dancing lights flowed from Silbrey and streamed throughout the city.

The little girl who had called Silbrey "the acorn woman" stepped into the rain from the wreckage of her house to see the blue light shoot past. The girl jumped back as the saplings broke through the ground and stretched skyward.

The waves of blue light spread across Aberton from west to east. Dahlia Tulan saw the blue light approaching. Her eyes widened.

The trees grew along the western border and the thorough-

fare. The trees were pliable. Silbrey willed them to grow
further, to weave in and around with the trees on either side,
creating a braided wall. The woven pattern reminded Silbrey of
the braid she saw Maricel wear when she was caged in the
aviary. Silbrey thought of Maricel's face—the dappled light
upon her. The plaited trees matured, tightening the weave,
strengthening the partition.

Despite the blue light, the darkness increased around them
as the trees grew taller. The walled street was a valley of
shadow.

Aubec cast another fireball and then another. This time, it
wasn't placed in the center of the army where it would do the
most damage. He hit the flanks, herding the gnolls toward the
center, guiding them to the thoroughfare.

Once the gnolls were close enough to throw their spears,
Aubec shouted to the soldiers, "Move back! Everyone move
into the thoroughfare." Aubec walked backward as the gnolls
moved faster upon them. The rain was heavy. Every command
had to be shouted so that the soldiers could hear him over the
downpour. "Behind me!"

Aubec cast the force wall spell, which now encircled
Aubec, Silbrey, Tom, and the remaining soldiers, just as the
gnolls pressed against it. Some gnolls tried to penetrate the wall
with their spears and swords, but the wall blasted them back.
As more gnolls pressed against the wall, the gnolls were unable
to escape the blast. The spell punished them until they were
bloody husks.

The spell held back the gnolls, but the rain passed easily
through the barrier, which made the storm even more
menacing and unwelcome.

Aubec moved the translucent wall far enough back so that

they were well within the darkened thoroughfare. It would be a long walk to the other end, and Silbrey remembered his words from the last time. The spell wouldn't last.

The gnolls continued to hurl themselves at the wall. They kept coming until the soldiers had difficulty seeing anything other than the mangy gnolls pressed against the flickering force.

"Aubec, will you be able to maintain this spell all the way to the other side?" Silbrey asked as she watched the gnolls pile onto the top of the protective barrier. She brushed her wet hair from her face. The purple and red dawn, turning a vibrant orange, was barely visible with the summiting gnolls who blotted out the morning sky. Some began to climb the trees to get over Aubec's wall and to the other side. The gnolls surrounded them.

"Eventually, this bubble is going to pop," Aubec strained to get out the words, "and we're going to have some new problems that look like our old problems."

"Hounds?" Tom asked.

"These damn hounds," Aubec said.

Each soldier within the barrier stood back-to-back and held out their drawn weapons. They moved down the thoroughfare, while Aubec maintained his magic. The gnolls swarmed the barrier. The numbers were so great they were as much at risk from trampling each other as from the force blasting any gnoll trying to pierce the barrier.

"I can put them into a deep sleep," Silbrey said. "But the last time I focused on so many, I couldn't do it again without getting dizzy. But it should buy us time to get out from under them, create some space, and continue to the eastern border."

"I should remind everyone," Tom said, holding out his stiletto daggers, "the goal was never for us to make it to out alive. Our goal was to lead these hounds to Dahlia's army. If the hounds keep going this way, truly, we played our part."

Silbrey gave Tom an incredulous look. "I'd like to live. Let's make that one of our goals."

"Dare to dream," Tom shrugged.

More gnoll bodies slammed against the barrier.

Silbrey could see beads of sweat gathering on Aubec's forehead as he struggled with the spell. His eyes were bloodshot. The muscles in his neck strained. She placed a hand on his shoulder. "Let the spell go. It's okay. I'll take it from here."

Aubec exhaled. All energy drained from him. The barrier blinked out of existence, and the gnolls on top of the barrier collapsed upon the people below. With nothing to press against, the gnolls stumbled forward. The ones at the front were trampled. But the ones who maintained their footing rushed toward Silbrey and the rest.

Motes of light flickered around Silbrey. The shimmering blue rippled from her staff, her surrogate tree, toward the marauding gnolls. Their eyelids grew heavy. They wobbled where they stood, and then all fell asleep, falling over, one after another.

The soldiers disentangled themselves from the unconscious gnolls.

Many more gnolls crowded into the thoroughfare. They brandished their jagged weapons, ready for a slaughter. The braided trees confined them to the street.

"Run!" Silbrey yelled to the soldiers. Everyone heeded her command except Tom. He stood his ground.

"I can hold them back," Tom explained. "I can give you and the others a better head start."

"A head start right into Dahlia's army," Silbrey said. "I need you by my side. You have nothing to prove here."

Something in Silbrey's words struck Tom. He looked over at her. He was soaked from the rain. Droplets clung to his hair and face.

"Okay then, let's go."

No hound could resist a chase. When Silbrey and Tom started running, the gnolls dashed after them. As a pack, they pursued. In the shadowy recesses, they moved as a darker mass against the dark. It reminded Silbrey of Kret Bonebreaker, now titanic in scale and formless. Their steps upon the cobbled street sounded like a low rumbling thunder.

Silbrey and Tom raced down the thoroughfare, catching up with the other soldiers. Unlike the meandering cart paths in most cities, this thoroughfare carved a straight shot from one end to the other. Up ahead, they saw Dahlia's waiting army. The plan was working. The sun rose along the horizon where the storm had not yet reached. Silbrey had never seen such a magnificent sky before.

Sven from Guldur looked at Silbrey as they sprinted from the gnolls. They both had noticed the beautiful morning sky, framed against the moody storms. He smiled. They had made it this far. A serrated spear pierced his back and tore through his chest. His smile faded and turned to confusion. He fell to the ground, hitting his head against the cobblestone street. Silbrey stopped running. She saw Sven's vacant face, partially submerged in the puddles accumulating on the street. He was gone. Her heart twisted. Silbrey thought of Annet, Sven's mother, the fortune teller who worked at the market in Guldur. Silbrey had saved Sven from drowning, and she had promised herself she'd return him safely to his mother, but that wasn't a promise she could keep.

Then her twisted heart burned. The heat of this anger spread across her chest and face. Silbrey screamed at the gnolls. White light radiated all around her. She thought about commanding the braided trees to enclose the thoroughfare and crush all the gnolls. The trees shook in response, but the braiding was too strong to allow them to move. The gnolls halted. They were terrified of this woman. Some ran back the other direction. The anger also scared Silbrey. There was no end to it. She could drink from this cup, and it would never empty. It would never quench her thirst. More anger poured out. She knew where it came from.

As a child at Dahlia's estate, she never slept easily. She was always afraid of the sound of a door opening, of a mother-shaped shadow against the wall, of a clinched fist. She would curl into a ball to survive Dahlia's violent episodes. She would think about the beautiful queen from Timon's dream—if she would ever come to rescue her. Silbrey cried and begged for the beatings to end, hoping Dahlia would grow tired and go back to sleep.

There were so many things she never talked about, but these thoughts were never far from her. The particulars of the abuse she endured. The babies she lost in childbirth. The husband taken from her.

The anger was itself a storm.

Silbrey wasn't of this world. She knew that. Like Kret, sometimes she wanted it all to break and burn. This world was so bent upon its own destruction. Her husband was dead. Two unnamed children buried. Sven would never return home. Maybe the world deserved its fate.

Silbrey heard the flitting noise of hummingbird wings and the voice that sounded like tiny bells.

"Ald'yovlet," the sprite's voice was gentle. It stirred Silbrey from her rage. "The hounds are afraid of Ald'yovlet. They will not continue while one shines so bright, but Ald'yovlet needs them to go forward, not back. That was the plan, yes? Ald'yovlet is so close."

"I couldn't save you from Kret," Silbrey said.

"Ald'yovlet saved some and not others," Fig said. "Always how it would be and will be. Ald'yovlet must keep running. Ald'yovlet has unfinished work."

\* \* \*

Whenever a surviving soldier would convene at a tavern, people would always want to hear the story about the Siege of Aberton. The soldier would oblige if their bar tab was covered and the drinks flowed. By the time they got to the part of the story where the gnolls were led to Dahlia's army, the soldier, without fail, would chuckle as they recalled the look upon every face of every person waiting for them. The soldier would try their best to mimic the wide-eyed, open-mouthed confusion, accompanied by the realization they were doomed.

They would talk about how a handful of soldiers ran out, looking as though they wanted to fight the army all by themselves, death by valor. But right on their heels came the gnolls. More hounds than any of those mercenaries had ever seen in their lives. Kret was dead, and these gnolls had no warlord to command them. The hounds saw more humans, and so they fought.

The soldier at the tavern would explain how they moved

out of the way, content to sit out this fight—and let the gnolls and mercenaries settle the matter between themselves, fighting in the mud. All except Tom the Barber and Silbrey, the close friend of Bren Caius.

Even though Silbrey had barely known the high general, she became part of the Northern Light myth. Sometimes, she was described as a childhood friend, and in other tellings, as a cousin. The tavern would hang on every word either way.

Silbrey fought with her staff, taking down both hounds and mercenaries. The soldier would delight in explaining Silbrey's odd fighting style, wielding a staff in one hand and a shield in the other. Then, the soldier would share how Tom faced a goliath, a true goliath in service to Dahlia Tulan. Tom climbed onto his back and slit the goliath's throat, which gave Tom a second name: Tom the Giant-Slayer.

The battle did not last long, shorter sometimes than even the retelling of it. Despite the many variations of the story, it always ended the same. The gnolls wiped out every treasonous mercenary. A few hounds remained. Aubec Skarsol cast a fire spell, which incinerated the rest.

Only Dahlia Tulan survived, or so the story goes. The Penderyn guildmaster, covered in mud, stumbled before Silbrey and fell to her knees. She held her arms out, asking for death. Dahlia was not afraid to die. She laughed, a hideous crazed laugh. She repeated the words, "Kill me. Kill me." Silbrey would not do it. She knew Dahlia Tulan had conspired with Kret Bonebreaker to kill Bren Caius, to destroy Thistle, and to besiege Aberton. She knew Dahlia Tulan's crimes required something greater than death. It required justice. Silbrey had Dahlia bound in chains and taken to Rhyll where she would face the families of the victims, day after day, to get a full accounting of her wickedness—and only then would she receive a proper sentencing for her many crimes.

The soldier would provide as many details as they could remember about that horrible night when *Il Van Naran* struck and the floods came, of the miraculous walls that sprouted from the ground, and of the final battle, a generation later, to end the War of the Hounds.

But the soldier would never share one detail. It was just one word. It never fit easily into the narrative and was simple enough to omit.

Silbrey had called Dahlia Tulan "mother."

\* \* \*

Maricel woke up in her old bed. She was back at the farming community. Her hair had been braided. Her mother had probably done it while she slept.

Maricel had slept so much over the past few days. She was still disoriented and struggled to put together the details. Gydan, the dragon, and that Taraki priest had found her. They removed the arrows. Maricel used the mistletoe to heal herself —a trick her mother had taught her, but she had never been able to perform until then.

The druidic magic was not academic, nor did it require some deep well of emotion. It was neither head nor heart—and so it never made much sense to Maricel. This magic occupied a liminal space, employing both natural objects and wisdom from a bygone age. In her near-death state, the old lessons had made sense.

Maricel vaguely remembered being taken back to her child-hood home. Her mother and father were horrified when they saw her covered in dried blood and her drooping face. Her mother applied more druidic salves to help with the healing, but nothing would fix the paralysis from the poisoned arrow. Maricel ached, and she felt chills, but only on her left side.

She remembered the second earthquake several days ago, which shook her out of bed. She knew the community's main barn and grain shed had fallen during the quake. She wanted to help, but she couldn't walk. Her right leg would not obey. She couldn't leave her room without someone to carry her. Maricel's whole world had been reduced to this room, but she could hear the destruction outside her open window—and it broke her heart. She remembered, as a child, the celebration when they raised that barn. It took days to build and seconds to destroy.

As Maricel stirred from her sleepy recollections to a wakeful awareness, she noticed her face felt sticky. She had been drooling again. She reached for a rag next to her bed and vigorously wiped her face. The drool had a thick, mucus consistency. And even though no one was there to see her, Maricel was embarrassed. She had never thought of herself as vain about her looks, but it mattered to her. She used to be beautiful.

She touched the right side of her face, and it felt like nothing at all. Maricel couldn't fully close her right eye, so her mother applied a sap-like adhesive to it. Crust formed around the eyelid. She couldn't help it; once again, Maricel cried. The sobs came out in an ugly, slurred moan. Unlike every time before, no one entered to console her. Usually, her mother, father, or Gydan would come in to check on her. On one awkward occasion, the Taraki priest, Timon, tried to offer some wisdom while rambling about the unknowable will of the twelve named gods. Cyru, the dragon, rarely came into the house—and instead occupied their time ratting. Ausdre told Maricel that, within a day, the miniature dragon had rid the farming community of every rodent, and then proceeded to eliminate the rat population throughout the region.

When no one came, she stopped crying and listened. The house was quiet. She heard footsteps. The floorboards creaked. Silbrey stood in her doorway. She was bruised, but alive.

"I would've come sooner, but I got lost trying to find this place." Silbrey smiled. She had a pitying look.

Maricel did not want Silbrey to see her like this. She rolled on her side and pulled the quilt over her head. She tried to say, "go away," but all that came out was unintelligible. Maricel cried again.

Maricel felt the mattress give. Silbrey had laid down next to her. Silbrey put her arm around Maricel and nuzzled her face into Maricel's neck. The closeness caused goosebumps to race along Maricel's skin. She missed having Silbrey in bed next to her. Silbrey's strong arms wrapped around her. Silbrey spoke. Her mouth was an inch from Maricel's ear. She whispered, "I'm sorry. This is all my fault."

Maricel cried even harder at the sound of Silbrey's voice. Silbrey misconstrued the crying as a rejection and so she pulled away, but Maricel grabbed her arm and held her there.

Maricel tried saying, "no, don't go." The words were a jumble, but Silbrey understood.

"I asked you to go find Gydan," Silbrey whispered into her ear, "but it wasn't safe. It's my fault this happened."

"Sil, you did nothing wrong," Maricel spoke slowly, putting space between each word, hoping to make herself more coherent.

"Nothing? We both know that's not true," Silbrey said. "Please, turn around, look at me."

Maricel turned. It took some effort. Silbrey was there, face to face with Maricel. So close they could kiss. Maricel forgot everything else. She just wanted to love this woman and be loved in return.

"You're still you," Silbrey said. "And nothing has changed about how I see you, or how I feel about you. I have plenty that I regret, but my biggest regret was not trusting you."

"Last time we spoke, you said you don't know me," Maricel said. Silbrey shook her head, indicating she didn't understand. Maricel said it again, slower this time.

"There is some truth to it. I don't know much about your life, but I know your heart. Your heart is pure, and that's why I need you by my side." Silbrey rested her forehead against Maricel's. This confession was not easy for Silbrey. "I'm damaged. I have so much anger in me. I feel like half a person. I need you to be my other half. Kret's spirit—or the Ancient Beast, whatever he's called—is still out there, and I can't defeat him if I'm giving in to his ways." Silbrey looked at Maricel again and stroked her cheek. "Here's what I think you should do. You're going to rest and heal, and when you're ready, I want you to come with me and Gydan. We have unfinished work."

"Where are we going?"

"We're sailing to Raustfweg," Silbrey said. "Your mother had a mission. Find me and bring me back to her homeland—and I think I know why she was asked to do that. We're going to Alda Feren, the great tree of life, to stop the world from breaking."

The glint in her eye and lift in her voice hinted at hope.

*"The mother preferred her sorrows to all the joys of this world.
The entire forest quaked, the earth fell in, and the huge oak,
with its castles and its silver-fenced village, sank underground."*

*— from Stribor's Forest,
a Croatian fairy tale*

# VI

A FEW DAYS after the second earthquake *Il Van Naran* toppled the barn and the grain shed, the community worked tirelessly to rebuild them. These two buildings represented the center of their world. They needed them to keep their farms running. Other tasks could wait. But even after all their labor, the barn and grain shed didn't look like before. Propped up and patched, not restored. It reminded Ausdre that the community was getting old.

Many of the children had grown up and left, taking spouses and raising families elsewhere. What remained was a collective of old hands holding old hammers. She knew it was time to sell the land to the Welton heir and move on. The young noble was intent on taking up as much land as possible, even if he didn't have the serfs to work it. The feudal ways had been in decline for generations, but the aristocratic families still had the money. They challenged anyone living on freely owned lands.

Guildmasters of the bay cities fixed their prices and bargained behind closed doors. They preferred to deal with the nobles instead of negotiating a fair exchange. Many farmers held out hope the high general would intervene, but Bren Caius never did. And now she was gone, so what else was left to them? The common joke was: a young merchant asks the old farmer, "When is a good time to be a farmer?" The farmer responded, "I didn't know 'good' was an option." Selling the farmland to Welton would be easier and inevitable, but the farmers would hold out if they could.

Ausdre took a break from her work to sit on the bench outside their house. She needed to quiet her worried mind. She had hoped sowing in the south field would distract her from thinking about her daughter—confined to a bed and unable to do anything for herself. As she worked, she could see Maricel's open window, and she didn't have the energy to continue. So, she sat on the bench. She focused on her breathing and placed her hands, palms up, upon her lap. The air was heavier, more humid. A warm breeze fought against the cooler morning air. Summer would come early this year.

The child, Gydan, sat next to Ausdre. She had helped bring Maricel back—along with the Taraki priest and the tiny dragon. They had saved her daughter's life. And now, the child rarely left Ausdre's side. Even if Ausdre left the house in the morning before anyone else was awake, the child would find her. It took a while for Ausdre to realize the child was waiting for chores. She wanted to stay busy. She wanted to earn her keep while waiting for her mother, Silbrey. Both the priest and the child had helped in repairing the barn and shed. The child worked hard. She had lived on a farm. That was obvious. Whereas the priest was finished after only half a day's work, sweating and flushed red, exhausted to the point of delirium. Afterward, he was reassigned to simpler tasks such as fetching water and "overseeing," as he called it.

Regardless, their help was another debt Ausdre owed these visitors.

Ausdre had been so worried about her daughter's condition she didn't even think about Gydan. If the Taraki priest was being truthful—and priests of the named gods were known to exaggerate—then the child had been through so much. A father murdered. Fleeing from not one, but two homes. And then, she had to escape Rhyll, leaving her family behind, to avoid Kret Bonebreaker. She escaped capture on her journey to Penderyn. Every step of the way, she had narrowly avoided death.

Ausdre struggled with the events recounted to her by the priest and the child. As a druid from Raustfweg, she believed in the impossible and the transcendent. The world was filled with unknowable, unnamed power and dark visions that must be heeded. Such mysticism put her on a ship sailing from Raust-fweg to Amon in search of a true fey, a child born from a tree, to help keep titans asleep deep under the earth. Ausdre wasn't sure she even believed that anymore—despite the earthquakes. But as a farmer from Amon, the world diminished and became knowable. The seasons came and went. Seeds grew under the right conditions, which varied depending on the crop. She used her druidic spells to improve the conditions, to yield a greater bounty. That became an acceptable overlap of her two selves, which made the mysterious feel even more mundane.

Ausdre looked over at the girl, sitting obediently next to her. She felt a twinge of guilt at not being more attentive. The child had survived, but not without scars. This child needed to be useful. She needed to be busy, occupied, vigilant. And when she felt her obligations were done for the day, she sneaked into the forest. Ausdre asked Gydan what she did in the forest. Gydan said she practiced with her sword. Ausdre's eyes widened. She hadn't noticed the child carrying a sword. Apparently, Bren Caius had given her the sword, and she needed to be worthy of it.

If this was the daughter of a true fey, the one Ausdre lost all those years ago, then Gydan herself was an impossibility. Ausdre had said so to Maricel. A fey and a human could not have a child together. It would be like a unicorn mating with a mule. Those were her words. Yet here Gydan was, having survived monsters and mages, and now in possession of Bren Caius's fabled sword. The pragmatic farmer in Ausdre dismissed it all in favor of a simpler explanation. Their mother must not have been a true fey after all. The vision which sent her to Amon was the rambling of zealots.

"My mother's almost here," Gydan said.

"How do you know?"

"Cyru has been scouting between here and Aberton. They saw my mother walking this way." Gydan tapped her head to indicate their psychic connection and then pointed to the northwest. Cyru was a small pinprick on the horizon. "I want to run to her, but you should see her first."

Ausdre felt Gydan's small hand on her back, pushing her to get off the bench and start walking.

"Why me?" Ausdre screeched. She reacted more strongly to this suggestion than she had intended.

Gydan gave Ausdre a quizzical look. "Isn't she why you're here? Aren't you why she's here? Your lives are, like," Gydan paused to find the right words. "It's like a braid. Your lives are all a tangle."

Ausdre wanted to correct Gydan on associating braids with tangled hair. The people of Amon didn't appreciate the weaving art quite like her Raustfweg kin, but she let it go.

Ausdre walked for some time until she saw a woman approaching. Silbrey was more battle worn and grim than Ausdre expected. She was muscular and walked with a menacing swagger, predatory. She carried her wooden staff like a weapon, not a walking stick.

"A steady journey," the woman said.

"And a clear path," Ausdre responded.

"Is this the farming community where Maricel was raised?"

"Aye. It is."

"Are you her mother, Ausdre?"

"Aye. I am."

"Is my daughter here? Is she okay?"

"Gydan is doing fine."

At hearing her daughter's name, Silbrey softened. She closed her eyes and breathed deep.

"You could post signs, you know," said Silbrey. "I got lost trying to find you."

"The farmers out here," said Ausdre, "we like being hard to find. If we need anything, we'll find you."

"I'm glad Maricel chose such a good hiding spot in the wide open—"

"She's been hurt." Ausdre interrupted. "Maricel ran into Dahlia Tulan's patrol. Your daughter and her friends, they found Maricel on the side of the road. They saved her life."

"Will she be okay?" Silbrey's voice went quiet and vulnerable.

Something about her words pierced Ausdre. Her voice cracked as she spoke. "No, I don't think she will be okay. She'll live, but I don't know what kind of life she can have."

"That's true of anyone," Silbrey said. "If she hasn't given up, then it's not up to us to decide what her limits will be."

Ausdre's eyes met Silbrey's. Ausdre wanted to see something of that infant she had carried across the icy river so long ago, but she couldn't. Silbrey looked away, uncomfortable with the focus on her.

"Is it you? The true fey?" Ausdre asked.

"That's what everyone keeps telling me," Silbrey said. Then Silbrey had a question for Ausdre. "If you came to Amon believing I could stop the titans from waking, why didn't you come for me when Maricel started having visions? She knew I was in Penderyn. Why the spying? The lack of urgency?"

Ausdre hadn't rehearsed her answer, but she always knew what she would say to Silbrey, if given the chance.

"The elders of my village spoke with forest spirits. They believed a true fey would be born in the Hazelef Forest in Amon. They sent me and three others. We needed to bring the infant to Raustfweg to Alda Feren. The ancient tree has roots extending across all four continents. Alda Feren, with the fey's help, could calm the waking titans and stop the world from breaking. I had faith in my elders. I came here ready to save the world. When you slipped from my hands into that river, it shook my faith. I thought, how could the gods let it happen? The elders must have misunderstood. So, I started a new life. I got married and became a mother. And the world didn't end. I came to doubt it all. Even when my daughter started having visions, I doubted. Living my new life was easier than correcting my previous failures."

Silbrey did not respond. She was deep in thought. Maricel had told her mother about this habit Silbrey had. She would pause for so long, Maricel would wonder if Silbrey had anything further to say, and only then would she speak.

"You don't look *that* old," Silbrey said. The response was unexpected. "You must have been so young when you traveled to Amon, when you got married and became a mother. I understand escaping to a farm and hiding under the role of wife and mother. And like you, my old life kept calling."

Silbrey reached out to take Ausdre's hand, but then brought it back, unsure about this gesture of familiarity.

"You knew who Dahlia Tulan was—how cruel she was," Silbrey said. "Maricel found me through a vision. She knew I needed help. Instead, you told her to . . . ," Silbrey swallowed. The words were hard for her. ". . . to keep an eye on me and just observe? I was suffering."

Ausdre nodded her head, and she knew Silbrey would not like what she said next.

"You were a murderer. Whether Dahlia Tulan put you up to it or not, you made the choice to follow her. I didn't know if it'd be safe to have Maricel around you. And once you moved away, I didn't know if you were still loyal to Dahlia. Maricel got close to you, despite my warnings. Look what happened."

"She got hurt."

"The people around you are in constant danger," Ausdre said. "I know you see it. Promise me, once you've gone to Alda Feren and done what you need to do. Leave Maricel alone. Let her go. Let her live."

Silbrey's face flashed with anger. She looked at the ground to avoid eye contact and walked past Ausdre toward the farm, bumping her shoulder.

"I promise."

* * *

The Amoet was different from the ships that sailed Tu'enya Bay, the ones that ferried people to and from Rhyll. The Amoet was built to transport trade goods between Raustfweg and Amon on the open sea. This ship was a cog, discernible by its larger fore castle and stern castle. The stern castle included an upper deck, accessible by a ladder, and a lower deck, which had room for whatever supplies would not fit in the hull. The lower deck was also where the trapdoor to the hull's storage was located.

Between the stern castle and mast was the whipstaff, which protruded from the deck. The whipstaff handle was wrapped in leather for the comfort of Captain Hrutib as he steered. The rest of the whipstaff post had the names of loved ones carved into it. Sailors believed the names of family and friends left ashore had the power to distract Golwin from claiming lives.

A gold coin was nailed to the mast, a custom to honor Sarna'vot, the named god of trade and commerce. As the sailors walked past, they would reach out and touch the coin. It reminded them of why they were at sea, why they were away from their families, and why they risked their lives. Sailors who saved their coin and made shrewd investments along the trade routes could retire to a comfortable life and a wealth of stories to share.

The square sail was a dull white, adorned with a few markings, which served as navigational guidelines and indicated the ship's originating territory. The markings were discernible by only the captain and his son, who served as proxy. Hrutib could look through the cloth sail to the position of the sun without being blinded. A rope ladder extended from the starboard railing to the top of the mast. The mast bore the sun sigil of Bren Caius, a reminder to pirating ships that this vessel was under the Northern Army's protection and not worth the trouble.

Carved on the side of the cog was the name Amoet, the Volir word for "Wisdom." The captain gave the ship this name as a joke, since this line of work mostly attracted fools willing to risk their lives for a few extra silver coins.

The ship had appeared larger to Silbrey when she first boarded with Gydan, Cyru, and Maricel. However, once they were at sea and land escaped from view, the ship diminished in Silbrey's estimation. With each day, the ship became smaller and smaller. The seafaring vessel with its eighteen people felt more cramped. As a result of the earthquakes, the open sea beyond Tu'enya Bay was capricious. Waves grew taller, and the ocean more unpredictable.

Having taken this voyage several times, the crew liked to tease the passengers—an assemblage of Silbrey's group and a Raustfweg dwarf named Udger—for their discomfort. The crew teased them about their lack of sea legs and other matters they felt were essential to the sailing life. But as the journey continued, the teasing stopped. The roiling seas made every day treacherous and every moment a step too close to death. The sailors, too, felt worn down by this voyage. They couldn't poke fun when their own exhaustion was so apparent.

The crew tried to keep their concerns from the passengers, but Silbrey knew what they said. Silbrey's fey senses extended across the wood of the ship and allowed her to glimpse into their private discussions. Silbrey could sense the interconnections of nature, and this cog was part of the natural world. The cog was once a copse of trees in a forest near Illuin Faire.

Silbrey could feel the ship yearning for the forest—to spread its branches and leaves once again, for roots to dig into the soil. That desire never left even after the trees were cut down, split with hammer and wedge, shaped into planks, wetted and bent across rocks. The wood remembered its original state, even as the shipwright formed the frame and then applied the planks with double-clenched iron nails. The wood remembered, even as the shipwright dragged the structure to Illuin Faire's dry dock where the hull was tarred. These wordless memories were embedded into the grain of the wood itself. When Silbrey boarded, she could feel Amoet welcoming her. The voices of the crew, the insecurities and fears, all vibrated across the ship, passed obediently along to its fey guest. Silbrey wished she could shut out the messages and have some peace, but the trees had served the fey long before being cut down, and the trees knew their allegiance.

The crew murmured about how this voyage was different. The earthquakes in Amon continued across the ocean floor. Silbrey could feel the deep tremors disturbing the normally calm water of the Great Thayl'em Sea. The voyage was from west to east, but also up and down, as they rode the waves. For this reason, the passengers spent much of the day in the dark hull storage, crammed in with the cargo. And whenever they were allowed on the deck to empty chamber pots and stretch their legs, the passengers were never allowed beyond the stern castle to prevent someone falling overboard as the ship teetered and tottered upon the unsteady ocean. The crew did not envy the passengers and their confinement, nor did they want to be upon the deck, either. They had to be vigilant, for fear the

Amoet would cast them into the sea. Each sailor had a story of how they nearly fell over the railing, and each one knew there was no return. This fear of being lost to the sea tempered their criticisms of the passengers and reminded them of how small they were.

Silbrey also sensed the sailors talking about Aegir's proxy.

No one is more practical than a sailor. No one is more superstitious. And nowhere is this contradiction more apparent than in the role of proxy.

A ship won't set sail without a proxy. Even fishermen, a few feet from the shoreline, would feel uncomfortable getting into a boat without one. Often, the proxy was the captain's child. Once the proxy reached adulthood, they would either be assigned as one of the crew or they might captain a ship of their own. The captain would then find a new proxy, sometimes a sibling or a dockside orphan. The proxy's function was quite simple. They were to learn as much about sailing and naviga-tion as possible. They followed the captain and learned their ways. The proxy provided continuity from generation to gener-ation. They lived most of their lives on the sea, and they earned the respect of every sailor. But that was their function, not their purpose.

The proxy was to act as the living embodiment of Aegir, the named god of the sea. In Amon, he was called "Aegir," but each continent and culture had their own sobriquet. Aegir assumed the appearance of a young boy, susceptible to the foolish whims and impulses of any boy. To gain the favor of Aegir, his proxy was treated well on the ship—given the best quarters, the best food and drink, the utmost respect. Treat Aegir's proxy well, and the crew honored the sea god.

Captain Hrutib's son Vindel was too old to serve as proxy.

The boy was a man and had been one for a few years. He was old enough to have a spouse and a few children, but Vindel preferred the deck of his father's ship and the lavish treatment he received as proxy to captaining his own ship, which required handling all the responsibilities that came with it. The captain loved his son and was loath to admit it was time for him to move on.

Vindel's age was not a concern until this chaotic voyage made everyone weary of Aegir's temperament. Also, the arrival of Gydan—and her being younger than Vindel—further contrasted Vindel's unworthiness as proxy. The crew saw it as an omen when all the rats abandoned the ship the moment Gydan boarded, but Silbrey knew this was because Cyru traveled with them. The tiny red dragon had almost wiped out the rat population across the bay. These rats felt the threat of Cyru's presence on an existential level. But the crew decided anything out of the ordinary was confirmation of their worst fears.

To be a sailor was to put one's faith in the unknowable, uncontrollable vastness of the sea, to be at the mercy of an irascible god. Silbrey felt these panicky conversations through the wood, once a forest, now the lumber of this cog.

"Aye, the girl, she's confusing the poor god," said one sailor.

"Aegir wants her as proxy, to be sure," said another. "We're making the god angry."

"The god has been displeased with us for some time. Vindel is no proxy. Not for a long time."

"Maybe so, maybe so. But are you going to say that to the captain?"

These mutterings continued unabated throughout the

journey, and it worried Silbrey. Maybe sailors were more disposed to complaining. From her time at Penderyn's docks, she knew sailors to find fault in every blessing or curse—but if the journey worsened, if the ship were in peril, what would the sailors do to appease Aegir? Silbrey looked at her daughter, wishing she could have left Gydan at Sage Hall with her brother, where she would be safe from the superstitions of scared men.

\* \* \*

Gydan was told how long the voyage would take, but as the days and weeks crawled on, she was astounded they had only traveled half the distance. At one point, Gydan dared to ask her mother if they were almost there. Silbrey gave her a glare that told Gydan she would be wiser not to test her mother's patience with questions she already knew the answer to. Gydan was bored, bored to a degree she did not even imagine was possible. She wanted to practice with Bren's sword while on the ship, but Silbrey wouldn't let her. There wasn't much room in the hull. Gydan insisted she would be careful, but that also elicited a glare from her mother. Her mother had a glare for every situation.

Cyru's companionship and their psychic connection were the only solace for Gydan. Her mother may not be listening, but Cyru never missed anything.

*We would be much larger if we were not caged for all those years. We could fly you to this other continent. No more of this tedious motion.*

"You would transport me? That's sweet."

*Not sweet, a terrifying dragon.*

"Apologies. You may be small for a dragon, but your ferocity is unmatched."

*And we're quite deadly.*

"Yes, and deadly." Gydan thought about the time at the farmhouse when Cyru, with the other two miniature dragons, lifted her into the air. She still had the scars from their claw marks. "Do you think dragons ever flew with people riding on their backs?"

*No, the dragons would eat the people.*

"That makes sense."

*If we did not know you, that's what we would do.*

"In that case, I'm glad I know you."

Cyru curled into Gydan's lap. The dragon's body vibrated like a cat purring. Eyes open, but relaxed, and occasionally chirping. During these moments, Gydan could open her mind and share with Cyru in their clairvoyance. At first, their connection was limited to unspoken communication, but as they spent more time together, the connection deepened. Gydan could catch glimpses of their surroundings. She was amazed at how natural it felt, the way Cyru saw the world in all directions without obstructions. The walls were there, but they did not limit Cyru's ability to see the other side of the wall. Everything at once. A whale swam far below, a pale leviathan twice as large as the ship. Out of curiosity, the creature kept pace with the ship and then dove deeper into the black void. The magnificent whale glided along as though flying. Everything was chaos upon the Amoet, but the world was peaceful not too far below. Gydan could feel the slightest twinge of sadness from Cyru. The dragon rarely showed any vulnerability, and it took a moment for Gydan to understand what she sensed. In this whale, Cyru was reminded of the true size of dragons, titans several times the size of this whale, by comparison making it no larger than a piper fish. Cyru was denied this magnificence. Cyru spent those years in the cage, their intended growth forever stunted. Gydan complained about being stuck in the hull, but nothing compared to Cyru's confinement.

"I'm sorry."

*You are not Speck. You do not need to apologize. And if you were that goblin mage, you'd be dead because I would slash your throat.*

"It's a different 'I'm sorry.'"

*I don't need your pity. I'm still a dragon.*

"Yes, dragons are to be feared," Gydan stuck out her lower lip in a playful pout. "Dragons eat people."

*Thank you.*

Cyru redirected Gydan's focus from the whale to Captain Hrutib on the deck of the ship. He was a dark-skinned old man with a long white beard. His beard was straight and extended past his chest. He wore a dark red shawl over a red robe. He wore a bronze helm with ram horns affixed to the sides. It appeared more fashionable than practical. Hrutib looked more like the ship's king than captain.

The ship rocked back and forth. Hrutib held onto the whipstaff to keep from tumbling into the ocean. The sailors on deck clung to a rope that ran down the middle of the ship from stern to bow. They moved as though half dead. They were exhausted from fighting the waves night and day without reprieve.

In the hull, the cargo was fastened, but the passengers were not. If they weren't holding on to the leather loops nailed to interior planks, they would slide along the lacquered bottom deck and crash into whatever cargo was on the other side. Gydan was convinced she could maintain her balance and move about freely, but when the ship took an erratic dip, Gydan went cartwheeling down the narrow aisle between the barrels and crates, knocking her head. The bruise turned a deep purple, almost black, and she had a splitting headache afterward. Since then, she hadn't left her spot on the lower deck.

The hull was dark at all hours, but a few lanterns hung from the ceiling, creating pockets of dim light. Gydan could see Udger the dwarf sitting across from her. He had long, dark hair threaded through beads of ivory and silver that glinted in the lantern light. Gydan sensed he was a wealthy man who tried to hide it. Silver instead of gold was the kind of concession only the wealthy considered. He hadn't said a word and instead sought to become invisible—appearing as inconsequential as the crates next to him. However, Gydan noticed how he observed her family. He would not let his gaze stray for too long as to make them uncomfortable or aware of his presence. But it was his cautiousness that made Gydan wary. Gydan had a dragon in her lap. Her mother dressed like a warrior. Any normal person would gawk and have a hundred questions. He did not.

Finally, Udger spoke.

"There are four cottages. Each one has a person from a different continent—one from Amon, one from Raustfweg, one from Karkasse, and one from Lunthal. Each one has a favorite drink. And each one has a different—"

"The unicorn is in the Karkasse cottage," Gydan interrupted. "I heard that riddle last winter. Maricel told it to me. It took me a week to solve it, and I cheated."

"You cheated?" Udger asked.

"I had to write everything down. I made a map to make sense of the clues. Maricel repeated everything several times."

"I've never known anyone to solve it without having to repeat it—or writing it down."

"I wish I would've heard it for this first time on this ship," Gydan said. "It would've been a way to pass the time."

"Time does move differently at sea."

"Everything moves differently at sea."

Udger's eyes widened. This statement caught his attention, as if he was hoping the conversation would turn this direction.

"Do you think Aegir is upset?"

"Aegir doesn't have as much control over the sea as people would hope."

"How would you know?"

Gydan was about to respond, but how did she know? She said it with such assuredness, but she wasn't a priest. Even Timon framed any discussion about the gods with the caveat that the gods' ways were unknowable and that confident priests were liars, while the honest ones weren't any use to anybody. She liked this sardonic nature about Timon. He knew more about people than he did the gods, and that's what made a good priest.

"Why should he control the sea?" Gydan mused. "We appointed him to the role. Who decided? It wasn't me."

"Perhaps he told us himself," Udger said. "Sometimes the gods take human form and dwell among us."

"And perhaps we tell ourselves that, so we can feel more important than we are."

Udger nodded his head. "And we're back to riddles, then. How do we know anything of the world beyond our experience of it?"

"Through stories," Gydan replied before Udger even finished what he was saying.

"Through stories," Udger agreed.

Udger pointed to Gydan's sheathed sword. "There's a riddle I haven't been able to solve since we first got on the ship."

"My sword?"

"Is it yours?" Udger asked. "I don't know any reason why a child your age should have such a sword. The markings on the scabbard are distinctive. Something the legendary Bren Caius might have. But you are no Bren Caius. Did you steal it? Doubtful. Was it gifted to you? But why?"

Cyru chirped and trilled, interrupting him. *Don't tell him anything.*

"And right there," Udger continued. "You turned to the dragon as if you understood him."

"Them," Gydan corrected. "All dragons use 'them.'"

"How would I know?" Udger countered. "How do you? Unless you can speak to dragons."

"Any Ayler with a poem about dragons could tell you that."

"But what about the sword?"

Gydan scratched Cyru's neck as the dragon hissed at Udger.

"If I told you about this sword, then you wouldn't be able to enjoy trying to solve the riddle. Why would I take that from you?"

"Can I have a hint?"

"The sword isn't magical," Gydan shrugged. "It's just a sword."

"Is this your way of telling me it doesn't belong to Bren, or are you trying to lead me astray?"

Gydan shrugged again, refusing to answer any more questions.

\* \* \*

Silbrey stroked Maricel's hair, but Maricel was irritable and swatted away Silbrey's hand. Silbrey resumed her grooming, acting as though she didn't understand what Maricel wanted. Maricel had such beautiful hair, but it was getting knotted while they were at sea. Silbrey couldn't help but fuss with it. Maricel slapped at Silbrey's hand a second time. Silbrey wrinkled her nose and playfully slapped back. Maricel shook her head and gave a wry smile.

The ship jolted to one side. Maricel and Silbrey both grabbed for a leather loop. They were getting used to the routine. Silbrey heard Gydan, farther down the hull's port side, tumble onto the floor, punctuated with a *"sah'le vuk."*

Silbrey and Maricel had relocated to this end of the hull to give themselves more privacy. Gydan and Cyru were near the center of the ship, while the sailors stayed toward the bow and rested there on the alternating shifts.

"What are we doing here?" Silbrey asked.

"We're going to Alda Feren to stop the world from breaking," Maricel's speech had much improved, but she still spoke slowly with a slur—unnoticeable to anyone except people who had known her. The right side of her face still sagged and would possibly stay that way. Her paralysis had not changed. Instead, she learned how to manage through it.

Maricel was able to walk with the use of a crutch and a wooden brace. The brace curled around her right leg, fixed to a wooden boot. The boot was carved by Maricel's father. The brace was something Silbrey had conceived back on the farm by commanding a maple tree to twist around Maricel's lame leg. Since the siege of Aberton, Silbrey's ability to command trees had improved. After growing and weaving the trees in Aberton, simple commands required little more than a focused thought and a wave of her hand. It took a few tries to create a comfortable brace secure enough to stabilize Maricel's leg, but not so tight it couldn't be taken off. Silbrey wrapped the brace with strips of a beaver pelt to keep it from chaffing. After several days of practice, Maricel could move about with the assistance of her crutch. However, on the Amoet, she struggled to use her crutch and brace. The ship was too unreliable. The floor, too slippery.

Silbrey thought about Maricel's words. *We're going to Alda Feren to stop the world from breaking.* She was repeating back to Silbrey what she had said when they reunited at the farm. The statement felt more prophetic than practical. They knew little about Alda Feren—the great tree of life—or where it was in Raustfweg, or even if Silbrey could calm the earthquakes through this mythical tree.

"I shouldn't have brought you and Gydan," said Silbrey. "It's not safe."

"Nowhere in the world is safe right now," Maricel responded. She raised her voice, annoyed at the suggestion she should have been left behind. Silbrey noticed the change in her voice but did not react. "That's why *we* are going."

"What if this leads to nothing?" Silbrey asked. "What if there's no tree of life, no hope of stopping the earthquakes?

What if I dragged you across Efre Ousel, only to die in a strange land without a copper to our name?"

Maricel grabbed Silbrey's hand, giving it a squeeze. "Neither of us ever had a copper to our name. We die together. That's our lot."

Silbrey wrapped her arm around Maricel and nestled close. "That sounds horrible."

"It was supposed to be sweet," Maricel laughed. "Let's not die."

"I'll talk to the tree and see what it says."

They both laughed.

Gydan heard the laughter and peered over the crates to see what was going on. She saw her mother and Maricel, laughing like idiots. She rolled her eyes. Gydan got the glares from her mother, while this lighter side belonged to Maricel. The ship jerked and again Gydan tumbled to the floor.

Another eruption of laughter from the two grown women. From Gydan, more cursing.

Silbrey looked at Maricel. The lantern light outlined her light skin against the dark surroundings. She appeared to glow. One side of her face was blank, unmoved, but the other side contorted in childish mirth as she unleashed peals of unrestrained laughter, followed by snorting. Silbrey had never heard Maricel laugh like this before. She had always thought of Maricel as quiet and restrained, offering little more than a slight snicker or amused head nod, acknowledging the humor but not taking part in it. That was who Maricel was to her.

Was that all an act before, as Maricel tried to get close to Silbrey, taking notes and observing? Or maybe, because Silbrey's grief was so raw after Callis had died, Maricel held back out of respect. To love life felt like a dishonor to the dead.

It was nonsense to think that way. The dead were gone, and that was that, but grief rarely made sense. It was also possible Maricel's experience on the road, almost dying, had changed her and opened her up to be bolder.

This past year, the person Silbrey knew as "Maricel" had changed so many times. Maricel the friend and neighbor, who helped Silbrey and her family relocate after Callis's death. Maricel the new mother to Yurig and Gydan, who told them bedtime stories and cooked meals for them. Maricel the deceiver, who had been spying on Silbrey and who Silbrey wrongly thought was working for Dahlia Tulan. Maricel the captive. Maricel the savior. Maricel the wounded. Now, this incarnation—a Maricel who refused to be defined. She laughed when she wanted to laugh, and she said whatever was on her mind. Silbrey wasn't sure what to do with this Maricel.

"Come here," Maricel said to Silbrey, placing her hand on the back of Silbrey's neck, bringing her close. "Kiss me."

And so, Silbrey did. It wasn't like the secret kisses they exchanged in the middle of the night while the children slept. It wasn't the desperate kisses of someone starved of affection. It was better, something both earned and unearned. Something close and intimate. It felt like love.

Later that night, Silbrey, lying on her thin woven blanket, looked up at the ceiling. She listened to the creaking of the boards as the crew walked the deck and to the lower-pitched groan as the waves buffeted the ship. She could hear the soft snoring of Gydan on the other side of the cargo. The lantern closest to her shone brightly, while others throughout the hull were low on oil or burnt out. She noticed shadows along the ceiling, which hadn't been there before. Her eyes focused and saw the shadows were from tiny roots that had emerged between the planks. She felt the Amoet yearning for its old life. It wanted to return to the forest.

Silbrey's arrival felt like an invitation for growth.

She did not fully understand what this urge from the ship meant. If so, she might have stopped it.

\* \* \*

Silbrey would've woken up with a seax (a razor-sharp short sword, commonly used by Raustfweg warriors) at her throat, but the Amoet reached out with a warning. The natural world —even the wood of a ship—spoke in a language that didn't rely on words, but the message was clear enough to Silbrey. Before opening her eyes, she reached for her staff and swung it around, placing her weapon at her attacker's throat.

"Do not come at me while I'm sleeping. Show some respect."

Silbrey opened her eyes to see she had Captain Hrutib grimacing and pinned against the side of the hull. He dropped his seax.

The lantern swung near Hrutib. The light danced madly about the darkened confines.

"I wasn't going to kill ye, but I needed to make the message clear." Hrutib spoke in a raspy voice common to old captains who spent their life on the sea, shouting orders to his crew. His peculiar, thick accent originated from the place between places. It was the accent of merchants from far-off lands and of vagabonds.

"You have your words. That works." Silbrey lowered her staff. "What's the message?"

"Yer daughter has brought devilry upon m'ship."

At first, the statement confused Silbrey, but then she noticed the roots. What had been a few wisps of root tendril before she went to sleep matured into thick appendages, fingers digging through the deck and across the hull. Silbrey and Maricel were surrounded by the roots, like a canopy enveloping them as they slept.

She looked to where Gydan had slept and saw Vindel, the captain's son, standing nearby with a seax. Cyru, teeth bared, was next to Gydan. Vindel wisely decided to not move any closer.

"Gydan, Maricel, wake up!" Silbrey raised her voice. She saw the off-shift sailors from the other side of the hull make their way to the deck to see the devilry Hrutib spoke of. "My daughter is not to blame."

"I'm to believe a tree grew out of the ship's stern castle on its own?"

"Your ship is made of wood. A tree, once. I don't see what's so hard to understand."

"Are ye making fun? Ye think I'm ignorant? I'm the captain of the ship, and if I want to throw yer daughter overboard—"

Silbrey swung her staff faster than anyone could track and hit Hrutib upside the head. He stumbled backward, tripping over a sack of dry goods, falling onto his back. His bronze helm fell off his head and skittered across the floor. Silbrey moved upon Hrutib and put her knee on his chest. "You're the captain, are you?" Silbrey asked. Hrutib snarled at her but made no reply. "How about you go back to the deck of your ship and do some captaining up there? Down here, I'm in charge."

Silbrey was seething. She wanted to kill the captain for that threat. She was tired of violent men making threats—a world

full of them, all acting like Kret Bonebreaker. Silbrey felt a
hand on her back. She turned around. It was Maricel. Her
expression pleaded with Silbrey to be merciful. Silbrey spat to
the side of Hrutib and took her knee off his chest.

Hrutib sat up. He rubbed the back of his head and swallowed hard. He gave Silbrey a grim look from his sunken eyes.

"Why are ye going to Raustfweg?" Hrutib asked. "Don't
give me that story about being farmers who lost everything in
the earthquake, claiming a land inheritance from the ravens.
The farming is better in Amon. Better soil. Why do ye think
the people from Raustfweg raid and trade? Their land is too
mountainous, too rocky. And the areas that are farmable are
too cold and wet—with too many tribes fighting over those few
acres. Everywhere ye turn, there is someone who calls themself
'king' or 'queen,' trying to claim more land. No farmer ever left
Amon for Raustfweg."

Silbrey was silent. She had no interest in defending herself.

"I won't ask you again," she said. "Return to the deck."

"I don't know why yer going to Raustfweg, but yer
daughter has brought misfortune upon m'ship. That I know to
be sure. By and by, I'll see the curse removed."

"It's your son who caused this curse," Udger spoke.
Everyone turned toward him. "Your son is too old to be proxy.
Your crew knows it. Your son knows it. You've angered the god
of the sea, and you've broken from his ways. If you want to save
this ship, you'll throw your son overboard."

Vindel snarled at Udger's accusations.

"Damn liar! Blasphemy!"

Vindel swung at Udger with his seax, but before the blade
could slice open the dwarf's stomach, Cyru was there to inter-
cept the attack. So fast was the dragon, they seemed to pop into

existence wherever they were needed. Cyru's jaws were upon Vindel's hand. Cyru crunched their razor teeth into flesh. Bones snapped. Vindel shrieked. Blood poured out over his shaking hand, and he dropped his weapon. Cyru looked to Gydan, waiting for permission to kill. But Gydan was too shocked to respond. Silbrey saw something of herself in that dragon. She remembered how easy it was to take a life when she was younger and worked for Dahlia Tulan. What everyone else saw as violence, she understood as restraint. She yelled to Cyru, hoping the dragon would hear or even care.

"Cyru, do not kill him. If the captain and son die, we're lost at sea. No one else knows how to navigate this ship. They die. We die."

Hrutib adjusted his shawl and red robe and placed his helm back on his head.

"I'm glad ye understand that much," Hrutib said.

"But navigation be damned," Silbrey turned back on him. "If you harm any of my people, I'll come after you. You don't harm the dwarf either. He's also under my protection."

"His name is Udger," Gydan said.

"Udger is under my protection," Silbrey said to Hrutib. She did not completely trust Udger, but he was also vulnerable to the whims of the captain, and they needed allies.

"There's a tree growing out of the ship's stern castle. Be glad I can still sail this ship."

Hrutib grabbed Vindel as he walked away. Vindel's injured hand was wrapped in his coat. The few remaining sailors at the other end of the hull looked to their captain for direction.

Hrutib took a piece of chalk from next to the ladder. The chalk was used to mark inventory as it was loaded onto the ship. Hrutib bent over and drew a line along the floor from port side to starboard. He then tossed the chalk to one of the sailors.

"If anyone crosses this line, kill them."

Hrutib climbed the ladder with Vindel following close behind. He struggled to scale the ladder with his one good hand.

After the father and son left, the Amoet rocked upon the unpredictable waves. Each person in the hull, in unison, shifted and then recovered their footing. Silbrey held her staff in one hand, and the other hand braced against the cargo to steady her as she moved toward the chalk line. The sailors moved a step back, unsure what to do if Silbrey decided to cross the line. Silbrey stood at the chalk line and looked at each of them in turn. The youngest sailor grabbed for his dagger. He shook with fearful anticipation.

"Do you think you could kill me?" Silbrey asked. There was no threat in her voice. She asked it as plainly as if she was wondering what the weather would be like tomorrow.

"No, m'lady," said the sailor.

"Lady?" Silbrey smiled. "I've been called many things. Never 'lady,' but I receive your courtesy. What is your name?"

"Jokull," he said. He didn't know if he ought to say more, so he added again, "m'lady."

Silbrey suppressed a laugh.

"Good lord, Jokull," Silbrey said, giving a curtsy. "You are young, but not as young as the captain's son, the proxy."

"I'm a year and a month older, m—," Jokull caught himself before saying "m'lady" a third time. "The captain would not hire anyone younger. He didn't want to displease Aegir."

"He allowed my daughter on board."

"I suppose he thought the age wouldn't matter if it were a passenger's."

"I see." Silbrey considered his words. She swung her staff around, more out of boredom than as an invitation to combat. "Do you think my daughter angered Aegir and cursed the ship?"

Jokull did not know what to say. He looked back at the other sailors, hoping for some guidance, but they wanted no part of it.

"It's not for me to guess at the what the gods want or don't want. One wants gold. Another wants ale and song. Another wants nothing at all. Who can figure them out?"

"Indeed," Silbrey responded. "One last question." She stopped spinning her staff and brought one end down on the wooden floor with a loud thump. The entire ship quivered, actually quivered, in response. Jokull jumped. Silbrey leaned forward over the chalk line. Her voice went low, all good-natured banter absent. Her voice filled with strength and savagery. "Do you think I could kill you?"

The other sailors drew their daggers. Gydan got to her feet. Cyru flew to Silbrey's side, ready for a fight. Maricel shook her head and cursed.

"I— I— I—" All color left Jokull's face.

"Think on it," Silbrey said, her voice trembling in anger. "If the captain asks you to give up your life, is that what you want to do?"

Silbrey took a few steps back. The sailors all lowered their weapons. Cyru flew back to Gydan. Silbrey walked away from Jokull to where the roots had penetrated through the deck, to where Maricel was.

"You didn't have to scare him," Maricel whispered to Silbrey.

"He's already scared," Silbrey responded. "I want to make sure he's more afraid of me than his captain."

Everyone was still looking at Silbrey. Everyone except Udger. He kept his eyes on Gydan. Silbrey's skin crawled when she noticed. It looked as though he was coming to some realization he couldn't quite put to words.

Silbrey leaned closer to Maricel. A whisper so low, she couldn't even hear herself amidst the creaks and groans of the Amoet, forever fighting with the ocean waves.

"I don't trust Udger."

"Me neither," Maricel responded.

Maricel struggled to sit up. She grabbed one of the roots to pull and position herself. The grim look on her face made Silbrey wonder if Maricel still trusted her as well.

"Come sleep next to us," Maricel called to Gydan. "It's not yet morning, and we'd like you here with us."

Gydan sighed but obeyed. Cyru followed.

Silbrey knew Gydan tried to keep her distance from them at night because she didn't want to see or hear Silbrey and Maricel being affectionate with each other. They tried to be discreet, but the hull wasn't large enough. They were still trying to figure out their relationship—and nighttime was when they turned to each other for comfort, for intimacy, for rediscovering each other.

In short, Gydan would've jumped ship long ago if she thought it was an option to avoid hearing them.

Silbrey rolled her eyes at Maricel, mocking her daughter's disgust, but when she laid back down, she gave Maricel a respectful amount of space. She didn't know if she would get any more sleep, anyway.

\* \* \*

The next day, the supplies within the ship's hull were redistributed to counterbalance the weight of the tree, which continued to grow. Even with the added weight, the front of the ship lifted out of the water. The ship wobbled and shifted direction without warning. The crown of the tree acted as a secondary sail, often competing with the mainsail. In defiance of everything Captain Hrutib knew about sailing, the Amoet was still able to make progress across the vast ocean.

The provisions within the Amoet included several boxes of salted beef and pork, pickled herring, and dried cod; wax-coated cheese wheels stored in a case; a crate with bottles of wine and brandy packed in sawdust; jugs of oil and vinegar; barrels of fresh water; a crate of hardtack biscuits; sacks of white peas, oats, barley, rye, flour, mustard seed, and beans; sacks of onions, garlic, and potatoes; a large bag of salt; ceramic pots of butter stored in a crate; and a tub of whale blubber, which had numerous uses, chiefly as fuel for the lanterns.

There were several rope coils of varied thickness; tools—for repairs the ship may need—including hammers and a lidded bucket of nails, additional planks, as well as a barrel of tar; two hay bales; stacked bags of sand; a folded replacement sail; extra lanterns and candles; netting and hooks; a row of lock boxes with the personal effects of the crew; scrub brushes, squares of cut cloth, brooms, and mops; and a series of pulleys hanging from hooks on the starboard side.

The trade goods were in the largest crates, packed with

sawdust and nailed shut. The contents were a mystery. Although, from the smell, Gydan guessed that a few of these crates were packed with sweet leaf. Each crate was marked with a family seal to indicate third-party traders and another seal to mark the intended recipient along with the agreed-upon cost. The first mate was paid extra to handle the coin and make certain every crate was exchanged for the correct amount.

These trades were often negotiated beforehand by sending messages with a special breed of white-necked ravens. These birds were trained carriers and had notes fixed to a claw ring. These ravens were beloved by the people of Raustfweg because, no matter where they were in Efre Ousel, they would find their way back to their nests in Raustfweg. The expression "white-necked" had come to mean someone who was devoted to their home and family.

Gydan wouldn't have so carefully observed the provisions, except she had spent many days in the hull, and she was bored. These items became fixed in her mind like landmarks along a familiar path. The crates with the bottles were ten paces from the ladder, and over there, the tub of whale blubber and the jugs and the coil of rope. Her world had been reduced to this dark territory under the ship's deck and then cut in half by the captain's chalk. She had nothing else to do but acquaint herself with every item in her domain.

One night, while sleeping, Gydan felt someone nudge her.

"Gydan, wake up. You're making noises in your sleep."

Her mother was a darker shape against the darkness in the hull. Over the last few weeks, Gydan had become a skilled identifier of sounds, smells, and silhouettes. Even with the lanterns, her eyes became less reliable in the perpetually dim surroundings.

"I was making noises?"

"You were crying and saying something about drowning," Silbrey said without a hint of compassion. "The crew already thinks you've cursed this ship. We don't want them saying the gods gave you worrisome visions."

Gydan sat up, annoyed.

"It's not my fault Vindel is old." She said his name with derision. She hated him, and she hated the position he put her in. "What if Aegir prefers me? Aegir is an ass."

"Now you know the named god of the sea?"

"Well," Gydan waved her hand around, indicating the general situation. "Doesn't he seem like an ass to you?"

"He seems like a child," Silbrey said. "And I've never been good with children." She said it as if Gydan, *her daughter*, weren't there. Gydan had come to expect this honesty from her mother. "Your father, he was better at calming you and your brother when you were having a tantrum. He was better at all things."

Gydan had always chosen her words carefully when talking about her father, but she needed to ask one question.

"Do you even miss him?"

Anger flashed across Silbrey's face and then calmed into a neutral expression. It startled Gydan. These flashes of anger were becoming more frequent. She could hear a pain in her mother's voice.

"I miss him every day," Silbrey said. Gydan thought she was done talking, but then she spoke again. "Do you think I want to be on this boat? I can't sleep. There's no relief from the constant motion. I'm so afraid I've put you and Maricel in danger by bringing you. I would rather be home, our old home, with Callis and with you and Yurig, tending sheep and keeping house."

"Mom," Gydan said. "You weren't the one tending the sheep or keeping the house."

Silbrey smiled. "I did my part."

"And in this dream, where Dad is still alive, would Maricel be part of it?"

"Maricel has always been part of my life. I just didn't know it. I think Callis knew. I keep expecting Callis to appear, maybe in a vision. There seems to be no shortage of visions. Why not one from him? I hope for his ghost to approach me and ask me to remember him or avenge him. I've been waiting for him to tell me it's okay to move on with my life. I wait, and I wait, and I wait. But there's nothing. Callis is gone. Forever silent."

The roots had extended farther into the hull. They became animated whenever Silbrey was near, tending to her as needed. One root tendril reached out to a lantern hanging from a nearby ceiling hook. It wrapped around the lantern's ring, lifted it from the hook, and carried to Silbrey's waiting hands. Silbrey looked into the lantern light. Her face illuminated from underneath, casting ominous shadows.

"Over the past year, I've seen such wonders," Silbrey said, lost in her own thoughts. "I've felt a connection to all nature, but there is no connection to the dead. Their bodies return to the earth with no special message for those they leave behind."

Gydan thought about her dream and if she should share it with Silbrey—if this dream was a message to her mother—of Maricel and her father occupying the same body. Like the named god Taraki, both male and female, brother and sister, one sows and the other reaps. Gydan decided to keep this dream to herself.

"The dead can no longer speak for themselves," Gydan said. "We must live in their silence or speak for them."

Silbrey handed the lantern back to the root, which obliged by returning the lantern to its hook. "But I miss him so much."

For once, Gydan was able to think about her father's death without crying. The pain was there, but it didn't sting like before.

"I don't know what's waiting for us in Raustfweg," said Silbrey. "Alda Feren, yes. A chance to stop the earthquakes, yes. But also, an opportunity to escape, to start over."

"You're not planning to return to Amon?"

"No," Silbrey said. "If I need to go to Alda Feren to calm the earth, I don't see how I could ever leave that place. It'll require vigilance." Silbrey paused before sharing another truth. "I need to get away from Amon. There's too much pain, too many memories. Beyond Callis. The things I witnessed in Penderyn, in Rhyll, and in Aberton—I close my eyes, and I still see the ones I hunted, the ones I couldn't save, and the ones I failed to save. I can't go back."

Gydan understood. Gydan was the one who had found her father dead in the alley. She had entered Speck's cave and was chased by the monsters hiding in the forest. She was abandoned by her brother at Sage Hall and sent away by Bren Caius. She saw the bodies hanging in Penderyn. She held onto Maricel as she struggled to stay alive. And the suffering continued on this ship—with a captain who wanted them dead because he believed some seafaring superstition. Gydan didn't want to measure her suffering against her mother's, but she had been there too. Gydan had also seen wonders and suffered for it. She also needed someone to hold her and comfort her.

"Mom?"

"Yes?"

"Even if you stay, I want to return to Amon, eventually," Gydan said. "Before we left, Aubec told me Dahlia Tulan must face the firstborn of every victim's family. It was a law established by the first monarchs. Dahlia Tulan must meet with over a thousand people before she's executed—and she'll stay in prison until that happens. It could take several years. Aubec told me they'd wait until I returned."

"Oh." Silbrey tensed at the mention of Dahlia Tulan. "I asked Aubec to join us, and he said he was staying to restore order."

"He might become the next high general."

Silbrey snorted. "He'd hate that."

"I think he'd make a good high general."

Gydan and Silbrey sat together in silence. Both held onto roots that snaked past, steadying themselves against the rocking of the boat. Gydan considered where Dahlia Tulan was right now, in her prison cell, waiting to hear her crimes. Gydan thought about the various cargo in the hull, tethered with nets and rope to the floor. These crates formed the walls of her confinement—and like Dahlia, she might never be free.

\* \* \*

Since Silbrey's confrontation with Hrutib, the passengers were no longer able to leave the hull. The days and nights blurred together. Getting a sense of how much time had passed was difficult. The restlessness settled into quiet surrender. Even the jostling of the Amoet did not bother them as much as it once had. They swayed with the irregular motions without resistance. Each one stared into the dimly lit space that receded into a dark void at the farthest reaches of the hull. That darkness became a comfort because it hinted at a greater expanse beyond.

The roots spread throughout the hull, weaving in and around the crates. To go anywhere in the hull, a person had to hunch over or risk getting tangled in the roots. Rather than being tossed about, they would find themselves caught in the mesh.

Cyru's head rose from Gydan's lap. Gydan's mind had been open to Cyru as their perception drifted across the ship, observing the crew at work. She saw what Cyru saw. Silbrey sat up as well, and her eyes met with Gydan's. Silbrey had sensed it too.

Jokull—the young, nervous sailor—had fallen overboard. He tripped over an exposed root and crashed into the railing. His feet lifted off the deck. It did not appear to be significant, but the imbalance was enough. Slow and awkward, he tipped farther over the side until he was upside down and falling into the black water. A yelp, and he was gone.

Maricel placed her hand on Silbrey's arm.

"What is it? What happened?"

A moment later, they could hear the crew above, yelling for rope and shouting out where they thought Jokull was last seen. He did not resurface. The waves were that violent. They consumed the young sailor and crushed him under their weight.

"Cyru!" Silbrey called. "Can you fly out and save him?"

The dragon gave a series of chirps and clicks, but did not move.

"Cyru says the boy is too far under the water," Gydan said. "There's no saving him."

"The captain is going to blame us," Silbrey said.

"The captain is going to blame *me*," Gydan corrected her.

"A steady journey and a clear path," Udger mused. They had forgotten he was there. "People think the expression refers to travel along a road, but the old blessing originated with sailors and spread through Amon and Raustfweg. This journey is anything but steady, and the path is not clear. Whether mother or daughter are to blame, we are all at the mercy of Aegir now."

"Every time you think you should speak, you should be quiet," Silbrey said. Her words came out like a snarl. "And every time you're quiet, I wish I knew what you were thinking."

"People who speak the truth often get that response."

"Then what are you not telling us?" Silbrey asked.

Udger looked hurt. "I told you. I'm as honest as a prophet. I'm speaking the truth, even if you aren't ready to hear it. The only way to appease Aegir is to throw the captain's son into the sea—or maybe your daughter can reason with the god."

Before Silbrey could respond, Captain Hrutib climbed down the ladder into the hull. He used his seax to hack his way through the roots. As he cut at them, the roots grew and reformed behind him.

"Captain, I believe you've crossed the chalk line," Silbrey commented. The captain looked around him and saw that he was on their side. The rebuke flustered him.

"One of m'men fell overboard. In all m'years at sea, I've never lost a sailor in such a manner. Every one of them knows their way on a deck of a ship. No matter how stormy the seas. Ye have an accounting for this loss. Yer daughter is cursed. I'm here to take her and do what needs to be done."

Silbrey stepped in front of Hrutib, standing in between him and her daughter. Silbrey held her staff at her side, braced against her forearm, ready to strike.

"You crossed the chalk line. You're now in my territory."

As she said this, the roots loosened from their netted pattern and, like tentacles, wrapped around Hrutib, squeezing him.

"Who are you?" Hrutib said as he struggled for air.

"I'm Gydan's mother, and if you thought you could come down here and threaten her, that's not a wise thing to do in front of her mother."

"The child'll kill us all."

"I'll kill you before she ever gets the chance."

The roots tightened around his throat. Hrutib grunted. His eyes bulged. His neck strained.

"Silbrey, don't," Maricel said. "Let him live."

Maricel was trembling, resolved in what she knew to be right, fearful that Silbrey wouldn't listen.

"I spared Dahlia Tulan's life in Penderyn," Silbrey said. "I showed mercy, and she conspired with Mendal Caius and Kret Bonebreaker. She slaughtered everyone who supported Bren. She marched her mercenaries to Aberton. People died because I couldn't bring myself to do the necessary thing."

"And Dahlia is now in a prison cell on Rhyll," Maricel said. "She'll pay for her crimes."

"But it won't bring back the people she killed."

The roots squeezed. No noise came from Hrutib, only the gaping mouth of a soundless scream.

"Hrutib is not Dahlia," Maricel said. "He's a scared man who wants to save his crew."

"Scared men are dangerous."

The anger Silbrey felt had become familiar. After all, the world was falling apart, and anger was a reasonable response. And she knew every time she indulged in it, she pushed the people she loved away.

"Let him live," Gydan spoke, and her voice carried an authority beyond her youth. "Have you forgotten what you said? Hrutib and Vindel know how to navigate this ship. If they die, we die."

The roots let go. Hrutib gasped for air. There were red whelps where the roots had been. He reached for his seax. Motes of blue light shimmered across the hull, and he collapsed to the ground, asleep. Silbrey grabbed Hrutib by his red shawl and dragged him across the chalk line, now smudged.

"He can sleep on his side of the line."

\* \* \*

The crew kept their distance from Silbrey and the other passengers. They gave over the entire hull to them and to the ever-expanding tangle of roots below, while the tree continued to flourish above. The captain knew—short of sinking the Amoet—he couldn't get rid of Gydan or Silbrey.

The passengers didn't spread out after the crew left. They did not search for softer, dryer places to make their beds. They remained where they had been. Familiarity became a prison, which bound them to their routine.

After Silbrey's encounter with the captain, she had become restless and untamed. She was a caged creature, desperate to strike. Gydan kept her distance. Maricel did not. The two of them needled each other and acted indignant when the other snapped. Any reconciliation was short-lived and then they were at it again. Gydan missed the earlier days of the voyage when she was embarrassed by their open affections in the close quarters. She preferred that to their stupid arguments.

Udger remained strange. He spoke infrequently, but cryptically, offering his theories on fate and the gods and the state of the world. And when he spoke, he narrated as though addressing an entire village instead of the three people and one dragon who shared in his confinement. Often the topics would come from nowhere, as though he were completing a thought or a having conversation with some other unseen member of their group.

"You call him Olar," Udger said, breaking a long silence and causing Gydan to jump. "In Raustfweg, we call him Albjorn. You call him Wedril. We call him Dodrik. Aegir is Gymin. Tian is Efrynir. I could go on."

"You don't need to," Silbrey said from across the hull.

"What do the people of Lunthal and Karkasse call the named gods?" Udger ignored Silbrey. "I'm sure it's different from what we call them. I'd wager they each have a hundred names, and there is power in every name."

"I doubt it," Silbrey said. Her commentary continued to fall on deaf ears.

"Except Golwin," Udger mused. "Golwin is not a name. It's a title like *for'win,* the Volir word for blacksmith, or *ald'win,* meaning carpenter. Golwin simply means a person who makes death their business. There's no name specific to Golwin on Amon or Raustfweg. She is always Golwin the Fated. Her nameless nature is why she likes to collect the true names of the living. Silbrey isn't a name either. It means—"

"Beautiful flower," Silbrey cut him off. "Thank you for explaining my name to me."

"Beautiful flower," Udger agreed. "You also claim lives. It's in your nature. You've tried to be someone else, but you cannot escape who you are."

"Udger, please." Gydan was desperate to change the subject. She knew her mother's patience would not last, and Udger would regret it. "We don't know much about Raustfweg. Could you tell us a story from your land? Something we haven't already heard."

The dwarf pondered this request. He reached for a strand of the silver and ivory beads threaded in his long dark hair and twisted it around his finger.

"I have a poem."

"A poem would be good," Gydan said, before her mother could protest.

Maricel had been ignoring most of the exchange, but the mention of a poem caught her attention. Even Cyru appeared to perk up.

"The poem is called 'the Peddler who visited Elara Brok,'" Udger said. "I've heard it many times, and I've heard many variations of this poem. This is the version I remember and love best."

Udger's voice became low and measured like an Ayler performing for his next meal. The lantern lights flickered, and the ocean calmed for a moment. To Gydan, it seemed as though the world paused so Udger might share these verses.

> Deep within the Angnavir mountain range,
> A gentle river carves through a valley,
> A winding way that few will ever take
> To the ivory doors of Elara Brok.
> Many sail along and pass unaware,

*When searching for treasures of gems and gold.*
*Sail with pure intention and open eyes,*
*The doors will appear, unlocked, unguarded.*
*Discover the city of gems and gold.*
*Listen all to this tragic tale unfold.*

*Within the high vaulted mountain cavern*
*Is an ancient city hewn from the stone—*
*A marvel, a wonder beyond compare.*
*Winding stairs climb to impossible heights.*
*Neighborhoods built on top of each other,*
*All balanced in circular symmetry.*
*Farther within, the castle keep takes shape.*
*Beyond the walls are twelve gates with twelves*
    *traps*
*And a maze of circular symmetry,*
*At the center, a king's grand treasury.*

*Golden coins and golden bars, heaped in piles,*
*Hills of gold, as far as one could see, and*
*Gemstones, every color imaginable,*
*Each one, a prism projecting rainbows—*
*Chromatic ghosts dancing about the walls.*
*To reach down and grab only a handful*
*Of the scattered treasure would be enough*
*To live comfortably the rest of one's days.*
*The mind cannot grasp wealth in a handful.*
*The ambitious, the foolish feel its pull.*

*Old King Stoneheart guarded his treasure well,*
*And timeless spells pervaded the mountain.*

Reach for what's not yours, and the mountain
      strikes
At the hapless thief, collapsing on them,
All vice buried. All avarice consumed.
So confident in the wards and watchmen,
The king proclaimed whoever takes one piece
Of the vast treasure from the mountain keep,
Past the safekeeping of wards and watchmen,
Would then be given the entire fortune.

For such a prize, heroes have tried and failed.
For those heroes, no poem shall be shared.
In failure, we know no song shall be sung.
And while it may seem so simple a task,
To take just one piece from the treasure vault,
Old King Stoneheart would not have risked
      his all—
If he thought it were even possible.
Yet, still they search and they strive and they fail.
They leave defeated. And they risked it all,
For treasure untouched, from behind the wall.

One day unlike any other, there came
A plain peddler to the ivory entry.
The doors opened because he posed no threat.
The people of Elara Brok watched him
Walk in without fanfare, without escort.
The peddler said, "I'm here to see the king.
I have come eager to take his challenge.
Someday, his treasure will belong to me."
The peddler bowed to the astonished king.

*He bent his knee and kissed the royal ring.*

*The peddler's bold statement moved King*
    *Stoneheart.*
*He gave his guest a room in the palace.*
*And every morning, the old king would ask,*
*"Have you stolen anything from me yet?"*
*And every morning, the peddler would say,*
*"Not today, your grace, but all in good time."*
*Days turned to weeks turned to months, then a*
    *year,*
*But the peddler never took anything.*
*No charity, no favors in that time.*
*No offense or trespass, no theft, no crime.*

*The peddler became a familiar sight*
*To all the people of Elara Brok.*
*His plainness made him truly peculiar*
*When compared to the wealth surrounding him.*
*And not once did the peddler's eyes linger*
*On a coin or bright gem, nothing of gold.*
*King Stoneheart's only daughter took notice.*
*She began to despise Elara Brok.*
*To her, the peddler was adorned in gold,*
*Something uncommon, worthy to behold.*

*The peddler did not woo her, not at first.*
*He would repay her kindness with a nod,*
*Any good word would be met with a smile.*
*The princess could have anything at all,*
*But she burned for the peddler, only him.*

*In modesty, he offered courtesy.*
*She would send for him, and he would decline.*
*"I am a peddler. What could I provide?"*
*She swore off her wealth and his courtesy.*
*She wanted more than court ceremony.*

*Then one morning, the king asked the peddler,*
*"Have you stolen anything from me yet?"*
*The peddler said, "Today, your grace, I have*
*Stolen the greatest of treasures from you.*
*Gone forever. You cannot take it back."*
*The king laughed at the peddler's confession.*
*"Is that so, my friend?" The king urged him on.*
*"Tell me then what you could possibly steal.*
*What did you lift? Give me your confession.*
*If you speak true, then state your transgression."*

*At this command, the princess stepped forward.*
*"Father, the peddler has stolen my heart.*
*From now until the end, I will love him.*
*If he'll have me, I will walk by his side."*
*The peddler smiled and gave her a brief nod,*
*But it said everything. The two were one.*
*He reached out his hand. She took it in hers.*
*No ceremony could further unite*
*And no decree could divide. They were one.*
*What is joined in love cannot be undone.*

*The king lowered his head, removed his crown.*
*He placed that royal top upon the ground.*
*"If I esteem my great treasure higher*

*Than my daughter, I'm a foolish father.*
*But if I esteem my daughter higher*
*Than my treasure, I'm a destitute fool."*
*So the king left Elara Brok that day.*
*He left everything behind to wander*
*The world and think on how he became a fool,*
*Giving his kingdom to a peddler to rule.*

*The Peddler King took the throne and his*
        *queen—*
*The treasures of Elara Brok, now his.*
*If happiness comes from wealth, it is brief.*
*The gold could not ease his unsteady mind*
*As he considered how he tricked the king.*
*Did he truly love King Stoneheart's daughter?*
*Maybe once, but now lost in his deceit.*
*His vault could hold riches beyond compare,*
*But his heart could not hold the king's daughter.*
*What despair had this deceit brought to her!*

*The halls of Elara Brok were silent*
*And empty, except for the king's treasure,*
*And the Peddler King alone on his throne.*
*The queen had left in search of her father,*
*To care for him in his few final years.*
*She would never return, young love denied.*
*Within the high vaulted mountain cavern—*
*Each lonely step echoed the peddler's loss.*
*What is lost in love cannot be denied,*
*And what is gained instead cannot provide.*

*The peddler left Elara Brok behind.*
*Treasures within, there for others to find.*
*He tells his story to all who will hear,*
*How he lost what was so near and so dear.*
*That gemstones and gold cannot replace love,*
*Truth is better than to be devoid of*
*People who know you and care for you still.*
*Who walk with you and wish you no ill will.*
*Of loss and of love, this tale is now told—*
*Wealth is wasted on the foolish and old.*

\* \* \*

Silbrey and Maricel had been arguing.

Silbrey didn't even know what had started it or if this argument was the continuation of some unresolved matter. Whether it was true or not, in these moments, she recalled that she and Callis hardly ever argued. Even when she wanted to get into it, Callis would wave it off or concede her point. He rarely gave her the satisfaction of conflict. The man's patience with his young wife knew no end. And now that Silbrey was older, he was gone. Silbrey was inexperienced in the fine art of disagreement. She didn't know how to navigate the conflicts and bitterness, so she sailed into it head-on, taking every look and every misspoken word as a slight to be addressed.

Maricel, for her part, was not the soft-spoken, gentle woman Silbrey had originally taken her to be. Maricel's dry humor was a cudgel, which struck at Silbrey when she least expected it. Maricel stuck up for herself, and to Silbrey's frustration, she was right most of the time.

Maricel was concerned about Silbrey's anger. Silbrey was

restless. The lighthearted playfulness they felt when they were first on the ship was gone. The moments of affection had disappeared. Everything was difficult, all the time.

They had spent so much time together on the boat. They were exhausted by each other's presence. They needed space, but space was in short supply. The roots had taken over the hull. Even if Silbrey stepped away, she was connected to everything and everywhere. Maricel, Gydan, Cyru, Udger, Hrutib, Vindel, and the rest of the crew were always there.

Silbrey moved through the hull, among the roots, which uncoiled and made a path for her. She ran her hand along the tendrils as she walked. She went to the darker half of the hull, where no lantern light could reach. In the darkness, she remembered the cavern where the goblin war mage Speck brought the ceiling down on her, burying her alive. The cavern wasn't dark, though. The phosphorescent runes had provided light. But then, like now, she was trapped. She felt a crushing weight and did not know how to survive. The tree above had saved her, restored her, and lifted her to the surface. As she thought about that moment, motes of blue light flickered around her.

Was she Golwin or was she Ald'yovlet? Did she deal in death, or was she a child of the forest who brought life wherever she stepped? She bristled at the comparison to Golwin, but Udger's words hit hard. *You claim lives. It's in your nature. You've tried to be someone else, but you cannot escape who you are.* What did Udger know about her? Yes, she nearly choked the life out of Hrutib, and yes, Silbrey wanted to kill him, but it felt right. She felt justified.

The blue lights hovered around her. The roots thickened. Tiny leaves and white flower buds sprouted from the roots.

Silbrey looked down at her bare feet. A patch of grass grew from the wooden floor where she stood. Scattered throughout the hull were small signs of flora she hadn't noticed before. Flowering vines twisted around some of the crates. Mushrooms grew from a burlap sack. Moss and lichens covered portions of the hull. The Amoet was returning to life. For growth, there must be the decay of death, rich nutrients in the soil.

Life. Death. Whatever helped the plants grow.

Silbrey stood still and breathed, feeling the natural world expand around her. The blue light pulsed with each exhale. She sensed Udger was not in the hull. He had snuck up to the deck and was talking with Captain Hrutib. Silbrey could not make out the conversation. She could only sense he was seizing an opportunity. She would need to confront him about it later.

Silbrey extended her consciousness across the ship and noticed her blue light had put some of the crew to sleep. Fortunately, they had been tethered to the mast to prevent any other crew from falling overboard.

After abandoning the hull to Silbrey's group, the crew took shelter under the forecastle and stern castle. The tree had extended past the main sail, creating a canopy over the whole ship that provided some relief from the elements. The weight of the tree should have caused the whole ship to capsize, but it maintained an uneasy balance. Silbrey felt the tree continually shifting its weight to keep the ship steady. Silbrey sensed that the tree had kept them from tipping over several times throughout the worst parts of their voyage.

Silbrey sensed Vindel was not with the rest of the crew. He leaned against the massive trunk of the tree, rejected by the other sailors and his father. Silbrey felt pity for him. He didn't ask to be the son of a captain. He had lived his whole life as a proxy on this ship and then was cast out for being too old for the role. It appeared Vindel had a change of heart about his role. That was the terrible thing about faith. When the water was still and sailing easy, no one thought twice about the proxy —but when the water was rough and the journey uncertain, every eye was on Vindel, blaming him for not leaving when he was younger. The only life he had known. Silbrey also thought about Timon. The two were much alike, Vindel and Timon. Timon lived his entire life within the temple. The temple was his Amoet, a comfortable life that felt like a higher calling.

Silbrey didn't know if she believed in the superstitions of sailors and priests, but she knew what a true calling felt like— and it did not lead one to comfort. How did Gydan fit into this proxy mess? She was innocent. A girl who was a victim of peculiar circumstances. Everyone looked for someone to blame. Vindel was too old, and Gydan was too young. The god of the sea didn't know who was supposed to be the proxy, so he caused the whole angry ocean to conspire against one ship— such a terrible faith to place meaningless people at the center of meaningless circumstances and call it higher truth, to sit in judgment of a bad situation.

What about Silbrey? She knew she was in no position to criticize the faith of others. Traveling to Raustfweg, in search of Alda Feren, to save the world from breaking, because an ancient evil wants to wake the titan birds sleeping deep under the earth. She had been through too much to doubt her experience. Even across the great ocean expanse, she could feel Alda Feren calling from somewhere on that distant land.

\* \* \*

Gydan stirred awake from the violent jolt of a wave crashing against the side of the ship. Often the water from the deck would pour through the gaps in the trapdoor where the ladder was. The splashing water would also wake up Gydan. She would wake up several times through the night for several different reasons. Each time, Gydan would reach out to grab Bren's sword, hold it close, and she would feel safe. Something about the smell of the scabbard's leather, the soft texture, the bumps and ridges where it had been tooled, made her feel comfortable. She reached out for the sword but could not find it. Gydan opened her eyes and began to search. Anger swelled in her.

"Where is my sword? Where is my sword?"

Silbrey and Maricel came to Gydan's side. Maricel was able to hold on to the roots and use them to aid her walking.

"Don't you mean Bren's sword?" Udger asked.

"Where is it?" Gydan directed her wrath at the dwarf.

Udger steepled his fingers, tapping them to his lips, relishing the attention.

"I solved the riddle, and I shared my theory with the captain," Udger said. "You are not Gydan. No. You are Tian, the named god of mischief, luck, and misfortune. I've listened to your stories. You have a way of avoiding death by sheer happenstance. Everywhere death follows you, and yet you remain untouched. You're lucky."

Lucky. Udger thought she was lucky. After everything she had been through, that was the conclusion he came to? The time at sea had driven him mad.

"Of all the gods, Tian most enjoys dwelling among the people of this world," Udger explained. "People may love Taraki, but Tian loves the people. Adores them. She is their defender. She was the one who humbled herself before the Fey Court and convinced them to send their children to Efre Ousel to protect it. You are that Tian, the first named god. You are no child. You are a god—the living avatar of one. Aegir is not angry about the proxy. He's happy to see his sister, and he's showing off. That's the solution, however improbable, to the riddle you presented."

"You're deranged," Silbrey said. "I birthed this child. I saw her brought into this world, cold and crying. Trust me, she's no god."

Udger's voice lifted in response. "You're a mother. Another mystery. But not impossible for a god to arrange. Tian would choose her mortal mother carefully."

Udger was spouting nonsense. The gods didn't dwell among people. Gydan knew this. Those were only stories. She certainly wouldn't have chosen her mother.

"I told the captain you're a god," Udger said. "And I suggested a test. I stole your sword. No easy task with your dragon guardian. And I gave the sword to Hrutib. He's going to throw your sword into the sea. You love that sword. It's special. Bren Caius gave it to you. Perhaps Bren sensed your divinity. If you are a god—and I know you are—you'll get the sword back."

Udger's assertion was absurd. She loved her father. He wasn't coming back. She cared about Bren Caius. She wasn't coming back either. Gydan cherished Bren's sword and what it stood for. She wanted to believe the sword had a greater purpose, but it was only a sword. If it were tossed into the sea, the sword would just be another thing Gydan loved that was taken from her and would not return.

"And since you are a god," Udger said. "Hrutib needs to

make peace with you, not further antagonize you. If Hrutib can be convinced of this, we can have peace on this ship."

"Hrutib has my sword?" Gydan asked.

"He's on the deck of the ship."

Without hesitation, Gydan ran for the ladder leading to the deck. Silbrey and Maricel both called for her, but she did not stop. The roots reached for her, trying to keep her from the ladder, but Cyru cleared a path with their sharp talons. If Gydan wanted her sword back, Cyru would help her get it.

Gydan reached the top of the ladder and scrambled onto the deck. She looked out and saw the endless ocean.

She had been in the dark hull for so long that the openness of everything was disorienting, despite spending much of her time bonded with Cyru and viewing the ship through their draconic perception. This was different. Now, she could see out to the far horizon as the ship bobbed up and down. Her mind could not comprehend it. The light above, filtered through the tree's canopy and cloudy sky, was blinding. She tried to steady herself, but everything was moving and immeasurable. She slipped and fell on her back.

*Gydan, get up.*

"Udger, she doesn't look like a god." Gydan heard the captain's voice. "Her mother almost killed me. I'm risking a lot here."

*Gydan, get up.*

"Don't worry, Hrutib." Gydan heard another voice. "You didn't do anything. The girl came up here on her own. You can't be held responsible."

*Gydan, get up.*

"I'm responsible for everything. That's why I'm doing this. We need to settle this proxy matter."

*Gydan, get up.*

Gydan rolled over and pushed herself up. Her knees wobbled, but she stood on her feet. She reached out to steady herself but couldn't find anything to hold on to. In the hull, there was always a crate or roots she could grab to keep from falling over. On the deck, she only had herself. She placed her hands on her knees and tried to find something she could focus on. She saw Captain Hrutib standing next to the railing. The bastard had Bren's sword, sheathed in its leather scabbard, and held it over the railing.

"*Yakost*, girl. Are you Tian, the named god of gamblers and prostitutes?" Hrutib said.

"*Ya*, I'm only Gydan, menace to ogres, daughter of Silbrey and Callis."

She didn't mean to give the title Oren assigned to her. Menace to ogres. The words slipped out. She saw the sword, and she thought of Bren Caius, which made her think of Oren.

"A menace to ogres?" Hrutib said. "That's almost better than Tian, the goddess of drunken brides."

"If that's what you think of Tian," Gydan said, "you wouldn't recognize her even if she were right in front of you."

Her bold words impressed Hrutib. The captain then looked at Udger. Gydan hadn't even noticed before where the dwarf was standing, but she saw he was close to her as he had climbed up the ladder too. Silbrey and Maricel were also there. Maricel held onto Silbrey's arm, leaning against her. Silbrey had a stricken look on her face, forbidding whatever Gydan had on her mind.

"Let's see then," Hrutib said.

Hrutib let go of the sword. It fell into the violent sea.

Gydan's thoughts reached out to Cyru. *Grab me as soon as I resurface.*

Gydan ran for the railing and dove into the water headfirst.

Silbrey screamed as she saw her daughter leap over the railing. Silbrey felt such stifling anguish, she couldn't breathe. Her throat seized up. She nearly fainted.

The world could take everything from her, but not her daughter. Not her. Pain shot through Silbrey. Her knees buckled. Then she felt a white light of anger burning across her chest and face. The white light she remembered from Aberton. White light radiated all around her. The Amoet lurched in response. The tree bent over and opened like a hand grasping at the air, reaching for Silbrey's daughter, who was already gone. The roots shot through the bottom of the hull and into the water, seeking out Gydan, hoping to find her. Water flooded into the hull where the roots had rent the sides of the ship.

Cyru chirped frantically at Silbrey and Maricel, but they couldn't understand the dragon. Cyru shot out over the water's surface, faster than an arrow, changing directions at sharp angles. So fast, it was impossible to track where Cyru was.

Silbrey found her strength again and tried to move toward the railing, but someone was holding her. She brought her elbow back, hitting them on the bridge of the nose, dropping them to the ground. Only then did Silbrey realize she had hit Maricel. Without her crutch, Maricel had been holding onto Silbrey. Maricel fell backward, hitting hard against the deck. Her wooden boot twisted behind her. Maricel cried in pain.

Blood poured from her nose. Silbrey was bewildered, forgetting for a moment what she was doing, where she was.

"Go save Gydan," Maricel waved her off.

Silbrey turned, ran for the railing, and looked at the open sea.

Gydan was gone.


The water was hard when Gydan hit the surface, but then she was pulled below into the crushing current. She tried to hold her breath, but water pressed against her on all sides and her breath escaped, bubbling out from her open mouth and nose. She thought the ocean would be calmer under the surface, but that was not the case. She remembered seeing with Cyru the whale soaring through the depths of the ocean. The pale leviathan appeared so serene, but such creatures were massive, built for this world. Gydan was nothing in the ocean. The immense void devoured her.

She twisted around, cartwheeling, pushed this way and that. She had no sense of which way was up. Gydan looked around, hoping to see the sword. Her lungs tightened. She panicked and started flailing.

Far above her, she saw a shadowy form that was the Amoet on the surface. The ship was smaller than her hand as she held it up. The depth she had sunk was an insurmountable distance. It didn't seem possible she could have descended so far. She would never be able to reach the surface.


Silbrey had lost Gydan. She screamed and clawed at the railing of the ship, screamed until her voice gave out. She could hear

Maricel on the ground, crying. It broke Silbrey's heart because she knew Maricel was anguished—and because Maricel felt terribly alone. Now was not the time to grieve. Silbrey would have the rest of her life for that. Silbrey needed to act, but she was unsure what to do. She wanted to dive in after Gydan. She watched as Cyru repeatedly dove into the water and then resurfaced. The dragon was looking for Gydan and could not find her. If Cyru couldn't, what hope did Silbrey have? She tried to extend her fey senses beyond the Amoet, but the depths only offered a dull hum. The ocean created a darkness she struggled to see through. She only felt the tremors along the ocean floor of the Great Thayl'em Sea. All between was unfamiliar territory.

Captain Hrutib stood next to Silbrey. She was about to throw him overboard, but then she heard him crying. Silbrey looked to see his face racked with grief.

"I'm sorry," he blustered. "I don't know what came over me. The ocean, it's driving us all mad. I can't think straight."

He grabbed his bronze helm and tossed it into the ocean.

"I didn't think she'd jump. I wanted m'crew to think I was taking their proxy concerns seriously. They were conspiring against me and m'son. Udger sounded so convincing. I—"

He had no more words. Silbrey hated the empty excuses, the rationalizing a person does to excuse their crimes. Silence was better.

"That is the way of the gods," Udger said, standing behind them. "Everyone loses something when they intervene. A sword. A crown. A daughter. The gods will reward these sacrifices."

Silbrey wanted to tear Udger limb from limb, like she had done to Kret. Before she could, one of the sailors spoke.

"Captain, the roots from that cursed tree, they tore through the ship. We're sinking."

"This is m'reward," Hrutib said. "A well-deserved reward."

Gydan continued to tumble through the watery abyss. The light of the surface dimmed as she sunk deeper. She felt the ever-tightening squeeze. The pain became so excruciating it ceased to have any meaning. The pain was worse than anything she had ever felt, and to feel that pain increasing couldn't do any more to her than it already had. Throughout her body, she was in agony beyond agony, but her mind had become calm. All panic had left her. She was perfectly still as she descended, appearing serene, like a leaf floating to the ground. She was dying. She was dead. All because—in an irrational moment— she had thought Bren's sword was worth saving.

A light flickered farther below. Gydan thought it was the glint of Bren's sword, but that didn't make sense, since her sword was sheathed and tied. Also, there was no light to reflect. The light flickered again and grew brighter. Something was swimming toward her. A young boy. He was a little older than her and shirtless. He wore ragged pants. His bare feet were large with long webbed toes. Luminescent fins extended from the ankles. He had dark, curly hair. He moved through the water almost as fast as Cyru flew through the air, a whooshing noise and a trail of bubbles followed him. After swimming circles, he stopped in front of her. His face studied hers. He smiled.

"Hello, sister."

He tapped her nose with his index finger. All pain left Gydan. The sudden absence of pain was euphoric. She opened her mouth and found she was able to breathe the water. It took some effort at first, but it felt natural. She didn't know it then, but this curious gift would stay with her for the rest of her life.

"Yurig?" Like him, inexplicably, she was able to speak underwater.

"Your other brother. We've been siblings for much longer."

"Aegir?"

"Is that the name we're going with?" The boy winced. He didn't appear to like that name. "Fine. Aegir. And what are you calling yourself now?"

"I'm Gydan."

"You are, and more." The boy smiled again. He reached behind his back and held out Bren's sheathed sword to her. "You lost this. I thought it might be important."

Gydan reached out and took the sword.

"I don't understand."

"You do," said the boy who was her brother who was Aegir. "You haven't forgotten anything. In your human body, you're using your human mind to do that very human thing."

"Which is?"

"You're trying to make sense of everything," said Aegir. "Humans will forget who they are, if it helps them make better sense of the world."

"I'm a god?"

"No and yes, but mostly no," Aegir said. "As I said before, you are human. Fully human, by choice. You hurt as they hurt. You die as they die. You have all their stupid ideas and limitations. But that's not to say you don't have a certain providence that most mortals lack. You are destined for great things—or more to the point, great things will seek you out. Sometimes, you succeed. Other times, you fail. But it's always—"

"Wondrous," Gydan said, realizing a bit more about herself. Some truths hide in plain sight. Since language is limited in describing certain experiences and some things defy reason, these truths dwell in the periphery. Yes, she was Tian. Udger's faith allowed him to see the impossible truth, which Gydan had been ignoring. "I chose to become human because I want to experience true wonder at this fragile world. I want risk, adventure, and that is something a god can never have. And I chose my mother because I want to help her save this world."

"That sounds like something you'd do," Aegir said. "Even though I don't get it."

As they talked, Gydan was unaware of the blackness surrounding them. They had plunged so deep into the ocean that no light, except the illumination of Aegir, reached them. This world was a black curtain, as though they were inverted shadow puppets.

"You're a god," Gydan said. "I'm talking to a god, one of many siblings."

"Sister, I'm always a god," Aegir said. "Every family has an odd one. That's you."

"Since you're Aegir, can you calm the ocean?"

"I wish I could, but I have no control over the four titans." Aegir smiled at Gydan. She felt the playful condescension in his look. "They're waking up, and they're the ones making your voyage so miserable."

"The world is ending."

Aegir did not seem too concerned. "The world is always ending. Reality is not very kind to worlds. Be wary. This time, you may fail. Even if the daughter of autumn, the one you think of as your mother, is able to put the titans back to sleep, there is another who could start an unending war between the gods and the Fey Court."

"Kret?"

"No. Mendal Caius. The true son of winter, the adopted son of summer's daughter. Their family is filled with odd ones. He will make you suffer. Ten years hence." He kissed her on the forehead. "Until next time."

Several minutes had passed since Gydan had gone into the ocean. The ship, even while sinking, had drifted far from the point where they last saw her. Silbrey and Maricel had both given up looking. Hrutib left their vigil at the railing and was trying his best to save the Amoet from sinking further. Udger stared at the ocean, still expecting a god to re-emerge.

Cyru continued diving into the water to search for their friend. When Cyru stayed under longer, Silbrey took notice. Then the dragon surfaced, pulling at the shirt collar of a pale and unconscious Gydan. Even still, she was stubbornly holding on to Bren's sheathed sword with a tight grip. When Silbrey first saw Gydan, she thought she was dead. Cyru had recovered the body and nothing more. Then Gydan began coughing up water. An intense warm sensation spread across Silbrey's body. A joy like the moment she held her daughter for the first time. Her daughter was here. She was alive.

Waves of blue light emanated from Silbrey. The tree spread its limbs as the light weaved around it. The wooden boards of the ship groaned as they tightened together. The boards shifted, sealing the tears the roots had caused. The roots coiled around, pressing against the larger holes to plug them. It was a miracle. Whoever Silbrey was—demon, devil, or demigod—it no longer mattered to the crew. Whatever power she had over the Amoet, they were thankful for it.

Hrutib was able to pull Gydan up out of the water with a fishing net. She was barely conscious, lying in Silbrey's lap. Her eyes fluttered a bit. She looked up.

"Mom?"

Silbrey held her tight.

"Gydan, don't you ever do that again."

"If someone throws Bren's sword into the ocean a second time, I definitely won't dive after it."

"What happened out here? How were you able to reach the surface?"

"I can't remember," Gydan said. "It's all a blank."

This was true. She couldn't remember anything that happened.

Gydan—exhausted, frail, and broken—curled into Silbrey's embrace.

Udger looked defeated. This girl was too broken to be a god.

"I was so certain," was all Udger said.

He wouldn't speak again for the remainder of the voyage.

\* \* \*

Maricel heard the shouts. Land had been sighted. She grabbed her crutch and made her way to the ship's bow in hopes of seeing the Raustfweg shoreline. She was walking better now. Her right side was still numb, but she could get where she needed to go with the aid of her crutch and the wooden brace around her leg. About a week after Gydan went overboard and the ship nearly sank, Hrutib steered the ship farther north.

This was a good decision. The water was still rough, but not as much as before.

Maricel reached the railing and looked out across the sea. Maricel's mother had told her so much about her homeland, a beautiful and magical land, a land that existed in her mother's heart and in Maricel's imagination. Every praise and every complaint her mother ever had was in the context of her original home. "The food is better in Raustfweg." "The weather is much cooler and more agreeable." "The people in Raustfweg are wiser and honor their families." It was never-ending. Maricel wasn't sure what to expect, but she was disappointed to see the heavy fog had obscured her view of the shore. All she saw was a darker line along the horizon, which to the sailors was "land," but to Maricel, meant nothing.

They would soon be off the ship, and they would begin the next stage of their journey to Alda Feren. Maricel knew the journey would be difficult, not because of anything they might face. Alda Feren could be on the other side of the continent, along the most dangerous, twisted paths—or it could be right along the coast, waiting for them. She did not know. No, the journey would be difficult because Maricel didn't feel the same about Silbrey anymore.

Her mother once told her if a person wanted to know someone, travel with them. Maricel felt she knew Silbrey much better now.

Silbrey could be kind and attentive. During the early days of the voyage, she saw the best of Silbrey, but as things got difficult, Silbrey became angry, bitter, and inwardly focused. This anger was a survival instinct Silbrey had developed from her years of being abused by Dahlia Tulan and from the pain of losing Callis. Maricel also knew Silbrey enjoyed the violence. Udger was right. Violence was part of Silbrey's nature. No matter how much Silbrey said she regretted what she did, part of her liked the power she had over other people. And Maricel, even though she had devoted her life to finding and following Silbrey, did not know if she could stay with Silbrey after their journey. Maricel had hoped they could reconcile and become what they once were at the farmhouse near Barcombe, but too much had happened since then.

Maricel wasn't mad about Silbrey elbowing her in the face. It hurt, but it was an accident. What concerned Maricel was how violent Silbrey became whenever something was in her way. Maricel did not have a place in Silbrey's life, no matter how much she wanted it.

As they sailed, Maricel could make out more of the Raustfweg coastline. What she did not expect was how mountainous it was. The areas of Amon Maricel knew best, along Tu'enya Bay, were mostly flat. She had never seen anything like this before. The mountains soared high, beginning at the edge of the shore and shooting almost straight into the sky. The fog had lifted, but all the mountain peaks were still covered by the clouds, causing the range to look like an impenetrable rocky wall—something built not by giants, but by titans. Maricel couldn't take her eyes off it. She saw vertical snaking lines along the mountains, actual paths worn into the mountainside. How was it possible for people to travel along them? She hoped they would not have to go along those routes, but how else would they get anywhere?

Since they had traveled so far north, the Amoet had to sail south along the coast for a few days to get to the docks at Vasterghent. They would pass a few smaller villages, which clung to the shoreline or were set farther back in one of the many fjords.

Every village was destroyed—collapsed buildings with a scattering of people trying their best to survive amidst the wreckage. They looked like Rhyll and Penderyn had looked after the earthquakes. In far worse scenes, she saw areas covered by rockslides, consuming entire villages that were once there.

The earthquakes were not limited to Amon. Raustfweg had also experienced the destructive preamble of a breaking world.

# VII

Ausdre's husband was a quiet man. He was a gentle person who made sensible decisions. His name was Rue, but everyone called him "Rooster." The nickname was intentionally ironic because he was not a person who made a lot of noise.

Ausdre and Rue had met when she first came to the farming community. He lived on the other side of the pasture, so Ausdre and Rue saw each other often. They politely acknowledged each other with nods and waves for a year before either of them said a word to the other. Even his proposal of marriage was quiet and understated. They often disputed the particulars, but Ausdre swore he said, "There might be a better man out there, but I think you like it here." Rue said it was an endearing moment and that she told it wrong. Ausdre loved her version of the story, which made him appear more awkward. He happily endured her teasing like many spouses do.

Rue worked on the farm and helped the neighbors who

were too old to maintain their land. In the evenings, he focused on his whittling. He enjoyed carving forest animals and legendary heroes. The finished figures were small enough to fit in the palm of his hand. He had a whole set of Bren Caius figures on the hearth mantle. Rue's Bren Caius was always with a sword and shield—always Bren the Beloved who saved Amon from Kret Bonebreaker.

When Rue discovered Gydan had Bren's sword in her possession, he refused to believe it, but asked if he could hold it on the second day.

"Rooster, are you even listening to this?" Ausdre pleaded. Rue looked up from his carving. He was whittling a figurine of the late Oren of Angnavir. Ausdre gestured to their obstinate daughter.

"Yes," he said, even though he had lost track of where the argument had gone. Ausdre and Maricel had been at it for so long. "Can you remind me again of what you were trying to say to Maricel?"

Ausdre looked like she could've strangled Rue. He was used to it.

"Maricel can't even walk. She was dying on our doorstep. And now, she wants to accompany this strange woman and her daughter to Alda Feren." Ausdre turned back to Maricel. "How are you going to do that if you can't walk?"

"*Strange* woman?" Maricel spoke over her mother's last question. Maricel looked like she could've strangled her mom. "The whole reason you came to Amon was to find her! Did you forget the visions I had? The seizures? I followed her. I documented her every moment. I know more about this strange woman than I know about my own family."

"The elders of my old village asked *me* to find the fey child, return home, and then take her to Alda Feren, not you."

"Our fates are connected!" Maricel countered.

"You know nothing of your fate."

"Mother, come with me."

"My life is here now."

At this point, mother and daughter were talking over each other, and Rue couldn't make out any more of the argument. How they kept track was beyond him. He put down his carving knife and wood block. He held up his hands, asking for a momentary pause. They obliged, each hoping he would take their side.

"Fate or not, your mother makes a good point. How would you travel through Raustfweg if you can't walk? If the world supposedly will break unless Silbrey finds Alda Feren, wouldn't you worry about slowing her down?"

"I feel myself getting stronger every day," Maricel said. "Give me a week, three weeks. I'll be able to walk again. I know it."

"Three weeks?" Ausdre balked at this idea. "It's a long journey. What if Silbrey doesn't have any time to spare?"

"If you had rescued her sooner, in Penderyn, like I suggested—she would've been there years ago."

And again, the argument resumed a similar path to where it had already been. Rue was a patient man, but he hated when these quarrels went around in circles like this.

"Please." He didn't raise his voice in a way that any person, except his wife and daughter, would notice. Again, they quieted. "Let me speak."

They both waited for what he would say next.

"If the world is breaking—if these earthquakes are the

result of titans waking up under the earth—then no one is safe wherever they go. And if Silbrey is the one to save us, we should ask Silbrey what she wants."

Maricel smiled. Ausdre buried her head in her hands.

Rue didn't realize it, but they already knew Silbrey's opinion. Silbrey had said she couldn't go to Raustfweg without Maricel. She wouldn't be able to make it to Alda Feren on her own. Silbrey needed Maricel by her side.

Assuming the conversation was over, Rue returned to his whittling. He cut grooves into the soft wood that became Oren's two-handed sword. He thought to himself how sometimes heroes wield weapons, and other times, people can be heroic just by supporting each other or offering the right judgment on a difficult matter. Rue's wife came from Raustfweg, and they were people directed by omens, visions, and dark prophesies. Rue, on the other hand, was a practical man. None of this made much sense to him—and he doubted any of this ominous talk about waking titans was true. However, right then, Rue thought he was rather heroic.

Maybe he even helped save the world.

Rue didn't believe in miracles or the intervention of the gods, even when Ausdre worked her druid magic. But over the next few weeks, he was inclined to change his opinion. His daughter, who had suffered seizures throughout her childhood, who nearly died on the road home, showed greater strength and willpower than he had ever seen before. With the help of a crutch and the wooden boot that Silbrey had formed for her, Maricel pushed herself every day to relearn how to walk. She moved one foot in front of another, and she was able to step forward. Rue decided that was also heroic.

\* \* \*

The Amoet arrived in the port city of Vasterghent on the Raustfweg coast. News of the peculiar tree growing from the ship spread. People gathered at the docks to gawk. No reasonable explanation for the tree could be given, but rumors circulated. The most common theory was that the captain had lost his mind and wanted to plant a tree from his homeland so he could carry it with him wherever he went. The story was a sentimental one, but it failed to explain how he could navigate a ship with the additional weight on the stern. The crew charged curious visitors two copper coins for the opportunity to board the ship and inspect the tree. The people who touched the tree and examined it closely attested that, yes, the tree was a tree and not some illusory spell. One captain was so enamored by the tree, she consulted druids to see how she might grow a tree on her ship. By the time she set sail again, the captain had a sapling in a barrel filled with rich, black soil and strapped to the mast—not as impressive as the Amoet tree.

With all eyes on the tree, Silbrey, Gydan, and Maricel were able to disembark without arousing any attention. Most travelers between Amon and Raustfweg were merchants, and none traveled with a shoeless fey, a sword-bearing child, and a small dragon.

Before parting ways, the dwarf Udger gave Silbrey a small sack of coin as restitution for the harm he had caused. Silbrey weighed the sack in her hand and told Udger any amount he would willingly part with was not enough. He gave her three more sacks of coin. Silbrey asked for one more, and Udger obliged.

"When you come back from wherever you're going,"

Udger said, "look for me in the town north of here, Solenstrig. I'll cover your journey back home. Then we will be even?"

"Then we will be even," Silbrey confirmed. She said the words, barely opening her mouth, little more than a mumble. She didn't know what "even" meant. How could she put a price on Gydan's life or forgive Udger's recklessness? But she knew she'd never see Udger again. She wouldn't be returning from Alda Feren once they found it.

Udger had other dwarves from his village waiting for him at the docks. They were ready with a cart and several mules. Udger looked at Gydan one last time. Silbrey saw a great sadness in him. Udger wanted to believe he had met a living god, but he had made a terrible mistake—giving Hrutib every reason to throw Gydan overboard. And although Udger did not toss her over himself, he pushed a distraught captain to do the unthinkable.

Silbrey put the coins in her haversack. Since leaving the farmhouse near Barcombe, Silbrey had lived off the charity of whomever they were staying with. Now she had more coin than ever. Even as Dahlia Tulan's ward, Silbrey never had any wealth of her own; whatever she needed was given to her.

They took Udger's offering and walked about the city to purchase supplies for their journey into the mountains as well as some warmer clothes. It was summer, but the weather in Raustfweg was much colder than they had expected. Ausdre had warned them before they left, but it didn't occur to Silbrey that it could ever be this cold at this time of year.

Vasterghent was unharmed by the earthquakes. The city was an anomaly—a floating island in the middle of a fjord, connected to the mainland by seven bridges. When the earthquakes came, Vasterghent had rocked upon the water but did not shake or crack.

The greater challenge was handling the survivors from inland towns who came seeking aid. Silbrey passed families on the street who were clearly destitute and displaced. They had lost their homes and had nowhere else to go but here. The coin weighed heavily in Silbrey's haversack and on her conscience. She could give it away to the refugees, but it wouldn't be enough, not to save them all. Silbrey knew they might need the coin for their journey.

The refugees came here because Vasterghent was a cross-roads for travelers and merchants. People journeyed from across Efre Ousel to trade stories and goods. In this way, Vasterghent reminded Silbrey of Penderyn.

The buildings were densely packed. A maze-like series of narrow alleys—intended for the locals—connected all of Vasterghent, while the wide main roads led visitors from the docks over the bridges and into the mountains. Plumes of smoke rose from the chimneys of each building and drifted far into the sky. Hearth fires and lanterns shined from every window. The travelers would gather around bonfires set at the open markets. Vasterghent was illuminated throughout the night. From the mountains, the city looked like the stoked glowing embers of a campfire.

Silbrey found a fur merchant near the center of town. After some haggling, Silbrey bought a soft double-lined black shirt with gray fox fur trim on the shoulders and back. The collar had silver buttons and, beneath it, a woven leather pattern with silver studs at the intersections. It was the most extravagant outfit she had ever worn.

Maricel opted for a modest wool dress in a style common

to the maids of Raustfweg. Unlike Silbrey's ornate fur-lined shirt, Maricel's dress was embellished only by the clasp beading of the cloak that accompanied her outfit.

Silbrey looked like a conquering warlord and Maricel, her attendant or adviser.

Gydan dressed for warmth and comfort. She selected a hooded white fur jacket that engulfed her small frame.

Silbrey couldn't help but smile when she saw her daughter waddle in the oversized attire.

"You look like a dandelion puff ball. I keep expecting you to float away on the next breeze."

Cyru hissed at Silbrey.

"You won't be laughing when we go into the mountains," Gydan said, "and you all are freezing to the bone. Are you not even going to buy a pair of boots?"

Silbrey hadn't even thought about buying boots. She had been barefoot this whole time and hardly noticed the cool air on her exposed feet.

"Halflings don't wear shoes," Silbrey said, looking down at her feet.

"That's a myth," Gydan corrected her. "They only go barefoot in their hometown. They wear shoes everywhere else."

Silbrey didn't know any halflings and had no reason to doubt her daughter.

"I like having my bare feet on the bare ground," Silbrey said. "And if my feet get cold, I'll tear off one of your sleeves and make slippers."

Gydan stared at her mother, unamused by the attempt at humor. Cyru mirrored this empty expression.

Silbrey, Gydan, and Maricel each bought a new rucksack along with a bedroll, a knife, rope, hardtack biscuits, and a stoppered jug of fresh water. They purchased a mule and a cart. In the cart, they had a series of wicker baskets that contained the rest of their supplies. The cart still had room for Maricel to sit so she wouldn't have to walk as much.

Outside the city, the mountain road was wide enough for the cart and not much more. To lead the mule, Silbrey had to walk in front. Cyru flew ahead of them. The road wasn't as steep as it appeared from below. The road cut back and forth across the face of the mountains in a gradual, perpetual incline. Only when Silbrey looked down was she aware of how high up they were. The world tilted whenever her eyes tried to focus on the city below at a dizzying height.

Maricel and Gydan both said they felt lightheaded as they continued up the mountain. Breathing became difficult. Even the mule struggled at this altitude. The air was much colder. Snow covered the road near the summit. Visibility was limited by the swirling snowdrifts.

Silbrey felt no discomfort, even though she walked barefoot through the snow. It was not that she was numb or immune to any sensations. She had a fey perspective that allowed her to move through the elements without being at odds with the elements. As natural as her heartbeat, she didn't know any other way.

Before reaching the mountain's peak, the road cut eastward, along a series of ravines, deeper into the mountain range. Other adjoining mountains formed a shield against the wind, and the path descended to a more comfortable altitude for Maricel and Gydan. The light filtered down to them, casting everything in a blue tint, like the light from the low-hanging sun after a thunderstorm. The ravine pass was silent and absent of other travelers. After weeks at sea, Silbrey had forgotten such stillness was even possible. The silence felt sacred. No one spoke during this part of the journey.

\* \* \*

The small, unnamed village was easier to find than Silbrey expected. They only had to follow Ausdre's tattoo.

The runic tattoos on Ausdre's face held deep significance. The tattoo along the left side of her face, closest to her ear, was called the "home mark." The home mark was given to people when they first left for war or to raid—or any other great journey. The tattoo helped others bring the bodies home for burial.

Although the ink had faded, Maricel remembered her mother's marks by heart. The vertical line that ran down her cheek represented the coastline. The crosshatches designated the larger fjords with a triangle to indicate the essential port city. The triangle had one dark corner to stand for the west, east, or south coastline. From the triangle, a line extended horizontally with hashmarks and a circle to mark the villages along the path leading inland. Underneath, there was a rune, which identified the village. Ausdre's village had a seven-point star as its home rune.

It wasn't a perfect system. For instance, few settlements lined the northern coast. They were so scattered that instead of a home mark, the person had a mark, which essentially meant, "I'm in the north. Good luck finding my home." Also, villages sometimes relocated or died off. Five hashmarks from the port town might be one or two marks off. Also, some of the more popular home runes, such as bears or ravens, were employed so frequently as to be useless for identifying a village.

In the case of Ausdre's village, her home mark was accurate

and easy to follow. Silbrey, Gydan, and Maricel continued east along the ravine pass until it opened to a wooded valley, still high in the mountains. The valley road consisted of soft-packed dirt and stones lining each side. Ausdre's village was the third one they encountered. The seven-point star hung upon a wooden archway extending over the road.

The star, with its interwoven lines, reminded Silbrey of the floral crown she had once worn while working for Dahlia Tulan.

The houses in this village were dome-shaped, built with interconnecting stone. Each home was set a few feet into the ground with a set of stairs leading down to the front door. Each home had an irrigation path to drain any runoff from the pits to a water well. The water would not be drinkable but could be used for other purposes.

Each house was painted black with white markings that looked like a starry sky. A single chimney protruded from each dome. The villagers kept their weapons outside—swords, shields, bows, and quivers leaning against the side of each home. Possibly the weapons were kept out of the house as a symbolic commitment to peace in the home or maybe they just wanted to be ready to arm themselves if the village should be attacked.

At the center of the village was a long house with a grass sod roof. The window flaps were propped up around the building to allow light and ventilation. Silbrey had seen a similar long house in each of the other villages they passed through. The front half of the house appeared to be a common meeting place, while the back half was a residence for the head of the village.

The people in the village went about their business. Each

gave the visitors and their dragon a sidelong glance to determine if they were a threat, and then they continued their work.

Silbrey froze, staring at a boy tending sheep among the villagers. It was Yurig. She was so certain of that child being her son it gave her a jolt.

She looked again, and Yurig was gone. A trick of the mind.

Maricel got out of the cart and hobbled with her crutch to join Silbrey and Gydan. An older woman, streaks of white in her blonde braided hair, walked past. She held a roll of tanned leather hides. Maricel stopped her with a raised hand.

"Excuse me. Is this the village where Ausdre once lived?"

"Ausdre is a common name," replied the woman. "We have five Ausdres in this village."

Her Raustfweg accent was thick and melodic, more so than the people of Vasterghent. Silbrey recalled that Oren, also from Raustfweg, spoke with a subtler intonation. The woman's accent must have been distinctive to this village or this region of Raustfweg. Her voice lifted at the end of each phrase. To Silbrey, the accent sounded as though everything was pronounced at the front of the mouth. "Vill-udge" became "vill-eege."

Maricel tried to explain. "Ausdre is my mother."

"Then you should know if this is your home or not." The woman shifted the roll of hides from one arm to the other.

"I'm not from here."

"Aye, that I know. Are you another spirit here to play tricks on me?"

"My mother left the village and traveled to Amon with three other people. They were searching for a fey child."

The woman spit and then rubbed the saliva into the dirt

with her foot. Silbrey knew the gesture meant something, but wasn't sure what.

"What was that for?" Maricel asked.

"If that Ausdre is your mother, then I just found out that I have another granddaughter," the older woman said. Her eyes welled up, but her face remained firm and expressionless. "My name is Olvi. The Ausdre you speak of is my daughter, my only daughter. I thought she had died."

"Your daughter lives," Maricel said. Her voice lowered at the realization of who stood in front of her.

Silbrey could see a resemblance she hadn't noticed before. Olvi's long neck and strong jawline were a family trait, and there was a gentleness in her eyes. Others in the village stopped their chores and looked at the visitors with new eyes.

"Why didn't she come home? Why did she leave me wondering what had happened?" Olvi looked around them as she spoke in the hope that Ausdre would be standing behind them somewhere, but she was still in Amon.

"I can tell you everything in time," Maricel said. "My mother thought she had failed in her mission, but she didn't. The path wasn't straight. That's all. Olvi, meet Silbrey. She is the true fey they were looking for—and I am bringing her to you."

The people of the village approached, curious and cautious.

"Let's go to the long house," Olvi said. "One of your uncles would like to meet you."

\*\*\*

Maricel's uncle called himself a sage and a king of the valley. To Gydan, he didn't appear to be either. He looked like an extravagant fool.

Soren wore a fur coat, dyed the most garish colors Gydan had ever seen. She didn't know such colors even existed— radiant reds and oranges, blinding pinks and yellows. Soren was proud of his coat. More than once, he mentioned how he had obtained the pigments from a Karkasse merchant. He said the colors were worth five times their weight in gold, and Gydan believed it. Such colors must be rarer than any metal from the ground. Even Cyru was impressed by it.

Soren wore no shirt or tunic under his coat. He was hairy and muscular—not muscular like a farmer who worked the fields, but like a warrior or mercenary who spent their time in a fighting pit and wanted to appear as intimidating as possible. He rubbed some sort of oil or lard on his muscles to give them a shine. It struck Gydan as a strange sort of vanity.

He had long, greasy hair and a well-groomed beard. The sides of his head were shaved. His hair was a black obsidian. Another peculiarity, since almost everyone in the village had blonde hair.

Soren laughed loudly and often for no reason at all. He spoke as if addressing a nation of followers, even though there were only a few people in the longhouse to hear him.

"Does my sister Ausdre miss me?" He shouted this question, even though they heard him just fine.

"She speaks of you often, your grace," Maricel lied. She understood the way to gain his approval was to feed him with flattery.

Soren laughed, but it wasn't a real laugh. He laughed in a

staged, exaggerated manner to show Maricel she had gotten something wrong.

"How old do you think I am? I was born after she left. Was Ausdre seeing visions of my ascent to greatness?"

"My apologies, your grace," Maricel corrected herself. "I mean to say she loved her home and her family. She spoke fondly of her six brothers. She will be pleased to know she has a seventh. You honor your family."

"I honor myself," Soren said. "But do not feel the need to call me 'your grace.' You may call me *franduri*. It's an old word that pre-dates the common tongue. It means 'uncle!' Unless you feel more comfortable addressing me as 'your grace.' I understand the impulse when standing in my presence."

"You are most wise, *franduri*." Maricel bowed her head.

Gydan chuckled. Soren glared at her and then returned his attention to his niece.

"Have you seen any unexpected people since coming to the village? People from your past?"

"I'm not sure I understand."

"You will, soon enough." Soren shifted to a new topic. "What happened to your face?" Soren gestured to the side of his face as he said it. Silbrey took a step forward, wanting to confront him for his rude question, but Maricel held her back with an outstretched arm. Soren was not being malicious. He was like a child who asked whatever question was on his mind.

"I was struck by arrows. I would've died if it wasn't for my friends arriving and some druidic healing magic my mother— your sister—taught me with the use of mistletoe. The arrows were coated in a poison used to paralyze large game. I survived, but the poison did its cruel work on the right side of my body."

Soren nodded his head.

"We haven't had any druids in our village for some time. The druidic elders who sent my sister on that mission have all died, and I took over as sage and king. Since then, we have only prospered."

Gydan looked out the window to see the modest collection of stone huts. The farming looked more like subsistence than anything that could be taken to market. But she kept her mouth shut.

"After all these years, you decide to return home?" Soren asked. "What's your business?"

"We're here to complete the mission," Maricel said. "This is Silbrey. She is the true fey they were searching for."

"And?" Soren asked.

Gydan assumed it was a momentous event, but he acted as though they were sharing what the weather was like on the other side of the world. There was a long pause until Silbrey spoke.

"We need you to take me to Alda Feren. We're here to stop the world from breaking apart."

"Oh yes," Soren said. "The earthquakes. They haven't been as bad here in the valley. But elsewhere?" Soren grimaced to emphasize how bad it had been.

"So, you will take us?" Silbrey asked.

"Probably not, no. How is it any of my concern?"

"If the world is destroyed, you die with it." Gydan spoke for the first time.

Soren raised his voice in response.

"If I die on the battlefield or from disease or from the world breaking apart, it's still just one death." He held up one finger to illustrate his point. "One death. My death. It's not any concern how many die by my side. Everyone dies. I'm sorry if you're just now figuring it out."

*The fool makes sense*, Cyru communicated to Gydan.

"*Franduri*, you are right," Maricel said. "We cannot ask for so great a favor without expecting to pay you back. We have coin. What would be a fair exchange?"

Gydan was impressed by Maricel's role as diplomat. Maricel knew what to say. Even from their brief time among the Vasterghent merchants, Gydan sensed that "fair exchange" was an important concept to the people of Raustfweg. Everything given must be compensated. Nothing could be requested without offering something in return. Soren took Maricel's words and mulled over them.

"I cannot take you to Alda Feren," Soren said, "because I don't know where it is. Most people believe it's a fey story, that it doesn't exist. But in this village, we know the truth. It's all real. I can take you to the person who knows how to get to Alda Feren. He's a strange fellow named Jack Stag. He doesn't live here, but it's not far. He can help you."

Jack Stag wasn't a real name. That was the name parents gave to any magical creature that appeared in bedtime stories. Jack Stag helped the clever princess get home after grandmother witch turned herself into a pig. Jack Stag tricked the wolf into fighting his own reflection in the river. Jack Stag stole the moon once a month and gave it to the fey queens. And sometimes, Jack Stag was the trickster, leading children astray with promises of cakes and spiced drinks. Jack Stag was not a real person.

"And what do you want for this generous service?" Maricel asked, ignoring that Soren had said he was going to introduce them to the mythological Jack Stag.

"I am a king without an army," Soren said with an exaggerated sigh. "I have a rightful claim to this entire valley, but it means nothing if I can't defend it, fight for it, or expand my territory and wealth. I have a war band, thirty warriors, but that's nothing compared to even the smallest army. I need more soldiers."

Soren pointed to Gydan's mother, waggling his finger up and down, sizing her up.

"You. You have a fighter's build. You hold your staff like someone ready to strike, even when you're in the company of friends. You would make a great addition to my war band."

Soren leaned back in this throne and held out his arms to make his offer. His chest muscles stretched with new definition, a reminder of how strong he was.

"You want me to help you find Alda Feren? Once you return from your mission, you owe me ten years of service."

"Ten years?" Maricel interrupted. She choked on the last word. Silbrey placed a hand on her shoulder.

"I can't. Once I reach Alda Feren, I'll need to stay there. I won't be able to return."

Maricel's eyebrow lifted in confusion. She turned to Silbrey, silently asking for an explanation. While Silbrey had talked to Gydan about what would happen once they reached the great tree of life, she did not have this discussion with Maricel.

"Fine," Soren stood up and walked toward Gydan. He looked her over. Gydan's nose wrinkled—not that he smelled bad, but the perfume he wore was strong and artificial. She would have preferred the manure of livestock. "The youngling has a fine sword. She can take your place, and I'll teach her how to use that sword. Once you return, this child and the small dragon that follows her will be in my service and under my care for ten years. After ten years, she'll be an adult, and she can make her own decisions on where she will make her home."

*Once again, the fool makes sense,* Cyru expressed to Gydan. *He would benefit from having a dragon as part of his war band. We would subdue the region in no time.*

Silbrey dropped her staff. It clattered to the ground. "She's just a child," Silbrey's voice, normally so steady, wavered.

"And how old were you when you first learned to fight?" Soren asked.

Silbrey didn't reply. They knew she was Gydan's age when she'd first learned to fight with Dahlia Tulan.

"It's okay, Mom," Gydan said. She wanted to reassure her mother. She didn't want her mother to look so sad. "Cyru and I can do this."

"I need a day to think about your offer," Silbrey said to Soren.

Silbrey walked to the doorway of the longhouse. The light from outside surrounded her, casting a long shadow across the ground.

Soren, always laughing, lifted up Silbrey's staff. "You forgot your stick."

Silbrey said nothing as she walked away.

* * *

Silbrey burned with rage. She didn't know where to go, but she didn't want to stay at the longhouse. She didn't want to be at the mercy of that oiled-up loon. She was afraid if she had stayed any longer, she would've burst into tears in front of everyone.

The farther they journeyed from Amon, the less sure she

was of the destination. Everything had a cost. Everything required sacrifice, and she didn't know how much more she could give up.

Silbrey should have never given Bren's sword to Gydan. She thought she was honoring Bren by keeping it out of Mendal's hands. That monster would wave her sword around as if it were a scepter. He would take his mother's legacy and ruin it. Instead, that sword put ideas into Gydan's head, filling her with a misguided sense of purpose. Gydan loved that sword as she loved Bren Caius. Now some self-proclaimed king was offering to train her, and she jumped at the opportunity. If Silbrey allowed Gydan to serve in Soren's war band, firstly, she might be paving the road to an early death, but secondly, it would be no better than when Timon allowed Dahlia Tulan to take Silbrey. It would be worse. Timon didn't have much of a choice. He couldn't stand up to the guildmaster of Penderyn. But Silbrey would be giving her daughter over to a person she didn't know. If such a thing were possible, he might be worse than Dahlia Tulan. The thought twisted Silbrey's stomach.

Silbrey looked for a private place where she could be alone with her thoughts. The village was a humble collection of huts and plots of farmland—hardly a kingdom worth ruling over—and not much privacy, except for the nearby forest. Silbrey walked to the other side of the village, down a sloping hill to the edge of the forest. She walked among the trees, and she felt like she could finally breathe. She placed her hand on each tree, feeling the bark—a tactile delight of bumps, ridges, and small grooves—and in that moment, she wished she could leave the civilized world behind and just live among the plants and animals of the forest. That was what her kind did, the tree-born fey. She knew this impulse made sense, and she had been denied the life for which she was made. She grew up in the city, far from the comforts of the wild. She was drawn to Dahlia Tulan's garden as naturally as water flows downhill.

Silbrey wasn't meant to have children either. She had two. One apprenticed to Aubec Skarsol, a good man. The other might be indentured to Soren, king of the valley. What kind of man was he? Silbrey hoped that underneath his bluster and bravado, he was an honorable man. Within a year of her husband's death, she would be without both Yurig and Gydan. In her heart, she knew her children were safer away from her, even if it was in a war band.

Silbrey saw a butterfly navigating the ferns of the forest undergrowth. The butterfly transformed in front of her, taking the form of a tiny human, twiggy arms and legs, and silky clothes that looked like they were spun from a spider. Papery wings of vibrant orange, outlined in black, sprouted from the pixie's back.

Silbrey smiled when the pixie looked at her. To her amusement, the pixie smiled back and waved. The creature flitted around her, then turned into a shining, diaphanous wisp and disappeared.

Silbrey felt Maricel enter the forest. It wasn't anything she heard or perceived through her other senses. Soren had his kingdom, but these trees belonged to Silbrey—and nothing within this domain escaped her.

"How did you find me?" Silbrey asked without turning around to face Maricel.

"Silbrey, I don't think you realize how predictable you are." Maricel's voice was gentle and kind. "When you get angry or confused, when you need space to think, you go to the trees—or you grow your own."

Silbrey looked around her.

"It feels like home."

Maricel came up behind Silbrey and leaned against her back. She placed her head on Silbrey's shoulder and wrapped her arm around Silbrey's waist, resting her hand right below Silbrey's belt. Maricel needed support when not placing her weight on the crutch.

Silbrey stood there, feeling Maricel against her, taking in the quiet moment.

Whatever arguments they had before, it was pointless. Silbrey loved Maricel, and that was all that mattered. This moment, with her. Whatever happened on the Amoet was the irritable ramblings of a person who was sleep-deprived and feeling the burden of those unending moments on the ship. Silbrey placed her hand on Maricel's.

Maricel turned Silbrey around and looked straight at her. Such intense eye contact made Silbrey uneasy. She looked away, but Maricel placed a hand on Silbrey's cheek and guided her back.

*Look at me*, the gesture said.

Silbrey looked at Maricel. They held each other's gaze for a long time.

Maricel's face still drooped on the right side, but she could now open and close her right eyelid. They had been worried about her eye drying out, and if she might lose it. But it looked like the paralyzing effects had eased some. Silbrey thought she saw her lips twitch into the faintest smile.

As they looked at each other, Maricel's eyes began to water and turn red. Her face twisted in sadness. Silbrey tried to look away again in shame at the pain she had caused Maricel. Once again, Maricel placed her hand on Silbrey's cheek.

"Why are you crying?" Silbrey asked, but she was afraid of the answer.

"I'm crying for you," Maricel said. "You have an impossible decision to make. And it's okay to grieve."

Silbrey teared up. She convulsed as the tears started to come. It was the beginning of a good cry, a cleansing one. Despite Maricel's permission, it still embarrassed her, and she laughed.

"Damn it," Silbrey said. "What's wrong with me?"

Maricel held Silbrey's face in both hands.

"It's okay," Maricel said. "You don't have to be strong. I don't mind."

Maricel and Silbrey both started crying, but there was some laughter in those sobs as well. They kissed—a powerful kiss, which sent a warmth from Silbrey's stomach up across her chest and then her face.

When they pulled back, their foreheads touching, Silbrey laughed again.

"We could torture your uncle until he tells us where Jack Stag is." Silbrey raised her eyebrows to indicate she was joking.

Maricel placed her arms around Silbrey's waist.

"Maybe that's how things are done in Raustfweg?" Maricel pondered in jest. "He might disapprove if we don't torture him. We should keep it as an option."

"I agree," Silbrey said as she wiped the tears from her eyes. "Soren doesn't know what he's in for. If he touches a hair on my daughter's head, Cyru will cut him to pieces."

Silbrey then wiped the tears from Maricel's eyes.

Silbrey was thankful for the dragon. It made an impossible decision more tolerable.

* * *

Gydan and Cyru stayed behind in the longhouse. Soren looked at them. They looked at him. All were unsure of what they were supposed to do next.

"Let's start with your first lesson as a member of my war band," Soren said.

Gydan unsheathed Bren's sword. Soren waved his hands, baffled by her actions.

"By the named gods, put your sword away," Soren said. "I'm not sparring with someone who doesn't have a shield. No, this first lesson is more important."

He walked to a table. It was almost the length of the meeting area in the longhouse itself. From there, he grabbed a clay jar, gave it a shake, and then removed the cork stopper. He picked up a cup and poured a golden libation.

He held out the drink to her.

"What's your name again?"

"Gydan, your grace."

"Gydan." He gave the cup to her. "This is mead. Drink up."

She sipped at it, but Soren shook his head in disapproval and tipped the cup higher, so she took a larger gulp.

"Delicious, isn't it?" Soren smiled and laughed. "Some say it's the best mead in Raustfweg, if not all of Efre Ousel. The druids spent generations perfecting it. Sweet, but not too sweet. It warms your belly with just a little tickle in your throat. The taste grows in your mouth, even after you've had a gulp, and it stays with you."

And it was true. This mead was the most delicious thing Gydan had ever tasted. She felt that warmth in her belly.

Soren took the cup from her. Gydan was disappointed to be parted from it.

"When you fight and you live, you return to this house and you get to drink more mead. But if you die in battle? No more mead."

Soren gave Gydan a serious look. "Do you want to die, or do you want mead?"

"I want mead." Gydan said it with wide-eyed earnestness. Soren laughed. Cyru had already flown to the table, had uncorked the jar, and was checking to see if any mead was left for them to try.

"My warriors drink often, and they've earned it," Soren said. "Your mother be damned. Let's take the oath now."

Soren set the cup on the floor. He knelt before it, bowing his head to the ground. He patted the floor, inviting Gydan to also kneel. She hesitated. If she took the oath, if she became a member of Soren's war band, would she ever return to Amon? Would she see her brother again? She agreed to serve for ten years, but her heart swelled at the idea of this new life, and she wondered if she could ever leave it behind. Gydan knelt next to Soren.

"Gydan?"

"Yes, your grace."

"We look like idiots. Don't tell anyone you saw me kneeling like this."

"Yes, your grace."

"Repeat after me." Soren cleared his throat. "Oh mead, I bow before you."

"Oh mead, I bow before you."

"I pledge my sword to this arrogant ass beside me."

"I pledge my sword to this arrogant ass beside me."

"But I pledge my belly to mead."

"But I pledge my belly to mead."

"Kings and generals will fail and fall."

"Kings and generals will fail and fall."

"Mead will never disappoint me."

"Mead will never disappoint me."

"May I live for many days, so I can drink again from this cup."

"May I live for many days, so I can drink again from this cup."

While bending over, Soren looked at Gydan. His brilliant fur coat outlined his gleeful face.

"Don't come back until you have a shield. I won't train anyone without a shield. Understand?"

"Yes, your grace."

Soren patted Gydan on the head. "Get out of here."

\* \* \*

Silbrey woke up the next morning filled with dread. She felt a tremor in the earth, and she was certain the earth was breaking apart. The confusion from the morning faded. It was just a falling sort of dream—the ones that startle a person awake. As Silbrey breathed deeply to recover from her awakening, she knew they needed to get to Alda Feren as soon as possible. To do that, she needed Soren to take her to Jack Stag. What did it matter if she kept Gydan from a warrior's life if she died within the crevasse of a broken earth?

They were given a vacant hut to stay in for as long as they wanted. The huts were large enough to accommodate a small family. The sloping interior walls of the dome-shaped house were painted with a twisting, knotted pattern reminiscent of the popular Raustfweg braids. All the lines were outlined with gold leaf paint, which shined when the light hit it during the day—and glowed at night.

The doors and windows in the house were positioned to capture the morning light and allow a cool breeze to move throughout. The tiled floors were covered with colorful rugs of different styles and textures, including a few animal pelts. Potted plants lined all the places where floor met wall. The beds were straw-stuffed mattresses on the floor. All sitting surfaces were firm pillows, and the tables were low to the ground as well. The low furniture made guests feel the need to crouch while moving about the home, though it was unnecessary.

Silbrey stepped outside, staff in hand, and walked up the steps into the open area at the center of the village. The morning chill raced across her bare arms and neck. She could see her breath in the cold air. Soren was there, holding a wooden practice sword and shield. He was not wearing his colorful coat, which hung nearby on a fence post. The sweat glistened on his muscular form. Soren inclined his head to Silbrey, greeting her.

"Your grace," said Silbrey.

She swung her staff around and circled Soren, a silent offer to be his sparring partner. He pointed to a shield on the ground. Silbrey, not taking her eyes off Soren, reached down and grabbed the shield. She braced her staff against her forearm and gave him a slight nod, welcoming the start of their match.

They moved toward each other. Silbrey's staff had the longer reach, so she took the first attack, which Soren blocked with his shield, and then he countered with a swing of his own. He was much faster than Silbrey expected. She assumed he was more of a brutish warrior who depended on strong swings and a lot of noise. Instead, Soren was a finesse fighter, like herself. He swung, and Silbrey barely blocked it with her shield. Silbrey followed Soren's eyes. She saw him make note of her close call, but he expressed no reaction.

They paused and then exchanged a flurry of strikes and parries. This sequence repeated a few times, creating a rhythm to fight. The sound of the wood clacking against the wood was loud in the quiet village.

Silbrey took a few steps back. She wiped the sweat off her brow. Soren did the same. Silbrey showed Soren the back of her hand, three fingers extended. Soren laughed at the unfriendly gesture.

Curious villagers came out to watch the fight. Some were drinking their morning tea. Gydan and Maricel were also awake now and watched with interest.

Soren smiled when he saw he had an audience. He went in for a few meaningless strikes at Silbrey's shield.

The outcome of this match meant nothing. What did it matter if Soren was the better fighter? Who cared if Silbrey bested the king? Soren had little to teach Silbrey. She had spent much of her life training with her staff. Likewise, she had little to teach Soren. Instead, she needed to see how Soren would train Gydan. What kind of person was she trusting to raise her daughter?

Silbrey stepped forward. Soren stepped back. His footwork was impeccable. She took a few more quick steps, and he bumped against the back of the fence. Instead of targeting for more vital areas of his body, she took that moment to jab at his feet, which made him appear to dance. She could hear snickers from those watching. The attacks made no sense in an actual fight. The intent was to make him look foolish, to embarrass him. He looked at her, confused, but he was not upset.

Silbrey intentionally overplayed a move with her staff, which left her shoulder and back exposed. She offered Soren a tempting and vulnerable target. Silbrey anticipated the wooden sword striking her back. She had been hit hard many times by Dahlia Tulan's wooden training sword. She did not want to feel that ever again, but here she was, inviting it.

With his sword, Soren tapped her lightly on the back.

She turned to see him there, right where she expected him to be. Instead of revealing in his victory, he gave a cordial bow to his competitor.

"Again?" he asked. "You're trying to get me angry with those silly jabs. You should worry about your own anger."

"Me?" Silbrey said, but she knew what he meant. She spent her time in the village with a scowl. "Worry about yourself."

She began a series of strikes against Soren. He blocked all but the last one and winced from her hit.

"That's how it's going to be?" Soren asked.

They sparred throughout the morning until the early fog had lifted, and the dew clinging to the grass faded. The villagers had lost interest and were now going about their chores.

Gydan continued to watch. She sat at the edge of the fighting circle, fascinated. Silbrey had stopped with her games to test Soren's temperament. Sometimes, she won. Other times, he did. He was cordial in defeat, often pointing out where his mistakes were and committing to doing better next time.

Both were tired. What had started as a simple morning

exercise had turned into an exhausting brawl. Neither of them had ever been so evenly matched with an opponent, and they knew it was an opportunity they didn't want to pass on.

The workout calmed Silbrey. After so many weeks in the hull of that ship, it felt good to test herself physically and to sweat.

Silbrey took a swing, but she didn't give it any power, and it grazed at Soren's shield. He moved forward and bumped Silbrey with his shield. She lost her balance and fell on her back. Soren stood over her with his sword pointed at her neck.

"Am I the king of the valley?" He wanted to know if Silbrey saw in him what he saw in himself. It was also his way of asking if he was worthy to train her daughter.

"If ever I've met a king, it's you," Silbrey said. She grunted as she got back to her feet.

"That's good enough for me," Soren said.

Soren might be a braggart. He might even be a delusional fool, but Silbrey respected him. If someone had to be king, Silbrey decided this fool was better than most.

"If Gydan agrees, she can fight in your war band for ten years after we return from Alda Feren." As Silbrey said these words to Soren, she looked at her daughter. "You must protect her, train her. And when you expand your kingdom across Raustfweg, she returns to Amon a wealthy woman. In exchange, you'll take us to Jack Stag."

Soren reached for his coat. "Tomorrow morning, before the sun rises. His home is in the marshland a few miles north. Maricel won't be able to make the trip, not with her—" Soren alluded to her weak leg and wooden brace. "Once we get the map, we can come back for her."

"If Maricel stays," Silbrey responded, "Gydan needs to stay behind too. I'm not leaving Maricel alone again."

"She's home. She's among family."

"She's among strangers."

Soren didn't argue. He had what he wanted. He walked back to the long house with his wooden sword resting on his shoulder.

\* \* \*

Gydan grinned while skipping through the village, without a care of where to go or what to do. She had taken the mead oath. She was joining a war band. Soren would train her to become a great fighter. She replayed the morning events in her mind—Soren sparring with her mother. She had never seen such grace and power. Surely, his skill would have rivaled Bren Caius in her youth. What was ten years to Gydan? She would return to Amon with stories to share and the gratitude of a king. Her mind was filled with wild visions of her future greatness.

Cyru flew by her side, bobbing up and down. Then the dragon stopped mid-air. Cyru sensed something and, in a blink, shot into a nearby bush. There was a rustling and a terrified squeak. Cyru emerged with a dead rat in their claws. The dragon tossed the rat aside and rejoined Gydan.

Cyru chirped to bring Gydan out of her dream-like state.

*Do you think in the war band we'll be able to kill people?*

"I hadn't thought of that," Gydan said.

*What do you think that sword does? What do you think our claws are for?*

"I'm not stupid."

*The rat we killed, its last moment was one of terror and pain and confusion. That's how most things die. We enjoy the feeling of taking a life. But we don't think you would. You want battle without violence, adventure without consequence, and domination without enslavement. Don't be naïve. A king is a terrible thing.*

"More terrible than a dragon?"

*Nothing is more terrible than a dragon.*

Gydan could hear the smile in Cyru's voice that moved like ocean waves through her mind.

Cyru's warning about kings stayed with Gydan. She knew better than anyone that Cyru reveled in violence. She had to restrain Cyru's murderous impulses on a daily basis. She couldn't imagine Cyru would lecture her on the bloody nature of war. For the first time in a long time, Gydan felt like a child. She was ashamed of her enthusiasm.

"Do you think I shouldn't join the war band?"

*We think you should be wary of anyone who calls himself a "king." We think you shouldn't be too excited to use your sword. We think, for now, you should leave the violence to the dragons. But we see how fate works, and maybe this outcome is unavoidable—unless we die at Alda Feren. And if that happens, none of this matters.*

Gydan agreed with Cyru's grim outlook. She could worry about the next ten years after they traveled to Alda Feren.

No matter what the future held, Soren said she needed a shield. She could start there. It would give her something to occupy her time. Gydan asked Oma Olvi about where she could find a shield. Olvi told her to ask the mason on the east end of the village. The mason told her to ask the ravenmaster on the other end. Each person pointed her to someone else who might know where she should go. She was convinced the villagers were sending her on a fey errand, passing her from one person to another, but finally, she got an answer.

An old man with a long white beard—who had no noticeable trade—told her to travel a mile north of the village. She would find several shields leaning against a stone wall, and she could have any one of those shields. No one would mind.

Gydan thanked the man and left the village. She walked past the north gate, along the dirt path, with Cyru at her side.

The path winded down a gently sloping meadow and into the forest. The forest was alive with animal noises and bird calls, insect trills and creaking branches. Gydan walked deeper into the forest. Then, as though passing from one world into the next, all the animal noises stopped. The trail opened to a gated cemetery, bordering it was a swamp. The graves were marked with smooth stones, large enough to hold in two hands. Each stone had a rune carved into it, which matched some of the village runes Gydan saw as they journeyed through the valley.

Gydan and Cyru moved among the graves and saw several round wooden shields—each with different runes painted on them—leaning against a stone wall. This cemetery was for the fallen soldiers of the region. Gydan sighed. Another heavy-handed lesson about the fragility of a life lived by the sword. She walked toward the wall to get her shield and get out of there. She heard a still voice beyond the shallows of the swamp, but she couldn't make out what was being said.

She looked to see if Cyru heard it as well, but the dragon wasn't there at all. She was alone. Even though it was the middle of the day, a darkness covered the forest as though the sun were behind a cloud. She looked up but couldn't see the sun. The whole sky was a pale gray. Then she heard the voice again. "Come closer," it said.

Gydan walked to the other side of the cemetery to the swamp. She stood at the water's edge. She looked out at the undisturbed, mossy water. Dragonflies skimmed the surface. Gydan's eyes had trouble focusing. For a moment, the winged insects looked like something else, small fey creatures flitting about. She blinked, and the dragonflies returned. Gydan was about to turn around when she heard the voice again, like a faint echo. She could not see who was speaking.

"Tian, it's such an honor to have you in my swamp."

"My name's not Tian. It's Gydan."

"My mistake. The named gods go by many names. This is a new name."

"I'm not a god."

"The god says she is not a god. I'll have to remember that. Last time I saw you was right after the Great Firestorm. You came to the Fey Court and begged us to protect the mortals. We tried our best."

In the last few words, the voice rose a bit and trailed off. It felt like a taunt.

"You can try harder."

"Your mother should have been at Alda Feren years ago, but I will see her soon enough. Right now, let's talk about you. I sense great worry."

Gydan wanted to step into the swamp, but she resisted.

"I'm worried I might not live to see my brother again."

"Which brother?"

"Yurig. My only brother."

There was a long silence, as though whoever was speaking had to make an important decision and needed time to think.

"What would you give to see this brother again?"

"Anything," Gydan said without hesitation.

"Anything?"

"Anything," Gydan repeated more adamantly.

"Fine then. You will see your brother again. You will have many adventures together. You will be the best of friends. But —you will never see your mother again after she leaves tomorrow morning."

"What?" Gydan realized who was speaking. She remembered the stories. "Jack Stag?"

"That's what they call me. Do you accept the terms? Your brother or your mother. You must choose one or the other."

Gydan knew there was only one choice. Her mother would say she made the right decision.

"My brother. I want to see Yurig again."

"Slick, slack, tickety-tack. Deals made can't be taken back." He said the rhyme as if sealing a contract with wax and a stamp. "You will live, and you will reunite with Yurig. But after tomorrow morning, you will never see your mother again. No tricks. If you tell your mother about this agreement, you will lose both."

The shadows lifted. Gydan heard Cyru chirping again. The dragon flew to her side.

*What is it? Gydan, what happened?*

Gydan did not respond. She walked over to the shields and grabbed one painted blue with a white seven-point star on it. "Let's go back. We don't belong here."

When they returned to the village, Gydan looked for the old man with the long white beard, but he was nowhere to be found. When she asked Olvi about him, the old woman said she didn't know of such a person.

\* \* \*

The villagers weren't happy with their king. In his wisdom, Soren announced they were moving the midsummer feast, which was several weeks away, to that evening. He said he wanted to honor the arrival of his estranged family. All the preparation that normally went into this celebration was put aside. Instead, the villagers rushed to put something together that might please their capricious king.

People hung colorful fringe banners throughout the village. They gathered the floating lanterns they would light and send off later in the evening. Others raced throughout the valley, wrangling bards and poets. They were hoping to have these performers for the midsummer feast when it normally occurred—the middle of summer. A delicacy made from figs, walnuts, and soft cheese had to be prepared in copious amounts for the evening—as well as barrel-aged mead and ale brewed for this special night.

Everywhere Maricel, Silbrey, and Gydan walked, they received glares from the villagers who had hoped for a lazy day and instead were commanded to celebrate. As the evening neared, however, the general frustration cooled, and everyone became sincerely excited about the feast. Musicians arrived, cracking jokes about the leap forward in time. They smiled and went to work because coin was still coin in whichever village needed their services. They tuned their instruments and played.

Silbrey strayed from the group. She strolled by herself through the village and observed the people. They laughed and embraced each other. Some started drinking early. Others stepped away to smoke sweet leaf or play festival games. Children ran around with wooden swords and yellow ribbons, hunting whichever poor soul had been targeted as "it." Young lovers snuck off across the meadow and into the north forest. The sun had set, but the sky was still ablaze with oranges, blues, and purples. Fireflies pulsed around the fields beyond the village. Silbrey heard the hum of cicadas. The natural world was ablaze with life, noisy and bold in its declarations. Silbrey felt at peace. Alda Feren was calling, but for tonight, she wanted to not worry about what would come next. She wanted to enjoy what was here and now.

Silbrey saw a man she hadn't noticed before. He was tall. He stood with his broad, muscular back to her. He had long, dark hair tied into a bun. When he turned around, Silbrey first noticed his clean-shaven face. It was Callis.

All breath left Silbrey.

"A steady journey!" He smiled and called to her.

"And a clear path," Silbrey responded, not sure what else to say.

Silbrey felt connected to nature. From the tallest tree to the smallest blade of grass, she understood on an intimate level how both needed the water to nourish them and the sun to shine upon them. Nature breathed and exhaled. It depended upon so many elements, and Silbrey sensed how everything impacted everything else. This man had mass and form but left no true footprint upon nature. Not that he was an illusion, but whatever space he occupied was not of this place. He was something else.

"I see you took my suggestion of talking with our neighbor, Maricel," this strange man said. "Is she a good lover? It hasn't been a year, and you've already moved on."

"You're not Callis," Silbrey said. "He would never be so

coarse. He was never jealous. He did not view me as a possession. And he would want me to be happy and to find love."

"What would Callis say to you?" This man, in this world, but not of this world, taking the form of Callis, but not Callis, stood inches from her. She could feel his warm breath.

"He would say, 'I love you and I always will,'" Silbrey's words tumbled out of her as she struggled to keep herself together. "He would tell me to not be sad anymore, to forgive myself, to live a happy life, that I'm worthy of love. He would tell me Maricel is a good person, and if she makes me happy, then I need to not hold anything back. He would tell me he misses our children, and he hopes they live well. He would say all that, and he would not say anything at all, because I know him as I know myself. He would just hold me and that would be right and good. Please do not torment me with his appearance. Take any form but his."

As she said these words, all the anger she had held onto, all the feelings of injustice, and all the rage directed at everyone who had wronged her, she was able to let it all go. Silbrey knew whatever magic was at work could not lead her astray from the truth of her words. Everyone Callis had left behind knew who he was and what he cared about. That was never in question.

Silbrey blinked, and he was gone.

* * *

The feast was about to begin. Gydan had been searching for Soren and found him sitting in front of the longhouse as another man braided his hair. Soren looked pleased with himself as he admired all the work the villagers did that day.

"Your grace?" Gydan gave a formal head bow.

"Yes, Gydan. How are you enjoying our midsummer celebration? Wait until we release the floating lanterns. It's stunning."

"Your grace." It didn't take Gydan long to realize that "your grace" could be used to mean many different things when addressing Soren. When she said it this time, it meant she wanted to change the topic. "Why are the other children in the village trying to hit me with practice swords? Only me."

"You have a shield now. I thought this would be a good start to your training. I equipped the children and told them to go after you. Hopefully, you've been deflecting their strikes?"

Gydan looked at her new shield as if it were cursed.

"But your grace, some of those kids are twice my size."

"Oh, yes."

"A little warning would've been nice," Gydan said.

"Not fair, is it?" Soren asked. He was proud of his efforts. "It's good training."

"I got mad and bashed one of the kids with my shield. His nose bled."

"More good training! And a bit of a lesson for that kid, too."

Gydan looked around. She'd been on edge ever since children had begun jumping from every corner wielding wooden swords.

"Your grace, there's one more thing. I saw an old man with a long white beard. He was in the village, but I found out later such a man doesn't live here."

"That would be the fey," Soren said plainly. "If I had a silver coin for every time a fey spirit snuck into our village, taking the form of someone else, I'd have a greater fortune than all of Elara Brok. I'm sure our midsummer festival gained their attention, and there might be a few around here right now."

Soren grabbed the chin of the man braiding his hair and looked at him closely, turning his face to one side and then the other. When Soren was confident this man was no fey, he continued.

"Don't mind them. They're harmless. The border between our world and theirs is hazy in this part of the valley, especially around the solstices." Soren tapped the star on Gydan's shield. "It's what this village is known for."

Gydan realized this village's fey affinity might be why their druids knew to travel to Amon in search of her mother. If Gydan was to spend the next ten years here, then she would need to learn to not trust everything she saw. This lesson felt more valuable than not getting hit by other children swinging wooden swords.

Cyru hovered nearby.

*Was this what you were keeping from me earlier today? Did you speak with a fey spirit at the cemetery?*

She did not want to say anything else in front of Soren, so she sent her thoughts to Cyru that, yes, she did speak with someone at the cemetery, but she wasn't willing to share any details yet. Jack Stag's words about her mother rang in her head, and she did not want to think about it. She wanted to pretend she had misheard or that this was further fey trickery.

Cyru accepted her answer, although the dragon was not pleased. They had never kept anything from each other before. Cyru flew into the sky to explore the valley.

"Your grace," Gydan excused herself, "thank you for your lessons."

"Today, we feast," Soren called out to her as she walked off. "Tomorrow, we conquer Raustfweg!"

A boy about her age jumped out from one of the carts. He had been waiting there while she talked with Soren. He yelled a battle cry as he swung his wooden sword in a wide overhead arc. She adjusted her grip on her shield, holding one end with both hands, and swung her shield at him. Gydan was faster and was able to slap the unfortunate child upside his head with the flat of her shield. A white speck flew from his mouth, which might have been a tooth.

His battle cry turned into a normal cry as he fell on his back and dropped his sword. He scrambled to his feet and ran in search of a parent to comfort him.

Soren clapped and cheered on Gydan's ruthlessness.

"Your grace, if an opponent drops their sword, can I take it?"

"Is such a thing prohibited in war? Fight for your life, Gydan."

Gydan grabbed the boy's sword. She raised it into the sky and howled in triumph. She then ran into the fray of children waiting to avenge their kin.

* * *

The longhouse table was brought to the center of the village as a place of honor for their guests. Each family also moved their tables outside, encircling the long house table. The tables were draped with ornate cloths and decorated with beaded strands and wildflowers. Candles were set at each table, producing a bewitching, other-worldly glow as the sky darkened.

Unlike the hardy winter festivals with fatty roasted lamb,

seasoned potatoes, and dark ale, no meat was served at the midsummer feast. Instead, the meal consisted of small-portioned foods, which were eaten by hand. Each family had their contributions, and everything was delicious.

Silbrey looked around the table. Oma Olvi was chatting with her granddaughter, Maricel. Soren was laughing at something he had just said. He slapped the back of a squat warrior visiting from a nearby village. Gydan looked like she had fallen out of a tree. She was covered in bruises, but she looked happy and content, so Silbrey decided to leave it be. Silbrey lifted her cup to her daughter.

They spent the next few hours picking at the food and drinking. The night sky was filled with stars. The beads on the table sparkled in the candlelight. Silbrey got up from the table. She felt light and off balance from the mead. She walked around to Maricel, placing her hand on each chair she passed to steady herself. Silbrey whispered into Maricel's ear. Maricel blushed and her eyes widened.

Silbrey stretched her arms wide, an exaggerated yawn, and announced she was tired and her belly was full. She was going to retire for the night.

"But you're going to miss the floating lanterns," Soren said, knowing full well what Silbrey had planned. "We're about to send them up."

"I'll come outside to watch when it's time." Silbrey tried to act casual, but her ruse wasn't as clever as she assumed—especially since she walked in the opposite direction of the guest hut, down the grassy meadow toward the forest's edge. She stumbled a bit as she walked down the gentle slope. She could hear Soren laughing. Was there anything he didn't find humorous?

Once Silbrey stepped into the forest, her senses quickened, which helped her sober up. She could feel everything happening around her. She could feel the trees breathing, the roots digging into the earth, and the leaves curling inward, anticipating a cool night and hoping for the warm sun tomorrow. The skittish woodland creatures retreated farther back toward the edge of the marshland as a few other couples—to the east and west—laid out blankets on the ground to have privacy in the dark wood. Young couples tentatively exploring each other, and older couples reminiscing about their wilder, foolish days when their love was nervous and uncertain. Now they enjoyed the greater intimacy of a life lived together, and they smiled as they relived their earlier adventures. Silbrey could feel all of it, and it was exquisite.

Other ethereal creatures floated through the forest, curious fey spirits caught between worlds, invisible to all except Silbrey. It must have been one of these spirits that had appeared to Silbrey and took the form of Callis. The fey were not cruel. Their mischief was innocent, but seeing Callis sent her mind reeling, reliving the pain of that loss.

Maricel entered the forest not far from where Silbrey was. She walked deeper into the woods and then waited for Silbrey to come to her. Silbrey could sense Maricel wasn't comfortable alone, but from Silbrey's perspective, Maricel was already in her world and beside her.

Silbrey walked to her. The leaves crunched, and Maricel turned around. Silbrey felt a nervous ache in her stomach, a good feeling, a feeling of anticipation.

Silbrey wanted Maricel. She needed her, a hunger that made it difficult to focus on anything else. And knowing they'd soon continue their journey to Alda Feren, this moment felt like a merciful pause before they had to travel again—a space created just for them.

There had only been two people in Silbrey's life, two people that she allowed to get this close: Callis and Maricel, him and her. They had so much in common. Both were kind and gentle, annoyingly so. They both appeared innocent to the dangers of the world around them, but like the fey, this was a deceptive idea taking flesh and form. In truth, Maricel knew about the dangers of a life lived close to Silbrey. She had suffered and survived, and she stayed. Maricel had stayed for her. Silbrey moved closer, taking in her beauty, looking her over with brazen, ravenous confidence.

Silbrey lightly touched the back of Maricel's neck. It startled Maricel at first, but she relaxed at the feeling of Silbrey's hand. Silbrey looked at Maricel for consent. Maricel smiled and nodded her head. Silbrey unclasped Maricel's cloak and lifted it off her shoulders. She laid it on the ground. Silbrey grabbed the hem of Maricel's wool dress and pulled it up and off. Maricel helped in removing her undergarments, one piece at a time. Silbrey looked at Maricel's fair, delicate form, and the scars on her body from the arrows. They had healed so much since she had last seen Maricel undressed. Now, Silbrey undressed in front of Maricel. She pulled off her fur-lined shirt and laid it next to Maricel's cloak. Silbrey could feel the breeze across her skin. Every inch of her skin was awake and waiting to be to be touched, caressed.

Silbrey whispered into Maricel's ear, "What would you like me to do next?"

"Kiss me."

Silbrey moved behind Maricel. She reached around her waist, placing her hand below Maricel's belly. She kissed her on the back of the neck. A lighter kiss followed by a stronger one. Maricel let out a tiny moan and reached around for Silbrey. She turned around and kissed Silbrey on the lips. Silbrey felt a chill go up her back at the sensation of being touched and kissed. Silbrey opened her mouth, inviting Maricel to kiss her more fully.

Silbrey then took Maricel's hand and invited her to lie on the cloak. Maricel placed her hands above her head ready for whatever came next. Silbrey straddled her, making sure to avoid Maricel's wooden boot. She clasped Maricel's hands in hers, holding her down.

Silbrey kissed Maricel's neck and delicately bit at her earlobe. Silbrey moved her hand down past Maricel's smooth belly onto her pelvis and then between her thighs. Maricel grabbed Silbrey's hand, guiding it. Maricel spread her legs wider, making herself available.

Maricel started breathing faster as she became more aroused. Maricel continued to guide Silbrey's hand and fingers. After a while, Maricel let go—allowing Silbrey to continue. She felt comfortable and safe.

Maricel whispered, "faster." And Silbrey moved faster. Maricel whispered "slower," and Silbrey moved slower. Maricel whispered, "harder." And Silbrey applied more pressure.

Silbrey could feel Maricel was nearing completion. Her moaning reached a higher pitch.

Maricel's back arched in pleasure. Her breathing became irregular and shaky from the waves of tension. "Don't stop." She moaned louder and louder, letting herself be in the moment.

Maricel's whole body tightened. The tension rose higher and higher. Maricel screamed in pleasure and held Silbrey close, clawing at her back. Maricel's body started shaking involuntarily. After a moment, she relaxed and sighed with contentment.

Maricel and Silbrey lay together. The forest noises surrounded them. The two women were lost in each other's attention. Maricel's eyes welled with tears.

"Why are you always crying?" Silbrey asked.

"These are good tears," Maricel placed her hand on Silbrey's cheek. "I had given up on us. With all the arguing on the ship, I was certain whatever there was between us was gone. I felt like I didn't know you."

"I'm sorry."

"No, we're going to be okay."

Silbrey had to share what happened with the fey, but she didn't know how it would be received. "Earlier today, I saw Callis."

"What?" The words stunned Maricel. She looked at Silbrey in disbelief. "How?"

"It wasn't him. This forest, the fey spirits live here. And they play their games with people in the village. This was their ruse."

"That must have been so hard for you."

"It shocked me, and then once he spoke, I knew it wasn't him. He wasn't Callis, not at all."

"You loved Callis," Maricel looked away as she spoke. It was a sensitive topic for them. "You're still grieving. I only want a place in your heart somewhere."

"You have my whole heart," Silbrey said. "And I can give you something I couldn't give to Callis—the rest of my life. Up until the very last moment. You and me."

A light flickered in the night sky. It was one of the floating lanterns, which the villagers had spent the day preparing.

Several more lanterns joined the first, and then more—until the entire sky was filled with candlelight.

Watching those lanterns, lying next to each other, neither one of them would forget this moment. Time slowed down. They forgot the weight of their obligations. The past was pardoned, and the future did not taunt them like it often did. There was nowhere to go and nothing they had to overcome. They were together and in love, and the night lasted forever.

"I want to know," Maricel was the first to break the silence. Her tone was teasing. "Why did you think it was a good idea to have an assignation in a forest haunted by fey spirits?"

"You don't like being around my kind?" Silbrey teased back.

"Can we get dressed and go back to the village?" Maricel reached for her clothes. "I don't want to stay the night in a haunted forest. We can enjoy the rest of the evening in the hut."

The night was getting cooler, and what now felt brisk could soon be more uncomfortable. The cold didn't affect Silbrey, but she didn't want to spoil the evening with Maricel freezing.

Silbrey remembered her conversation with Ausdre before they left for Raustfweg. She promised Maricel's mother that she would let Maricel go once they had gone to Alda Feren. It was an easy promise to make since Silbrey did not believe there would ever be an "after Alda Feren" for her. She couldn't leave the great tree of life if there was a possibility the titans could wake. Silbrey wanted to enjoy this evening because she knew there might not be another.

"Sil, what are you thinking?" Maricel asked as she touched Silbrey's lips.

"Nothing," said Silbrey, which couldn't be further from the truth.

Silbrey kissed Maricel again, and they resumed their loving intimacies, touching each other and exchanging noises of contentment, postponing their return to the village.

Eventually, they got their clothes back on, and they snuck back to their hut. Once inside the warm, comfortable enclosure, they both collapsed onto the mattress—and burrowed underneath the layers of blankets and pile of pillows. They fell asleep almost immediately, wrapped in each other's arms.

\* \* \*

Gydan always woke up before everyone else, but today she was up especially early—even Cyru was still asleep. It was dark outside. The sky was starry. Below the horizon, the valley was a pitch-black void. A few midsummer revelers staggered to their homes, singing songs about wars won, lovers lost, and the interference of gods. The morning air was icy cold. Gydan was thankful for her fur coat, but the air still bit at her exposed face. She wondered how she would survive the winter here.

Gydan sat on a bench at the back end of the longhouse, which blocked the wind. A dying bonfire kept her warm. Her mother wouldn't wake until the sun rose, but if Jack Stag was right and this was the last time she would see Silbrey, she wanted to say a proper goodbye.

Gydan had Bren's sword. She laid the sheathed sword across her lap and ran her fingers along the tooled bumps, ridges, and grooves of the leather. Gydan often did this whenever she was anxious and needed something to calm her.

"Are you ever going to give me back my sword?"

Gydan heard Bren's voice from a few feet away.

"You're not Bren," Gydan said without looking up. "You're a fey spirit trying to trick me. Soren explained how this works."

"You're no fun," the fey said, pouting. "This midsummer feast is always one of my favorite days—and you're ruining it. Your mother was also a boor."

"Are you Jack Stag?"

"No, I'm just a spirit that wears many faces. Jack is something else and far more dangerous."

Gydan looked at the fey. Yes, it was Bren, but to Gydan's surprise, it wasn't the older, infirm woman she remembered from Rhyll. This Bren Caius was a much younger Bren, the brave warrior who had led a small army during the War of the Hounds.

"Why aren't you older? I never met Bren when she was young."

"I am as you know me best. This is the Bren Caius you see when you close your eyes."

Gydan thought about it, and it was true.

"What do you *really* look like?"

"I have no name, no appearance other than what I borrow from the minds of others." The fey that looked like Bren sat on the bench next to Gydan. "No one has ever spoken to me so plainly. Are you not taken aback?"

"I've seen some things," Gydan said. "You asked for the sword. What would you have done if I'd given it to you?"

"I'd toss it into the swamp."

"That's rude."

"I'm a spirit of mischief."

Gydan looked at the creature and marveled at how intimidating this Bren was. Her sharply savage features were the countenance of a clenched fist. Bren looked like someone who would fight anyone. After all, Bren was one of only two people who had survived single combat with Kret Bonebreaker. The other person was Gydan's mother.

"Can you fight like Bren Caius?"

"I can, possibly, if that's how you know her."

The fey spirit, however puckish, could be befriended.

"If you want to visit again as Bren Caius, I wouldn't mind. I could use some friends in this place."

The fey responded with a nod. She touched the hilt of the sword on Gydan's lap.

"Keep it," the fey said. "Next time, I'll bring my own."

With those words, the fey disappeared.

* * *

Silbrey opened her eyes and saw that Maricel was still sleeping. She looked so lovely and a little sad, as though her dreams were fraught with visions.

An orange beam of sunlight reached across the ceiling. Soren would be waiting for Silbrey outside. Already she was running late. He said they would leave to see Jack Stag before the sun rose. He would, no doubt, ridicule her for sleeping in.

Once they learned how to get to Alda Feren, they could leave the village later that day. Silbrey liked it here, and she wouldn't mind staying if she could. Whenever Gydan returned from Alda Feren, she hoped the village could be for her what Sage Hall was for Yurig, a place where they could grow into adults—if Gydan survived her time in Soren's war band.

Silbrey got off the mattress and dressed. Instead of her black fur-lined shirt, she wore her plain linen tunic and strapped her breast plate over it. She ran her fingers through her hair to comb out any tangles.

Silbrey knelt next to the mattress and kissed Maricel on the cheek. Maricel's face relaxed. The nightmares chased away.

"Only sweet dreams," Silbrey whispered to the sleeping Maricel. "And when I return from the swamp, we should get married. Because whatever we face at Alda Feren, I want to face it together, and I want to be by your side as your wife. That's who I want to be." Silbrey stroked Maricel's hair. She thought about the three questions Maricel had posed to her at the farmhouse. What are we? Who am I to you? Who are you? In truth, it was one question, and it had one answer. "I want to be *yours*. I don't know what that will look like afterward since I must stay at the tree. Maybe we could build our own little hut, just like this one. We can hunt and plant and forage. We can make love under the stars and have new adventures. It might be a good life."

Silbrey gave the sleeping Maricel another kiss and then stood up, grabbed her shield and staff, and left.

Gydan and Soren waited outside the guest hut.

"A fey spirit appeared to me as Bren Caius," Gydan said.

Soren was unfazed.

"Wait until you see yourself standing a few feet from you. That'll throw you."

"I think the fey spirit liked me."

"Be careful. They have many tricks. It's dangerous to trust someone so changeable."

Soren shifted his weight, restless. He had been standing in

front of the hut for only a short while, but he acted as though her lateness was an intolerable imposition.

"I'm going in," Soren said.

"My mom will be up soon enough," Gydan said. "If you go in there, you're likely to get hit by her staff. She won't hold back this time."

"You thought your mom was holding back when she sparred with me?" Soren gave Gydan a playful shove, knocking her off balance. Gydan enjoyed the playful way he pushed her around. Gydan shoved him back, but he stood unmoved. He smirked at her attempt. "Nice try."

Silbrey walked out of the hut, dressed for combat, blinking at the morning light.

"Did you and my niece have a nice evening?" Soren asked. "Enjoy the midsummer feast?"

Rather than respond, Silbrey tilted her head as though considering a response, which was response enough for Soren. He let out a laugh. Birds flew from the limbs of nearby trees.

"You're so loud," Silbrey said as she walked to a table left out from last night. She grabbed a stoppered bottle, unplugged it, took a sniff, and then a swig. She swished the liquid around and then spat.

"I am loud," Soren said with pride. "My people never sleep in."

"Be careful your people don't rise up against you."

"They're welcome to try. Are you ready to go?"

"No," Gydan answered for her mother. She ran to Silbrey and gave her a hug. It confused Silbrey. She patted Gydan on the back.

"We won't be gone long. We need to talk with this Jack Stag and then we'll return. I need you to stay with Maricel."

"I know," Gydan pulled back and looked at her mother, trying to commit her mother's face to memory.

Gydan knew her mother was beautiful, as all children know this about their parents. And maybe it was because she had just seen Bren Caius, but she realized how similar her mother and Bren looked. One had blonde hair. The other, dark hair. But otherwise, they could be related. Cousins. Maybe all warriors had a certain look—serious and vigilant, but underneath, a weariness. For Bren and Silbrey, there was also a beauty. Silbrey once described herself as plain and boyish. Gydan didn't see it. She looked at her mother, and she saw a woman with a warrior's strength and a mother's heart. Her mother lacked her father's compassion. This was true. Gydan had endured many glares and scoldings and awkward attempts at affection, but perhaps she hadn't been seeing her mother with the right eyes. Love requires strength, and her mother was the strongest person she knew.

"Gydan, is everything okay?" Silbrey asked.

Gydan smiled. It felt false, but she tried her best to not give away that she was breaking apart inside.

"I'll see you when you get back." She hugged her mother again. "I love you."

Silbrey wrapped her arms around Gydan, harder than before. "We haven't talked about your covenant of service to Soren. You made a big sacrifice to help us get to Alda Feren. And it was an unfair decision to be forced into, but everything is going to be okay—"

"Mom, I'll be fine." Gydan found herself reassuring Silbrey. "I've made it this far, haven't I?"

Before Silbrey could respond, Soren stepped in. He was

eager to lead Silbrey to Jack Stag and fulfill his obligation. "Gydan, you're in charge of the valley while I'm gone."

Soren tussled Gydan's hair.

"Is that a good idea?" Gydan responded.

"I have complete faith in you."

"You barely know me."

"And yet, I have complete faith in you," Soren said, tapping the side of his head as if this made perfect sense. "I'm a sage. I know what I'm doing. Don't let the power put any treasonous ideas in your head. I'm coming back."

He patted Silbrey hard on the back to say it was time to go. Silbrey hugged Gydan once more and gave her a curious look. She knew something was being withheld.

Silbrey and Soren walked to the north forest. Gydan watched them the entire way. Her heart was heavy. If Jack Stag was right, she would never see her mother again.

\* \* \*

Soren and Silbrey waded into the swamp. The water line reached Silbrey's waist. Occasionally, they would step into deeper areas, which brought the water uncomfortably close to her neck. The first time this dip happened, it surprised Silbrey, and she gasped. Soren found the whole thing hilarious and imitated the noise she made to amuse himself—until he fell into a trench and went fully underwater. Silbrey cackled in delight.

Silbrey felt the muddy bottom with her bare feet. Every step required her to pull her foot free and sink it back into the mire. If she had been wearing boots, they would've been lost. Moss and scum gathered on the water's surface, which broke up and scattered from the ripples as Soren and Silbrey trudged through. Dragonflies flew over the water, darting in search of something. Clouds of gnats gathered. They were so widespread Silbrey would swallow them and get them caught in her eyes as she blinked. Swatting at the air did nothing to dissipate the swarm. Frogs, turtles, snakes, and other small creatures swam away, wanting nothing to do with the humans.

Larger, toothier creatures kept their distance.

Soren was right. Maricel wouldn't have been able to make it. She would've needed a raft to be pulled along. The effort would have made the journey more difficult for everyone. Maricel had made incredible progress with her leg, but part of that process was accepting her limits. She pushed where she could push herself, and she was patient whenever she faced something too difficult.

After Soren and Silbrey had been in the swamp for the better part of the morning, Soren broke the silence.

"You're wondering how I met Jack Stag."

Silbrey didn't care, but she knew it would pass the time.

"Tell me."

"I heard him calling to me once when I was in the forest. I followed his voice through the waters until I reached his home. That's where I'm taking you now. He fed me a wonderful meal, and we drank strong sack, the best wine I'd ever had. He so enjoyed my company—and who wouldn't—that he gave me a prophecy. He told me I would become a great king of a great land. He said the land would extend across the whole of the valley and the western coastline, even part of Angnavir to the south. This land would belong to me and my descendants. It would bear the name of my choosing. In exchange, I'd give up both my eyes. I will lose them the day before my conquest comes to an end. Once my eyes are gone, I can stop the fighting and begin my rule. Those were Jack Stag's terms."

"And you agreed?"

"Obviously, I agreed to it! Two eyes? That's a small price for a kingdom. You grow old, you lose your sight regardless. At least, this way, I get something in return. I wish I could give up my nose, my ears, every limb, and whatever else that can be hacked off for the whole of Raustfweg. Why stop there? I'll trade my left bauple nut for Amon too. In fact, I'm hoping after Jack Stag gives you what you need, he might be willing to negotiate away a few more of my parts."

"That's lovely," Silbrey said dryly.

"I'm serious."

"I know you're serious. You'll be ruling all of Efre Ousel, and you'll be nothing but a bloody stump upon a throne."

"Heh. King Stump."

"What are you going to do if it costs your head?"

"Many kings have already proven they don't need a head on their shoulders to rule." Soren laughed at his own insight. "Silbrey, let's be friends."

"Take good care of Gydan, and I will be your friend for life."

"Silbrey, I would not give up Gydan's littlest toe for a promised kingdom."

"And yet, she's part of your war band."

"With a dragon watching her back? I'd like to see anyone get close to her."

"Keep her safe."

"I will," Soren promised.

"Then, *franduri*, you have my friendship."

Soren looked at Silbrey. Strands of his greasy hair clung to his face. He pointed straight ahead. "We're almost there."

They reached dry land at the far end of the swamp.

"Couldn't we have walked around?" Silbrey asked, pleased to be out of the swamp but irritated about the journey.

"Strange thing. I've tried that. You can't get here any other way. This place doesn't exist unless you go through the swamp."

This area appeared normal. It was identical to the forest they had first entered—mostly spruce but with a wonderful blend of birch and rowan trees evenly spaced on level ground. Nothing about it felt particularly strange.

Soren walked toward a glade of high grass, much taller than them. When the sunlight—filtered through the tree canopy— hit the grass at a certain angle, a momentary path appeared in the glade. When Silbrey moved forward or tilted her head, the illusion disappeared. A few more steps and the path became clear again. The high grass formed an arched tunnel that extended farther than the glade itself.

"You think that's odd? We'll return to the village sooner than our time here will account for. You'll go mad trying to figure it all out."

Soren and Silbrey entered the arched tunnel. The path curved to the left and then to the right. It was well-trod and easy to follow. The sounds of the forest quieted, not completely silent, but muted. Silbrey tried to reach out with her fey senses to see the forest beyond the path, but nothing was there except the trail. They were walking on a bridge over a great void. To step off the path would be to fall into oblivion. She couldn't even sense any deeper soil underneath them, nothing deeper than the surface they walked upon.

"Stay on the path," Silbrey whispered.

"You don't have to tell me. The first rule when things get weird: follow the new rules. I'll stay on the path."

As they continued, Soren whistled a tune Silbrey had heard last night.

"What's that?"

"A Raustfweg song about the end of the world."

"It sounds so cheerful."

"Our folk have many songs about the end of the world. They aren't all miserable."

The path opened to an enclosure—with grass three times their height, along with brambles and twigs, all interwound to create a domed space. From the ceiling hung several stick dolls, dangling from twine. Each doll was suspended at different lengths. The overall effect disturbed Silbrey. It made her think of the scattered bodies she had seen in Rhyll after the earthquake.

In the middle of this enclosure stood a man. His face was goat-like, eyes spread farther apart, and his nose was snout-like. He was covered in fine, dark fur. He had large, curved horns protruding from the sides of his head. Silbrey had seen him before. He was the horned fey statue Silbrey saw in Dahlia Tulan's garden. She had pulled her staff from that statue, and then it had disappeared.

The horned fey also recognized her.

"The daughter of spring lives," his voice echoed. It filled the space. Not loud, but full. "And she arrives with autumn's son. The court will be so pleased."

"You're the statue in the garden."

"You misremember. That was no statue. That was me in

the flesh and fur. Jack Stag. I was there to protect you, but—tell me your name. What do they call you now?"

Jack Stag's movements seemed unnatural to Silbrey, as if he moved in reverse, as if he moved both faster and slower than the normal pace of things.

"I'm Silbrey."

"Silbrey." Jack Stag spoke the name as if it were an incantation. "Not a name I would've guessed."

"It's not a common name."

Jack Stag gestured for Silbrey and Soren to come closer. As they stepped forward, tree stumps appeared for them to sit on. They sat while Jack Stag crouched lower, observing them both.

"You said you were there to protect me," Silbrey said. "Why did I never see you again? You knew I needed to go to Alda Feren. When the earthquakes started happening, why didn't you come find me?"

Jack Stag turned a complete circle, a slow-motion dance. The movement had meaning, which Silbrey could not decipher.

"I'm Jack. I travel great distances through this world—in the blink of an eye, in the batting of a butterfly wing—not by flight or footstep, but by names. Mim, mam, mare, tacky-tare. By naming the thing I want to visit, I am there. 'Piper' was the name Spring wanted for you. She spoke it to the priest in a dream. But when you went to that woman in the garden, the wicked mother, what was the first thing she did when she adopted you?"

"She gave me a new name."

"And I couldn't travel to you or find you again. Not without your name. A terrible twist. I doubt she even knew the power of renaming someone." Jack Stag continued to turn around as he spoke. "There was a moment not long ago, when I thought I found you again. I sent a shield to you."

Silbrey recalled being buried in Speck's cave. She was pulled through the earth, mended, and given a new shield. Gydan was right. Someone was looking out for her.

"But you knew other names," Silbrey insisted. "Why not say 'Timon' or 'Dahlia Tulan?' I would not be far from them."

"Fitty-foles, bitty-boles. You cannot deceive fey magic or search for loopholes. That's the boundaries of this game. Since my purpose was to find you, I needed *your* name."

"You mentioned Spring. Who is that?"

"Another time, I'm afraid. You need to go to Alda Feren."

"Yes," Silbrey agreed. She didn't know what to expect from Jack Stag or how willing he would be to fulfill her request. From the way Soren talked about him, everything came with a steep price. "I need to know how to get to Alda Feren."

"No, no, you don't need to know anything. You only need to arrive. Alda Feren is to the east on the other side of the Raustfweg continent. Traveling over land, it would take several months, almost a year by how you experience time."

Silbrey did not know what to expect, but she had assumed it would be closer. Maybe not right on the western coastline, but she thought the longest part of their journey would've been crossing the ocean.

"If it takes longer, it takes longer, but we're not going to give up until we get there."

Jack Stag took a few steps back, another spin, and then crawled closer to Silbrey.

"Once again, you misunderstand. There's no map. There are no helpful words of guidance. The next earthquake will be the one that ends everything, and it's imminent. While you were celebrating midsummer several weeks early, you were casting bones on the fate of this world. Be thankful the titans did not stir last night. But now you are here, we can't wait another minute. We must travel by name to Alda Feren. And we must do it now."

"Now?" Silbrey felt like she got the wind knocked out of her. "Right now? But I need to bring Gydan and Maricel with me. I promised. I can't go without them. I need them."

"Does the word 'now' mean something different than what I once remembered?" Jack Stag asked. His echoing voice became more distorted. "We cannot delay. We must leave this very moment."

"Why can't we travel by name to Maricel and Gydan? You said you can do it in the blink of an eye. Then you can take us to Alda Feren."

"Alda Feren is like no other place—older than this world and not even of this world. I can only take one person there, and I don't know if I'll be able to make the trip again."

"But I might never see them again," Silbrey looked to Soren for help, but Soren didn't know how to respond. Panic crept into her voice. "I never said goodbye to Maricel." She clutched onto Soren. "I can't do this without them."

Jack Stag began to spin around and around. His arms outstretched. The whole grassy enclosure vibrated.

"In the end," Jack Stag said in a sing-song voice, "all mortals are alone. Even when surrounded by loved ones, each takes a path worn for one. You were born to be alone."

Silbrey grabbed tighter onto Soren. He held her hand. It was a kind and tender gesture. She took several deep gasps as she struggled to keep back her tears. Her face twisted in anguish. She thought of leaving behind Gydan and Maricel.

She knew she'd have to stay at the tree, and that might mean saying goodbye to both. The knowledge became real, and it was agonizing.

"I can't do this. I can't. I can't do this."

Jack Stag began chanting the name: Alda Feren, Alda Feren, Alda Feren as he spun around. The stick dolls spun as well.

Soren looked at Silbrey, his heart breaking for her.

"I'll take care of them," he promised. He gave her hand a squeeze.

"Tell Gydan and Maricel I love them," Silbrey pleaded. "Tell Maricel to find—"

Before Silbrey could finish what she had to say, she and the horned fey disappeared.

* * *

Maricel waited until it was evening. Everyone else had retired to their homes. The feast from yesterday had worn down the villagers. The sky also hinted at some late night storms, which urged people inside before the rain rolled in.

Maricel had been quiet most of that day. When Soren returned much earlier than either Maricel or Gydan had expected, he told them about what had happened. Soren looked shaken by what he had witnessed. He comforted Gydan as she cried. Gydan understood what it meant. Silbrey was gone, and she wouldn't be coming back.

Maricel did not react. She accepted the news with a nod and went for a walk through the farmland. People assumed it was so she could be alone with her thoughts. Actually, she was collecting supplies—mushroom, a honeycomb, wolfsbane, bloodroot powder, wormwood, and juniper. She couldn't find any pomegranate. It was too early in the season to harvest, but she found another fruit native to the region, which might suffice. She gathered large quantities of mistletoe. She would need these materials for her trip.

That night, she loaded her rucksack into the cart. She collected several stoppered jugs of water and plenty of feed for the mule. They hadn't yet given the mule a name. She decided Whisker was a decent name. She missed her draft horse, Mustardseed, but Maricel and the mule would become fast friends. She scratched Whisker on his neck, right under the jaw. He seemed to like it. She made some soothing clicking noises with her tongue and harnessed Whisker to the cart.

"Were you planning to leave without telling me?"

Gydan stood at the doorway of the hut. She looked older to Maricel. In the past year, she had grown so much. Maricel had to remind herself Gydan was still a little girl, but she carried herself like someone twice her age.

Maricel hadn't decided if or how she was going to tell Gydan, but it seemed Gydan already knew.

"Do you know where you're going?" Gydan asked.

"I talked with Olvi. If I continue on the path that brought us to this village, there are nine more villages in the valley I'll pass through. From there, the road forks—and I need to go to the right, which leads south, but will eventually take a more easterly direction. From there, after a week, I'll arrive at the city of Apalwaite. It's one of the largest and oldest cities in Raustfweg. That's when the journey truly begins.

"The city marks the starting point of Raven's Road, which connects western Raustfweg to the east. I will take that highway all the way to the other side of the continent. At that point, I'll need to start asking around—see if I can find anyone who knows how to get to Alda Feren. Hopefully, they're not a fey trickster that lives in an enchanted swamp."

Gydan forced a smile. "It sounds like you know what you're doing."

"I have no idea what I'm doing," Maricel said. "But I have to try to find her."

Several emotions crossed Gydan's face. There was sadness for being abandoned, anger about her lot in life, and resignation to her fate. It was all different shades of grief in the end. Gydan's life hadn't been fair, and there wasn't much she could do about it.

"It's going to rain tonight." Gydan gestured to the thick gray clouds moving in like behemoths taking possession of the valley. "Do you want to wait until tomorrow?"

"I need to leave tonight. Otherwise, I might lose my nerve."

"Would that be so wrong?"

"A day will come in your life when you must choose between a comfortable life and the possibility of something greater," Maricel said. "The poets and philosophers act like the correct choice is always to pursue greatness, but that's not true. In the end, it doesn't matter. A life is a life, and a well-lived life can take many forms. The real point is you get to choose. You. That's the important part. And a long time ago, before your mother even knew me, I chose her. I saw visions of her life in Penderyn. I saw the suffering she endured, and I knew I could be what she needed. I fell in love with her. That was my choice. Wherever she goes, I go too. If I die on the way to Alda Feren, if the world breaks before I even get out of the valley, I still lived the life I chose for myself."

Gydan nodded. She didn't understand everything, but she knew it was important. Gydan pointed to Maricel's weak leg.

"Can you make it?"

"We will see. Every day, I'm a little stronger."

Maricel walked toward Gydan and gave her a hug. Gydan wrapped her arms around Maricel tightly. She held on for a long time. Maricel would remember this moment whenever her journey was difficult or dangerous, whenever she thought of giving up. She would remember Gydan, and it would give her strength when her own ran out.

Eventually, Gydan let go, and Maricel left the village as the scattered raindrops began to fall.

# VIII

TIMON STAYED BEHIND AFTER MARICEL, Silbrey, Gydan, and Cyru left the farming community and set sail for Raustfweg. Timon continued to make himself a guest of Ausdre and Rue. The couple was unsure how to get rid of him.

He wasn't an annoyance. Timon had figured out how to make himself useful. But Ausdre and Rue had questions about his presence. How long was he planning to stay? Was he planning to live with them? After all, Ausdre knew his temple home was destroyed in Penderyn after the first earthquake. Ausdre and Rue did not know how to ask these questions without breaking the common practices of hospitality. Surely, Timon knew his obligation to let them know how long he was staying.

All day, Timon was there.

In the morning, he would rifle through the pantry wondering if they should take a trip to the crossroads market for more food. He would then add the priestly adage, "Rise and dine, work through sunshine. Sup and retire, when the sun expires." Ausdre never knew what to make of it. Was he suggesting there wasn't enough food or was he worried they'd forgotten how the day functioned?

In the afternoon, Timon would walk with Ausdre wherever she went. She could not avoid him. He would talk about the blessings of good farmland and honest work. He would praise Ausdre for how well she had raised her daughter.

After dinner, while Rue whittled and Ausdre practiced her slipstitch, Timon would comment on how quiet it was around the house with everyone gone. Ausdre would focus harder on the knitted patch, resisting the urge to say that Timon was the only one making noise.

At night, from across the house, Timon's snoring would keep Ausdre awake. Her eye twitched from exhaustion and irritation. Something about the snoring of strangers was far more disruptive than the familiar noises that came from her husband.

One evening, she got up and walked into Timon's room. He was fast asleep, probably dreaming of full pantries and good farmland. Ausdre moved his cane, resting across the wooden chair next to his bed. She picked up the chair and slammed it down, startling him awake.

Timon made unintelligible noises as he looked around in a panic, then he saw Ausdre sitting in the chair.

"When are you leaving?" Ausdre asked. She was done with being polite, and she couldn't wait until morning to endure any more of his rise and dine routine. "We appreciate what you did for our family. We're thankful for the work"—that word was more strained than she intended—"you've done around here. But please, you've got to go."

"It's funny you should mention that," Timon said. He sounded so casual, as if he wasn't being confronted by a woman who had reached the end of her patience. "I've enjoyed the work around the farm so much. It's made me realize I've spent much of my life being useless. The other priests and I would joke about it. Our lot in life is a unique one. Sometimes you have to laugh about the eccentricity of a life devoted to the gods. But it struck me while I was here: I can do more."

Ausdre nodded. Her lips were drawn tight as she waited for him to get to his point.

"I lost my friends, the other priests, in the first earthquake," Timon said. "I thought about returning, but there's nothing left. I thought I could help in Penderyn, but I don't know if that's true. There's an orphanage near Aylebridge, founded by one of the old noble families. I'd like to go there. It will be my pilgrimage. I will offer my services at the orphanage."

Ausdre was touched by Timon's calling. She had been so annoyed with him she forgot how sweet he could be to the people he cared for, especially Silbrey, whom he had called "Piper" when she had lived at the temple in Penderyn. He talked about how he wanted to make amends for failing Silbrey, and it looked like he had found what he needed to do.

She patted him on the shoulder as she stood up from the chair.

"Leaving tomorrow?" Ausdre asked. She was sympathetic, but Timon still had to go.

"Leaving tomorrow."

Ausdre looked at Timon's cane. She knew he wouldn't make it halfway to Aylebridge if he walked.

"Silbrey left her horse here. Feste. You can take him."

"Thank you."

Ausdre walked to the door. Before she left, another idea came to her.

"At the orphanage, some children never find parents?"

"Many, I would assume."

"When these children come of age, if they don't have any vocation waiting for them, send them here. We have good farmland, plenty of it, but our community is old. We could give them land to work, a house of their own, and a way to make a living."

Timon began to cry. He hiccupped through his tears. These were happy tears. Ausdre's heart warmed. Little did she know that this offer to Timon would change her life and the farming community forever.

"I will remember your offer," Timon said.

"One of them might be a fey child hiding in our midst. It's happened before."

Ausdre returned to her bedroom. If Timon snored again, she didn't notice.

\* \* \*

Silbrey stood before Alda Feren, the great tree of life, in the vast wilderness of east Raustfweg. Jack Stag had brought her here in a blink, far from her family. Then Jack, with a nod, also blinked away. And she was alone.

She looked to the left and to the right. The entirety of the tree could not be taken in. The curvature of the trunk was so slight, the tree appeared as a great wall that stretched into the sky, past the clouds swirling around it. The tree felt to Silbrey as the titans must have appeared when they first walked upon

Efre Ousel. The tallest mountains were diminished in comparison.

Silbrey placed her hands on the bark. She loved feeling the deep fissures, the textured complexity of its grooves and ridges. When she tried to connect with the tree, Silbrey felt something like when she wielded her staff. What was a gentle whisper of the world around her—with her staff—was a roaring wave with this timeless tree. She felt everything, and everything came to her at once. The world became known to her on a level no one could grasp, not even herself.

She did not just feel the bark against her palms. She felt the whole tree. She sensed the roots as thick around as the walled cities of Aberton and Penderyn. The legends said that the roots extended across the entire world, connecting to all four continents. The roots cut through all layers of rock, tapering to small, exposed ends that surfaced on other sides of the world. A person in Lunthal could trip over such a root without realizing it was part of Alda Feren.

The moisture that the roots pulled from the earth could fill an ocean. The roots moved these rivers throughout the tree with such force that Alda Feren emitted heat. Silbrey placed her ear against the tree. She could hear the pumping, churning of the waters that nourished the tree. All the water of the world—moisture from the sky, the lakes and rivers, the ocean—had at one time siphoned through Alda Feren. The roots pulled nutrients from soil across Efre Ousel, the decay of all life clung to these roots. Generation after generation of animals and plants, worms and insects, bacteria and magic. The history of civilizations could be felt through the roots of Alda Feren.

All within Silbrey's grasp.

The great tree inhaled in deep gulps. Silbrey could feel an

actual drop in the pressure near the massive trunk. Alda Feren, with each inhalation, tasted the world carried on a breeze. The tree would then exhale, and it felt like Alda Feren could sustain all life with each breath.

The canopy of leaves extended across the sky, blocking out much of the sunlight so that everything below was in the continual glow of twilight. With Silbrey's touch, she could feel the sunlight upon each leaf. The light traveled across boundless space to this point in time, all to be absorbed, just as Silbrey felt herself being absorbed by the immensity of this tree. When the tree spoke to Silbrey, it came with echoes of a distant past. All Silbrey had to do was listen, and the mysteries of creation could be opened to her. The sun spoke of the present and the future. The light brought hope that nothing ends, not on a celestial scale. The energy was everlasting, and every living thing was part of it.

As Silbrey pressed her hand to the tree, she felt the force of creation.

She felt the force of the primordials Terron, Ignasi, Aylo, and Cael. These were respectively the elemental forces of earth, fire, water, and air. All creation came from and would return to these four elements.

She felt Al'taru, which weaved all the elements together.

There was greater wisdom within the great tree than anything she had ever experienced. If only everyone could feel what Silbrey felt. If it were possible, the most sensible thing for anyone to do would be to sell everything, make a pilgrimage to this tree, and spend a day in its shade.

The wisdom was intoxicating as was the power. Every moment held forever within a single creation. Nothing could be taken from Silbrey. Nothing denied.

As Silbrey touched the tree, she felt a white light glowing from her. She saw white petals floating down to the ground, falling from the branches far above. The light from Silbrey reflected off the petals. It looked like stars floating to earth and dying upon the ground.

The ground rumbled under Silbrey, not another earthquake but smaller roots trying to break through the earth and reach out to her.

The tree opened, a sliver of space, a doorway of light. Silbrey needed to step forward. It was her purpose. The reason she was born. Her whole life was a winding path that led here to Alda Feren. But she hesitated. She was afraid. The world was on the verge of breaking apart, and in this moment, she only wanted someone to tell her it would be okay—that it was a noble sacrifice. Silbrey thought of Soren who shrugged off such heroics. He said, "If I die on the battlefield or from disease or from the world breaking apart, it's still just one death. One death. My death. It's not any concern how many die by my side. Everyone dies." Despite his warped perspective, he was right. Silbrey could walk away. She didn't have to save anyone or anything.

She beat her fists against the tree and screamed. She didn't want to do it.

No one was here to see her struggle, and she was thankful for it.

"I don't want this life," Silbrey said through her tears. "Let someone else be Ald'yovlet."

She hit the tree once more, and the frustration left her. "Maricel, I will come back for you. I will find a way."

It was time.

She took a step into the tree, and a prickly sensation came

over her entire body. The space closed. The tree tightened around her, but it did not hurt her and she did not fight it. Alda Feren then pulled Silbrey downward into the earth.

Motes of light glinted across Efre Ousel, over the four continents and the seas separating them.

* * *

Ausdre saw the lights while she looked at the open pasture, waiting for her husband to return from work. The lights reminded her of the floating lanterns from her old village. It occurred to her why they released the lanterns. They did it to honor the lost fey children who were summoned to the mortal world—a promise to find and care for these children. Melancholy settled on Ausdre as she observed the lights.

Callis' parents, Wardi and Igvan, saw the lights as they sat on the porch of their home. The sheep bleated. Wardi got up from his chair to calm his flock. The lights made him think about the embers that rose and fell in the air from his son's funeral pyre. The image had stayed with him.

Timon saw the lights as he journeyed to Aylebridge. He was riding Feste. The colt was unceasingly energetic and determined to race the whole way there. Timon tried to slow him down. They compromised on a trot and frequent breaks for apples and water. Feste did not respond to the lights. Timon took the glinting lights as a sign from the gods. He had made the right decision to go to Aylebridge. Timon snorted in amusement, which Feste did respond to, turning his head to check on his travel companion. Timon gave Feste a reassuring pat on the neck. Timon watched, filled with awe at the lights. He knew the impulse to favorably interpret signs said more about a person's desires than the will of the gods. In the end, a decision was right or wrong, independent of the gods. And the lights, he knew, were not for him.

Aubec and Yurig were studying their spells within the quiet of Sage Hall's library. They had lost track of time, absorbed in the mysteries of their research. Yurig tapped his index finger twice on the table, an unobtrusive signal to Aubec that he needed help. Aubec leaned over to see what his apprentice was reading. Aubec gave a breathy whistle, impressed at the complexity of this spell. At first, neither of them noticed the lights among the many lit candles in the room. Then Yurig saw them and nudged Aubec as if to say, "Did you do this?"

Dahlia Tulan saw the lights while she sat within her cell far underneath the palace in Rhyll. She held out her hand and tried to cradle one in her palm. The light passed through her hand. She waved her hand over it, amazed at its incorporeal nature. The light gave off no heat. Dahlia Tulan leaned forward and observed the lights. It had been a long time since anyone had visited her—mostly victims' families. They would yell and cry and curse. It might rend the heart of most people, but Dahlia Tulan looked forward to these encounters. Better than being alone.

These lights were something different.

"Hello, little one," she said to one of the lights. "Hello. Are you here to keep me company?"

Dahlia Tulan waited for a reply, but none came.

Not too far from the palace where Dahlia Tulan was imprisoned, Mendal Caius walked the street toward his estate. The two-story timber-frame manor had served as his second home when he was younger and Bren Caius was high general. Now this estate was his sole residency. The lights appeared, and he sneered at them. He swatted at the lights, hoping they'd disperse.

Tom the Barber saw the lights in his shop, where he sharpened blades. He smiled at the lights as if seeing an old friend. He put down his oil and cloth. He poured himself some port wine and raised the glass in honor of Silbrey, his friend who had saved Aberton.

Udger saw the lights as he stood on the balcony of his mountaintop home, which overlooked a turbulent sea. He had been so happy to return to his homeland and his family. However, part of him wanted to be back on the Amoet, to be close to something crucial and meaningful. Udger looked at the lights and thought about how vast and unknowable the world was.

Soren and Gydan saw the lights as they sparred with each other. They had been practicing for some time, and Gydan was getting distracted. She learned fast, but she was still a child and learned like a child. They paused for a moment and lowered their swords in respect. Gydan looked at the lights, and she knew her mother had made it to Alda Feren.

As the lights glinted, Maricel slept soundly in the cart with a blanket wrapped around her. She had moved the cart off the path and into the nearby forest, so she could rest without worry of being discovered by other travelers. Maricel dreamed of Silbrey. She dreamed of reuniting with her lover. Every inch of her body felt alive and tingled. For a moment, feeling returned completely to her body, both halves. She awoke with a gasp, and the lights disappeared.

\* \* \*

The physical world faded away when Silbrey stepped into the tree—or more accurately, the world expanded in Silbrey's consciousness. Everything was experienced as energy, a vibrating world of minuscule interconnections, pure understanding. Everything was as it should be. No past and no future. Silbrey could look back to the origination of Alda Feren and every moment leading up to this perpetual now.

The elements were in balance and could be felt everywhere. Al'taru, a concept that mages devoted their lives to understanding, became tangible and practical. There was fire and not fire, water and not water, air and not air, earth and not earth. All elements had to be distinct from the other elements. Al'taru was not a thing. Al'taru was the invisible borderline between real and unreal, which made the elements possible. Silbrey understood it all. Nonsensical as it was, she understood. The elements and Al'taru were the antithesis of abstraction, while the fey world where she originated—a place of story, of ideas and meaning, of imagination, of dreams—was a waystation along this border. A place where the abstractions were made real, a magical reality that willed other worlds into being.

As tall as the tree was, extending well past the clouds, the tree descended much deeper into the earth. The roots were a system of forked paths that stretched endlessly in all directions. Silbrey explored the roots as a person wandering the world with no destination in mind. She didn't even know if this place was real or if it existed only as an illusory backdrop to something beyond her understanding—a transcendent labyrinth, a vast table set for parley, or possibly, a battlefield. Silbrey's consciousness moved along these paths. Even in her heightened state, she could not fully comprehend the trails available to her. Much like a life, every decision—left or right—led to another set of options, and then another, until life had been lived. Each path, a story.

Silbrey had lived many lives through the roots of Alda Feren. And in every life, her daughter and son were there—a constant centering truth. Without them, she would have lost her mind and her way. She did not know what the future held for them, but she knew their shared path branched into perilious places.

Because of the scale of Alda Feren, getting lost in the maze deep below the earth was always possible, but to lose oneself was far easier. Silbrey was divorced from her physical body and her place in time, which made her doubt everything she knew. Silbrey. Piper, the name given to her by Timon, or Ald'yovlet, the name the tiny sprite called her. These were ideas, nothing more, and ideas can be forgotten. But she would not forget her daughter, her connection and obligation to that life. Like Al'taru, a mother's love was nothing in itself. It was the in-between, the invisible borderline that connects and makes things possible. It was the ball of twine that allowed Silbrey to find her way.

* * *

As Silbrey journeyed through the root maze, searching for the waking titans, she heard a familiar voice. It was distant at first, but closer with each utterance.

"Hello, little mouse, I see you."

Who called her "little mouse?" She remembered someone used to call her that.

"Little mouse," the gruff voice repeated. His voice was the growl of a nightmare, a monster hiding in the shadows. "Do you even remember me? Last time we saw each other, you tore my body to pieces. Savage. I respect that. I do."

"I'm sorry." Silbrey spoke, not sure he could even hear her.

"I told you I am inevitable as the elements that make up this trash heap of a world. I told you that if you killed me, I'd come back. I told you there's no end to me. Well now. Here I am."

"Kret?" The memories of this portion of Silbrey's life returned to her. She fought this wolf, a big bad wolf—or was it a hound—or was it just the idea of all things with sharp teeth that hunt wayward children in the forest. All things cunning and sinister and dangerous. "How did you find me?"

"I can always smell the fey."

As the memories returned, so did Silbrey's anger, and with her anger, Kret's essence in this place expanded, drawing him nearer.

"I will fight you, and I will defeat you," Silbrey said.

"Will you now?" Kret asked, his tone dripping with malice.

Kret drew nearer. He had caused so much suffering. He delighted in it all. And though Silbrey knew she must confront him, she did not know how she could defeat him. She must keep him from waking the four titans underneath the earth, underneath Alda Feren at the center of Efre Ousel. Silbrey struggled to hold on to these thoughts or any memories. The intoxicating omniscience that this tree granted was too much for one life. She needed to find the titans, but she lost more of herself as she descended.

"If you go to the titans, I will follow." Kret finished her thoughts for her. "You cannot escape or defeat me, and you cannot keep them asleep if I'm there. I make a disturbance wherever I go." Silbrey could sense his toothy grin with these words. "You have failed. The titans will wake, and the world will break."

The darkness surrounded her, and she wondered if there was any way to face him without losing herself. More of her—memories from the past, people she cared about—slipped away as the darkness expanded.

\* \* \*

In another time and another place—ageless and filled with wonders—Tian walked into the great hall of the Fey Court. Tian appeared as a young woman, strong and poised, wrapped in a white fur cloak. Underneath her cloak was a silk tunic and wide-legged pants. The silk was embroidered with gold thread in elaborate swirls. She wore slippers with a similar gold swirl. She moved with the relaxed gait of someone who never felt unsafe or unwelcome. She was, after all, a god.

By Tian's side was a red dragon, with black accenting patterns along the wings and snout. The dragon was about twice her size. The dragon slinked across the smooth stone floor, prowling, and scanning the room for threats. Tian placed a hand on the dragon's side, a gentle request to stand down and be at ease. The dragon's siblings waited outside the tower, flying around it, ready to come to Tian's aid if summoned.

But Tian had no reason for concern. After all, she was a guest here.

The tower was a sublime work, carved from the wood of a massive hollowed-out tree—smaller than Alda Feren by half, but still large enough to dominate the city. Several ages from this moment, Tian—living a mortal life as Gydan—would see Bren's palace in Rhyll. The spiraled columns and curved archways would remind the child of this otherworldly tower. She wouldn't fully understand how she made this connection.

At the highest point of the tower, the royal members of the Fey Court sat upon their crystalline thrones. They were a family, of sorts. Being eternal and without parentage, they were not related by blood but by their connection to each other. Each ruled their domain in this world. The borders were marked by the seasons they represented. Winter was always winter. Summer was always summer. Spring and autumn, likewise. Like so much of this world, the nature of it bled over into Efre Ousel. Winter existed in Efre Ousel because it existed in the fey world.

All the seasons met at a single point within the city and this great hall, the Fey Court.

Willow Bud, the spring queen, slouched in her throne. Even reclining upon the hard surface, Willow appeared rested and at ease. She wore a translucent dress adorned in elaborate frills of green leaves and flowers. Sapphires lined the dress from top to bottom. The gems looked like dew drops, glistening in the morning sun. She had dark hair and light blue eyes. Everyone in the Fey Court was exceedingly beautiful. Each was lovely in their own way. Willow's loveliness was a gentleness. Her face brightened with kind eyes. It drew people close.

Willow slouched, but Kyran Bloom, the summer queen, sat tall and proud as though she held the whole realm in contempt. She wore a brilliant gold robe. The gold was layered like scales, and it sparkled. Kyran had short hair, shaved closed on the sides with a blonde curly mass on top. She wore a jeweled headband that served as her diadem. From the band were a series of golden needle-like spikes like a sunburst. The summer queen's facial features were sharp and dramatic. Her beauty was regal, a superiority that demanded the worship of others.

Arelius Fall, the autumn king, was standing with one knee on his throne—as if that knee was sufficient to fulfill his courtly role when receiving guests. Arelius didn't have the appearance of a noble. He wasn't slovenly, but he dressed in a more casual manner than his brother and sisters. Their presence exuded power. He looked roguish. He wore a simple wool tunic and baggy tan pants tucked into leather boots. He wore a cape, which was the only token of his high status. It was made of red, orange, and yellow leaves. But everything was more muted and lacked the brilliance of Spring or Summer. His beauty was a mischievous charm, a half-smile, a raised tankard, a devilish wink.

Eirwen Frost, the winter king, sat upon the throne as though everything inconvenienced him. He wore black. Black cloak over a long black tunic dress, black boots, and black armbands. Even his hair—long, past his shoulders, and straight—was black. The blackness contrasted with pale blue skin and his piercing eyes with white irises. He was beautiful in the way that all strange things are beautiful. He was intriguing and mysterious.

Tian walked to the center of the great hall and spun around once and then took a deep ceremonious bow to Willow Bud, Kyran Bloom, Arelius Fall, and Eirwen Frost. The gesture, staged as it was, surprised the Fey Court—a god bowing to them. They were ageless as she was ageless. They had power as she had power. In a sense, their domain was greater than hers. They controlled the very concepts of nature and creation, which helped shape reality across untold worlds. Tian spent too much time among the people of Efre Ousel. The Fey Court agreed it diminished her in their estimation. But Tian was still a god. And gods were dangerous, unpredictable, and it was wise to give them an audience whenever they asked for it.

Tian held out her hand. A seedling appeared above her open palm. The plant rotated in the air. It transformed with each season as it turned—blossoming during the warmer seasons, drawing inward during the colder seasons. It was one seedling and also four.

"As a gift, I bring you a seedling, which originated from Alda Feren. You may plant it within your domain, and it will grow as Alda Feren did. A part of the other world will always be with you."

Eirwen Frost was unimpressed with the gift, but the other three were pleased.

"Thank you, Tian." Willow Bud had already summoned the seedling to her side, admiring it more closely. "The other gods give gifts based on what they love. Taraki gives grain. Olar gives weapons. Hebren plays sad songs. You are wise enough to know every gift has a recipient, and one should consider what *they* would love."

"Indeed," Eirwen Frost said with disdain.

"Don't listen to him," Arelius Fall said. "He hates everything."

"Not true," Eirwen responded. "To love the absence of music is not to hate music but merely to appreciate the wonder of silence all the more. I am very fond of the space between things."

"Absence makes the heart grow fonder," Arelius Fall mused. "And a fondness for absence makes Eirwen's heart grow."

Tian gave the winter king a respectful nod.

"The seedling is yours to do with, or do away with, as it pleases you."

"I will watch it die," mused Eirwen.

"I'll bring it back every time stronger than before," Willow Bud said. "I undo all his best work."

"Tian." Kyran Bloom said her name, but the tone implied it was time to move the conversation along. "I doubt you came here only to give gifts. Lovely as the seedling is. You have a purpose in requesting an audience with the Fey Court. Circling the tower, you have a hundred full-sized dragons, not like this pup here." The summer queen gestured to Tian's dragon companion. "How are we not supposed to take this as an act of war?"

"If this were a war, I'd only need one dragon." Tian's voice was playful, but the threat was not missed on the Fey Court. "These dragons are my attendants. They accompany me to honor you."

The dragons could be seen from a series of windows carved into the walls of the great hall. The dragons passed one after another and then another. Every time, the shadows would move across the room, a relentless reminder of the threat outside.

"What do you want?" Kyran Bloom punctuated each word to indicate her growing irritation. The hall shook as she spoke.

"First, I would like to tell you a story," Tian said.

Each member of the Fey Court made a noise in response— a sigh, a groan, a murmur, and a gleeful squeak. Willow liked stories.

"A seed floated on the void of space, pulled along by distant forces. For how long? This would be the wrong question. Time in the vast expanse, in this isolation, was meaningless—with no frame of reference, no other mass to chart its movement and relation to all other things. No fire, no wind, no earth, no water. All that could be known was that something existed, and it was this seed. The seed was as alone as one thing can be.

"But it wasn't always this way. The seed once existed at the center of a white flower surrounded by a cluster of leaves on a large tree in a wondrous, distant world. Magical? Yes, such a word would be appropriate. The world was magical. The seed waited to fall from the flower and land upon the soft, wet ground. The tree was at the top of a hill. If the seed ever fell, it would roll down until it found a level place. But this would not come to pass.

"The seed's world broke apart, torn asunder by corrupt and violent forces. Everything would end in screaming, suffering. Everything around the seed was consumed in fire. The seed was spared. Its shell covering resisted the chaotic forces, and the seed was flung from this devastation into the void.

"The seed floated along, unbothered, unbeaten—tethered only by the slight something out there. Over an infinite period of infinite space, eventually, the seed could feel other beings that exerted no pull. These were the unnamed gods. A whole universe of unnamed gods. Their job was to speak worlds into existence, to create and call upon titans.

"One unnamed god approached the lonely seed as it continued a journey without a destination. The god saw a story within the seed, one of luck and misfortune as the last inhabitant of a doomed world. The god spoke to the seed, marveling at its history, such a small artifact, the final witness of a great beauty.

"The god did something no god had ever done before. The god breathed upon the seed—a thing without form acted upon something of substance. With this single act, the god gained the right to a name. The first named god came into being. The god would have many names, but on Amon, she would be known as Tian. That would be me.

"Eleven other unnamed gods noticed this act and followed. They were curious to see where the seed would go. These gods would eventually become known as Olar, Cyruth, Golwin, Taraki, Fen, Aegir, Hebren, Wedril, Sarna'vot, Yoon, and Verin, but first, they would need to earn their names like I did.

"My breath moved the seed off its original path, and it took a new course.

"For an eternity of eternities, the seed traveled, followed by the gods—until the seed arrived at a world. The seed entered the upper reaches of the sky, and the air created resistance. The resistance created heat. Within the air was water. Then, the seed collided with the earth itself. All four elements—air, fire, water, and earth—greeted this distant visitor. Within those elements, there was power.

"The seed was the last living thing of its old world and the first living thing of this new world. It spanned an impossible gap from one reality to another, a reality it would have missed, if not for the single breath of a god who liked to interfere with the world around her. Once again, me."

Kyran Bloom rolled her eyes, but Tian continued her story, unhurried by the summer queen.

"The seed sunk into earth. The heat and moisture of the earth caused the outer shell to open. The seed, feeling the embrace of these elements, opened further, small wispy roots extended into the earth, and a seedling climbed upward, breaking the surface and growing.

"This growth was good. It connected the elemental power

toward a common purpose. 'Good' was the first magic of this new world. From the goodness, an evil manifested in opposition. 'Evil' was the second magic. The evil was without form. It drifted across the earth, seeking a way to take shape and destroy the small seedling. The evil would become known as the Ancient Beast. I called upon the other eleven gods, my siblings, to protect the seedling from the Ancient Beast. They earned their names when they agreed to protect this world—each in their own way.

"The seedling grew. It became a sapling and then a tall and mighty tree. Its branches spread out and provided a cover to the world below it, casting shadows across the earth. The gods dwelled in and around the shadows. At the ends of the branches, flowers bloomed. Seeds like the original seed sprouted and fell. More life sprung from the earth. The good increased as the evil also expanded, and the gods grew in strength as they strove against the Beast."

Tian got down on both knees. She looked to the summer queen. There were tears in Tian's eyes. The Fey Court was stunned.

"Consider what I say," Tian spoke softly, which gave her words greater power. "Life is fleeting on Efre Ousel. The Ancient Beast dwells upon the surface and takes many forms. He wants to wake the four titans sleeping underneath the earth. And if they ever wake, they will destroy everything. The Beast hungers for destruction. I need your help to keep Efre Ousel safe."

"As you said, isn't this the providence of the named gods?" Arelius Fall asked. He spoke as if the question bored him.

"It's true. The gods committed to fighting the Beast, and for centuries, we did. It grew stronger, more determined. The

Great Firestorm tested our resolve, but we persevered. Afterward, the gods became distracted by the petty affairs of that world. Willow Bud, you said it best. Taraki gives grain. Olar gives weapons. Hebren plays sad songs. They became comfortable in their roles. We were once united in our cause, but no more. That's why I come to you. I need your help. Do what the gods cannot do."

"If the gods cannot do it, then how could we help you?" Kyran Bloom asked.

"The gods are big," replied Tian, "but so are you."

Kyran Bloom looked to her sister and two brothers. Her expression was stern and unsympathetic.

"No," said Kyran. "We will not help you. That world is no concern of ours."

Tian lowered her head, feeling the weight of this decision.

"I agree," said Arelius. "Their situation is unfortunate, but there's nothing we can do."

"Mortal's life is precarious by design," said Eirwen. "The rain falls. We do not mourn every time a drop hits the earth. You are trying to save a dying people in a world that was never meant to last. I fail to see why this should occupy your time or ours."

While her siblings addressed Tian, Willow Bud's focus was on the seedling. She admired its tiny leaves, delicate stem, and wispy roots. She was so enamored by it. When she spoke, it surprised everyone in the great hall.

"I disagree with all of you," Willow Bud said. "Especially Eirwen Frost, but that should surprise no one. We never agree. The rain falls with purpose. The earth absorbs it, and life is possible. Plants grow. All because a drop of rain fell. We celebrate the rain. There is no cause for celebration when mortals die on a doomed world. They are denied any possibility of a greater purpose, and even from my throne, I weep for them. I disagree with Arelius. There is something we can do. Otherwise, why would Tian be here? And I disagree with my dear sister, Kyran. We can decide to make their world, our concern. We can take up a higher purpose. We can do whatever we want. And I want to help this world. I want to see it grow."

There was a long silence. The low-droning whoosh of the dragons outside could be heard, and then Kyran spoke.

"Tian has an army of dragons at her command. She can use them to save Efre Ousel."

"Dragons are not good for keeping titans asleep," Tian said with a wry tone. "They tend to wake up everything around them. But the fey often have one foot in the world of dreaming. Some of your kin are even known for sleep magic. A fey once put an entire kingdom to sleep for a hundred years, or so the story goes." Tian moved from her knees to sitting on the floor. Legs crossed. Feet tucked under. She rocked gently. "Also, I've instructed the dragons to stay away from the Beast. He can possess living creatures, and the last thing we need is for the Beast to find a new home inside a dragon."

"This makes sense," Willow said. "Sister, this makes sense."

"The Beast would not be able to possess the fey," Tian said. "And I'd like to try a different approach to fighting the Beast. The gods oppose him, and he becomes more godlike. He is a force that grows to match whatever he confronts. We need to be clever. We need tricksters. We need fey."

Kyran was about to speak again when Willow interrupted her.

"I never ask for anything," Willow said. "Let's do this. I'm so bored."

"If you're bored, we can find you a new pastime to—"

"Kyran, dear sister, let's hear what Tian's plan is," Now Eirwen interrupted Kyran. Willow Bud beamed. Eirwen—who often antagonized her—had taken her side.

"Fine." Kyran sighed, surrendering to the realization she had lost control of the Fey Court. "Tian, tell us what you have in mind."

Tian got up and smoothed her attire with a few pats.

"To every generation, I want you to send some of the fey children over to their world. Let them grow up among the people of Efre Ousel, live as they live. In time, they will mature and stand up against the evil of their age. With an unseen hand, I will lead them to the Beast. Some will fight. Others will work to pacify the sleeping titans. And still others will keep watch and protect other fey children, preparing them for what they face. I will not ask you to do something I'm not also willing to undertake. I'll live among them and join in the fight—not as god—but as a mortal."

"You would have us sacrifice our children?" In her anger, the summer queen's skin glowed a hot white. "I don't care how many dragons you have outside our tower. You will regret even suggesting we offer up our children for that pathetic world of yours."

"The cause is great," Tian held up her hand, hoping to stay Kyran's anger. "The cost is greater I'm afraid. You are a good queen, and your obligation is to your people. However, Efre Ousel will make a sacrifice as well. For every child of yours given to their world, they will offer up a child to your world. A life for a life. Their children will live in your kingdom, and you will grow to love them. Your worlds will be connected."

"My fey are worth far more than their children."

"Not in the eyes of a mother," Willow said. "A child is a child. To the parents? It's their whole world. We can't weigh such value on scales. The sacrifice is painful but fair."

Kyran stood up from her throne.

"I'm tired of arguing. The spring queen has made up her mind, and we will support her—not Tian, but her. You want to trade lives to save their world, then you are a far sterner ruler than I am." Kyran Bloom looked around the room but avoided Tian's gaze. She turned and exited the great hall. "I leave you two to work out the particulars of this madness."

Arelius and Eirwen followed Kyran out of the hall, leaving Willow alone with Tian.

"My sister will come around."

"I don't think she will."

Willow Bud hardened at this response. She did not like being contradicted.

"The Beast. What do you think he will do when we send the fey to Efre Ousel?"

"He will hunt them and kill them. He will try, at least."

Willow Bud looked so innocent as she took in this information. She did not grasp the weight of it.

"If he hunts our people, my sister's anger will rage against him. She will go from being your greatest critic to your closest ally."

Willow walked from her throne to Tian's dragon companion. She gave the dragon a pat. The dragon warmed to Willow's touch, nuzzling their head under Willow's hand, asking for more attention.

"And what about you?" Tian asked.

"Send me more gifts from Efre Ousel," Willow responded. "I like the trees."

\* \* \*

The roots of Alda Feren twisted through the earth, each path breaking into more paths. The woman navigated the paths, and the Beast followed her every step of the way. If she continued to the four titans, the Beast would be there as well. She had to stop and allow for the inevitable confrontation.

"No more games, Beast," the woman said. She had another name for the Beast, but she could not remember it. "I'm here. You're here. I defeated you once, I think." The memories were fading fast. "I can defeat you again."

"You destroyed the flesh, a vessel, nothing more," the Beast snarled. "But you will never defeat me."

"Sounds like an excuse."

"We're in a world beyond flesh and blood, but my claws and teeth can still tear at you."

The shadowy form of the Beast surrounded the woman, blotting out everything else. Alda Feren disappeared; the complex root structure gone. All that remained was the darkness of this void and within the void a deep despair.

This was the Beast's first move against her.

The woman felt a staff materialize in one hand, a shield in the other. The heft of both items was familiar, comforting. Beneath her feet, a stone floor appeared—level ground on which to fight.

The Beast took the form of a massive crab-like creature. The Beast had two pincers like fortified towers, looming over her. The Beast was covered by a mottled carapace of overlapping plates. Six legs on either side of his body. Each segmented leg came to spear-like tips, which clicked along the ground, creating a nonstop tapping noise. The Beast's new form had a razor-like tail that whipped from side to side.

The creature was an incarnation of despair. Hopelessness emanated from the Beast.

Despair was a deceiver, a liar that spoke truth, treacherous movements hidden within false assurances. Surrender. Lie down. Find strength later, but for now, give up. But the woman was acquainted with despair.

The woman had nowhere to run, no cover to hide behind. No strategic advantage from her environment. The roots and the foliage, which had always been hers to command, were absent from this darkened wasteland. Without any other options, she held her shield high and ran toward the crab. The crab brought down one of his pincers, crushing the floor, and the woman cut to one side to avoid the attack.

She looked for a weak point in the crab, possibly the eyes, but she couldn't reach them on this behemoth. The legs were a possibility. They supported the great mass of the crab, and the final segment of the legs were small enough for her to grapple.

The way to fight despair was to keep moving, to keep living. Hold the grief close. The grief would travel, but it was better to not give over to despair. Hope for another day. There were moments of joy to walk alongside the grief. Thoughts of her children. She could remember them, but their names escaped. Thoughts of a woman, a beautiful, kind woman, a gentle maiden who had suffered for her. She was worth fighting for, but once again, the names slipped by. The woman recalled hazy moments of beauty that left her speechless, but if despair had its way, then nothing else was possible.

The woman ran underneath the crab in an abrupt, unpredictable pattern. The legs stabbed at her. She was quick enough to dodge them. She held out her shield, and one leg pierced through it. She let go of the shield and braced the staff behind this leg. She held onto the staff with both hands and pulled toward her with all her might. She heard a cracking noise. The crab screeched in pain.

She ducked and rolled as another leg stabbed at her. When she got back to her feet, she swung her staff at a joint between the segments. The leg bent at a severe angle. More screeching came from the crab.

The Beast's tail swiped at her, slashed at her stomach and knocked her back to the ground. The cut from the tail burned. The woman winced from the pain, but she refused to cry out. She gritted her teeth and kept fighting.

She swung the staff about her like a whirlwind, both deflecting attacks and taking more strikes against the legs of the Beast. The crab collapsed to the ground.

"There's nothing you can take from me that hasn't already been taken," the woman said. "Maybe it would work against someone who lived a brighter life, but you can't break me."

The crab form disappeared, dissipating into a black mist that returned to the surrounding darkness. The woman was hurt. Her shield was broken, but she could still fight.

The darkness split into beams of light. There were places that could be seen and not seen, and shadows between. Horrible things lurked in the uncertain places. The despair transformed into fear.

This was the Beast's second move.

Within the shadows, the woman could see something that resembled a lion. The creature had horns like a ram, curling around on either side of his head. As he roared, the jaw opened much wider than seemed natural. The woman could see the elongated fangs. The lion foamed at the mouth like a rabid animal. The matted mane was black and gray. The eyes were dark, caved-in pits.

The Beast had become a nightmare. Terror and dismay swirled about him.

The Beast lunged at the woman—jaws gaping, ready to tear at her throat. She held up her staff and the Beast clamped onto it. The woman tried to pull the staff from the Beast, but he only bit down harder. The Beast swung its head to wrest the staff from the woman, but she held on.

The woman was well acquainted with fear. In that moment, she remembered a wicked mother. She first met her mother in a garden filled with white flowers. The woman was just a child at the time. She had climbed over a wall to get to the garden. She had grown up in the city and had never seen such beautiful flowers. The mother nearly killed the child for trespassing. Instead, she decided to raise this girl as her daughter.

The mother beat her. Punitive slaps upon her hands and legs, but also her face—with clenched fists and leather straps. The girl often feared for her life. The mother felt it had made her strong, that it would prepare her for a cruel world. The mother would send her out to do terrible things, and the child did them because she knew if she didn't, there would be more beatings waiting at home. And if she escaped, the mother would find her—and that would be even worse.

The child was terrified of her mother. She was afraid of footsteps approaching her room. She was afraid of doors creaking open. She was afraid of threatening voices calling her name, the one her mother had given her. She had never gotten over the strange fear of hearing her own name.

The lion reared up, and then came down, sending the

woman against the ground. She hit the floor hard and felt something inside her break, but still she held on. The lion reared up a second time and again sent the woman to the ground.

Then, the staff snapped in the lion's mouth. The woman didn't even think such a thing was possible. The staff broke.

The woman held the broken halves of her staff. The staff had once been gifted to her, first used to protect her against the wicked mother. Now, it would be used one last time. The lion was on top of her. She stabbed the lion with sharp, broken ends. She pushed and twisted it into the creature's side. Blood poured out. And like before, the Beast dissipated back into the darkness.

The woman tried to regain her breath, and she couldn't. She looked down and saw that the lion had torn at her with his claws. During the fight, she wasn't even aware of the damage she had taken, but she was dying. She too was broken.

"I have faced far greater fears than you," the woman said in gasps. "Nothing is more terrifying than a cruel parent. Maybe your shadows would work against someone who lived a brighter life."

The darkness and the light shifted into a swirl of anger.

This was the Beast's third move against her.

The Beast transformed into a dragon—fearsome, ruinous, unassailable. The dragon had black scales like layers of an impenetrable shield wall, long claws of the sharpest steel, wings that stretched across the void. The dragon appeared, and the air became thin. The woman's ears popped from the change in pressure. Her skin vibrated, sensing the end.

"If I were you," the woman said, "I would've led with the dragon."

The Beast had been testing her. Anger was her great weakness, and it took the shape of this dragon. She was without her shield, without her staff, and she was mortally injured.

In her life, anger had kept her safe. It had made her powerful. It allowed her to fight back. It was her antidote to the despair. It allowed her to see her world for what it was. She knew how to fight against despair and fear, but anger had always been like an ally to her. She felt like she had control over it, but that was an illusion. It would be her downfall.

The woman remembered moments throughout her life when she had given into her anger. The anger was always under the surface, a sense of injustice in her life. She would never be able to hold on to the things that mattered in her life. It would all be taken from her, and all she could do was burn with rage.

"This dragon, I have known it for most of my life," the woman said. "I can't defeat it. It's become so much a part of me. I don't know who I am if I let it go."

The Beast grew stronger. He was reaching within her, taking over. It would be so easy to give in. And what then? The Beast would find his way to the titans. He would wake them, and the world would break. The end she had been trying to prevent would be imminent, but what did it matter if she could not remember herself or the world she was trying to save?

"I will not fight you" was all she could say.

The stone floor disappeared. She was back at the rooted labyrinth of Alda Feren. The Beast—in this dragon form—stood before her, but it did not strike.

The word "imminent" stuck with her. She defeated the Beast once. She tore the Beast apart in a grove of old trees. She had commanded the thick branches to wrap around him and rip him to pieces. His spirit descended into the earth. Why didn't he wake up the titans months ago? He's been here this whole time waiting for her to arrive. It occurred to her that he was lost in the maze. He couldn't find his way. He was a prisoner here. She may have lost herself, but she did not lose the way. He needed her.

There was another woman, a great warrior, a cousin perhaps. She had kept the Beast imprisoned below her palace within the dragon pit in a cage of magical steel bars. The warrior knew the Beast couldn't be defeated, but he could be contained.

This great tree, with its unending pathways, was a greater prison than the one behind the palace, and the woman could be his jailer.

The woman knew what she had to do, before he took over and all was lost.

\* \* \*

Tian walked along the worn path in the dark woods. Tian's red dragon companion had grown and was now the size of a house. The dragon glided overhead, keeping pace with their divine friend.

Tian stepped cautiously while on the path. Life was abundant in this world, and it came in all sizes. She did not want to step on one of Willow's attendants who might be standing ready to escort her the rest of the way. It would make for a poor introduction into Willow's domain.

Tian could see sprites flitting about in the warped trees. The sprites kept a cautious eye on the visitor. Tian lifted a hand and waved to them. They scattered farther into wooded sanctuary but then slowly approached again. The only illumination in the forest came from tiny glinting lights. To Tian, the forest appeared as if the night sky had descended upon the world. She thought of her first encounter with the seed of Alda Feren floating in the void of space, surrounded by stars, before Tian had earned a name. A simpler time, if ever one existed.

The air was cool. A thick mist hovered low along the ground. The mist roiled around the trees and across the under-growth, twisting around Tian and down the path. Tian under-stood. The mist was alive. This was Willow's attendant.

"Lead on, then. Take me to your queen."

Tian followed the mist until the path opened to a meadow. At the center was a tall tree with white flowers blooming on the branches. The white petals glowed, casting a purplish light upon the open area. Underneath the tree's canopy was a wrought-iron table set for two. Willow Bud sat, waiting for her guest to arrive.

This part of the fey world was cast in perpetual dawn, and it suited the lively monarch.

The mist thinned out across the meadow. In the distance, past the tree line at the far end, Tian could see the jutting towers of the spring queen's sapphire palace. Tian noted she wasn't invited to the palace as a visiting dignitary. This locale was intended as a casual gathering place for friends.

Tian neared the spring queen. When not around her siblings, Willow appeared lighter, more cheerful.

Willow pointed to the tree, which—while strong and mature—was nowhere near the size of Alda Feren.

"You said it would grow as Alda Feren did. I wonder if you overstated its potential."

"Give it time," Tian said. She gave Willow a kiss on the cheek and then sat at the empty chair. "Even Alda Feren was once this size, but it kept growing as will this one. I fear this tree may overtake the whole forest."

"We're immortal. We have time to see if you're correct," Willow looked up to the dragon circling overhead. "Your dragon companion has grown too."

"And they aren't even at full size, not even close."

"Everything takes time it would seem." Willow looked around with childlike expectation. "Have you brought me anything?"

"You knew I would." Tian held up her hand and another seedling appeared. Willow clapped and reached out to it.

"Is it another tree like Alda Feren?"

"This tree is different. It's named after you. A willow tree."

"Lovely!" Willow was utterly charmed by the gift.

"When it's full grown, you will like it. Very distinctive."

"You named a tree after me?"

"The people of Efre Ousel came up with it on their own. Ever since you started sending more fey into their world, they've picked up bits and pieces from your world. Things I would never anticipate."

"Such as?"

"Their food has gotten better. I don't know how they did it, but they've discovered dishes like your own. They combine foods, adding herbs and spices to create new flavors, not unlike here. And they've also figured out how to make wine, mead, and ale."

"Good for them," Willow responded. With a thought and wave of her hand, two glasses of wine appeared before them. Willow lifted her glass. "I doubt their wine will ever taste as good."

"You might be surprised," Tian reached for her glass.

"Time moves differently there. Things are perishable. Mortality is more of a concern. Time ages the wine in ways you can't imagine. When you drink their wine, you are tasting the slow death of a fragile world."

"How poetic," Willow took a drink and frowned. Willow did not like being corrected, even if it was on matters she didn't know anything about. Monarchs in both worlds shared this trait. "Forget the seedlings," Willow said. "Next time you return, I want a bottle of their wine."

"As you wish."

They sat for a while in comfortable silence. After a while, they exchanged a few words, which developed into the kindly banter only kindred spirits can share. As Tian observed, time moved differently there—and under that tree, time stood still. It felt as if they could sit there forever and enjoy each other's company. But eventually, they had to get to the matter at hand.

"My friend, you said you would give me a report on our enterprise to keep this fragile world, Efre Ousel, in one piece. How fare our fey heroes against the Beast? I was impatient and sent some of my sprites across the divide, but their reports have been incomplete. Tell me what you know."

Tian had been rehearsing what she would say.

"You were right about your sister. The Beast struck a terrible blow. In response, the summer sword has been raised against the Beast, and the queen sent her own daughter to fight him. She's committed to the cause."

"Good, good." Willow nodded. "A princess of the Fey Court. I would think our victory is all but certain."

"Not so." Tian hesitated. "The Beast is raising an army in response. It will be a terrible war."

"Aren't all wars terrible?" Willow's gentle voice hardened.

"This one is far worse."

The whooshing noise of the dragon circling overhead became more pronounced. Willow wanted to respond, but hesitated. The spring queen had been so happy to see Tian. She had been expecting a cheery greeting and a positive update. She did not want casualty reports and setbacks. She did not want a war.

"What do you want me to do about it?" Willow asked, but she didn't want the answer.

"Aid the summer queen. Produce an heir of your own; send them to fight alongside Kyran's princess."

Tian had offended the spring queen. Willow's eyes went wide at the suggestion of an heir.

"I'm not a brood mare. We may be friends, but don't ever be so casual with me that you forget you address a queen. My reign is eternal. I don't need to produce an heir."

When Tian had first approached the Fey Court, Willow Bud seemed like an ideal ally. And it some ways, she was. The spring queen was interested in helping, but in the abstract sense. She was not one for the hard realities of war and death. She didn't want to speak about sacrifice. The summer queen, who had put up the greater resistance to Tian, was the greater ally. She was more than ready to send her child to fight in this war. Whatever it would take to defeat the Beast.

"My words have offended you," Tian said.

"Your words do not offend me. Your presence does. Please leave."

"If you only—"

"Leave!" Willow shouted this command, and the forest surrounding the meadow curved forward in malice. The skies darkened. The glinting lights faded to nothing. Tian's dragon companion roared in response. Even they knew it was no longer safe here. "And I reject your gift. We do not need any willow trees."

The seedling rotted and crumpled into dust.

\* \* \*

The woman remembered a story. Maybe it was a true story. Maybe it was a bedtime story.

A girl in the forest was being followed by a wolf. She wasn't being hunted, not really. Secretly, she lured the wolf along the path to a cottage. The wolf went into the cottage, thinking it was so clever. The wolf wanted to catch the girl, but the cottage itself was a trap for the wolf. The girl returned with the hunter. The wolf died in the cottage, unable to escape. In some versions of the story, the girl was the hunter.

The woman always thought the story was odd. If the girl was in the forest and the wolf was in the forest, why didn't the wolf just eat the girl while she was walking the wooded path? The woman concluded the forest did not belong to the wolf; it belonged to the girl.

The woman decided she could be like the girl in the story.

"Beast, are you still there?" She called out coyly to the darkness.

"I'm always here, little mouse."

Little mouse. Yes, that's what he called her.

The woman took a moment to sense her way in the darkness along the roots. She chose a direction, and she ran. In her injured state, each step was like a hot iron striking her. She didn't know how long she could last.

Her movement was like the skittering of prey, dashing into

the brush. Instinct took over, and the Beast pursued. She could almost sense the sharp teeth ready to tear into her, saliva dripping from his jowls. He wanted the chase. He needed it.

"I never knew you to run away. You've forgotten yourself. You don't even know what has been taken from you."

The woman did not respond to his taunts. She may have forgotten herself, but the Beast had forgotten his way—and down here, that was far worse. She pushed the pain aside and moved faster. He followed. He could not tell she was curving and weaving the path ahead of them. The roots twisted, one over another and under the next and over again. They went around and around. The roots took the form of a crown wreath. She wasn't sure why she chose the shape. It felt significant to her. A prison for a more vulnerable version of herself, and now, a prison for the Beast.

As she shaped the roots, the Beast caught up to her and struck at her heels. Pain. She did not imagine such pain was possible. Greater than even what she had endured before. She kept running. He struck at her again and again—with no limit to what could be inflicted upon her. The Beast took pleasure in the pain he caused. He would let her get ahead so he could tear at her once more. She let out a scream, and the roots tightened in response. It was agony, but she kept going. If she stopped, he would collapse on her and feast, and then the real pain would begin and might never end.

Alda Feren guided her to the past. A time she couldn't remember, but she saw it and knew she had lived it. A druid was holding an infant and running from not one wolf but several. Gnolls, they were called. The druid stepped into an icy, rushing river to get away from the hungry pack, and that's when she lost the babe in the river. The infant had turned into a fish and escaped. The gods had acted to save the infant, but they also saved the druid. The gnolls stopped their pursuit once the babe was gone. A path her life could've taken, forever changed.

That is the way of the gods. When they intervene, everyone loses something.

What would have happened if the infant and the druid had made it across the river, if the druid had taken the child to the great tree of life? What lives would have never crossed her path? What lives would have never been born or taken, or changed?

Ahead was a series of forked paths. She moved faster, took one path, then the other, then a different one. She moved to the left and the right, taking each way seemingly at random. The woman could sense the Beast's frustration, and then she held back. She tried to make herself as small as possible. She thought to herself: *I am a fish in the river. You cannot catch me.* She found a corner in one of the paths and waited. She held her formless breath. The Beast rushed past without noticing. The woman waited and then went back the way she had come to further distance herself from the Beast.

She could hear the Beast's taunting voice far down the root path.

"Little mouse, little mouse, where are you?"

The woman moved along the path until she reached the point where she had started the chase.

"Oh little mouse? Are you being sneaky? I do love it when you're trying to fight back. So many of my victims stand there while I rip their heads off. Where's the sport?"

She needed to cut the root. She wished she had an axe, something to sever the path from the rest of the system.

"You are clever. You went back to the beginning—trying to trap me, are you?"

The woman shook at his words. He had figured out her plan, and he was racing back.

"When I catch you, no more games. No more playing with my food. I will kill you. I will crush you in my jaws."

The woman tore at the root, twisting it around in an attempt to break it. The root was tenacious, and the Beast was getting closer.

"And when there is nothing left of you, I will find those titans, and I will wake them—and the world will break. Everyone you love will die."

The woman yearned to hear those forgotten names once more, to be reminded of who she once was.

As the Beast neared, the woman heard another voice, a tiny voice like bells jingling. The voice spoke quietly, the whispering of a secret. It was the voice of a sprite.

Children played a game where they knotted twine between two cups with holes in the bottom. They pulled the line taut and could send messages to each other by speaking into them. The sprites voice came to the woman in a similar manner. The sprite was far away, on the surface, speaking to a tree in an ancient grove—a grove older than the surrounding city. The tree's roots connected to Alda Feren. She knew this sprite.

The sprite spoke words meant only for her. Words of power. They were the names of people she loved and a promise for the future.

The words were like an incantation. Upon hearing them, the woman was able to focus a sliver of herself into light, sharper than any blade. It cut clean through the root. The woman could see the Beast, but she had cut off his only way out. She moved the root's end, tucking it under another part of the path, completing the circle—and separating the Beast from the rest of the tree and the world itself.

The Beast howled when he realized he was trapped. He howled and howled. The Beast was contained in a jail cell, far under the earth. He paced across the braided circle, knowing he was trapped.

"Little mouse! You may contain me, but you cannot defeat me. As the creation grows, I grow in strength. Chaos to the order, ruin to the rise, spoil to the splendor. I oppose what is good, and I become greater. You cannot defeat me!"

The effort it took to create the blade of light exhausted the woman's remaining essence until all that was left of her was a wisp, a mote of fading light, no larger than an acorn. The wisp lacked anything distinguishable as a thinking, sentient being. All that remained was a sense of purpose and direction.

Reach the titans before it was too late. Float away from the howling Beast—raging on the other side of an impenetrable divide. Float along another root system. Find what it had come here to do.

* * *

As Tian had predicted, the tree grew to overtake the whole forest. However, because few things wither and die in the spring queen's realm, the smaller trees conjoined to the trunk of the larger tree and lifted upward as it grew—a forest on the ground and a second forest clinging to the massive tree trunk, reaching into the sky.

Tian did not find Willow Bud at the base of the tree as before. Not too far off, closer to the sapphire palace, the queen sat at the edge of a pond where she could view the spectacle of this titan tree and the forest it carried with it. Two swans coasted along the surface of the pond. The twinkling lights of this world reflected on the water. Willow's bare feet dangled in the water. Her eyes were red with tears.

"I found you," Tian said. The last time they had seen each other, Willow was angry, and Tian wasn't sure if she was welcome to return.

"You didn't bring any of your dragons."

"No, just me this time," Tian said. "It's not a formal visit. I'm only checking on you." Willow nodded and kicked her legs a bit, splashing the water. Tian reached into her travel sack and pulled out a bottle. "However, as promised, I did bring you this."

Willow smiled weakly and took the gift as Tian held it out to her. "Wine from that other world," Willow mused. "Thank you. I will try it later."

She set the bottle down and patted the ground, inviting Tian to sit next to her. Tian did so, and to her surprise, Willow rested her head on Tian's shoulder. Willow began to cry. From living among the mortals, Tian had consoled many tearful people. Most of them after having had too much to drink. For the first time, Tian comforted a person next to a corked bottle of wine. As the whimpering progressed into full sobs, Tian understood there was more going on than just a vulnerable moment.

"Your grace, what's wrong?" Tian asked. "After all these years, I've heard nothing from you. What is it?"

"The War of the Hounds." When Willow said these words, Tian felt a pit in her stomach. Willow had received updates on the war. Maybe it was from her sprites who had crossed over—

or she got the news from her sister who had given up her daughter to lead the battle.

"What about the war?"

"I did as you said. I sent more of the fey from my realm to fight, and they're just being slaughtered. All of them. The Beast finds them and hunts them down."

Tian knew the details of the war. Her brother Olar, a god of war, had been tracking it with great interest. Tian had asked him to intervene, but he had wanted to see what the summer queen's daughter could do. He had great faith in her. Tian wasn't so certain.

Willow lifted her head from Tian's shoulder. She gained her breath and spoke again.

"I can't do it anymore. I can't send any more of my people's children over to their world, which is why—"

"I understand."

"—I sent my own child over there."

Tian felt a chill on her neck. These words shook her. This issue of Willow's heir had been contentious with her last visit. Willow Bud had been offended by the idea of producing offspring to fight a war. Tian had replayed the conversation several times in her head during the intervening years. She felt guilty about what she had said. The summer queen was willing. She couldn't expect the same of the spring queen. But it appears Willow had a change of heart.

"You didn't have to do that. Your child would be too young to fight alongside Kyran's daughter, anyway. They belong to different ages."

Willow looked at her bare feet in the water, kicking back and forth.

"It is already done. Do you think Kyran's daughter will be able to defeat the Beast?"

"I don't even know if that's the right question."

Tian had seen what the Beast was capable of. But Kyran's daughter had proven herself a worthy opponent. In some ways, she was a greater threat to the Beast than the gods had ever been, but she needed help. If two children of the Fey Court could have fought him, they might've had a chance.

Willow's face was downcast. Her sacrifice, while commendable, was poorly timed. A good decision made too late was barely of any use.

"Maybe we can't defeat the Beast," Willow said, "but the titans still sleep under their world—and you need the tree-born fey to keep them asleep."

"Yes, the Beast and his soldiers killed the tree-born fey during the war. That seems to have been his plan all along. The titans will wake."

"My child is one of the tree-born, a wood nymph gifted with the ability to send others into an enchanted sleep. Hopefully, that will be sufficient for you."

Tian's eyes widened. This bit of luck, this twist of fate! The spring queen had conceived a child in her world, birthed from a tree in the other.

"We'll need to send people who can care for her and direct her to Alda Feren. There's a village in Raustfweg that communes with the fey. We can send druids from the village to recover her."

"Right now, my child rests in Amon."

"They can make the journey."

Tian wanted to ask about the particulars of Willow Bud's pregnancy. She wanted to know about her partner, if she had one. Was this child intended? Wanted? Was there great fanfare throughout her domain with news of a child from the queen— or was the whole matter handled in secrecy? Tian felt deep shame at urging Willow to produce a child for the war.

"Willow, I am sorry."

"This was my choice. I don't do anything against my will. This child is mine, but the child was not conceived, carried, or birthed as mortals would."

Being a god, Tian knew about strange births and pregnancies. People had numerous stories about Tian, a trickster, shape shifting in various beasts and getting impregnated by a lonely goatherd or down-of-his-luck miller's son. These stories were nonsense. It was her sister Fen who was the shapeshifter—and not too particular about her romantic partners from Tian's perspective.

Willow trembled as the tears came. She cared about this child, and she was grieving this decision.

Tian placed a comforting hand on Willow's back.

"The tree I gifted last time, do you remember?"

"How can I forget my own name? The willow tree."

"In Efre Ousel, the tree is sometimes called a 'weeping willow' because of how the raindrops run down its hanging branches. But I understand now—the tree cries for its lost child."

"She won't be safe in that other world. She could be immortal in this one. Instead, I've condemned her to a brief and frail existence."

Tian tapped the wine bottle she had gifted to Willow.

"It makes for better wine. Perhaps it makes for a better life as well—to have a beginning and an end."

"I ache at that thought. It tears me apart."

"Then, you are like any mother I have ever known."

They sat in silence next to the pond. Tian watched the swans glide across the water as she considered whether mortality was a blessing or a curse. The ripples from the swans' path disturbed the reflection of the tree.

\* \* \*

Four titans slept far beneath the depths of Alda Feren, each one larger than the tree itself, which did not seem possible. The world couldn't contain one, let alone four. Wherever they were, these titans dwelled in a reality where space and time were of little consequence.

The first titan slept soundly. The second and third titans slept, but it was a fitful sleep, filled with dreams of flight. The fourth titan was awake and ready to be free, like a seed bursting from its outer shell. It wanted to shake off the earth, launch itself into the sky, and expanse beyond. If it broke free, the world would break as well.

A small mote of light floated above the titans. The light was afraid, feeling it, not as an emotion but as an antithesis to its purpose. The light came here to lull titans to sleep with its fey magic. The light had taken a great journey, and here was its end.

The light crept closer.

The fourth titan rumbled, sending shockwaves to the surface far above, destroying whole villages and cities, sending great waves across the ocean, and scarring the earth with deep cracks.

The rumbling ceased. Then, the fourth titan spoke, sending tiny ripples upward.

"Where am I?" The fourth titan's voice was a distant thunder.

The light could not respond.

"How long have I been asleep?"

Once again, the light had no way to answer. It gave a faint pulse of acknowledgment to the titan.

"It is time for me to be free."

To this, the light could answer.

The light drew within itself one last time and then released the last bit of itself across the four titans. Motes of blue light sparkled before the four titans.

The first titan continued to slumber. The second and third titans fell into a deep, deep sleep, abandoning whatever dreams they once had. But the fourth titan resisted the fey magic.

"It's not right to keep me down here when I was created to fly, to be out there."

The light persisted with its blue light, hoping to lull the fourth titan to sleep.

Justice. Mercy. Fairness. These were matters for gods and monarchs. The light knew what it had the power to do—to use up the last bit of itself to give the titans rest and to still the shaking world.

"I must be free. Don't do this."

The Beast was made a prisoner as a punishment for his crimes against all that lived. He wanted to see the world break. The titans were prisoners too, but of circumstance, not of any transgression.

For many to live, the few must suffer.

An odd rule for an odd reality, but it had to be so.

Sleep.

"No, I don't want to stay down here in the dark."

Sleep.

The fourth titan begged for its freedom.

With each plea, the titan grew weaker and more oscitant until it drifted into sleep. A sleep that hopefully would last until the end of time.

Only the light would ever know how close the world had come to breaking apart.

With the Beast imprisoned within the roots of Alda Feren, the fey could return in greater numbers. And with the fey came hope.

The motes of light blinked out, one after another, until one light was left.

Then it too disappeared.

All that remained was darkness and the dreamless sleep of titans.

* * *

The spring queen tore down her sapphire palace and built a new home into the side of the great tree. Half the tree remained untouched. The other half appeared as though it were coated in white wax with twisted strands drooping from the waves and curves of the ivory surface. The sapphire palace had appeared as a distant, shimmering dream. This white palace, warped and weeping, was an expression of melancholy.

No guards were at the gate. Tian walked through the entrance, across the courtyard, to an archway that led to an interior spiral staircase. No attendants were there to greet her. Tian could sense only one person occupied this palace, and she waited for her at the highest point. Tian walked up the stairs. She placed a hand on the ivory wall. The surface was soft with an unexpected sandy texture. It felt good to the touch.

The repetition of the spiral stairs, with no windows to the outside, had Tian feeling as if she were trapped in an endless loop. Eventually, she reached the royal hall.

The spring queen sat on her throne, weary and restless. She blended into her surroundings with a white layered lace dress. The dress had a high collar and long billowing sleeves. Willow's loveliness remained, but her gentleness was gone. She had the hardened face of someone who had known sorrow. Tian wondered if this change had driven away her courtiers. But some things about Willow did not change.

"Have you brought me a gift?"

Tian smiled at the infantile way Willow greeted her.

"I brought you a riddle."

"Oh," she said with a sullen pout. "I was hoping for a dragon egg. Something like that."

"The dragons respect me because I don't do things like hand over their eggs, even to a dear friend like you."

"Dear friend." Willow repeated the words. Her petulant tone questioned the sincerity.

"Yes, you are a dear friend. I imagine you haven't had many friends visit lately."

Tian held out her hands to indicate the vast emptiness of the hall. Willow ignored this comment.

"Let me hear this riddle."

Tian took a step forward.

"A god and not a god. Unborn, yet birthed. Ageless, yet maturing. Undying, yet dies. All powerful, yet compromised. This girl will accomplish great things when greatness is taken from her."

Willow pursed her lips.

"The answer is you. You're the gift. You're going to become mortal."

"I've done it a few times."

"How is this a gift for me?"

"Your daughter has been trying to have children," Tian said. "Both times, her babies were stillborn. As a fey, she can't have a child with a person from that world. But how would she know? It might be the death of her. Perhaps, if she gave birth to a god, she'll have better luck."

"You're entering the world as my daughter's daughter."

"Hello, Grandma." Tian was not sure how Willow would respond.

Willow leaned forward in her throne. She was about to say something but stopped herself and tried again. After a few false starts, the words came out.

"I sent Jack Stagg to protect my daughter. He can travel between worlds and across great distances if he has her name. But my daughter lost her name, and we lost her." Willow trembled so hard it worried Tian. Her face was a flood of anger, sadness, and relief. "My daughter is alive? You found her?"

"I didn't know you had lost track of her," Tian said. "Otherwise, I would've told you."

"Lies."

"My sister Cyruth is known as 'the All-Seeing.' Helpful, when trying to locate someone. But yes, your daughter is alive."

"And her name?" Willow asked.

"My other sister Golwin has everyone's name, but she won't give it to me."

"More lies. More deceit."

Tian did not like being called a liar. This was not her way. Not usually.

"She is Golwin the Fated. If I could explain her ways to you, I would be a much more powerful god."

"Anything else you can tell me?"

"I don't know much about where she is," Tian said. "Still somewhere in Amon. Cyruth told me it was a farm, and she rarely leaves it. Before that, she lived in a city."

"Penderyn."

"Yes, and life was hard for her there. But it will prepare her for what she must face."

Willow's expression darkened.

"You're a liar, a deceiver. You kept her from me so you could turn my daughter into a soldier. You didn't want my fey to interfere, to stop the training."

Willow's harsh words flustered Tian.

"There's nothing I can say—"

"And now that my daughter is safe, you're going there to put her back on the path to war."

"That's not it at all."

"After you first visited us, I told the Fey Court we should trust you. My siblings weren't so sure. After all, you are Tian the Trickster. I defended you, but I was wrong." Tian could feel the palace shake. "Everything you've done is to send more of *our* people into *your* war. My daughter!"

"My mother!" Tian shouted back. "Already I feel connected to her. My whole world begins with her. My heart is with her, and I would rather break the world myself than give her over to the Beast. But do you think he's going to stop once he destroys their world? No. After he's done, he's coming here next. He won't stop unless we stop him. And so, we must sacrifice. We must fight."

Willow left her throne and walked toward Tian. As she did, a sword materialized in Willow's hand. Far outside the palace, a hundred dragons roared—all ready to rush to Tian's aid.

The fey queen and the trickster god stood a few inches from each other. Neither would yield. If it came to blows, the war between these immortal factions might destroy several worlds.

"Tell me her name," Willow commanded.

Tian remained silent.

"I want to know my daughter's name," Willow raised her sword. Tian did not flinch.

"You are not a warrior. Don't act like one."

"Tell me her name," Willow repeated, but her tone was less threatening, more pleading.

But Tian did not answer, instead she spoke of her transformation.

"When I take the form of a mortal, I'll struggle to remember anything of my time as a god—including these meetings. The memories will be there, but hazy and uncertain."

"Tell me her name, please." Tears rolled down Willow's cheeks.

"The mind of a mortal can't grasp the eternal. However, in my heart, I will carry a deep intuition for what must be done."

"Tell me her name." Willow knew she wouldn't get a response, but she had nothing else to say.

"I will put her back on the path to do what she was destined for."

"Tell me her name."

Tian shook her head and left. Tian could hear sobs behind her. They followed her down the staircase and echoed across the empty yard.

* * *

The birth would happen during the month of Tia'noth. There was disagreement on whether a child born under the goddess of luck, misfortune, and pleasure was a good omen or not. All the stories about Tian were such a mixed bag—sometimes she was a hero of the people, sometimes she was the cause of the world's suffering.

The father-in-law, Wardi, always shared his perspective on the named gods and what everything meant. He wasn't a religious man as much as he was an opinionated one, and he disapproved of the timing.

"If you could've had the babe during Yoontide, that would've been much better."

"Two months early?" Igvan laughed at her husband's suggestion. "Let's be thankful you're not in charge of when and how we come into this world."

Igvan placed a gentle hand on her daughter-in-law's cheek. "Don't listen to Wardi. Tia'noth is a fine month. A child born under Tian is a mystery, and that's how all children are, anyway. Parents think they know what they're doing, and then a child comes into this world. Suddenly, parents know nothing. Tian is a great comfort to mothers because Tian does whatever pleases her." Igvan winked at Wardi. "Tian has no time for foolish men. And this close to your delivery? That's good advice."

"You call me a fool, but it was my suggestion to fill the

birth room with flowers and use the lapis powder. We'll gain favor with Yoon."

The powder was made with grounded lapis combined with flour. The lapis had been procured from a traveling merchant, and it was expensive, but Wardi was convinced it was necessary.

"Yoon has blue skin," Igvan said. "With the powder, so will you. It's a strange tradition, but I did it when I delivered Callis —and just look at him. He's the healthiest person I've ever known. He never gets sick."

Both Igvan and Wardi tried to keep the mood light, but they were worried. The last two babies had been stillborn. The grief had overwhelmed the whole family. With news of a third pregnancy, they weren't taking any chances, especially because three was a cursed number.

Igvan and Wardi prepared the birth room by filling it with flowers. They lined the walls with dried summer flowers. These flowers were bound with twine and hanging upside down, lined in overlaying layers, so that it was difficult to see the walls. Neighboring families made garlands, which they strung across the ceiling and the cornices. Callis—without anything else to do—picked wildflowers that bloomed in late autumn. He made bouquets, which he placed along the floor. The entire room was a vibrant explosion of color. It was impossible to move anywhere without knocking over flowers and then needing to place them back in position. The sweet floral smell was, at first, incredible. However, after two weeks in the birth room, the water for the bouquets soured—and the putrid smell was overwhelming. Igvan had to replace all the water and spent the day lighting sage and fanning the room.

The laying-in period lasted for several weeks. The family became restless. There was little to occupy their time and even less to talk about. Callis left every afternoon to pick more flowers—thinking it was a way to make himself useful, but it made the birth room more crowded. No one wanted to tell him to give it a rest because everyone was relieved to have him away for a few hours. He was a bundle of nerves, which put the rest of the family on edge. Callis was constantly asking if everyone was okay or if there was anything he could do.

Whenever Callis was out and Wardi was taking a nap, Igvan would invoke some of the rune magic she knew. Neither her son nor her husband approved of it, but she was willing to do anything to protect the mother and child. She would stand in the doorway and chant the phrase "gee-uh-den." The phrase originated from a dead elvish language, meaning "powerful protector." While chanting, Igvan would wave her hands, writing out runes of protection. No hum of arcane energy was felt. The sky did not not darken. The earth did not shake. But Igvan was certain these small rituals were important.

"Most magic is not seen or felt. It merely happens in its own time when we're not paying attention."

At the end of the third week of Tia'noth, early in the morning, the contractions began. The room was filled with the periodic, resonant moans of a woman as her body readied itself. Throughout the day, the contractions continued. By evening, the water broke. The contractions got closer together and more intense. Callis and Wardi were asked to leave. An older woman came from a nearby farm to assist Igvan with the midwife duties.

It was no time for modesty. Clothes were removed, and the blue powder was taken from the cupboard. The powder formed a sticky paste on the sweaty skin. Igvan and the older woman had to rinse their hands in the basin several times to get the powder off them. Both had blue streaks where they inadvertently rubbed their forehead or scratched their cheek. The three women looked at each other, and for a moment, despite the pain, they laughed at the absurdity of it all.

"I hope Yoon is happy," the older woman said.

"At least Wardi will stop bothering me. The ceremony is done. All that's left is to have the baby."

"I don't want to do this," the mother cried.

"Now, there," Igvan said, wholly sympathetic to these natural fears. She wiped the tears away with a cloth, much of blue powder came off as well. "It's a bit late to change our minds. The baby is coming."

At a certain point, the body took over. There was no controlling the rhythm of the contractions or the pain. It hit in waves, and all that could be done was to give in to what was happening. There was screaming and more tears and grunting through the pain—and then, everything happened.

With a series of pushes, the head emerged and then more of the baby appeared. Igvan grabbed the baby from the head, the shoulders, the back, and she pulled the baby out. The warm, pungent smell of blood was thick in the room.

No sound came from the baby. The baby was unmoving and pale. Igvan rubbed the infant's back vigorously, then a series of drumming pats. She flicked at the tiny feet. The baby began to wriggle. A solid, healthy cry came. The mucus cleared.

Everyone in the room wept with joy. None harder than the new mother. Once the older woman wiped the blue powder from the mother's face, neck, and chest, Igvan gave the baby to the mother. She cradled the baby and held her close against her chest.

The older woman took an axe, sharpened for this task, and cut the umbilical cord.

"What are you going to name your daughter?" Igvan asked.

"She will have her true name, but I won't share it." This secret name was a common custom to keep the baby safe, so Golwin the Fated couldn't claim the child. Part of the custom was for the midwife to try to get the mother to say the name. The mother would resist and then share the other name. "But you and everyone else can call her 'Gydan.' Powerful protector."

"Gydan is a beautiful name."

\*  \*  \*

Maricel was not like her mother. She didn't have a deep druidic sense of how nature speaks to people. She couldn't read signs in a cool breeze or sense danger with a slight change in temperature. She wasn't connected to the natural world. But while traveling, Maricel could sense a calm. The earthquakes had ceased, and she knew why it had happened. The struggle, the sacrifice, the pain, it had all been worth it.

This calm meant Maricel could travel to Alda Feren without fear the world would break apart before she ever arrived. All that remained was the hardest part—a journey spanning the entire continent of Raustfweg, even as she struggled to take a step without the aid of her crutch and boot.

Apalwaite was a large city at the start of the Raven's Road. It was the last outpost before a long journey into the barren expanse of Raustfweg. In the city, Maricel tried to find out as much as she could about Raven's Road and the journey ahead. Most people avoided eye contact with her. They were leery of anyone traveling alone, and Maricel knew some were put off by her drooping facial features.

A caravan of spice merchants gathered outside one of the taverns. They wore beautiful silk clothes—ankle-length tunics paired with embroidered vests, loose trousers with shawls and wrapped tops. They adorned themselves with colorful scarves and jewelry of thin gold coins dangling from beaded headbands.

This group traveled with their whole family—men, women, children, and pets. Something about the lively demeanor of the dogs made Maricel trust this group. They weren't raising guard dogs or training them for pit fights. These pups were beloved members of the family that followed them everywhere. The dogs happily wagged their tails and never snapped at the food offered to them. They rolled over for belly rubs. They yipped and barked, not to menace, but to say, "Come play with me."

Maricel observed the caravan at a distance—until they noticed her watching them. One woman waved her over. The woman invited Maricel to join them for dinner. She had never known such hospitality. She was treated with such kindness and deference. While they ate, she shared her story. The story began before she was born, when her mom as a young woman traveled to Amon in search of a fey child. She told them about her great love—a woman she had lost and then found and then lost again.

"It sounds like your family has been trying to catch this woman for a long time," one of the women observed. "She's slippery, like a fish."

The comparison amused Maricel.

"For this fish, all rivers lead to Alda Feren," Maricel said. "If I can get there, I can find her again."

The people of the caravan knew about Alda Feren, but none of them had ever been there. They agreed to help Maricel and offered her a place in their caravan as they traveled back to their homeland. She accepted, knowing it would be safer to travel with this group than by herself.

The caravan left Apalwaite the next day. They went along the Raven's Road. This path would take them all the way to the east of Raustfweg. From there, Maricel could ask around to find out how to get to Alda Feren.

Everyone in the caravan rode horses, stockier than the ones from Amon. These horses carried the entirety of the caravan's goods and supplies in large saddle bags. Maricel was embarrassed at how slowly she moved. They kept pace with Whisker, her mule. They'd go faster without her. Even when getting ready to leave, Maricel needed help loading her cart.

"I'm sorry," Maricel said to a man named Mellal, who rode alongside her. "I'm not any use to your group. My mule is slow. With my lame leg, I'll only—"

Mellal held up a hand to indicate he wanted to say something.

"It's a good thing to travel with strangers. They bring unforeseen blessings."

"But you could go twice as fast without me."

"It's true. We have a saying, 'If you want to get there quickly, take one horse. But if you want to go far, take your family.' And look around, you're surrounded by family. You may not know it, but even though you started as a stranger, soon you will be like my sister and I will be your brother, and we will go far on this road."

# IX

AUSDRE DIED ten years after her daughter left for Raustfweg. She died soon after the death of her husband. Rue fell ill from a pox, which had spread throughout the bay region. Ausdre's druidic spells eased his discomfort, but they couldn't cure him. Rue's last moments were spent holding his wife's hand. He gave her a gentle smile and kind words. He wanted her to know he was returning his body to the elements. Everything would be okay. He had lived a good life, and he had no regrets.

The reason for Ausdre's death was less clear. She was not old, but her health declined. Every day, it looked like she had aged a year. She wandered the community, talking to herself, saying how she planned to return to Raustfweg to see her daughter and to see her mother, Olvi, one last time, and her brothers. She wanted to apologize to the fey child for a request she made of her. Since the world did not end, either the fey child was successful, or the quest which led Ausdre to Amon in the first place was nonsense. The earthquakes ten years ago were just earthquakes, and no sleeping titans would ever wake.

Regardless, Ausdre's daughter never returned. This meant either she was with the fey child—or Maricel had died while in Raustfweg.

Ausdre talked often about returning to Raustfweg, but she never made plans for a journey. She became forgetful, sometimes calling people by other names or walking into the forest without cause. Once, she made it all the way to the river. Others found her up to her waist in the water. She said she was looking for a fish she had lost.

Then, one morning, Ausdre was found dead outside her house, next to the bench.

The cause of death was unknown. Her spirit faded, and then she died.

Ausdre's funeral was a grand affair on a scale only seen for priests and nobles. The village had tripled in size—because of the promise she made to Timon. The Aylebridge orphans came here as adults. They were given land to farm. The village prospered. Everyone worked together to build new houses, barns, and even a small temple and a market square.

The village had become a community of outcasts—children without a family or a home found both here. When the village grew large enough to be included on a map, the community decided to give it a name, Dumeil. The word was a Raustfweg concept Ausdre had taught them, meaning a well-earned love. She said it was what she had found there.

For the funeral, everyone wore white floral crowns to honor Timon's legacy and Ausdre's as well. They spoke about her life, the person they had known—a druid immigrant from

Raustfweg with a strange accent and runic tattoos on her face, a person who had lost her child but gained several more.

Ausdre's body was lowered into the ground in keeping with the tradition of those who worshipped the unnamed gods. Exposed roots from a nearby tree protruded from the side of the grave pit. The roots reached toward her like tiny hands. Ausdre's body was wrapped in cloth. The orphans took their crowns and tossed them onto her body. They each grabbed a shovel to bury Ausdre, returning her to the earth.

The people of Dumeil marked her grave with a large stone. Upon the stone, they carved the rune that was on the left side of Ausdre's face, the home mark—a long straight vertical line to represent the Raustfweg coastline, crosshatches for the fjords, a triangle for the port city of Vasterghent, a horizontal line extending from the triangle. Underneath that line was a seven-point star to mark her birthplace.

She would never return home, and yet, she was home.

*　*　*

Gydan sat at the bar. She leaned back on her stool so that only the back two legs touched the ground. She rested one finger of the rim of her cup and also tilted it back. She looked at her mead and her nose wrinkled. She did not care for the mead of Amon. Soren had been right. The best mead was in Raustfweg. This Amon mead was both too sweet and a little flat. The aftertaste felt stale. While serving in Soren's army, Gydan drank a lot of mead—and now, having left the army, she missed it.

"Do you have any mead from Raustfweg?"

The barkeep looked at her. He was a portly man with a wiry red beard. He laughed at the request.

"Yes, ma'am, let me hop on a boat so I can overpay for a keg of mead."

"You wouldn't be overpaying."

"My patrons don't need imported drinks. They're happy with what we offer here."

"Your patrons don't know what they're missing."

During the day, this open area was a small market where two of the main roads in Rhyll intersected. All horse and carriage traffic was routed around it. And at night, out came the tables, stools, and a makeshift bar set across stacked crates and pallets. The barrels of beer, ale, and mead were rolled out from the home of the barkeep. Bottles of wine and other spirits were lined up behind the bar. Lanterns were lit and hung on the hooks of surrounding storefronts.

This outdoor, makeshift tavern was a popular gathering place for the soldiers in Rhyll. Gydan remembered this place. It was the night of the shadow puppet performance that Bren commissioned for her. That night, Gydan left and wandered the city with Cyru. She remembered coming here and seeing Maricel.

The tavern hadn't changed a bit. Much of Rhyll had been rebuilt after the earthquakes, but this space remained unchanged.

A tall, brutish man approached Gydan from behind. Gydan kept her back to him, but she could tell what he looked like—his flat broken nose, his braided blonde beard, the knotted scar down his neck, and the sword he kept at his side—because Cyru, ever-faithful Cyru, patrolled the sky above her, and she could see the brute through the dragon's eyes. This complete view had saved Gydan on the battlefield several times. They disagreed on how many life debts Gydan owed the dragon. Cyru placed the number at ninety-nine, while Gydan's pride placed the number much lower.

"Good evening, traveler," Gydan said without turning around. She could tell he was from Raustfweg. She had fought enough people from that part of the world to know them by smell alone, the earthy musk of grazing animals and damp fur coats.

"You're Gydan, the first general of Soren the Blind, the king of the valley and the coast."

"That I am." Gydan turned around. She rocked back on her stool so the other two legs were now on the ground. "Pleased to meet you."

She held out her hand to shake his, but he did not take it.

"You killed my brother."

"What did he look like?"

The chatter at the tavern died down. The soldiers looked up from their drinks but did not intervene. They knew to be cautious when someone from Raustfweg was causing trouble. It was far too likely the person was an ambassador here to talk with the high general.

"He looks like me, only taller."

Gydan eyed him, up and down.

"Taller than you? I find that hard to believe. And no, I didn't kill him."

"You did."

"I didn't. Are we going to do this all night? I'm meeting someone here."

*Do you want me to kill this one?*

Gydan waved off Cyru's suggestion. The brute wasn't much of a threat.

"Honor dictates a life for a life." He spoke through

clinched teeth. He gripped his sword hilt tightly. His knuckles turned white. His free hand shook.

"But I didn't kill him." Gydan's voice remained calm.

"Lies!"

The brute began to draw his sword. Gydan kicked out the stool she was leaning on. It flew at his feet and tripped him up. He fell over. His head slammed against the gravel. Gydan grabbed a washcloth from the surprised barkeep's hand. She kneeled on the brute's back and tied the washcloth around his belt and the pommel of his sword.

She got off his back. He fumbled on the ground, getting to his hands and feet, and then standing upright. In the time it took, Gydan was certain she could've killed him twice, sailed to Raustfweg, killed the rest of his family, and returned to finish her mediocre mead.

He swayed a bit while standing. He had a gash on his forehead where he had hit the ground. It bled down his face. He wiped the blood with his hand to keep it from getting in his eyes. He only smeared it further. He reached for his sword but couldn't pull it free from the scabbard. He hadn't realized Gydan tied it with a washcloth. She couldn't help but snicker at the pathetic scene.

Gydan grabbed the stool she had knocked over and swung it at his head.

The brute fell on his back. Out cold.

Gydan righted her stool and returned to the bar. The soldiers stood and drew their swords.

"Hold on now," Gydan said. She took a sip of her mead and winced. It wasn't good. Next time, she'd try an ale. "My mentor once told me you never draw your sword unless you plan to kill the person across from you. And I don't believe that's what you want to do. You're just trying to intimidate me, and that's not wise."

"You accosted that man," said one soldier who appeared to be the ranking officer.

Gydan looked at the man on the ground, groaning and regaining consciousness. His head was bleeding profusely. If his injury wasn't looked to, Gydan might have to explain his death to whatever brother or sister remained from their family.

"He tried to accost me." Without thinking, Gydan took another sip. Another sour expression. She handed the drink back to the barkeep. "Take this away from me."

"Maybe you'd like to discuss this with the high general?" the officer asked.

"I'd love nothing more than to talk with High General Aubec Skarsol. That's part of why I'm here. But first, I'm meeting someone else. Look. I didn't draw my sword. He didn't draw his sword. It was a simple bar fight. Nothing more. But one of you should take him to get his head stitched and wrapped. He's bleeding out."

The brute struggled to get off the ground. He was too dazed to do anything, and he looked much paler.

"Friends, lower your swords."

A young man in a green cloak stepped out from around the corner. He had a serious face, and he spoke in an even, more serious tone. The man was attractive in a conventional way—piercing blue eyes, high cheek bones, symmetrical features, all that. Gydan was sure he had broken a few hearts. He walked with confidence and authority. His long unkempt hair reminded Gydan of her mother's.

"Yurig?"

The young man looked at Gydan, and his face softened.

Gydan jumped from her stool and ran to him, wrapping her arms around her brother. She hugged Yurig. He kept his arms at his side. He was not the hugging sort. He stepped back and looked at her more closely, unsure. He had been much younger when they last saw each other. Gydan knew it was harder for him to recall those early experiences together. He stared at her for such a long time. Gydan didn't know if he would say anything, and then, finally, he spoke.

"Gydan, is that you?"

"It is," Gydan said. The tears flowed easily for her, just like her father. Yurig appeared to share their mother's stoic demeanor. "It's me. I'm back. I came back for you."

The soldiers sheathed their swords—complying with Yurig—and tended to the brute, helping him stand and leading him to the barracks for medical help. The brute mumbled protests as he was taken away.

Yurig and Gydan looked at each other. Gydan couldn't control her tears and laughter, which came in equal measure. All these years, she had held on to Jack Stag's promise that she'd see her brother again. It had been a great comfort on the eve of war when the night offered little assurances. And when she missed home, she thought about how Jack Stag promised they would become the best of friends.

She looked at her brother, and she was overcome with joy. In response, Yurig's face was blank.

"What took you so long?" Yurig whispered. "Where's Mom?"

"Mom went to Alda Feren to stop the earthquakes. She never came back. I owed a king ten years of service before I could leave Raustfweg. He taught me how to fight. I helped him expand his nation." She said it with great pride. "He was like a second father to me. Yurig, I have so much to tell you, but let's sit awhile. Talk to me."

Yurig pointed down the street to where the brute was taken.

"What was his issue with you?"

"I didn't kill his brother." Gydan spoke the truth. On principle, she tried to avoid lying whenever possible. "Cyru killed him." But she had become quite skilled at not telling the whole truth. "There was a brawl outside Vasterghent. That man's brother felt he had to prove something by fighting me, and Cyru took issue with it."

Yurig had no response. He exhaled. His sister's life was very different than the life he had known.

Gydan and Yurig sat at the bar. Yurig held up a finger. The barkeep, knowing what he liked, grabbed a bottle wrapped in burlap. The bottle was hidden away in a wooden case. The barkeep poured a bright green liquid into a cup. He diluted the drink with water, gave it a few stirs, and slid it over. Yurig picked up the cup and took the tiniest of sips and set it down again. Absentmindedly, Gydan ordered another mead. She reached in her belt pouch for some coin, but Yurig reached out his hand to stop her.

"I am the esteemed apprentice of High General Aubec Skarsol. Drinks are always on the house."

Gydan nodded, impressed. "I should've come home sooner." She took a drink from the cup handed to her and then recoiled. She glared at her drink.

"Thank you for your letter," Yurig said. "It arrived at Sage Hall, and they delivered it to me. I wish you had written more."

"I'm not much of a writer."

They sat quietly, each lost in their own thoughts.

"I hardly remember our dad," Yurig said after taking another sip. "Maricel and Mom, I have a few memories. But it's difficult to know how much I remember and how much is a fabrication from the stories Aubec told me. Memories are made, more than they are recalled."

"Do you remember anything about me?" Gydan asked, but she was afraid of the answer.

"I remember waving goodbye to you from the tower. I remember sailing to Rhyll for the first time. I remember the ogre in the barn. You saved my life." Yurig struggled with these words.

"No, it was dumb luck. I didn't want us to both die. You ran one way. I went the other. The ogre went after me."

"And somehow, we both survived. You saved us," Yurig insisted. "I also remember Speck in the cave. I remember the dragons." Yurig pointed in the air to where Cyru circled, high above. Gydan didn't think anyone would notice. "You and your dragon are still close."

"We're stitched at the ankles."

"What?"

"It's a Raustfweg expression. It means we can't escape each other, even if we wanted to."

"You know, sis, you have a bit of a Raustfweg accent."

"I do not!" Gydan was surprised by this observation. "Everyone in Raustfweg said I had an Amon accent."

"No, you sound like one of them."

"I *was* one of them. I was good at being one of them."

Yurig inclined his head. Gydan could tell he was conflicted about who she was now. More Raustfweg than Amon, more raven than owl. Rather than give voice to his disappointment, Yurig continued his recollections.

"I remember that winter in the farmhouse. I remember when we were at the market, when dad died—and we had to bring his body home in the cart."

"You weren't at the market. It was only me and dad."

"I could've sworn I had been there."

"No, I was alone in Penderyn after he was murdered."

"Are you sure? It was such a formative moment. I can see him so clearly dead among the sheep."

Gydan did not feel the need to correct him on this detail. He had been killed in an alley away from their livestock.

"Memories are made, more than they are recalled," Gydan repeated Yurig's own words back to him. She could see the truth was hard for him to accept.

"Dad's killer, Dahlia Tulan, is still imprisoned here."

"Is she? Have you met with her?"

"Once. She's in the dragon pit underneath the palace."

Gydan noticed how Yurig, when he mentioned this woman who had ordered their father's death, placed his hands upon the bar and sat up straight. He was trying to control his anger, steady himself.

"How is the high general, by the way?" Gydan asked.

"Not great," Yurig said. "The past few months, his mind has been slipping. It's not uncommon among old mages. I encouraged Aubec to retire as high general. Even though it's an elected position, most treat it like a lifetime appointment. No one votes out the incumbent. But now, we're a few weeks away from electing a new high general. Everyone's on edge. Mendal is one of the candidates."

"Mendal?" Gydan said his name louder than she intended, and everyone turned toward her. She lowered her voice. "Bren's adopted son, the same person who poisoned her?" Hearing

Mendal's name unsettled her. Like trying to recall a lost memory, something was just out of reach. *The true son of winter, the adopted son of summer's daughter. He will make you suffer. Ten years hence.* These words came to Gydan, but she did not understand them.

"Mendal denies poisoning her. The people who support him deny it too. And the people who oppose him keep quiet, because they don't want to deal with his supporters. No matter who he is or what he's done, he's the son of a legend, the Northern Light."

"*Sah'le vuk,*" Gydan cursed under her breath.

"If Mendal discovers you've returned, he'll want that sword." Yurig pointed to the sheathed sword hanging from Gydan's belt. "People believe you stole it."

"It was a gift from Bren," Gydan said. She placed a protective hand on the tooled leather sheath. "If Mendal wants it, I'd be happy to give it to him. He can have the sharp edge."

Yurig shushed Gydan and looked around to see if anyone heard.

"Maybe you know how to handle yourself on the battlefield, but Rhyll is a place of politics. Swords aren't as effective."

"You'd be surprised how effective swords are in matters of politics."

Yurig rolled his eyes. She had a comeback for everything.

They spent the next hour sharing stories.

Gydan told Yurig about her many battles in Raustfweg, how she spent much of her life encamped outside besieged cities and towns, eating her meals around a fire with other soldiers—people who served King Soren as pikemen, archers, shield bearers, scouts, and calvary. She held many positions, gaining experience in every facet of war. Cyru had given them a critical advantage when it came to scouting and assassination. Cyru could swoop into an enemy's camp and take out their commanders before anyone even noticed. Cyru referred to it as "ratting." When people—without warning—would fall over dead, their necks slashed, sometimes that was enough for them to surrender. Eventually, Gydan earned the rank of high general, second to Soren himself. Despite her youth, she commanded the army, winning even more territory. When it was time for Gydan to return to Amon, Soren had begged her to stay, bargaining with riches and the whole of his kingdom once he died. He already treated her like his daughter, but now she would be the rightful heir. However, he knew she was ready to leave—and anything he could offer would be received as another responsibility, another burden. She was content with good food, good mead, good music, and the company of good people.

Yurig told Gydan about his time on the island of Rhyll. A few weeks after Kret Bonebreaker's attack on Thistle, most of the Sage Hall students were relocated to the small village, tasked with the rebuilding effort and the farming. Yurig was familiar with farm life and took to it naturally. But many of the children who grew up in wealthy households, each with their own banner and sigil, were intolerably useless. It put a greater burden on Yurig. During the day, he'd work the fields, and at night, he'd study his spells. Eventually, they were able to move back to Sage Hall. Those were the quiet years. He was able to focus more on his magic. It was a period of tremendous growth. Aubec struggled as a mentor to keep up with him. After Bren had died and the siege of Aberton ended, the region was without a high general. As one of the few surviving veterans of the War of the Hounds, by reputation alone, the title fell to him. He protested, but the city state representatives insisted. Aubec's time was consumed with his new duties and maintaining the peace between the southern and northern areas. He didn't have time to study like he once did. Aubec gave up his life as a mage and bequeathed his spellbook to his apprentice. Yurig left Sage Hall for a time, traveling to House Varya, north of Il Strig Deep. There, he continued his studies under the tutelage of Archmage Onrik. With his help, Yurig transcribed Speck and Aubec's books into a third book. When Yurig returned to Rhyll, he decided to live in Thistle and often traveled to the city to advise the high general on important matters. In Thistle, he met a weaver named Catherine. A few months ago, they moved in together.

"Are you betrothed?" Gydan's eyes grew wide.

"I share my life story, and that's what you took from it? No, Catherine and I haven't made any commitments."

"Does she know?"

Yurig changed the subject.

"Mom went to Alda Feren and never returned. What happened to Maricel?"

"I don't know. Mom was taken to Alda Feren by Jack Stagg—"

"The character from the children's stories?"

"The same. Then, Maricel loaded up the cart and went after her. She also never returned."

There was still so much to share and so much left unsaid, but it was getting late. Gydan gave Yurig a playful push.

"They wrote a song about our mother," Yurig said, lost in his thoughts, observing his green libation.

"I'd love to hear that one." Gydan, without a care in the world, addressed the whole bar. "Everyone! Did you know they wrote a song about our mother? And my brother is going to sing it."

Yurig sighed. He knew this was coming. He began to sing. Gydan marveled at how beautiful his voice was—bright and melodic. It felt as though the whole city stopped to listen to him.

> *Titans stirred, the earth shook,*
> *And the walls came down.*
> *The hounds rushed toward the city*
> *Like a terrible flood.*
> *They poured into Aberton*
> *With a roaring sound,*
> *With death in their hearts*
> *And a hunger for blood.*

> *We call for aid. We make a stand,*
> *Even when we fall.*
> *With Bren the Beloved gone,*
> *Who will answer our call?*
> *Who will help us to rebuild*
> *Aberton's wall?*

> *The oak-born knight, a wood nymph*
> *With staff in her hand.*
> *A friend of the Northern Light*
> *Until the very end.*
> *She whispers to the acorns,*
> *And they obey her command.*
> *The trees sprout, weaving a bulwark,*
> *No hound could bend.*

*We call to you. Stand with us.*
*The trees grow so tall.*
*Bren's dear friend rebuilt*
*Aberton's wall.*
*A friend of the Northern Light*
*Has answered the call.*

*The wood nymph warrior*
*Disappeared that same day.*
*To see a new sunrise was*
*Aberton's only concern.*
*Where Bren's friend went,*
*What beckoned her, none can say.*
*But if we need her again,*
*We know she'll return.*

Gydan hadn't heard this one before. Occasionally, merchants from Amon would make their way to Raustfweg, and they'd share their stories and songs. Gydan always enjoyed hearing these fragments of home. There had been other songs about the siege of Aberton, and her mother was never named in any of them. She was most often referred to as the friend of Bren Caius, as if they had always been in each other's life. Gydan had even heard a few stories about the War of the Hounds that inserted her mother into the narrative, even though she was an infant during the war.

"That was a beautiful song," Gydan looked behind her to the street where the brute had been led away. The lanterns cast a warm glow across the outdoor tavern, but the streets beyond remained dark. "We should move on. I'm not in the mood for another fight. That man has had plenty of time to bandage his wounds and his pride, and he may have more siblings with a score to settle. Shall we go to the palace? I'd like to see Aubec again."

Yurig kicked back the rest of his drink. He shuddered and then smacked his lips.

"He may be asleep."

"Then there's a half a chance he's awake."

Before Yurig could argue with Gydan's logic, she was already walking toward the palace.

\* \* \*

Yurig knew the guards. They let Gydan and Yurig enter without asking questions. Gydan's brother seemed to know everyone in Rhyll—either as a former Sage Hall classmate or as the apprentice to High General Skarsol.

They walked along the palace's main hallway. The white limestone walls curved in a way that limited a person's ability to see farther ahead. The hallways acted as a choke point. If Rhyll were attacked, the palace could be easily defended with only a handful of well-trained guards. And the stone itself was a wonder, imbued with a magical property that made it impossible for Cyru to use their clairvoyant sight. A contradiction in design, both inviting and foreboding, open and opaque, this palace was the perfect home for a high general.

Gydan thought about the last time she was here. The palace of her memory was a colossal maze, a place to explore and get lost in. Tonight, everything felt diminished, narrower than she remembered. The hallway opened to a courtyard with a vaulted ceiling. There were holes carved into the ceiling, a repeating cluster like a honeycomb, revealing the night sky.

This space was the center of the palace where the menagerie once was. Cleared of the animals and their cages, it now served as a space for entertaining guests. Gydan realized this must have been its original purpose. The menagerie was at Bren's request.

"Before a new high general is elected, representatives from all the cities will meet here for a banquet to honor the nominees." Yurig looked back at Gydan as he explained. "It's a time for people to make their last plea for consideration. This room will be packed with the most influential people in Amon."

Gydan nodded, not sure what she could add. She had been a high general in Raustfweg. She knew what a folkmoot was. Yurig just didn't use that word.

They continued through the palace. All of Bren's trophies, tapestries, and banners still hung from the walls—only Kret Bonebreaker's axe was missing.

Yurig led Gydan up the flight of stairs to the high general's room. He continued to give a narrated tour, explaining the significance of everything in the palace. Gydan wasn't listening. Her mind drifted to visions of a much younger Gydan sitting on these stairs and crying. Cyru had nestled next to her, trying their best to comfort her. Bren Caius had snapped at her and told her to leave. Gydan would always remember her words: "I do not hold court with children." Gydan had looked forward to meeting Bren the Beloved, and these words had broken her heart.

At the top of the staircase were a set of double doors.

"No guard at the doors," Gydan observed.

"No need," Yurig said. "Master Aubec placed warding runes throughout the palace. If anyone made it this far, the guards wouldn't be of any use."

Yurig swiped his finger through the air. The doors opened with this wordless spell.

The high general's room was lit with several candles. Curtains lined the walls and were tethered at the bottom to small hooks. The room was much stuffier than Gydan remembered. The same canopy bed was here but no longer in the center of the room. It was positioned against the far wall. The honeysuckle vines were gone.

Aubec was slumped on the floor next to the bed. He had a quilt draped over his shoulders. The shadows from the candlelight flickered across his face, rippling, so that it looked like he was underwater. Even though the room was cool, beads of sweat gathered on his forehead, dripped down his neck. Sweat stains marked the front and the pits of his gown. His braided strands of hair had been cut. His hair was a woolly shock, untamed and gray. The lines on his face were deep and well-defined. He had aged considerably. No longer the dashing, sophisticated man Gydan once knew.

"Master Skarsol, are you okay?" Yurig, with a wave of his hand, disappeared from where he stood, and blinked across the long room to the space right beside Aubec. Yurig's casual use of magic startled Gydan. Mages were rare. She had encountered many druids in Raustfweg, but no mages.

Aubec tapped his index finger twice on the Yurig's hand, a signal between the two of them. Yurig nodded and wiped the sweat from Aubec's brow with a cloth.

"I'll be okay," Aubec said. "I had a bad dream and tumbled out of bed."

"You shouldn't be sleeping with the candles lit." Yurig chastised him like a son caring for an elderly father.

"It's fine."

"What did you dream?"

"I was tangled in the netting of a ship as it was sinking. I wake up, and here I am, tangled in this quilt."

Gydan walked toward them. She looked to either side, taking in the familiar room where she had last seen Bren Caius alive. There was a writing desk near the bed. Wax-sealed scrolls piled on top of it. She couldn't remember if this desk had been here before or not.

"Who's this?" Aubec asked, nodding toward Gydan.

"This is my sister," Yurig said. "Remember my sister?"

"Yes, yes," Aubec recalled. "You were a child when I saw you last. How's your mother?"

Gydan sat on the floor with Yurig and Aubec.

"She's gone. She went to Alda Feren, and she never returned."

Aubec nodded as though Gydan's words reassured him. He then mumbled something unintelligible. Yurig continued to fuss over Aubec.

"I'll find you a new gown," Yurig said. He got up and walked to the wardrobe.

Aubec leaned toward Gydan and spoke in a hushed voice.

"In my dreams, I'm always drowning. I should have died that day. Instead, I die every night." He patted Gydan's hand. "Yurig took my book, but it's okay. I said it was okay."

Yurig returned with a gown. He raised Aubec's arms to pull the sweat-stained garment off him. Gydan looked away to offer Aubec some modesty. As Yurig put the new gown on him, Aubec continued to talk in his soft, unhurried way.

"Do you remember the oak tree at Sage Hall? Such a beautiful tree. You sat under that tree almost every day. You liked to study there. Whenever I couldn't find you, I'd look over at the tree, and there you were."

"You tell me that every time I come to visit."

"You were such a good student. Diligent. That's the word I would use."

"We disturbed you tonight," Yurig said. "We shouldn't have come."

"Nonsense. My bad dreams disturbed me. Seeing you always puts my mind at ease."

Yurig dutifully helped Aubec back into bed. Yurig pulled the quilt up and smoothed it out on the bed. "Gydan, you wanted to see Master Skarsol. Was there something specific you needed?"

Yurig turned around to Gydan, but she was nowhere in the room.

\* \* \*

Gydan descended the dragon pit staircase. The white stone steps extended from the curved wall of the sinkhole. Bits of crystal flaked the walls, sparkling in the dark. At the bottom of the staircase was a large dome steel cage. The cage was furnished with a bed, a table, a dresser, and numerous personal effects. It looked like any bedroom, except it was behind adamantine bars. Overlapping rugs covered the mossy stone floor. The rugs appeared damp and stained.

Within the cage was a woman. Her face was marked with a scowl—always a disapproving downturned mouth. Gydan had known people like this while serving in Soren's army. They were cruel-hearted people who did not fight for a cause or for coin. They only wanted to hurt others. This woman's short black hair had streaks of gray, which looked almost like the markings of some poisonous spider. She wore a sleeveless tunic with buckles down the middle. Her arms were muscular. The veins bulged.

This was Dahlia Tulan, the woman responsible for all those discolored, bloated bodies hanging from the beams along the Penderyn coastline. The woman who had raised Gydan's mother. Gydan felt knots in her stomach.

Dahlia leaned forward against the bars of her cage. She saw the sword on Gydan's hip.

"You're here to kill me. Is that it? To get your revenge for whatever I did to you or your family?"

"I haven't decided yet."

"I don't believe you."

"You don't have to."

Dahlia enjoyed this banter. She had been a guildmaster. She worked with mercenaries. Dahlia was a person who made her livelihood by being intimidating and by controlling the room with her words. Down in the pit, she was alone.

"You wouldn't be the first person who came down here with a sword on their hip or a dagger in their boot with thoughts of seeking justice. Did you bribe a guard?"

"My brother let me in."

"Your brother?" Dahlia thought for a moment. "You must be Yurig's sister. I can see the resemblance. You've returned."

Dahlia leaned with more force against the bars. She pressed her face between two of the bars, taunting Gydan to strike.

"It's easier to kill a person in your mind," Dahlia said in a singsong voice. "Much harder when they are standing in front of you."

"I've killed before." Gydan stood a few feet from Dahlia.

"It's not the moral struggle it once was, especially with some of the people I've faced." Dahlia stared at Gydan, waiting. "At first, I thought I came here to fulfill my legal obligation, to declare your crimes against my family. Instead, I'm curious about something. I'd like you to help me resolve it."

Dahlia walked to a table and grabbed a high-back wooden chair. She dragged it toward the bars. The chair made a grating noise across the stone. She positioned the chair in front of the bars, and then sat down, ready to hear what Gydan had to say.

A pristine spider's web hung in the corner of the cage. And even though Gydan was the one with the sword, and Dahlia was on the other side of the bars, Gydan felt very much like a fly flitting about the webs.

"I've thought a lot about your name, 'Dahlia Tulan.' I don't think I've ever heard a given name like that before, Dahl-ee-ah. Maybe it's because people in Amon and Raustfweg don't end their names with an 'ah' sound, not to my knowledge. In Volir, ending a word with an 'ah' signifies possession. 'Dahli of Tulan.' But I don't know of a city, village, or region called 'Tulan.' However . . ."

When Gydan said "however," Dahlia Tulan looked up and snarled at her, actually snarled.

"However," Gydan resumed. "There is a small village, not even on the map, next to Sage Hall, which is called 'Two Lanes.' It's where the servants live. A professor told me about it when I visited Sage Hall. From what I hear, those wealthy, aristocratic students treat the people of Two Lanes very poorly. Maybe Dahlia Tulan is instead Dahli of Two Lanes. Perhaps her family served at Sage Hall—back when it was only one building. Dahli grew up cleaning the dormitory and polishing boots and emptying chamber pots—"

"Enough. You've made your point," Dahlia Tulan said. "You can leave now."

"Don't rush me."

Dahlia Tulan slumped in her chair and glared.

"My theory: Dahli of Two Lanes wanted to escape her miserable life and reinvent herself as a person of means and power. She gave herself a surname, so people would think she came from a higher class, but it was also a reminder of where she came from. She went to Penderyn. And why not? A bay city with good fishing, a good market, and a burgeoning trade port. After the War of the Hounds, it would need a strong hand to guide it."

Gydan had a moment of recollection, a memory she couldn't quite bring to the forefront of her mind, watching Dahlia Tulan sit uncomfortably in the wooden chair—like the throne of a despondent monarch. This memory felt older than herself, if such a thing was possible. Gydan shook off the feeling and continued.

"You preferred using orphans, rejected by the world. You would train them, turn them into killers, and send them against the wealthy of Amon. It had to be cathartic. Wretched children, victims of the elite, striking out against their oppressors. I'm guessing some of your targets—the ones you had my mother kill—didn't even cross you as a guildmaster. You remembered them from those earlier days at Sage Hall. Even if they forgot you, you remembered every slight. You were hungry for a reckoning. With their blood, you amassed your riches. You became wealthy enough to help fund Bren's Northern Army. She looked the other way while you continued your vendetta and tightened your control over Penderyn. Kret Bonebreaker helped you. He put the ideas in Bren's head to expand the power of the guildmasters. The advice he gave bankrupted her army. And during that time, you built your own sellsword army with the hope of overthrowing Bren and claiming the region."

"My crime was my ambition?" Dahlia Tulan leered. "I was too successful at achieving my goals?"

"No, you did the very thing to my mother that the people of Sage Hall did to you. You hurt her and used her and sent her into the world filled with pain and anger. But she found something." Gydan paused, waiting for Dahlia Tulan to guess at this prompt. Dahlia kept silent. "She found my father. She found love. Her happiness upset you, and when my father came to Penderyn, you had him killed—"

"That's where you're wrong."

"You didn't have him killed?"

"I did. But her happiness didn't upset me. I was indifferent to the life she chose. She wanted to shovel manure on a farm. That was her lot, so I abandoned her to it."

Gydan unsheathed her sword. Soren had told her to never unsheathe her sword unless she planned to kill the person in front of her and to interpret anyone doing the same as a threat on her life. She wanted to kill Dahlia Tulan. The guildmaster had practically dared her by sitting so close to the bars that separated them. It would take little effort to leap forward and thrust the sword between the bars and into the center of Dahlia's chest. Gydan imagined the sword cracking the sternum, sliding through the flesh, the heart and lungs, and out the other end with the sword point lodging into the chair. Dahlia Tulan would convulse in pain. Some pitiful noise would escape her mouth. There would be blood, and that would be the end of

Dahlia Tulan, the cruel guildmaster of Penderyn. Gydan imagined this death, and she wanted it. If Soren were here, he wouldn't stop her. He'd done far worse to less deserving people. If Gydan's mother was here, she might stand in the way. And this is what caused Gydan to pause. As she understood the story, her mother had at least two opportunities to kill Dahlia Tulan—once in Penderyn, and once outside Aberton at the end of the siege. Both times, her mother had shown mercy. Gydan always assumed it was guilt that caused her mother to hesitate. Now, Gydan wondered if there was something more to it.

Bren Caius spared Kret Bonebreaker, and her mother spared Dahlia Tulan. Killing demons made them more powerful. Was that it? Gydan looked into Dahlia's cold dark eyes. All she saw was rage, spite, and venom.

"You think our mother wanted to shovel manure?" Yurig's voice echoed through the dragon pit as he walked down the stairs. Cyru flew above him. "Then you do not know our mother. I doubt she ever shoveled any manure in her life. She had me and Gydan do it. I was young, but I remember the shoveling."

Yurig reached the bottom step, and Gydan sheathed her sword.

*Just so we're clear, I wouldn't have stopped you.* Cyru's voice comforted Gydan as she weighed the worth of Dahlia's wasted life.

Dragons did not have the same moral struggles. They acted on impulse. They felt little hesitation. Everything was beneath them. They soared over the world like winged gods of chaos. To snuff out another's life meant nothing to them. Gydan wished she was more like a dragon.

Dahlia Tulan ignored the arrival of Gydan's brother. She stared at Gydan, daring her to strike.

"You'll hang within a month," Gydan said. "Justice will be served."

"You think so? Once Mendal becomes high general, the first thing he'll do is pardon me."

Yurig placed a hand on Gydan's arm, urging her to calm down. Her face was warm and flushed. Gydan shook with anger. She was losing herself, and she needed to step back, take a breath.

Dahlia simpered. Gydan was nothing more than an amusement.

"What I did, I did for myself and myself alone," Dahlia said. "I served the privileged brats of Sage Hall. I cleaned their rooms, and I made their beds. I scrubbed those floors every single day. No one noticed me. I was a ghost to them. But I worked my way to Penderyn. I worked *hard*. No one gave me anything. And in Penderyn, I built an empire. I manipulated the fabled Bren Caius. I was the one to bring about her downfall. Not Kret Bonebreaker. It was me.

"I have no pity for people who think they're victims. Your dad died because he was weak and undisciplined. If someone hung from the gallows, it's because they couldn't escape their fate. I made your mother strong. I should be thanked for what I did. I have nothing more to say."

Gydan snorted, a few tittering giggles escaped her, and then she broke into uncontrollable laughter. Her laughter echoed throughout the dragon pit. She laughed so hard it was difficult to breathe. She placed a hand on her chest and through the laughter, she mumbled how it hurt to laugh so hard. Yurig took a step back. Even Cyru looked worried. After a while, the laughter subsided. She composed herself and then looked at Dahlia Tulan, who did not understand what was so funny.

"Those are your last words?" Gydan asked. "Your great apology is that you have no regrets for being an absolute monster? In my life, I don't think I've met anyone half as delusional as you—and you don't even know Soren the Blind, king of the valley and the coast." Gydan said the words with a dramatic flourish, emphasizing how ridiculous his title was. "You sit in a cage, and you think you defeated Bren Caius? Bren's legacy hasn't died. It lives on in me and my brother."

Gydan's hand went to the pommel of her sword. Dahlia Tulan's eyes followed her movement. Gydan saw this subtle shift of Dahlia's eyes.

Finally, Dahlia was worried.

"You think you made my mother strong by beating her? That my dad died because he was weak? You haven't escaped anything, and you won't. And when you die, I'll make sure they bury you in Two Lanes at the bottom of the hill. May your grave serve as a reminder. Cruelty has a cost. It made you who you are."

Dahlia Tulan tried to stand up from the chair, but Gydan was too fast. In an instant, she unsheathed her sword again, and she rushed forward. Before anyone could react or make sense of what was happening, the sword was already through Dahlia Tulan's chest. The blood poured out like foul water from a corrupted well. Dahlia looked down, in shock, at her chest. Her hands went to the wound in an irrational attempt to mend herself, to reseal the hole. The blood coated her shaking hands. She went limp and died.

Gydan pulled at her sword, which had pierced through the

chair, and freed it from Dahlia Tulan. Gydan exhaled, astonished by her own action. She felt like a dragon.

\* \* \*

The moon shone brightly over Rhyll. Yurig led Gydan and Cyru through the city streets. He walked at a hurried pace. He would take a few steps and then look over his shoulder, back at the palace. Gydan did not move with the same urgency. She looked at ease, even though she had spots of blood across her face and her wool kyrtill. Dahlia Tulan's blood.

"Don't look suspicious or anything," Gydan chided her brother.

"Tomorrow morning, I'll go back to the palace," Yurig said, out of breath. "I'll meet with Aubec and explain everything."

"She was going to hang. I moved up the date and saved her from public spectacle."

Gydan sounded unconcerned, but it would be a problem. People in power did not like when others administered justice.

"You think what you did was okay?" Yurig stopped. "I told you Aubec's time as high general is coming to an end. If you're in jail while they're sorting this out and Mendal comes into power, this could be bad."

"We can lie low for a while." Gydan's tone was apologetic. "We'll set sail for Penderyn and visit the old farm. Stay with our grandparents. If Mendal becomes high general, we'll disappear. If someone else gets elected, I'll return and answer for what I did."

Yurig did not soften at these words.

"Aubec told me about our mother's past," Yurig said.

Gydan wanted to respond with something clever or feign ignorance, but she knew what Yurig was alluding to. "Violence led
our mom down a dark path, and it's one way I can honor her,
by not repeating her mistakes."

Yurig grew up at Sage Hall, learning Volir, studying Amon
history and his spells. He ate well, and, every night, he slept in a
soft bed. He lived a life of comfort. But Gydan was trained as a
soldier. She grew up on the move, marching across Raustfweg
and claiming land for Soren. She couldn't blame Yurig for
wanting to live a life of peace, but she knew it was a privilege,
an option she wasn't offered.

"Brother, what would you have me do?"

"Tomorrow morning, I'll go back to the palace. I'll meet
with Aubec and explain everything." He said again in an even,
reassuring tone.

*Six soldiers, armed with spears, are coming around the
corner.* Cyru communicated what he saw to Gydan, right as she
heard their footsteps.

They approached in the opposite direction of the palace.
They saw Gydan and leveled their spears at her. Gydan held her
hands up to show she meant no trouble, but she did smile.

One of the soldiers spoke.

"Are you Gydan, the first general of Soren the Blind, king
of the valley and the coast?"

"I usually go by just my given name, but yes to the full title
as well."

"You're wanted for murder—"

"The news about Dahlia traveled fast." Gydan said.

"What?" The soldier was confused. He was talking about
someone other than Dahlia.

"What?" Gydan echoed.

"You're wanted for the murder of Einar Wulfspaw."

"Who's that?"

"Earlier today, there was a fight between you and Einar at the market square tavern. He died from the injuries."

Gydan was dumbfounded. Today, she had managed to kill two people. She took a few steps toward the soldier, but the others raised their spears to keep her at bay.

"The brute? That donkey-headed fool fell over my stool." Gydan was indignant. "He lost his balance and hit his head. You failed to mend his wounds. You don't even have a druid with mistletoe available. And somehow, this is my fault?"

"By order of Mendal Caius," the soldier's voice trembled as he spoke, "you are to accompany us to his estate to account for this crime."

"Mendal Caius is not the high general," Yurig intervened. He took a formal, commanding tone. "Aubec Skarsol is responsible for mediating such offenses."

"Einar Wulfspaw was here at the request of Mendal Caius," the soldier responded. "He was his guest, so yes, it's by *his* order."

Yurig looked at Gydan and shook his head. Something was wrong. Gydan shrugged, apologizing for what she was about to do.

Gydan grabbed the soldier's spear and pulled it toward her, throwing off the balance of the soldier. She then thrust it back and up, jabbing the man in the throat. He let go of the spear as he struggled to breathe. She held the spear in her hands. Another soldier thrust his spear toward her. She parried it and moved in close. The soldier hadn't buckled his breastplate properly, securing it to his belt. Gydan grabbed the bottom of the breastplate and yanked upward. The breastplate went over his head. She left it there, and the soldier flailed about, like a child struggling to dress himself.

*May I kill the remaining four?*

Gydan waved off Cyru's request. Her brother had already been horrified by what she had done so far in Rhyll. Her visit had become eventful.

Mendal must have been tracking her for a while. Possibly even while she was still in Raustfweg. Were the Wulfspaw brothers hired to assassinate her and retrieve the sword? The brawl outside Vasterghent, months ago, may not have been as random as Gydan suspected.

One of the soldiers stabbed at Yurig.

Yurig blinked away with a wave of his hand and reappeared a few feet away. The soldier stabbed again and again. Each time, Yurig disappeared and reappeared. Gydan remembered this spell from that terrible day at the farmhouse when Speck used it to avoid the dragons' attacks. It was one of the few times she had ever seen someone quick enough to escape a dragon's claws. The spell itself must anticipate the strike and act on the mage's behalf, because Gydan doubted anyone had quick enough reflexes to dodge the dragons. This soldier was not nearly as fast. Yurig blinked in and around him, avoiding each attack. Yurig, now behind the soldier, placed his hands on the soldier's back. With a few words, a concussive shockwave shoved the soldier across the street and into a wall.

Gydan pointed to the soldier who collapsed to the ground after hitting the stone wall.

"Be careful." Gydan's words dripped with irony. "Violence. You're going down a dark path."

"You plan to throw my words back at me on a regular basis?"

Another soldier considered approaching. The mage held his hands out, inviting the soldier to try his luck. The soldier backed away.

"You plan to make *this* a regular thing?" Gydan laughed.

Gydan hadn't yet drawn her sword. Instead, she slapped the soldier in front of her hard across the face. She did it with such disregard and force it surprised him. He started to run away, but Gydan planted her foot on the soldier's heel, and he fell on the ground. Gydan gave him a swift kick across the face, knocking him out.

One soldier was left. Yurig and Gydan both turned to see where he was. To their surprise, he was already on the ground, bleeding and groaning in pain. Cyru perched nearby and chirped.

*He'll live. It's hard to tell sometimes. Humans are quite fragile.*

Gydan looked at Yurig. She had a self-satisfied grin on her face.

"You enjoyed that, you little delinquent, you ruffian, you lawless scoundrel—"

"Please stop," Yurig groaned.

"I'm never stopping."

"You can stop."

"My little brother, going down a dark path."

Yurig shook his head and walked past her, farther down the street, away from the palace. Gydan carried on with her teasing.

"I've been here for a few hours, and already he's a blood-thirsty warrior like his sister."

"I threw one person against a wall. One person."

"And it felt good."

Yurig sighed.

Gydan cackled. Yurig shushed her.

"It's late. People are sleeping."

"My apologies. Great dark lord."

* * *

Rhyll was a unique city that catered almost entirely to the military stationed there and the visiting representatives from the city-states across the region. The island in the middle of Tu'enya Bay was an easy destination to reach, even for the southern cities across the coastline. Rhyll didn't have much need for trade and commerce since Thistle provided essential goods at a low, fixed price. Most docked ships were used to ferry people across the bay. And so, the dock was quiet at this hour of the night.

*Stop and find cover,* Cyru warned. *About thirty armed soldiers are off to the right, behind the shipyard stables.*

"Thirty?" Gydan took a moment to look through Cyru's eyes to see the soldiers—none of whom looked any older than Gydan herself—holding their weapons and waiting.

*That's a hundred life debts you owe me.*

Yurig gave Gydan a quizzical look. To Yurig, the psychic conversation between Gydan and Cyru only sounded like a series of chirps from the little dragon.

"Cyru spotted about thirty soldiers gathered behind the stables."

"Mendal gained the loyalty of some people within Aubec's army," Yurig said. "The new high general hasn't even been elected yet, and they're already choosing sides. They're waiting to capture you trying to escape."

Gydan had spent too much time on the battlefield. She

knew it was difficult to read the other side. An action may appear obvious, but the rationale may be elusive. Yes, thirty soldiers could indicate an intention to apprehend Gydan. It could also be an effort to redirect them elsewhere—or it could be a random location to reconvene after searching the city. No way to be certain. And there could be other reasons. However, after their recent skirmish, Gydan needed to leave the city, and the docks were no longer an option.

"What about Thistle?" Gydan suggested. "I'd like to meet your Catherine. We could stay there."

"No, I have a friend who lives not far from here."

They retreated down the street, away from the docks, and through the narrow alleys. After a few turns, they reached an alley lined with small, perfectly round doors. These were not the sad, neglected doors of a back entry. Each door was painted a vibrant color of the rainbow and along the circumference was a decorative white border. Potted plants and modest gardens lined the buildings. Rope netting was strung across the top of the alley with colorful ribbons tied and dangling from it. This place was a halfling neighborhood, turned around from the main thoroughfares, facing inward, and hidden within the city.

Yurig stopped at one door and knocked. He waited and then knocked again. Gydan could hear someone on the other side complaining about visitors at this odd hour. Before Yurig's friend opened the door, Gydan already knew who it was.

"Roby Roundtree."

The door opened and out peered the familiar, ruddy face. Gydan remembered this woman, the sailor she had met while escaping from Rhyll, the sailor who had betrayed her. Roby had a scar on her cheek from where Cyru had attacked her.

Roby smiled as if nothing had happened between them.

"Gydan, my goodness. You're much taller than I remember. Your kind do that, I guess. Grow."

"Roby, can we come inside?" Yurig asked.

"Yes, yes, come in."

Roby opened the door wider and motioned for them to enter. Yurig and Gydan both crouched down and stepped in.

The home smelled of hazelnut and cinnamon. The sweet, spicy scent welcomed and overwhelmed. To Gydan, it smelled like a midwinter festival in the Apalwaite market with all the gentle associations she had with it. Roby moved about the drawing room, lighting candles for her guests. The room was cluttered, not because of neglect, but the opposite. The room had been so thoroughly lived in; every bit of it was adorned with knickknacks, mementos of a full and happy life. The carpeted floor had well-worn paths from the cushioned chairs to the kitchen and to the upstairs. At the top of the staircase, a landing was built out with a beautiful wrought-iron railing and furnished as a secondary sitting room. This auxiliary floor was not part of the original construction. It lowered the ceiling of the drawing room. Yurig and Gydan continued to crouch. Roby noticed them navigating the lower ceiling and smaller floor plan, all built for halflings.

"Half the size, twice the house," Roby said.

She led them to two larger chairs, intended to accommodate guests who weren't part of this neighborhood. Once seated, Roby went off to the kitchen down a hall under the staircase. Gydan sat with her sword resting across her lap. Dried blood was still on her face. She looked around the room, taking in as many details as she could. Cyru perched on a peg used for hanging coats. Meanwhile, Yurig observed his fingernails with extreme interest. In the silence, they could hear Roby fanning the kitchen and then rummaging for plates and cups. A moment later, Roby returned with tea, bread, and a glass jar of olive oil.

"One for you and one for you," Roby said as she distributed the late-night meal, a thick slice of warm bread on a pewter plate. The plates had a stamped swirling pattern. Gydan loved the whimsical details of halfling craftsmanship.

"Thank you for your hospitality," Gydan said. Roby bowed her head. There was no higher virtue or greater compliment to a halfling.

"By all means, make yourself comfortable—"

"But I feel we need to clear the air," Gydan interrupted. "Last time we saw each other, you betrayed me. If I hadn't jumped ship, I could've been handed over to Dahlia Tulan's people."

Roby had been busying herself around the drawing room, tidying as best she could. But when she heard the name of Dahlia Tulan, Roby stopped.

"I hate to contradict the offended party," Roby said, "but I believe you remember that moment differently than I do. I was trapped on that ship like you were. Our crew was at the mercy of Dahlia Tulan. When we got close to the shoreline, I tried my best to give you a warning so you *could* escape. Your dragon gave me this scar." Roby gestured to her face. "But I never meant you any harm."

Gydan was not satisfied with the explanation, but she also knew they needed a place to hide. It made no sense to drudge up the past. And yet, that was the subject of the past few hours —Aubec, Dahlia Tulan, Roby, and even her brother, all specters of a past, which began with the death of her father and her leaving home. Why was she here, if not to put these memories to rest?

"Those days were fearful and chaotic," Gydan said. "If my brother trusts you, I trust you."

Roby placed her hand over her heart, accepting this reluctant forgiveness.

"I have a sailboat," Roby said. "It's docked farther down the coast. I can sail you out of Rhyll to safety, wherever you want to go."

"My brother and I can set sail tomorrow. Penderyn."

"You're going to Penderyn," Yurig said. "I'm staying in Rhyll until the election is over."

"If I'm in danger, you're in danger too." Gydan was hurt that her brother didn't want to stay with her. They hadn't seen each other in so long, and already, he wanted to separate.

"The people of Thistle asked me to act as their representative and cast their vote. I can't leave."

"Then I'm not leaving," Gydan folded her arms as though daring her brother to challenge her on this matter. Yurig looked at Roby, who wasn't going to get involved.

"It's getting late. We can talk about it tomorrow."

"If you don't want me here, there's not much to discuss."

Yurig was about to respond, but he stopped.

The tension in the room was too much for Roby to bear. After all, she was the host. "Perhaps tea and bread aren't what's called for? I have some sweet leaf if we'd like to unwind?"

"Yes, please," Gydan said with a bit too much enthusiasm.

"No thank you," Yurig said. "Do you mind if I retire to the guest room?"

"Not at all," Roby said. "You know where it is."

Without saying good night or even looking in Gydan's

direction, Yurig stood up and walked down the hallway. It was late. He would be more reasonable in the morning.

Roby lit a ceramic pipe stuffed with dried sweet leaf. She gave it two puffs and then handed it to Gydan. The two spent the next hour smoking and making amends. Gydan felt herself sinking into the cushioned chair and drifting into a deep and inviting sleep. After the long voyage across the sea, it was the best sleep Gydan had known in some time.

Roby opened a chest and brought out a soft, knit blanket. She laid it across Gydan and patted her on the head. Gydan made a contented grunt. Roby blew out the candles and left the room.

*  *  *

Mendal Caius had been a sickly child. He had been weak, easily broken, always on the verge of tears. Having the great Bren Caius as a stepmother made everything worse. She was powerful and perfect in every way. She was beautiful and strong and wise. And, and, and. There was no end to the praise heaped on her, often in his presence. People would talk about the splendor of Bren, then look at him and sigh. He could feel the judgment and the dashed expectations. Mendal would never ascend to her level. Who could? His other two parents, Corrinae and Halsten, tried to comfort him, to appease him with gifts and empty words. It did nothing.

The first time he truly felt special was when he discovered the secret entrance to the dragon pit. He felt called to it. In the shadowy descent, he saw Kret Bonebreaker, but he was not scared, not the way some might be. The fear he felt was more like walking along a ledge. An intoxicating urge, that at any moment, he could hurl himself over. He wouldn't, but he could—the thrill of a catastrophic choice. This is what he felt in Kret Bonebreaker's presence.

Kret Bonebreaker saw greatness in Mendal. He could become greater than Bren Caius. Every time Mendal went to visit Kret, he left feeling powerful.

One day, after leaving the dragon pit, one of his bullies, a son of the palace servants, began to taunt him. Mendal decided he had endured enough. He bit the boy's face. Tore a significant portion of his skin right off the bone. Mendal's face was covered with the warm blood. The boy howled in pain, flopping on the ground like a fish. None of the other children ever bothered him again. He became their tormentor, and he decided he preferred this reversal of roles. The next time he snuck down to the dragon pit, Kret was so proud of him, approval like nothing he had ever felt before.

Kret confided in Mendal. Kret shared his secrets—things he knew about the world and about Bren Caius. Kret had a plan to return to power, and it required Mendal's help. Mendal would become his ambassador. Mendal met with Dahlia Tulan. She was already a powerful guildmaster and using her wealth to fund Bren Caius's numerous military projects. Mendal, with Kret's guidance, gave Dahlia Tulan the information she needed to expand her enterprise and pull the strings of the high general. Mendal, Kret, and Dahlia worked closely, conspiring.

Mendal passed messages back and forth between Kret and Dahlia, spying on Bren Caius and relaying what he found. He wanted to do more. Kret, his friend—and that is what he thought of him as—did not belittle him. Kret reminded him of his promise. Mendal would become greater than Bren Caius.

Kret shared with Mendal one more secret, something Mendal could never tell anyone. He made Mendal swear on his life to never share. Mendal loved these empty oaths Kret asked of him. Swear on your life. It made him feel like a child again, but in the best possible way—special access to mysterious and forbidden knowledge.

Kret shared with Mendal the mystery of the seven spirits, powerful forces that had existed since the first seed grew in the soil of Efre Ousel. These spirits could possess other creatures. If enticed, they also could grant power to people they deemed worthy. Kret taught Mendal what he must do to gain an audience with these spirits.

The first spirit, Oshmeldai, had the ability to overcome pain. This spirit would come to Mendal once he killed his stepmother.

The second spirit, Lilit, had the ability to overcome the body's weakness and frailty. This spirit would come to Mendal once he descended into the caverns of Mountain Keep and drank from the black spring water found there.

The third spirit, Belgore, had the ability to control what other people perceived. This spirit would come to Mendal once he wiped out the bloodline of a single noble family.

The fourth spirit, Durahal, had the ability to speak with all living things and the dead. This spirit would come to Mendal once he spent a full year within the Prophet's Tower in the city of Guldur.

The fifth spirit, Qotha'tunach, had the ability to harness shadows into a blade capable of cutting through anything of this world. This spirit would come to Mendal once he slayed a dragon and ate its heart.

The sixth spirit, Usios, had the ability to summon fire from the sky. This spirit would come to Mendal once he destroyed the summer sword.

The final spirit was the Ancient Beast, sometimes called "Cerneboch," and he granted nothing. He existed to break the world and bring darkness.

On the day of his stepmother's funeral, Mendal had still not heard from the first spirit, Oshmeldai. He had done what Kret had told him to do. He had placed the poison in Bren's cup. It should have killed her, but she was strong and stubborn. When Kret was freed from his prison, he finished what Mendal had started. He gutted Bren Caius and cut off her head. Mendal wondered if Oshmeldai had denied him because he didn't deliver the final blow.

During the funeral, that sycophant, Bren's faithful soldier Oren, had held Mendal to the flames of the pyre. The fire seared Mendal's throat, boiled the skin on the left side of his face, and damaged both his eyes. His left eye completely melted away. The pain roared across his body, drowning out all thought. Everything was agony.

Corrinae and Halsten took Mendal to an apothecary, but the earthquake that soon followed destroyed the building and all the precious salves and potions contained within glass vials. There would be no relief from the pain. Only his parents were there to care for him. They did not think he would survive the evening. In the middle of the night, in his delirium, Mendal called out. It hurt to speak, and the animal sounds he made couldn't be understood.

"Oshmeldai! Oshmeldai!" He said the name again, and he would keep saying it until the spirit responded, just as Kret promised him it would. Mendal had done everything Kret had told him to do. He could not endure the pain any longer and would rather die than continue in this misery. "Oshmeldai! Oshmeldai! Oshmeldai!"

*You expect me to listen to a sad, broken creature like yourself.*

The voice was clear and cut through all other sounds. It spoke with confidence and disdain.

"Oshmeldai, I did what was asked of me."

*You did not kill the Northern Light.*

"I did. She was dying. It was a matter of time. The poison was eating away at her insides."

*You did not kill the Northern Light.*

"I promise I tried. What else can I do?"

The other sounds from Mendal's surroundings returned, and he thought the spirit had left. He panicked, but then the voice spoke again.

*Kill your other two parents within the year and let me dwell in you. Give over a portion of yourself. I miss having a body.*

"Yes," Mendal said without even thinking. "Yes, make the pain go away."

And then, the pain disappeared. Like the last grains of sand falling through an hourglass, all pain was gone. Not a numbness, but a sense that nothing would ever hurt him again.

His face healed. The scars faded away. His face was smooth and unblemished once more. His missing left eye reformed in the socket. He could see again.

"Thank you," Mendal wept. "Thank you."

Corrinae and Halsten both fell to their deaths soon after, tumbling out an open window of their private manor near Gandryll. Mendal told everyone it was a terrible accident. No one had the courage to disagree.

Mendal journeyed to the Mountain Keep. He drank from the black spring water to invoke the spirit of Lilit. And like before, Lilit asked to dwell inside Mendal. He allowed the spirit a portion of himself. In exchange, he was given power. To invoke Durahal, Mendal spent a year within the Prophet's Tower. He gave himself over to this spirit as well, and he gained more power.

He had invoked three spirits, but the remaining three were more difficult to summon and the tasks were left undone. He slaughtered the noble Pennswyrth family to call upon Belgore. However, one family member had disappeared, a son. He couldn't find him. Mendal did not know how he could slay a dragon to summon Qotha'tunach. He put off this impossible task. Usios remained elusive. In his research, he could not find the "summer sword." If it were a sword of legend, those stories had been lost. The riddle could not be solved.

Mendal grew in power and gained respect throughout Amon. No longer the sickly child. No longer weak. No longer easily broken. And in a few weeks, he would become the next high general.

Mendal stood in the street where the soldiers had encountered Yurig and Gydan. The patrol guard, Quint, led him to where the fight had been. Quint had a dark bruise on his throat. He had lost consciousness during the fight. When he came to, the two siblings were gone and the other soldiers were on the ground. He and the others returned to Mendal's estate to give him the report. Mendal wanted to see where they had been.

Mendal wore black, but without the puffs and frills that had once adorned his outfits. His tunic was smooth, crushed velvet with a simple cut. Over his tunic was draped a black hooded cloak. The cloak was a patchwork of different fabrics, stitched together in such a way it appeared as scales. But what stood out the most, what everyone talked about, was the mask. Mendal wore a glass mask over the left side of his face, fashioned to his facial contours with a leather band to hold it in place. It had a reflective silver sheen on the outside. He could see through it, while it still hid his features.

Most assumed he used this mask to cover the disfiguring burns and the loss of his eye, but the mask hid nothing except his miraculous recovery. At first, he had worn a burlap sack over his head. Later, he was given this mask while at the Prophet's Tower. He learned from the oracles about the power of such masks—to hide intentions, to intimidate the weak-minded, and to persuade the naïve. He wore the mask because it reminded people he had suffered. He was sacred, the son of Bren Caius, the Northern Light. The rumors of his involvement in her death evaporated to nothing. The whispers of his greatness as the beloved adopted son only expanded. He was no commoner. The mask made him like a god.

"This is where it happened, sir," Quint said.

They had been standing there for a while. Quint felt the need to declare the obvious because he wasn't sure what was supposed to happen next. Mendal held up a finger to hush him. Mendal walked in a circle, marking the area where the fight had taken place. A few times, he would stoop down and feel the ground. He would whisper some words to himself.

"And you believe she had my mother's sword?" Mendal asked.

"She never drew the sword, but that scabbard was hard to forget. I remember the Northern Light sigil on it."

"Anyone could have that design tooled on their scabbard."

"But no one does."

This was true. After the death of Bren Caius, the sigil took on near religious significance. It was not invoked lightly, and he had never seen another scabbard like hers. Gydan had Bren's sword. He knew it, and she was here in Rhyll. Mendal was impressed. After escaping to Raustfweg, she had the nerve to return.

"Also, sir," Quint spoke cautiously, not wanting to further anger Mendal, "Gydan had a dragon with her, a miniature one, like the kind aristocrats once kept caged for display. I know this because my aunt once—"

"Stop talking."

"Yes, sir."

A dragon. The three spirits within him—Oshmeldai, Lilit, and Durahal—all stirred. To summon Qotha'tunach, Mendal needed to slay a dragon and eat its heart. He had a better chance to push a mountain into the sea than to slay a full-size dragon, but a miniature dragon should suffice, if it could be caught.

"Quint?"

"Yes, sir."

Mendal reached down and placed his fingers on the blood that had spilled on the street. The blood had begun to congeal. He liked the feel of it.

"Most of our soldiers have returned to Rhyll?"

"Yes, in preparation for the upcoming election."

"Let them know, there is no other priority than to find Gydan and bring her to me. Knock on doors. Break them down if you must."

Kret Bonebreaker had made a promise to Mendal. The gnoll warlord had set him on a glorious path. Mendal knew that his work, his rise to greatness, was just beginning.

* * *

Gydan woke up in the chair. The drawing room looked different in the morning with sunlight beaming in from the narrow gaps of the drawn shades. Particles of dust were illuminated and gently floating. It reminded Gydan of the motes of light that had appeared whenever her mother had used her fey magic. For a moment, it felt as though time stood still and all the clutter of the house was forever fixed in its place. All was peaceful, a perfect morning.

Gydan heard a clatter, and the spell was broken. Roby was fixing breakfast and heating water for tea. From the kitchen, Roby called out.

"Good morning, Gydan. I hope you slept well in the chair. I'll fix a bed for you next time you come to visit." Gydan heard more clattering. "After our meal, I'll take you to my ship. We can sail out today."

Gydan got up from the chair, making sure not to bump her head on the ceiling.

"Has Yurig woken up yet?"

"Yurig? He left about an hour ago."

Gydan felt a hollow pit in her stomach. Panic set in.

"Where did he go?"

"I'm assuming back to the palace," Roby entered the drawing room, wiping her hands on a dish cloth. "That's his home when he comes to visit."

Before Roby could say another word, Gydan was out the front door, buckling her scabbard to her belt, mumbling curses the whole time. At some point, her boots had been taken off. They were placed at the front mat. She grabbed them—scabbard not fully secured—and tucked them under her arm. She would put them on later. Cyru was still asleep, but Gydan knew better than to wake a dragon.

Gydan's scabbard dragged along the ground as she made her way through the alley. She tried to adjust the scabbard, which was turned at an awkward angle behind her back. She tripped over something and went crashing to the ground. Her boots flew forward and tumbled down the alley without her. Gydan skinned her forearms bracing herself and protecting her head as she fell. She turned angrily to see what she had tripped over.

It was Yurig, sitting on the ground, leaning against the wall of Roby's house. He had his legs out, which is what Gydan tripped over. He was there, studying his spellbook.

"Good morning?" Yurig was not sure what Gydan was doing.

Gydan was relieved to see Yurig, then angry, then embarrassed, but returned to angry. She wanted to throw something at him.

"A fine morning to wake up and find your brother left without you!"

"I'm right here." Yurig closed his book and slid it back into its leather case.

"Why are you out here?" Everything Gydan said sounded like she was yelling him, and she supposed she was.

"I prefer studying outside. Even when I was at Sage Hall, I'd read under the oak tree. The light is better out here. And I didn't want to wake you up." Yurig latched the case and pulled his legs from Gydan's. "Why are running from the house like it's on fire?"

"I told you. I thought you had left without me."

She sat up and examined the scrapes on her arms. She wiped off the mud smeared on her from the fall.

"Why would I leave without you?" Yurig spoke sweetly with real concern for his sister.

"*Sah'le vuk.*" Gydan shook her head. "If there's one thing about our family, we keep leaving each other."

These words struck something in Yurig—truth, like a hammer striking the bell, summoning the ghosts to come home.

"Early on, I was so focused on studying spells I didn't allow myself much time to think about it. I'd have bouts of sadness that seemed to come from nowhere. As I got older, I had questions about why I was left behind at Sage Hall."

"It was for your safety. Where she was going, we couldn't follow."

Yurig sighed. He had heard this all before. It did little to comfort him. Gydan replied with a sigh of her own.

"It has to stop," Gydan said. "Promise me. Promise me you won't leave, and I won't leave either. We'll stay together."

Yurig smiled. Yurig always had an expression of morose blankness. When he smiled, it surprised Gydan.

"We're stitched at the ankles?" Yurig asked.

"We can't escape each other, even if we wanted to," Gydan responded.

"I promise."

"I promise, too."

Brother and sister looked at each other. They would keep this promise, a promise that would reverberate from their shared history toward a shared fate. They would return to the palace and deal with whatever the consequences were for Dahlia Tulan's death. They would stay in Rhyll until the election was over, and they would take on whatever came next. They'd do it together.

Gydan was a sentimental person. Once again, she was on the verge of tears, so thankful to see her brother again. However, she was never good at these tender moments. She looked at Yurig and made a face—eyes wide open, nose and mouth in an exaggerated snarl. Yurig laughed and shook his head. Gydan got to her feet. She held out her hand and helped her brother up. Once on his feet, Yurig gave Gydan a playful push.

"Do you remember Lord Strawbottom?" Yurig asked. "We found him in the woods."

"How could I forget?" Gydan gave a bow in mock reverence. "He and his family rule over the forest."

"That straw dummy terrified me. I had nightmares about him."

"We saw actual trolls and goblins in the woods, and that's what gave you nightmares?"

Yurig had no good answer. He shrugged.

"In Raustfweg, I painted Lord Strawbottom on my shield," Gydan said. "He protected me in battle."

"You did?"

"For being so well educated, you are stupid. No, I didn't paint him on my shield. I had a dragon sigil. Obviously."

They continued to talk about sigils and symbols, their time apart and about shared childhood memories. The past was a dense and dark, misshapen forest, a place to hide and get lost within. The future was a mystery to explore together.

\* \* \*

Maricel sat outside her thatch-roof hut. Nearby, the tree trunk of Alda Feren extended like a wall into the heavens. White petals idly floated down.

Maricel replaced the fletching of her arrows. She had extracted tar from the tree bark by boiling it in water over an open fire. In a separate pot, she boiled beeswax, which she combined with the tar and a ground sulfur-copper mixture to make the adhesive stronger. It was a formula she had learned from her caravan family. She stirred the concoction with an iron rod, collecting the warm glue on the rod's end and lining the end of the arrow shaft. The feathers came from a turkey she had hunted months ago. After fixing the feathers, she set the arrow aside to dry. She had finished a dozen arrows, which were lined side-by-side.

Skuldi barked enthusiastically, jumping about Maricel. The dog knew arrows meant hunting, and he was ready to venture from the tree. Skuldi was a hunting dog, a breed known as a gazelle hound. These beautiful dogs were lean, long, and muscular. Skuldi was a great companion and an invaluable hunter. During the leaner seasons, Skuldi was always able to bring back a rabbit or squirrel, his tail wagging with pride.

Maricel was also ready to hunt. During yesterday's trip to the berry patch, she had seen fresh deer droppings. A new herd had ventured into the area. If the hunt went well, she could clean them and cure the meat in the shed next to her hut. It would help them get through the winter.

Maricel wasn't worried, though. She had been ambitious with her farming through the spring and summer. She had plenty of food. But if she were being honest, she enjoyed the hunt. She longed to make use of the salt and spices she had stored away after the last visit from Mellal, Grish, and their children. They came to the great tree twice a year to check on Maricel and offer any goods they thought might be useful. Early on, these visits had been essential. Now, Maricel had most of what she needed, but she appreciated their company and the stories they brought from the outside world.

"Calm down, Skuldi. We need to wait for the glue to dry. We'll hunt tomorrow."

These words meant nothing to her dog. He heard his name and the word "hunt," which made him more excited. Maricel smiled at Skuldi's excited dance. She waved her arm and shouted, "Go!" This, he understood. Skuldi took off down the worn path, which lead to the spring, where most of their hunting trips began. It would take Skuldi a while to realize Maricel hadn't followed him. It gave Maricel a moment of peace before he returned, wondering why she was still at the hut.

Maricel breathed in, held it for a moment, and then breathed out. She was in a reflective mood and wanted to savor this time, the sounds and smells of the crackling fire, the simple pleasure of fletching arrows. After her injury, she had felt weak and helpless. But living at Alda Feren had changed her. She was a stronger, more capable person.

When Maricel had first arrived, she had lived in a small tent. Eventually she built a hut for herself. She cut down trees. She learned how to make rope and twine from twisted plant fibers. With the flint deposits near Alda Feren, she was able to fashion axe blades, spear tips, and arrowheads from this wonderful, useful rock. The flint also helped with starting fires. She learned to forage mushrooms, roots, and berries. She learned how to tan leather from the hides of animals she had hunted. In addition to the hut and the shed, she had built a coop for chickens and pen for the goats she used for milk.

Her grasp of druidic magic had improved a little. She was a competent healer. She could purify water and extinguish small fires. Maricel thought her mother would've been proud of the few incantations she learned.

Her greatest triumph was the buffalo horn she had hollowed out. She had drilled four small holes on top and one on the bottom to create a musical instrument. Her caravan family had a variety of horns, stringed instruments, bells, and drums. They played in the evenings, and she always wanted to join in the song. She used her horn to scare off curious wolf packs with its loud bleating. It took longer to produce something melodic. She practiced, and in time, the sweet sounds came. The buffalo horn had a mournful quality to it. Maricel found it soothed her and helped pass the lonelier nights when even Skuldi's company wasn't enough—on the nights when she thought only of *her*.

When she first arrived, Maricel had hoped she would see her immediately. Maricel had approached Alda Feren, hoping to find a victorious hero—with a staff in one hand and shield in the other—running to greet her with a warm embrace. But it wasn't to be. Year after year, season after season, Maricel waited. She patrolled Alda Feren, walking with her dog around the base of this colossal tree. She built her home near the spring. If there was to be a return, Maricel would be there. And perhaps she would keep waiting and nothing would happen. But if there was a chance to see her again, it would be here.

Maricel heard Skuldi barking in the distant brush. He had found something and had forgotten all about the hunt. He was a good dog, but easily distracted.

Maricel finished another arrow and held it up, rotating it between her index finger and thumb, admiring what she had made. She set the arrow beside the rest. They were well crafted.

Then, a silence fell around Maricel, muting all the normal sounds of nature. So complete was this silence, she stopped everything. She could feel her heart beating faster. She heard a sound to the east of her hut, along the surface of Alda Feren. She heard the soft sound of gravel crunching underneath careful footsteps. Mellal and Grish were not to return for a while, and they always came from the west.

Maricel felt a crisp breeze like the arrival of a new season. The wind swirled around her, lifting the white petals off the ground. Maricel's skin dotted with bumps. Her whole body was alive with anticipation.

After all these years, she had returned.

"Silbrey."

# ACKNOWLEDGMENTS

To Holly Lyn Walrath who made the Dryad's Crown a better book and me a better writer,

To Daniel Irving Decena who put so much care and detail into every breath-taking illustration,

To Francesca Baerald who is quite possibly the greatest fine art fantasy cartographer ever,

To Lindsey Dorcus who brought the story to life with her narration, a flawless performance,

To Sissel Morken Gullord who played a haunting and beautiful song on the bukkehorn for the audiobook,

To Calvin Nicholls, a true master of his craft, who *hand carved* the paper to create that floral crown on the cover,

To Betsy Mitchell, the original editor of book one and a legend in science fiction and fantasy publishing,

To Alaya Swann who helped out early in the process as a sensitivity editor for the setting itself,

To Josh Rose who provided some much needed feedback,

To Tricia Klapprodt whose copy edits were damn near perfect, if there are any typos—it's my fault for fussing with later drafts (I'm sorry),

To Kara Robinson, Jarrett Rush, and Matt Cobb who got all the spoilers and kept me accountable to my aspirations,

To Rena Violet who designed the cover,

To Rowynn Ellis who designed the enamel pin,

To Pat Williams who designed the t-shirt,

To David Lizerbram who provided legal assistance on the Efre Ousel setting,

To John Wilker, my SFWA mentor,

To Taffeta Darling, a soap-maker and herald within the Dallas geek community,

To Pantego Books, Whose Books, and Zeus Comics,

To Alison Kimble, Rosaire Bushey, Helen Garraway, and Adrian Santiago for their encouraging words,

To Emma Roberts, Kiki Mora, Young Ragnar, and Ashley Georgakopoulos who promoted my book with their cosplay,

To my Patreon team Rachel Lane, Christopher Luther, Michael Mooney, Nancy & Randy Hopkins, Mark Buffington, Tonya & Jay Rosenberger, Curtis Glenn, Chris "Waffles" Wathen, Tad Lake, Kacie & Evan Elwood, Brian Holler, Alyssa Sable, J. Kyle Fagan, Shelby Cunningham, Daniel Miller, Eileen Miller, Erin Taylor, Steven & Miranda New, Tony Hawkins, Jolyn Redden, Joe Jenkins, Gian Cruz, Paul Milligan, Erkan & Caitlin Eyvaz, Bob Moser, Ariel Heaton, Costa Koutsoutis, Jesse Sowell, Carl Walter, and Pat Hauldren,

And to my wife April who bravely read this novel before it was edited, I love you.

A special thank you to the beta-readers: James Lane, Dana Flanders, Paul Lightfoot, Brian Johnson, and Sandra Lutfy

# THATDAVIDHOPKINS.COM

*The Dryad's Crown* reveals only a small piece of a much greater world. There are more secrets, wonders, and mysteries contained within these four continents and the seas between them than could be explored in several lifetimes.

If you'd like to know more about this series and the setting, visit thatdavidhopkins.com for:

- illustrations by Daniel Irving Decena,
- a high-resolution map of Northeast Amon,
- music that inspired the story,
- a pronunciation guide,
- an introduction to the mythology, cosmology, history, and culture (including common phrases and customs),
- official merchandise and high-quality prints,
- and information about upcoming novels set in this world, such as *The Summer Sword*, which picks up where *The Dryad's Crown* ends.

Sign up for the newsletter to receive special offers and exclusive updates from the author.

# ABOUT THE AUTHOR

David Hopkins is a fantasy author. His short stories have been featured in Infinite Worlds, Oni Press, and Image Comics. He's created a few best-selling "Red War" titles for the D&D Adventurers League, and he's written stories for a variety of magazines and newspapers.

David is a member of SFWA (Science Fiction and Fantasy Writers Association) and teaches classes through WritingWorkshops.com. He's married to artist, April Hopkins. They have two daughters, Kennedy and Greta, and a dog named Moose.

## ABOUT THE ILLUSTRATOR

Daniel Irving Decena is an illustrator and concept artist from the Philippines. He has worked in character and game design. His influences include Bernie Wrightson and Moebius. He generally loves fantasy, fairy tales, and adventure.

Daniel began collaborating with David Hopkins on the Dryad's Crown in February 2020 and finished his final illustration three years later in May 2023.

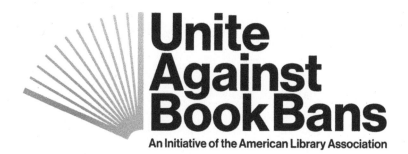

**Unite Against Book Bans**

An Initiative of the American Library Association

*"A library is a focal point, a sacred place to a community; and its sacredness is its accessibility, its publicness. It's everybody's place."*
*– Ursula K. Le Guin*

Unite Against Book Bans is a national campaign to protect the rights of everyone to access a variety of books, in libraries and elsewhere.

- Books are tools for understanding complex issues.
- Young people deserve to see themselves reflected in a library's books.
- Parents should not be making decisions for other parents' children.
- Individuals should be trusted to make their own decisions about what to read.
- Limiting young people's access to books does not protect them from life's complex and challenging issues.

Support the freedom to read. Oppose book bans.
Visit UniteAgainstBookBans.org